Zombies in my Hometown

Zombies in my Hometown

Gary Wedlund

Writers Club Press
San Jose New York Lincoln Shanghai

Zombies in my Hometown

Writers Club Press
an imprint of iUniverse, Inc.

For information address:
iUniverse, Inc.
5220 S. 16th St., Suite 200
Lincoln, NE 68512
www.iuniverse.com

ISBN: 0-595-22051-7

Printed in the United States of America

Foreword

"It's not what you think," he said, stepping over to the body that lay sprawled on the floor. In the process, he almost slipped on a piece of brain, the slip creating a foot long, grey skid mark on the floor.

Patricia put her hand over her mouth. She'd seen his stiffs before, but hadn't particularly gotten used to them. This one, on the floor, with his brains splattered all over the room, was too much to handle. She bent over the handrail, and tossed up three martinis, a vermouth, some beer nuts, two orders of tortilla chips and a little reminder from a guy named Mike; she doubted it his real name, though he hadn't been wearing a ring. To be fair, she'd taken her engagement ring off at the start of the evening as well.

"Sorry about that. I did warn you. It's not what you might think," repeated William.

"Well, what do you know about what I think?" Asked Patricia as William handed her a towel.

"There's some on your, uh, yeah," said William, brushing a bit of puke off of the top of her dress.

Patricia flinched, as if his hand was poison. "I can get it myself."

"Well, fine then. I don't know what you think. But...OK, just hear this and tell me what you think of it." William led her to a seat not too far from the door and well away from the stiff.

Patricia saw the gun and then the opened crate full of more weapons, and for the first time in her life, started to wonder if there wasn't more to William than met the eye.

William started, "This guy on the floor is dead."

"Duh!"

"No, I mean, he was dead before he came in here."

"Jesus, William. They're all dead before they come in here! At least I'm hoping they're all dead before they come in here! What are you, an idiot?" Said Patricia rhetorically. She was not too scared to still be Patricia.

"OK...um...he was dead, and then he walked in here."

I

"Come on, fishy. Just hop on, big guy. I'm not going to eat you," Joe said apologetically as he tossed the bait and bobber into the crisp morning wind. The red bobber rose and then drifted downstream in the rough direction of the rusty iron bridge a block downstream. The fish moved a little as the worm drifted above. He caught a smell of the wiggling delight. Then, his buggy eyes looked at the bait with a steadiness that gave Joe hope.

"You can do it...baby!" The moment passed as the fish rotated a few degrees away, as did the bobber swim downstream into the creek's swifter, shallower currents.

Pine Point is probably the universal worst fishing spot. Directly in front of Joe was the only place deep and still enough to house a fish—one fish—Joe's fish. At that bend, only for fifty yards or so, it was three feet deeper than the rest of the ankle deep creek. Flash floods had made the fishing hole by eating away a baby cliff made of fifty thousand year old Canadian glacial deposits. Just over the little cliff were the Pine Point Cemetery, Deadman Road's Curve and miles of suburban flatland called Central Ohio. Being below topsoil a few feet only offered Joe the illusion that he wasn't standing in the middle of town.

The fish could be gotten by just jumping in and grabbing it, Joe imagined, but that's not fishing. Besides, he'd already promised the fish that he didn't actually want him—he just wanted to catch him so that he could please a Neanderthalian instinct.

Up the creek, sparrows fought over the discarded corpse of Joe's last donut. They dunked it into the shallow water, maybe thinking the water coffee due to the water's color. The selfish bastards chirped sweetly as they pecked one another over the leftover, as if they had no sense. Closer, the early morning sun peeked over Joe's shoulder. The sun steamed the coffee colored creek in the distance to his left and right. He got a fresh worm out of his tackle box, stabbed it and cast into the brew.

The town had grown up, at places abutting Columbus housing. In the place of mooing cows was the clank of cars on the bridge a block downstream. There was a constant Doppler of engines moving from the road at his back, across the bridge, and every so often turning onto Deadman. He did his best to filter out the town noises and tune into the gurgling creek, buzzing insects or bickering sparrows. Sometimes though, like just before the big Lincoln flew over the bluff on the other side of the creek, it was hard to ignore the sounds of man.

The crash was rather sudden, though later Joe's brain replayed it slow motion. The car came right through the cemetery, up above Joe's view. The first thing Joe thought when he saw the thing was: I'm going to die!

He heard the car coming, but hadn't thought much of it until he saw the car loft itself off of the far bluff. A couple of tombstones cascaded over the bluff a split second before the grill. Brush and limbs were stuck in the car's fenders like horns. The wheels, no longer on land, spun out tornadoes of rock and mud. There was nothing but air between Joe and the front of the car. The engine screamed right at him as the car thrust itself off of the cliff and took aim. Pieces of exhaust pipe hung down off of the undercarriage, briefly visible before the front-heavy car rotated over and pointed itself at the creek.

Joe's body threw itself backward onto the rocky shore. There, in primal mode, he crawled backwards like a crayfish.

The Lincoln was too heavy to fly far though. It nosed over into the deep part of the water and landed on Joe's bobber before falling back onto all fours. In an instant the car's front wedged under. A wall of water exploded across Joe like a tidal wave. In three seconds the whole first act was over.

Joe shifted on the rocks. He slowly gathered his feet—no small task. The big yellow Lincoln gurgled as the back half leveled, sinking to match the front. Soon, the back of the car touched bottom. That left its windows half in and half out of the still churning brown soup. Joe smelled the stench of boiling antifreeze. Radiator steam bubbled like a high school chemistry experiment that had gone ugly; all of that in the water just a few yards in front of his feet.

Joe combed his hands through his hair until it no longer dripped in streams and he could see. He waded in some until he was up to his ankles. The driver moved around on the other side of an airbag. The way the driver's hands swam around the airbag had Joe thinking the man was a fat airbag tick.

"God damn bag!" Screamed the man from his driver's seat.

Joe didn't like the sound of that voice. The man's left arm shot out of the driver's window, wielding a huge nickel-plated revolver. The man pointed the gun across the hood and straight at Joe, but from there the gun wandered. It occurred to Joe that the man couldn't really see him with the airbag in the way, which of course helped Joe swallow his heart back down out of his throat.

Joe backed out of the deep water part, slowly making his way downstream. He'd been hearing the wail of a siren ever since the crash. In fact, the wail was coming closer. Joe thought the response a little too quick, as if the cops had been on the trail prior to the crash. Maybe that explained the gun, he gathered, thinking as swiftly as he could with both his head and his feet.

The nickel plating flickered as the gun was pulled inside of the far window. A gunshot cracked! The air bag puffed! Sheets of airbag were tossed out of the front window. With it, glass sparkled across the hood and splashed like ice rain onto the water. A little thread of smoke oozed in the air where the airbag had once been. It met radiator steam drifting across the side of the car, a literal premonition of Dante's Inferno.

Inside the cab, the driver was liberated from the airbag. A pair of deeply reddened eyes turned. Those loathsome eyes looked out of the passenger window, finding Joe. Joe instinctively ducked to his left, rolling a couple of yards downstream. "Bam," a bullet whizzed by, missing his back by inches.

Half in deep and half in shallow, Joe let himself sink, imagining that the next shot or two might have nothing to aim at. The water stung his eyes, but he forced them open, turning to face the threat. He moved away, crawling backwards again. His eyes tried to focus through the creek water. The water was too muddy for that, but he did manage to witness a line of bubbles submarine by a few inches to his side. Instinctively he jumped away from the bullet, breaching the surface with his back.

Joe put a hand out in front of his face, hoping to shield his head from the next bullet. A second later a hole formed in the back of his hand. A trial of blood arched out of the hole, caused by a slowing bullet. The bullet had just enough energy to land gently on the rocks under Joe chin. At first he couldn't believe he'd been shot, but then the stabbing pain found its way up to his brain. He yelled and gulped in a mouthful of water.

Joe grabbed a rock with his good hand, and leapt out of the water, choking for air. Just as the pistol fired, he rolled to his left again to put more of the car's back half between himself and the bullets. A bullet splashed where the ripples of his resurrection were still settling.

Switching hands with the rock, he threw it. The rock spun blood before hitting the back passenger side window. The glass disintegrated into slashing shards. A pain lashed up Joe's arm from the effort and he was still coughing up water. He grabbed the hand, the act slowing him for the briefest of seconds. When he looked back, there was a clear view through the smashed back window to the driver. Joe was looking at the deep, black hole in the end of the shooter's revolver.

Joe ducked into the same cliff that had launched the car. As he fell he heard a shot.

The car's rear window shattered. The madman ducked under the water that filled most of the car's interior. A second shot came right on the heels of the first, punching a hole through the top of the car. Joe did his best to stay still, not entirely sure if someone else was shooting, or if the madman was crazy enough to do that all by himself.

Officer Sandra Anderson jumped off of the bluff and ran into the creek, her service revolver held out in front of her with rigid arms.

Joe's head was spinning as he blinked back the pain in his lungs and hand. The blurry shape of Officer Anderson stood in knee deep water just a few feet off. The shape held a gun out in front of it, aimed at the car. Joe shook his head clear, and caught the color of her dark blue uniform.

"You are under arrest! Come out with your hands up!" Yelled Sandra.

"Bam!" Sandra's body jerked backwards downstream as if tackled. She splashed into the creek where she promptly disappeared. Only the trace of her brown locks waved upon the surface of the rippling brown water. Her gun seemed to hang in the air like something out of a cartoon. Then it fell into the water as if a rock. Joe got to his knees. He regretted the move, seeing that the madman's eyes had locked upon him next.

"What the hell," moaned Joe. He ran to the place where the officer had fallen and dove to grab the body. The pain in his hand made it impossible to pick her up, so he rolled her over onto her stomach and grabbed her black police belt with the one good hand instead. Getting a good grip, Joe pulling her across the rocks toward the shore downstream. Her limbs bounced across the rocks, the least of her worries, imagined Joe who'd seen her take the bullet dead center. With each step, he wondered why he was saving a corpse, and just as much, wondering why he was still alive.

Over in the car, the man took aim with his revolver and fired, the weapon hammering on an empty chamber.

Joe dropped the body behind a rock the size of a footstool. Both legs were still exposed, but at least the woman had a chance if she wasn't already dead, he thought. He'd thought about hiding behind the rock too, but there wasn't enough of it. Joe expected the crazy man to just walk over and plug them anyway.

"Click!"

All around Joe were red and blue reflections, flashs from the cruiser up on the far bluff. Sandra's siren was silent, but others were coming in the distance. They were at least a long minute away, guessed Joe.

"Click!"

The sound of the gun hitting on empty chambers frayed at Joe's nerves. He stood and glared at the gunman who'd become thirty yards away. The madman was out of his car and was standing on the other side of it. Holding his gun over the top of the car, the madman hammered on empty cylinders, either too enraged or too far over the edge to notice it wasn't firing.

"You're out of bullets, you freak! Come on out and fight like you have a pair! Come on! Let's see what you've got!" Joe yelled, stepping forward with one unhurt clinched fist and another that was throbbing all the way up to his elbow.

The man's eyes shifted out of their insane daze. He looked at Joe inquisitively. Then he looked at his gun. His head pinioned around as if he was physically doing a tour of the contents of his own brain. One hand felt at his temple for a second, rubbing away an ugly recent memory. Setting the gun onto the car top with an unexpected tenderness, the man dove back into the car. Literally diving underwater, he scrounged for more bullets.

Joe glanced at the officer's body, and then back at the spot of water where he remembered she'd dropped her gun. He could run, he figured. Chances were really good that the woman was dead and Joe knew that after fifty yards, hitting something with a handgun is unlikely. But then again, what if the guy ran off and kept shooting up the town? Joe looked back at the bridge that was a block away. The town's heaviest traffic came across that bridge—well, sort of heavy, a couple of cars a minute anyway. Joe thought about the kids out on Pine Point's streets in the summer. He thought that he had the drop on the guy—maybe. He decided that he had to go for the gun. Joe didn't feel particularly sure he'd win a fistfight, but the army had taught him how to use a weapon. He'd only need one hand for that too.

The sirens were still looking for a way in, the whole scene before him as if in slow motion, and thus, the cops seemingly getting no closer.

Joe sighed, leapt into the middle of the creek and reached down into the soup where he expected the gun to be. He found a rock. Time slipping by. He dropped onto all fours, searching desperately for a few seconds before his hand landed on the weapon.

The madman ripped a box of bullets apart. Some of the bullets splashed into the water. A dozen more scattered over the car top, them spinning. The man opened the pistol cylinder, and smacked the butt of the gun against the doorframe. Even unloading was done in rage. The spent shells spilled out of the cylinder. Several of the unused bullets on the top of the car rolled into the water from the jolt. Most didn't.

Joe wasted no time aiming the officer's gun at the madman. She'd hesitated, Joe realized, and it had cost her a bullet in the chest. Joe tried to pull the trigger, but his right hand didn't have the strength. He switched hands with the weapon.

The madman picked up a bullet and slid it into a slot in the cylinder.

Joe tested the trigger, shooting a bullet into the creek. The explosion and water spout seemed bigger than expected. "Damn!"

Not as much as a wince showed on the killer's face as he loaded slugs. He'd been practicing it all week and in spite of the fact that his mind had snapped, he was right-on loading the weapon, running on pure instinct.

Joe aimed the weapon again, his right hand trembling from the wound as it sought to steady his left hand. At that point, he didn't even think. Joe squeezed a round off, blowing one of the man's ear lobe to pieces. Joe was a good shot, but with a rifle, right handed and under conditions far less shaky. He knew that his problem was just plain nerves. Next time, he resolved, just a nice, slow squeeze!

"Just quit, man. I don't want to shoot you," said Joe hopefully.

The madman seemed unfazed by both the warning and the lost body part. He slapped the cylinder into place and lifted his weapon.

"Shit!" Joe pulled off a quick and dirty shot, this one lower than the last one and right through the side windows. The gunman's body jerked backwards, leaving behind a stream of blood that shot out of his upper chest as if from a water hose. As he fell backwards. His weapon fired into the sky. Joe was left looking at an empty window frame. The splash was followed by the muffled sound of an underwater gunshot. There was the decaying lap of receding waves on the shoreline beyond the car. The sparrows were no longer chirping, but the creek went right back to gurgling as if nothing had happened.

Joe ran around the front of the car, aiming his gun at the swirling currents. The place where the man had fallen was just about the only place deep enough to hide a body. Joe scanned the mud churned water for any trace of life. Nothing moved. Suddenly, there was movement of something reaching out to him from under the water. He fired nearly at his own feet. A two foot long carp dipped under the impact and then rose to the surface. It settled on one side, one eye looking at Joe accusingly as it slowly rode the current by the front fender. The eye seemed to say, "You lying jerk. You promised not to kill me." The fish floated on down the stream. "Put down the weapon and surrender with your hands up!" Screamed Officer Jimmy Baker from the top of the small cliff. Behind him, his cruiser's light-bars gave him a carnival halo of multiple blue and red strobe flashes.

Joe looked up and saw the heads of officers hiding behind doors, aiming pistols down at him. He dropped the weapon back into the creek and raised one hand, the other one aching mercilessly. "Hey, I'm the good guy!"

"You just let me be the judge of that and spread em on the ground over there. You're lucky we haven't shot you already," yelled the young officer.

Jimmy jumped the four feet down to the cliff shore, his weapon steadily in front of him. His finger was stiff from an itching urge to squeeze. The young officer had joined the force with delusions of shooting bad guys Dirty Harry style. It looked like his first rare opportunity to shoot a bad guy had slipped him by after three years of boring speeding tickets and Saturday night DUIs.

Joe found a good spot to lie on the rocks. There he waited for the late cavalry to treat him like trailer trash.

After wading across, Jimmy kicked Joe in the legs until they were splayed out. At six feet tall and a hundred thirty pounds, Jimmy's baby faced head seemed too large for a terrestrial. His hands were a little too large too, though quite steady as they kept the police automatic aimed at Joe's back.

The stout Chief Baker joined his deputy. Joe wasn't all that fond of Chief Baker, though he left the adult locals alone most of the time. Baker had a reputation for having made Pine Point into a speed trap, mainly on the four lane wide main drag that had a ridiculously slow posting of twenty-five. The extra money was spent hiring more cops who were then posted at other traps to help maintain the money flow that kept them employed. Considering the crawling traffic, High street was safe enough to surf a skateboard on, but that too was eagerly enforced in the pursuit of lawn mowing money. Baker's cops never missed a chance to pick on local kids for skating or spitting in the wrong direction. The more cop business they drummed up, the more powerful the Chief, Joe gathered.

Seeing that Joe was secure, Chief Baker wandered over to Sandra's body. In the mean time, junior slapped some cuffs on Joe's wrists, making sure to make them tight enough to stop all but the most determined blood cell from circulating. Joe's bad hand was already swelling, soon including the corresponding wrist where the cuff bit into the swollen skin. Jimmy noticed, smiling at Joe's back. He started patting Joe down roughly.

"You do much more of that and I'm gonna have to kick your ass in some dark alley, pink face," said Joe, earning himself a kick from Jimmy's knee.

"Jimmy? You see him shoot her?" Asked the Chief.

"Yeah. He did it alright. He had her gun when I cornered him! Shot some other guy over there too," He yelled back, kicking Joe as if using the kick to point.

"You lying pig. You saw no such thing," said Joe. Joe was exhausted and his whole arm ached, but he didn't want the deputy to know that.

"You shut up! Cop killer! You're going to feel my boot until they slip you the needle," answered the deputy as he finally holstered his weapon.

"Oh, that's nice. I like it rough. Can't wait until it's my turn with the baton. Sure I can't steal you away from your leather booted boyfriends?" Rode Joe.

"You shoot her?" Asked the Chief, knowing that it was usually easier to extract a confession at the crime scene. Later there were always lawyers, sure to shut up even the lamest criminal, he'd learned.

"I didn't shoot her. The guy who shot her is the guy who drove that car into the creek. He's lying in the water on the other side! I shot him with the officer's gun after she got shot. It was self defense," Joe said to the Chief. He ignored Jimmy who was closer.

"He threatened me, Chief. That's battery. That's ten days, automatic, regardless," announced the deputy.

"Eat me! I won't tell," said Joe between coughs of pain.

Baker was content to let his Deputy handle Joe, without comment. Two more cops walked up from the bridge, and the Chief nodded for them to check the car out. In the mean time, a par of medics raced up with equipment. They worked on Sandra under the slightly concerned gaze of Chief Baker.

"We got another one dead here," yelled the cops as they dragged the lifeless body of the madman onto the shore, dropping him next to Joe.

"This the one you shot?" Asked the Chief.

"Well, it'd be a hell of a coincidence if it wasn't," answered Joe.

"Any way you call it then, you're going to jail for murder. There has to be a grand jury for any death. For that we need to hold you, even assuming you're not a liar," said the Chief as he nodded to Jimmy.

"Oh, well of course. The American way; I almost forgot," said Joe angrily.

Joe turned his head and looked into the eyes of the dead man, both men lying nearly side by side. Those eyes are not quite as bloodshot as before, he thought. Joe absorbed the insult of being made to lie beside the corpse. He'd never seen a dead man before, outside of a funeral parlor, and it didn't help to know that this was one that he'd made that way. In just a few hours the body will start to rot. The man's relatives will be horrified. Lives will change. The more Joe thought about it, the more his stomach churned. He could only take solace in the fact that at least it wasn't him.

There was coughing over between the medics as Sandra showed she wasn't as dead as she'd seemed to be at the time Joe'd plucked her out of the soup. Joe felt a little guilty about celebrating the idea that he might have a witness before the idea that he'd saved a person from drowning. At that moment however, Joe wasn't feeling all that altruistic regarding cops. As if to add another reason for feeling that way, Jimmy reached down and pulled Joe to his feet, using the cuffs as a handle. The pain in Joe's wrist nearly caused him to black out even as he was made to stand. His head swam as he tried to not let on.

Joe watched a plastic gloved cop put his fishing gear into little Baggies as he was marched to the back of a cruiser. The back door slammed the second Joe sat down, his hand dripping blood all over the back seat. He lamented the inability to bring around a middle finger to show the dozen news cameramen shooting photos and videos of him through the cruiser glass. Jimmy's police radio talked endlessly, as if there were a hundred officers out there, all of them responding to emergencies all over town. Joe knew that police radios mainly send cops to places, and are notoriously vacuous of information. That knowledge only made it seem busier to Joe.

Downstream, Sandra struggled back to the living. She leaned up on one arm before falling back onto her stretcher as they put her into the medic van. Some cop I turned out to be, she lamented, feeling the prying eyes of her fellow male officers. To most of them it was concern, but to Sandra it felt as if they were saying, "See, a woman is just in the way out here in the real world." A medic above her peeled some scissors out of their paper wrapper as the squad took off with a wail He snapped her bra apart with practiced efficiency, (The only article of clothing above her waist not yet removed outside). She didn't know whether to laugh or to cry at the indignity, opting for neither, the pain in her chest definitely not worth it.

Joe's hand ached mercilessly. He found it bearable if he leaned over and got it up some from where it was cuffed. Everything had been taking forever, the cops content to let him bake in the back seat and wallow in his pain. Chief Baker measured things off at the creek with a tape measure, and then jotted down notes while the rest of his deputies walked all over the evidence as if they'd never seen Kojak. Jimmy dove down on the far side of the car and came up with both Sandra's and the madman's handguns in his hands, fingers in the finger wells; destroying all of the fingerprints.

The ambulance was long gone, and it troubled Joe to think that maybe the lady cop wouldn't pull through and her fellow cops would start a railroading, Texas style. He was of the mind that the evidence was on his side, as he watched them eliminate it. He'd seen, 'The Thin Blue Line', and he knew that dumb cops and innocent men didn't mix, particularly when they'd decided he was a cop killer. Shoot, even George W. had sat back and watched a few innocent men die for the thrill of a handful of cherry picked tough-on-crime votes. Look where a blind eye had landed Mister President Select, he mused! Joe had never in his life felt more expendable to the cause of inefficiency. Apathy kills, but the ignorance of the masses is the morphine that lets them sleep through it with a clear conscience, thought Joe. He fixated upon the desire for a little of exactly that drug to ease the pain running up his arm.

2

Andy was beating all over the bars with his metal cup again. Joe had no idea why the big man in the lower bunk didn't go over and whack Andy on the head. Perhaps he was getting some residual satisfaction out of it because every so often the guard came in and told them to cut it out, as if all three of them were one entity. Joe had to admit that at least that part of it was amusing. Andy could hear the guard coming. He was pretty good at hiding the cup on a brick overhanging the cell door and then dropping back a step with a sheepish look that said, "Who, me? I'm not even lucid!"

Joe wasn't getting that collective, "we," sense of satisfaction though. He'd let them put him in the cell without a word, other than an insistence upon dialing a lawyer. It had taken them an hour to arrange the call, and even then he'd had to call a friend and hope that, that person called someone worthwhile. Maybe a lawyer was coming, and maybe not, Joe wondered, as he watched the jailer reappear.

"You want to eat and you had better cut the crap!" Yelled the jailer to the room in general.

Joe said, "I think the Constitution says you have to feed us, noisy or not." May as well get a meal out of it, he mused.

"I take my orders from the Chief," said the jailer.

"Well, the Chief takes his orders from the law, and the sixteenth amendment says you have to feed us on time," said Joe, playing the jailer for as much as he could. As for the sixteenth amendment, he had no idea what it said, but he couldn't imagine it said anything more important than food.

"This can be a pleasant place if you want," said the jailer, changing his tactic for want of a good civics background. The man stood watching them for a second, and then walked back to the desk and coffee he'd left in the other room.

"That so? They got to feed us cause of the constitution?" Asked the big man in the bottom bunk.

"Not really. Just one of them says you have to be humane. He doesn't know that though, so I'm hoping for steak and onions," said Joe. His hand was throbbing again. The medic they'd waylaid had refused him pain medicine, the system apparently employing the doctrine that low-life were always addicts and should just learn to deal with it. Joe looked at the bandage. He wondered how it was possible that a quick dose of antiseptic and a bandage wrap were all he needed for what might otherwise require five hours of microsurgery.

"Ha!" Said the hyper Andy, him soon back to hopping around in front of the cell bars, looking to see if anyone was coming before clapping the bars again, in a slower cadence. "Steak and onions! Steak and onions!" He yelled.

"What you in for?" Asked the big man in the bunk under Joe's. His voice was a little more pleasant than Joe had expected.

"I'm in for being in the wrong place at the wrong time. If things work out, they'll soon be letting me out of here," answered Joe.

"Innocent, huh. So am I. I didn't knock that drunk around for messin with my bike. I just wasn't looking when he fell and hit my fist."

"You'll be happy to know that I drink like a temperance worker, and I have the utmost respect for Mr. Harley and Mrs. Davidson," said Joe, looking over the edge of the top bunk and offering his good hand down to be shaken by the giant.

"The Mr. and Mrs. appreciate it, but regarding temperance, I was more drunk than the guy I hit at the time, I'm afraid to admit. Name is Trunk."

"Joe. Glad to meet you. Hope you have a more prompt lawyer than I do."

"I can get that guard to make a fuss if you want," said Andy, his eyes beady and glossed over as he turned and made his claim. The man was out of his mind, thought Joe, jumping from one monkey act to the next. Joe came to the conclusion that Andy was here because jails are cheaper than hospitals.

"You go on. I'll tell you when I've had enough," said Trunk to the crazed Andy.

"That your real name?" Asked Joe.

"Been Truck ever since I took to the road and decided to make it my name. No need spreading around a mean man's name," he said, obviously making reference to an unloved father.

"That's cool. I never had the guts to stake out an entirely new life, but the older I get the more it appeals to me. What's Andy in here for?"

"Just being crazy. They emptied all the nuthouses out decades ago, and ever since then they've been sticking Andys wherever they can fit them. Of course, being crazy and all, there is usually some crime they can glue together to stick once they put him here. Truth be told, if they didn't find a crime to clean the street of him with, Andy'd probably do one for the free bed and food himself; especially around holidays. Hey Andy! What'd you do?"

"I didn't do nothin!"

Trunk continued, “See what I mean. You’re right, Andy! You didn’t do nothing! You keep beating on those bars and tellin em! So, Joe, what did you really do, besides bein innocent like the rest of us?”

“I killed a guy who drove his car into the creek and started shooting up the place. It was self-defense. I thought that if I didn’t take him out, he’d be in the streets next. They’ll sort it out in awhile, I figure.”

“You a murderer? Hey Andy, we got us a murderer here. This here fella’s done the big one. Capital C!”

“Hell! I’m not a murderer. I just had to shoot his guy. Trust me, the gun did all of the work. I was just standing behind it. It’s almost like I had nothing to do with it,” spat Joe.

“Well, that’s usually how it works, Joe. Damn near every time,” insisted Truck.

“Huh! You have a point, I guess. This is just nuts. All I wanted to do was go fishing. I was planning on Ponderosa for lunch.” Joe figured that Truck was at least as far along in his assessment as the cops had gotten, but on far less information. Besides, it was useful to be a criminal while in jail. It helped him fit in, so why argue details?

“God, Joe, you got to stop talking about food. I’m starving, and they even fed me breakfast,” warned Truck.

“Sorry.”

“Steak and onions! Steak and onions!” Yelled Andy, the cup rattling across the bars at an accelerated rate.

The cellblock door rattled, and Andy shoved his cup back up on the brick. He turned around so he looked like he’d been chatting with the group. The jailer came in with Chief Baker and a woman between them. The lady was tall with straight black hair that was tied back in a long ponytail. She wore deep red lipstick and long black lashes that matched her business suit. When she walked, she effortlessly made everyone around her seem secondary just by the way she carried herself, as if she'd been born with maids standing in all corners.

The cellblock was four cells, two to each side, and the one across the way had a pair of afternoon drunks in it. Their eyes licked at the woman's legs as her heels walked up to Joe's cell. The business suit was seamed stockings and a knee length black dress that well covered what everyone was guessing were garters.

"Hey baby!" One of the drunks yelled, after which the woman turned around and glared at him. The pause was a long half minute within which even Chief Baker failed to speak. The drunk stuck his tongue in his cheek and looked away. When she looked back in Joe's direction, Joe could see the ice that was still in her eyes.

"Which one of you is Joe Jefferson?" She said.

"Shit! It's him! He's the one who done it! He says he's a murderer! Steak and onions!" Yelled Andy. He jumped out of the way and pointed at Joe, Andy's social sensibilities always out of control.

"That's me," agreed Joe, sitting up and sliding off of the top bunk.

The lady looked at the jailer. She couldn't have been more than mid-thirties. The jailer had the looks of a man of fifty. She said, "Get that chair for me, boy."

Chief Baker nodded, and the jailer grabbed a wooden chair. He slid it behind her while Baker stood aside looking as if his afternoon was ending on a lower note than he'd expected at breakfast.

"Dominique Sawyer. I'm your lawyer, assuming the arrangement works for you. It does interest me."

Joe offered his hand. Dominique stuck hers through the bars and shook hands as if she'd never known a prisoner she couldn't trust.

Joe grabbed the lone cell chair and sat. Baker interrupted as Dominique sat down, "This isn't necessary. We can get the paperwork started and you can talk later. We're not interested in holding him any longer. You know how this works, Ms Saw..."

"Could you leave me with my client? You know that I like to talk to my boys while they're in a position where I'm sure they're paying attention," said Dominique.

Oddly, the words boys and attention seemed more directed toward the Chief than the client. She left the impression that she didn't expect a disagreement. Joe wasn't particularly fond of upper class bitchy women, not having had the need to actually get to know one, but in this case it was clearly an advantage. Even Truck sat up, admiring her caustic personality. Andy leaned back against the wall at the edge of the open bars and snickered, Joe imagining that, that was as close to respect as Andy was capable. Baker shrugged and waved for his jailer to follow him out of the block door. Beads of sweat glistened on the Chief's forehead as he left.

Over across the aisle, one of the drunks was peeing an arch into an adjacent cell's toilet. Dominique ignored the sound behind her; even that somehow commanding.

"I take forty percent. You can shop around for someone else, and maybe a hack will take you for thirty-five. Trust me though, I'll settle for enough more to make up for it and I'll squeeze it out of them in half the time, probably without a court date—assuming we win over a mind or two," said Dominique.

Joe sat back and asked, "Am I going to have to stand trial?"

"For what? Oh, that little shooting. Good Lord, I got a five minutes brief on that and there isn't anything to it. Nice footage on the local news to put between the fluff, but otherwise inconsequential for you. The case is embarrassing from the start. The state law says they have to have a grand jury in a shooting death, usually a formality. That doesn't mean that it's proper to arrest you. I'll represent you, but the criminal part is less than a couple of hours of work, which is already moot, though if they go insane I'll write it off, assuming you take me on in the civil case. In fact, the unnecessary arrest they've handed you is only half the case, so I don't care what they do to you; the worse the better. The hardship only means that there is more money in it. Any fool could have seen the shooting for what it was as soon as he drove up on the crime scene. Well, not every fool, it seems. We're lucky this happened in a small town and not Columbus. Small town police forces are more prone to overreactions than big ones, contrary to what you might see on TV. They just don't have the legal resources for on the job training that the big cities do. How's your hand?"

"Hurts so bad I can hardly move my elbow," said Joe.

"Good. What did they do for it? Let me guess. They brought a half blind, eighty year old medic in here and he wrapped it up and left you to suffer like a good boy. Prisoners are here to be punished. Prisoners don't need quality medical attention. Have they fed you yet?"

"I can see I have the right lawyer," answered Joe.

"So you can't move the hand, you're in pain, there's nerve damage, maybe a broken bone or two, and they just put a band aid on it, and locked you up. I'm surprised they don't make you drink out of the toilet." She paused, taking a look at the ugly cell john. "You got a good job, Joe?"

"Yeah. I work at the music store. Sometimes I get a gig or two. Sometimes I substitute teach."

"Every been in trouble?"

"Speeding ticket. So far I've excelled at avoiding the occasional bar fight."

"I like the speeding ticket. Nearly everyone on the jury in this town has one, and Baker knows it. Pisses people off. I'm thinking thirty thousand for false arrest, seventy thousand for the hand, and we settle on both for a discount at seventy or so, which is becoming something of a standard for minor police abuse settlements that result in injuries such as this. If you don't collect, I don't collect. I give it ninety percent that I get just under thirty, you get about forty and change, medical expenses and we both call it a good day of fishing. Whole thing takes about a year, mostly passing letters back and forth, if we're unlucky and don't get it in the first few weeks."

"Yes ma'am,"

Truck chimed in, "Hey, you wanna be my lawyer too?"

"Don't think so, Truck. You're guilty. There's no money in people who are guilty, unless they're rich, in which case it a gold mine. OJ had to sell his house and get a used Bronco," said Dominique, raising an eyebrow for Truck, but without taking her eyes off of Joe.

"Hey, how'd you know my name?" Asked Truck.

"Andy, John, and pissing Jolee over there. I know all you boys. If you find that a little mysterious...good. I like leaving an impression," said Dominique, getting up from her chair.

"Damn, a voodoo lawyer. And, all I get is a public defender who runs from room to room with a daily caseload a dozen deep. Dropping folders all over the hallway. The world ain't fair," proclaimed Truck, lying back on his bunk.

"Well, it has been super, boys. I'll see you out in the lobby in, oh, five minutes, Joe. Let me know if they give you any trouble on the way out of the cell door. Seriously. I have my fingers crossed," said Ms. Dominique Sawyer as she walked over and banged on the cellblock door.

She took one last glance at Jolee, the drunk who'd been doing his best to offend her behind her back since her arrival. "You know, it's a third DUI for you, Jolee. Most tell you it's six months on the license, two weeks in the real slammer and two in the rehab, but the law says they can keep you a whole year if they want to. Just depends on what kind of mood people put the judge in." She smiled at Jolee, as if she knew something he didn't. Scary, thought Joe. He was doubly glad that she was on his side.

The door opened almost before she'd finished speaking to the drunk. She stepped out. The cellblock was suddenly a lot less attractive. Even the smell of her jasmine was fading fast, as if she'd sucked it out with her. It seemed to Joe that all the nostrils in the place were working for the last of it. To Joe, she wasn't the dating kind—more the interesting, smelling kind.

"Weeeeeeeeeeeeeooooow!" Screamed Andy. "You got you a girlfriend! Joe's got a girl friend. Murderin' Joe's got a girl friend."

"Ah, shut up!" Screamed Truck, finally showing an end to his tolerance.

Joe apologized, "Sorry Truck. Seems that Dominique is exclusively an ambulance chaser. Considering, she might not be much good in a criminal case."

"Damn if I care. I just want to sit next to her through the trial."

"Better hold your hands over your balls if you do. Seems to me Dominique is the kind to collect souvenirs," offered Joe.

"Huh. Come to think of it, I did notice that her earrings looked kind of wrinkled and large," agreed Truck, his mood back to carefree.

"Want anything when I get out?" Offered Joe.

"Glossies?"

The wait lasted four minutes. "You got you one pain in the ass lawyer there, buddy," said the jailer as he let Joe out and led him into the processing room.

"I certainly hope so, and don't you think for a minute that I won't mention your disregard for the sixteenth amendment. I'll be checking on these guys to see if it's something we need to press.

I'm already suspicious about the quantity and quality of service," said Joe, hoping he'd sounded anything but cordial.

They gave Joe his wallet and keys, while Dominique stood behind him tapping her foot impatiently. Along with the release papers, Dominique shoved a contract of work under Joe's nose and told him to sign it right there on the police desk. Then she gave him her card.

She hurriedly said, "I'll see you day after tomorrow, nine AM. In the mean time, see Doctor Adkins. Her address is on the back. How's the hand?"

"Hurts like hell."

"Good. Try moving the fingers."

Joe curled them over one at a time. Each finger made it some degree to half way curled.

"Well, I imagine they'll stiffen quite a bit between now and the doctor's office," she told him, as if offering advise. "Got to go. Little case of whiplash over at my Columbus office. See that doctor; you're suffering, and will need to do this without delay before infection sets in and it not only becomes permanently debilitating, but perhaps even life threatening. Got my hopes up on that," commanded Dominique as she launched herself down the police building front steps.

Joe watched her leave, her legs churning in a near run, though they were no less appealing for the rush. Heads turned in the cars that crawled by on Hamilton Avenue. A tire squealed as a man was forced to hit his brakes at the last minute. The man had looked back at the road just in time to discover a pickup truck too close, she being such a unique distraction that she'd caught both drivers' eyes. Joe decided that as a physical being, Dominique was such a marvel to watch that she was a traffic hazard, though her personality required a stronger man than he felt up to. He felt a little sorry for the guy who called her his significant other; or her significant other; considering Dominique's unique and aggressive attack upon life one couldn't be quite sure. Joe added 'their' to his list of possibilities as he watched her disappear behind the wheel of a new black power car?

The powers in charge had kept Joe's fishing gear for evidence, so he was empty handed as he walked down Hamilton Avenue in his dried, but slightly fish scented clothing. The bridge and his car were a mile west, but the doctor's address was by the hospital, north on Hamilton a few blocks. That was roughly where the Ponderosa was too, and it had gotten to be nearly five o'clock. What kind of doctor takes appointments after five, wondered Joe as he picked up the pace?

3

"Yes dear. I know. Yes, I'm sorry. You're perfect right; I had no…Ok. Sure, sure. I told you…no, I'm not being…trying to be smart. I just wanted to assure you that…Ok then. And, I'm sorry if I spoke out of…But I love you, dear. I do. Well, you should know that I do. I tell you all of the time. Of course I mean it. Who wouldn't…Yes. Yes. I'd love to talk to you about the issue later. Yes dear. Anytime you want. Me too. I love you too. Please, just relax. No, I didn't mean that personal. I just want you to take a load off your…Yes, I do that sometimes. I never mean it the way it…I do care. Ok. I already said I was sorry for that. I'll give you…Yes. I know how that makes you feel pressured. I wasn't thinking. Yes. Ok. Ok. Ok. Ok. Ok. Ok. Ok. Ok. I understand. Ok. Yes, dear. I do too. I know how you like to hear…I love you very much. Ok. Bye then."

William sat the handset down and grabbed the top of his prematurely balding head. He leaned over as if he was in gut wrenching agony. "Aaaaah!" He screamed at the linoleum floor. Picking up the phone again, he listened for the dial tone. Satisfied that the line had been disconnected, he slammed the handset down five times until little pieces of plastic started snapping off of the handset and cradle. After holding his breath for a minute he thought that he felt a little better.

All six feet six of him stood up in his long, white, but body fluid splattered smock.

William was thankful that there was no showing that evening. He had a greater than usual and growing need for private space, and the weekend had been perfect except for when Patricia had started in on him. He felt that he was lucky to have such a good looking woman to go out with, but she came at a steep price—sanity. When it got to him badly enough, he found that nothing soothed him more than the solitude of his work. This evening was going to be a working one, realized the mortician—private time.

There was plenty of meat in the lockers, most of it what he called road kill as opposed to natural causes. When it rains it pours, thought Bill, doing an inventory of the closed lockers. Three new ones just that morning, and two from the previous evening. It had been an unprofitable weekend. Monday and Tuesday had made up for it with a literal bang.

Sticking his glasses back up onto the back of his nose and his hands into transparent latex gloves, William grabbed the spray nozzle. He sprayed the ample blood and chunks off of the table, the leavings of Mr. What's His Face. William had put the man back into his nice cool storage drawer before Patricia's call.

Aunt Millie had been left waiting on the second table, most of the gut work done at least. He sprayed her off as well. Hooked under a hole in the stainless steel bed near the corpse's head, a gallon bucket swung. A stream of water splashed against the bucket's galvanized sides. The swinging picked up with a jerk whenever a morsel added itself to the gizzards already dropped inside. A small hole in the bottom of the bucket pissed a steady stream of pink directly at the drain in the workroom floor, literally pissing on OSHA's rules regarding biological waste.

Aunt Millie was a dumpy lady with kind of fat, plain features. "The perfectly stretched canvas awaits its master. A little base, some tone, and...."

William had talent.

Directly after art school, he'd discovered how employable art students are in an age of fifteen dollar, framed and gloss sprayed Renoir prints. They sold the cheap stuff so cheaply that he used to buy them himself, just for the frames. After a line of minimum wage jobs, he'd met a government man who'd offered him a contract job painting dead faces to look un-grey. That first job had landed him in the basement of a VA hospital in Atlanta, doing cosmetics on stiff, pot bellied veterans who'd gone to that great Battle of the Bulge in the sky. He started out making a hundred and fifty bucks a pop to make grandma say, "My, doesn't Uncle Earl look like he is sleeping!"

In time, he'd gone through the motions that had earned him the whole license, so after five years of government work, he'd moved to the Midwest and started doing the entire requiem in his own parlor. There was a lot of money in burying or toasting corpses, but the painting was always the best part of the job, according to William. In fact he liked the makeup work so much that he'd have done it for free, though he wasn't foolish enough to tell anybody that.

He hadn't entirely given up on the art world either. In fact, imagined William, the art critics were going to cream over themselves when they saw his new stuff. Soon he'd explode upon the scene, he dreamed. His portfolio was already over a hundred pieces. That was his little secret for now—not even Patricia knew. For that matter, Patricia had never seen his work, neither that done for grandma, nor that done for art. The less she knew about his work though, the less stuff she had to pick on him about, and Bill welcomed that. If she saw his work, she'd add ghoul to the list of things she picked on him about; William knew that she was prissy about all things practical. As for the new 100 item portfolio, he couldn't imagine her reaction.

Last week he'd done his best piece. He'd made an eighty year old stock broker look like Carol Channing, complete with pearls and a frost hair job; using the guy's real hair too, (some of the back hair scalped and repositioned over the bald spot), so the roots showed, pulled nice and tight just to emphasize that point.

Shot on minimum aperture, every detail from the pores on the nose to the hairs in the ears were crisp; food for those critical New York gallery eyes. Most of the prints were the same chin level frontal, the angle meant to make the dead face appear towering. Only the makeover and lighting changed. Once in awhile he added a full casket view for perspective. Most of the visual art, realized William, was the makeover and the ever-moving light sources. Otherwise, the proportions and angle sought to simply accentuate a consistent theme. "If one does it once or twice, it's weird. If one does it over and over again, it's art," William said, reciting one of his old art professors. He'd tossed his hands up into the air at the last word, remembering Andy Warhol's Frankenstein.

"I am the Master, Ha Ha Ha!" William added his best madman imitation as he did a little dance by the table.

Anyway, he thought, collecting himself, this old dead woman will make another pretty fair Patricia. He wondered what that thought said about his relationship? He knew that if Patricia even found out that her likeness had been painted on over a dozen corpses, she'd not be particularly pleased. But, then again, if she did know, that would probably mean he had become famous already, and if that ever happened, Patricia would be number uno on his must-get-rid-of list. "Nice piece of tail, but Jesus, who can put up with her?"

William figured that abundant sexual partners were a fringe benefit of fame. He'd once noted that Andy Warhol was probably the ugliest pervert ever to lilt across the satin bed in any New York loft. Andy always had a woman under an arm. Any way William looked at it, Patricia was going to be history, sooner or later. With her personality, a stable relationship with a working stiff was not likely. Oh, she had him pussy whipped, he knew, but that wasn't forever. Those kinds of things never are for anyone. Sooner or later, magic of fame was going to carry him away on the arms of his corpses; he was sure of it.

Oh, why wait, thought William. Few places on earth are more private than a mortician's lab, with the exception of the bedroom, which was pretty much just the case with Patricia as a sexual partner. There had been a pretty one or two who'd lain upon his slabs. He'd been tempted. William pulled a flask of whiskey out of his hip pocket and took a swig, washing the unprofessional thought down. He had enough problems, not to let Patricia drive him to that.

He wedged a kidney pan upside down under Aunt Millie's neck, and filled a second one with yellow-blonde dye before lowering her hair into the solution. Forty minutes later, Aunt Millie's new blond locks were wound in neat rows of tight curls, and sprayed with a foam perm. Two hours after that, William was scrounging in the closet for his camera equipment. Behind him, a new Patricia likeness passively stared at the ceiling, awaiting its photo opportunity with peach lips and inch long eyelashes. Around the head, William had added an old ripped-up copy of Patricia's senior picture for background embellishment.

William sniffed the air. "When will I ever learn to not leave the cooler doors open?" He shut the cooler doors and then walked back to Aunt Millie, still following his nose. "Yo, Aunt Millie!

Been on a high fiber diet, I surmise. Seems it didn't work, but in my hands, my dear, you are at least looking marvelous."

William snapped a few photos, made a few adjustments to the makeup and then shot a few more. When he was done, he had to undo his creation. Bill thought he probably had the biggest stash of ratty grey and white hair dye in the state.

It took him half an hour to whip Millie back into shape, she finally prepared for the morning showing. He squinted when he looked at the redone Millie—not his best work, she having been too long in the process. She was quickly shoved back into the freezer.

Coupled with the one he'd done earlier, that left him with three to go. "That unfortunate family," mused William, sliding the first Keeder stiff out onto the table.

"So, Mrs. Keeder. What did you do? Hen peck him once too many? Call him on the phone just to give him hell? Now see where it has gotten you, my dear," said William, wagging his finger, Patricia's phone call still way too fresh in his mind.

He pulled her husband out as well, the two lying side by side for the first time since Mr. Keeder had started having those horrible and sudden headaches a month back.

William had another marvelous idea. He pushed the metal tables together. Fighting the rigormortis, he managed to force their fingers into a hand holding position. "There, just like the day you fell in love," proclaimed the mortician. The camera was still out, so he got a 'before' shot, Mr. Keeder with the ugly though curiously washed hole in the middle of his chest, and Mrs. Keeder with her head bent over at a forty-five degree angle. A bone stuck out of the unfortunate lady's neck. She had a thin, white nightgown on, the top of it stained brown from dried blood. The husband had been washed clean as a whistle in the creek. William was thankful for whatever color he could get. A corpses skin is made more ghostly contrasted against a little blood stain, good for his sense of camera esthetics.

Next came the makeup, the opportunity to make a Patricia pair, irresistible. Two rolls of film later, William switched on the Letterman Show, which he watched while replacing the couple's blood with formaldehyde. He was down to old reruns of the dating game by the time he'd made their faces ready for the more formal front room display. Apparently Mr. Keeder was going to be on ice several extra days, Mrs. Keeder and Mr. Keeder's relatives no longer on speaking terms and having chosen the same mortuary only by accident. If I have my way, thought William, neither group will ever know. He'd check viewing schedules to make sure of it.

"Four down and one to go." Shawn had only made it ten years as a Keeder before his dad had gone over the edge from a still undiscovered tumor and bashed the side of the boy's head in. There was no face making to be done on Shawn, thought William, not that he'd sink as low as to do the kid under any circumstances. William, after all, had some pride in his professional standards. Shawn was quick, routine and unfortunately, a closed casket case.

Bill switched the TV channel to Soul Train reruns after fixing a microwave pizza. Pushing the tables aside, he watched the TV across a wide-open floor while sitting on the edge of a wheeled stretcher. William spotted a couple of dancing beauties to look out for, and marveled at the psychology of intermittent reinforcement afforded by the spinning cameras.

"I just know I kept Aunt Millie out too long. That murderer is going to be in the cooler for half a week too. You get an ugly corpse twice in a row, and there goes the reputation," reflected William out loud, his words echoing off of the porcelain and brick walls in the funeral home basement.

"It's sooooooooooooooooooooouuuuuuuuuuuuuul train!" The television squealed.

"Yeah, what was that stuff?" William asked himself, getting up and going over to the corner of the underground room. There he slipped a small screwdriver blade into a loose brick and wedged the thing out. Reaching into the rectangular recession he pulled out a rag. There was a half-pint sized glass bottle inside of that, which he extracted and examined by holding it up to the florescent lights. Given a shake, the clear liquid grew a greenish-blue cast, and then immediately returned to clear. Nothing had evaporated, noticed William, the lid apparently well sealed.

The bottle had endured years behind the cool brick, mostly forgotten because William had wanted to forget about it. He'd taken an unexplainably idiotic chance buying it from his buddy on the off chance Ralphy's word of mouth claims had been legit. It had been marked for high temperature disposal by the high tech gurus in the secret west wing; that much William knew. Ralph had picked it up because his job had been to dispose of things at VA Atlanta, a task he sometimes didn't do all that faithfully.

Ralph was a biological sanitation engineer, and in spite of the special training and sensitive nature of such a posting, the job paid only marginally better than any other sanitation engineering job. Ralphy kept his ear to the ground though, in hopes of fencing something special, William knew. More importantly, Ralphy kept his ear to the ground regarding ambitious new employees gullible enough to buy things special. William had hid the bottle as soon as he'd bought the mortuary, imagining himself hiding a little bit of shame at having allowed himself to be so easily suckered by a trash collector who couldn't possibly know enough science to substantiate any of his wild, third-hand claims.

"Soul flesh, I think you called it, Ralphy." William read the tag on the bottle of clear fluid, "US Department of Defense, Surgical

Testing Services. XZ27741ENZ ver 6. Top Secret. If found, contact blah, blah, blah. What'd you say they called this stuff, Ralphy? "Dermatological nanobugs gone amuck. Worked a little too well for its own good. Fifty bucks, but keep it under wraps or we both lose our clearance!""

"I don't know Ralphy, but I think you got me there. Caught me at a moment of sheer stupidity. Well, we might as well check it out on Mr. Keeder before we shove what's left of it up his ass and burn it. Live and learn, test and burn," said William, pulling the dead killer back out of his cooler. He immediately thought better of it, sliding the dead man back into the freezer. Wednesday was going to be a long day, and experimentation will have to wait for a few hours of sleep.

William wiped down the tables with antiseptic and tossed the buckets of gizzards into a burn pan that he sat into the cool incinerator where they'd catch up to the next body. "Ashes are ashes. Let me think, who's next on the incinerator list? Hum, oh yeah, Aunt Millie's people are buying the Windsor model casket. The Keeders are going to St. Mary's in Greenlawn 320s. Hum…Mr. What's His Face is going VA in a Poorboy. Oh, of course, Mr. Keeder. Ought to smell good by then for you, Mr. Keeder. You won't mind though, will you Mr. Keeder? You're a bigun, but even big ones ain't apt to fill the whole urn without some filler. Besides, serves you right, Mr. Keeder for dumb-es-tic violence. Let em sort your giblets out in Hades; you'll probably appreciate anything by way of a distraction on the way down anyway."

William rolled a portable bed out from the storage room and set it up. No need to go home, he thought. He had his suit in the office, and he'd have to start on the final prep for Aunt Millie in five hours. Maybe, he considered, if testing the stuff on Mr. Keeder helped that complexion, he'd rub some onto Aunt Millie too? She'd not well withstood being out of the freezer as long as she had. "God knows she needs the help."

The mortician laid down on his cot between two steel autopsy tables, and without an ounce of concern about the macabre surrounding, was quickly snoring under a thin white sheet. Above his head, behind thick and shiny stainless steel doors, the others rested a bit more soundly.

4

At the same time that William was painting the face of the man Joe'd shot, Joe was stepping out of the Ponderosa feeling fat. The manager locked the door in the wake of his last customer. Joe had been ten hours late for brunch, but he'd made up for it. He patted his churning belly, instantly regretting the choice of hands. The numbness was fading a little too fast in Joe's opinion.

The hand wasn't in a cast, but there was a slight sling and a wrapping so complete that he could only see the knuckles of his fingers. Joe had expected Doctor Laura Adkins to be an incompetent quack; one of those lawsuit doctors who makes half of her money testifying in court, spinning reality in the direction of whatever tune the money dictates. Instead, she had proven to be a surprisingly competent surgeon, as well as a thorough examiner. A middle-aged woman with fairly long and greying hair that was barely brushed, it was clear that Doctor Adkins put more energy into her work than into her appearance. Joe liked her, her demeanor not unlike his own mother's had been. He'd decided to accept her bedside manner in just that way, motherly, though she was only a year or two older than Joe himself.

The x-rays had shone only one serious fracture beyond a chip and a hairline on a second bone. None the less, the doctor had managed to make a list that was a dozen items long. She had articulated all the nerves, minor veins, muscles and membranes damaged by the bullet's passage through Joe's hand. With such an eye for detail, it was no wonder Dominique liked her testimony, realized Joe. Doctor Laura Adkins kept saying, "You're really lucky. Bullets do more damage by suction than they do by anything direct. In your case, the bullet was nearly spent by the time it hit you. Do you have any idea how many bones and vessels are in a hand?"

"Well, a lot, I suppose,"

"Yes, a lot, honey," she said before pushing him down onto the paper covered bed and strapping his arm to a board that she extended from the bed's side. She picked up a Polaroid and snapshot his hand, reminding Joe for the second time that he'd been sent to Doctor Adkins by an ambulance chaser.

"If you think you can hold still, I can glue the bone to the one next to it, clean out the junk and tighten up the meat. That's your best bet. The glue might not work, and the skin is going to get black. If the infection is too bad, the black turns yellow, leaks infection and smells like an outhouse. Grafting skin into a palm is next to impossible. It could get to the point where I have to remove part of the hand, so we're going to see each other some more after this. Removing the stitches is particularly fun after the blood dries on them and the loose skin is nice and stuck. I'm sure you didn't want to hear any of that, but there it is. Oh, don't look so scared; I tell people the worst, just in case the unexpected happens and they get ideas that it's my fault. You'll probably be playing piano tomorrow.

I can do what I can for your hand right here and now in the office, but some people prefer to be under or think it isn't really surgery if it isn't done in a hospital that charges a month's pay for one night's bedding. Which is it, here or in hospital," she said, extracting a disposable hypodermic needle out of a wrapper and filling the syringe with local anesthesia.

"Damn!" Said Joe, realizing that the doctor was more confident of his answer than he felt. He answered by looking the other way and closing his eyes. A second later he felt the cold alcohol rub and the sharp needle prick. The worst part of the injection was the cold liquid as it flowed down his arm.

"Oh, and one more thing. I don't know if you found Dominique or if she found you, but this might not heal like new. At best, it might heal in a few days and itch every so often but otherwise seal up unnoticeable, save the scar. Either extreme is possible, but most of the time it just heals like any old scruff. Early arthritis is almost guaranteed though. Once in awhile people end up on lifetime pain medication, or have amputations, often just to ease the pain. I'll have you sign a form that you know the risks before you leave. Dominique hasn't sued me yet, but anyone who blindly trusts a lady like that is fooling themselves. It's not her, it's the breeding," confided Doctor Adkins.

Joe took it all in and then chuckled. "You ever have a patient referred by her that she didn't do the finding on?"

"No."

"That's what I thought. Don't worry. I figure you'll do the best that you can."

The local had him looking at flesh he couldn't feel. Laura set her instruments out on a table, and called for a nurse to help her scrub. Joe decided to turn his head away. He watched the wall as the doctor started her tugging on the numbed flesh.

"Besides the considerable pain, the skin is going to be really tight in the palm. I'll wrap it with the fingers curled. Keep it still until I see you Friday. You can change the wrap and clean it with alcohol, but that's it," said the doctor as she finished.

"Yes Ma'am," Joe'd said, happy that the worst was over. It occurred to him that the money he was suing for was going to be something earned instead of the windfall he'd at first imagined.

Later, from the front of the Ponderosa, he looked back across the street at the empty parking lot of the medical building he'd left a couple hours earlier. Another block down was the hospital. It had been a long day, and he was feeling woozy from the ceaseless excitement and the sudden contrast of a full stomach. In another twenty minutes he was going to need one of those pain pills, and then technically it would be illegal to drive his car that was still parked a mile away. He needed to be on his way. There was absolutely no reason that he could think of to go visit that cop who'd been shot, except for an acute case of curiosity.

Joe got off of the third story elevator, a wad of daisies and a balloon in his only good hand. There were a couple of cops down the hall, marking the room. They were standing with their backs to him, chatting over coffee, apparently unconcerned about the fact that visiting hours were over. Joe knew that to be an issue because he'd had to tell the candy striper that he was the woman's brother, "flown in all the way from Idaho. You know, potatoes, the stuff that they make French fries out of." Somehow he'd managed to convince the nurse that he was family without even knowing the cop's name.

The first officer to turn was Joe's worst nightmare.

"It's you. Who let you out?" Asked Jimmy. The name over the badge said Baker. Joe looked again at Jimmy's face and finally realized that he was seeing the Chief's son.

"My lawyer. She's writing a case regarding you and your daddy's bad police work right now. It's her idea really. If it was up to me we'd save ourselves the trouble and meet in that alley I promised," offered Joe.

The cop beside Jimmy bristled, which was quite a trick considering he was a round head who sported a crew hair. Jimmy, of course, had already bristled, it being his natural posture.

"You'd like that, wouldn't you," said Jimmy.

Joe suddenly felt childish for his part in the conversation. "No, Officer Jimmy, I'm just messing with you. I actually need the money. In fact, as much as it must pain me to be impolite, I didn't come here to chat with you. I came to see how the patient was doing."

"Sandra isn't up to it," said Jimmy, bracing himself.

"Let me see if I get this right. You are telling me that in America I'm not allowed to bring flowers to a sick person because you don't like me?" Joe put his flowers on a chair and pulled a piece of scrap paper out of his shirt pocket. The blue lines were all run together and the inside of the wad was still wet. "You got a pen. I need to write this down. I'm sure Dominique is going to love adding a constitutional issue to the lawsuit. Christ, that's another seventy K. You're making me rich, Jimmy."

Jimmy didn't budge, but his buddy shrugged and stepped aside. Apparently roundheads are a little bit smarter than daddy's boys, Joe guessed. He took the opening, and turned into the room with his flowers.

"Hello?" Asked Sandra when she saw the stranger. She grit her teeth from a sudden pain in her rib cage.

"Oh, sorry. Um, I'm Joe Jefferson, the guy down in the creek. Well, I just came to thank you for stepping up to the plate when you did. The guy had a bead on me just when you showed."

"Oh, I'm sorry. I didn't recognize you. Everything happened so fast," she said in a quieter voice. Sandra put a hand over her chest.

"Don't talk if it hurts. I'm kind of amazed that you're even awake and out of intensive care," said Joe.

"I'm OK. Bulletproof vest. Still, they say it knocked the breath clear out of me and that I cracked a rib. His weapon was a forty-five, and close. Didn't help that I breathed in a pint of creek water after I blacked out either. I can't even imagine drinking that stuff without a truckload of city chemicals to smooth it out," said Sandra, smiling.

She was mid-thirties, a few years younger than Joe. She also had a nice smile, Joe realized. The mussed up brown hair and hospital gown looked good on her for reasons that had Joe remembering the last time he'd woken up with a woman by his side. Joe mentally scolded himself for thinking that way about her; his mission was supposed to be one of compassion and friendship, not lust. Still, he was glad she'd lost the uniform.

"You know, I'm relieved. To be honest, I thought you'd bought the farm. I didn't have time to look and figure out how badly you'd been hit. I was even debating whether to pull you out of the creek or just run away. I figured you for dead. That must have been some cannon the guy had, because it lifted you right off your feet and planted you six feet back." Joe realized he's said enough, and apologized, "I'm sorry. You don't need to hear all that."

"Well, maybe I do. Baker had me thinking Jimmy pulled me out."

"Jimmy? The only thing Jimmy did was arrest me. Maybe that's good, because the rest of them were trampling on the evidence. At least he wasn't doing that while he was putting me in cuffs and shoving me into the back of his car."

"Now that's the police department I know," she said, her smile widening and her teeth fighting the pain by biting a lower lip at the same time. She looked over at the door and added, "Shut the door, will you?"

Joe went over, smiled out at the two eavesdropping cops and shut the door in their faces a little harder than he needed to.

Sandra started, "I need to thank you for saving my life too."

"To be honest, I don't have a clue why I pulled you out. Thinking back, considering you was dead and all, it seems perfectly stupid. That guy was definitely off his rocker."

"He killed his wife and child. I got the call. He was poised to shoot himself, thought better of it when he saw me and then bolted out the back."

"Well, I knew something was up. Figured it out, oh, pretty much about the first bullet he sent my way. So, how's it feel?"

"Hurts like hell when I laugh," said Sandra.

"Then I won't tell you any knock-knock jokes."

"Who's there?"

"Orange."

"Orange who?"

"Orange you glad I'm not going to tell you any knock-knock jokes."

Sandra looked at him with saucer eyes. Joe wasn't smiling, but he was biting his tongue so that he was completely deadpan on the outside. Somehow the deadpan face and the really bad joke started working on her. She bit her lip again. Then she squeezed her eyes shut. Then she started laughing and couldn't stop, as if the rules to laughing required either one big laugh or five minutes of suppressed little ones.

"God, I'm sorry. I didn't think it was all that funny," said Joe over and over again as the lady squeezed out the laughs.

Sandra rolled over onto her side, grabbing at her breasts with her arms. Ringlets of her brown hair fell across her face. Tears streamed down her cheeks as she finished. "Oh god, Joe...don't...do that...to me again."

"Absolutely," said Joe, seriously.

"I mean it. I don't know which hurts worse, the breathing...or the sharp pain in my ribs."

"Really, I'm sorry. From now on I'll stick to politics and religion; swear to god," said Joe, holding up his good hand. That, of course, got her going again, and in spite of the pain, they both felt a growing bond. They chatted awhile, Joe careful to keep it about the events of the day and his work in the music store. Sandra told him about being a cop in a small town.

Joe confided, "You know, in some places a person owes another person if they've saved their life. Have to follow them around until the debt is repaid."

"Oh, goodness," said Sandra, her face bright with mocked concern.

"Yeah. So the way I figure it, you saved me and I saved you, and so either we have to follow each other around awhile, or we can call it even, whichever is most comfortable."

"Hum. Well, I don't want to rush things. Maybe we can follow around a little, and decide later if we're even? Are you asking me out on a date?"

"Hum. Well, I don't want to rush things," Joe teased back.

"Jimmy thinks he's my boyfriend. We went out once, and it was horrible. I was into this younger man stage, and hadn't yet figured out that we'd have nothing in common to talk about. In Jimmy's case, it's more than that. It's..."

Joe finished her sentence,"...he has a chip on his shoulder. Likes people to think he's more than he is. Classic inferiority complex."

"Yeah. Well anyway, that was years back, and he still acts like he half owns me just because we dated one time, though I never miss the chance to brush him off. Talk about a guy who can't take a hint. Worst of all, his father is keen on us as an item, even though he pretends he's not watching. That's my boss, you know; makes for a very odd situation," explained Sandra.

Joe could take a hint, and was happy to at least know the score. "So, when do they cut you loose?"

"Tomorrow morning. Ten or so."

"Maybe I can pick you up, assuming they haven't impounded my car like they did my fishing gear. Not that it was much of a loss because my fishing isn't very good and the fish up and died. Call it a little date to your car at the station and maybe breakfast. You might not like me in the daylight," offered Joe.

"Oh, would you? I was planning on going out the back and walking to my car. Anything to keep from being driven by one of the guys. They're all full of this, 'I'm out in the hall protecting the pitiful female cop,' look. It feels like, 'See, told you women weren't up to it.' God forbid it should be Jimmy out there in the morning still, doing his male protector thing all over me."

"I can, and I'll consider it an act of mercy no less significant than you standing in that creek protecting me from that maniac's bullets."

"It's a deal, Mister Jefferson," said Sandra, holding out her hand.

Joe took it, noticing how cold and shaky it was, she clearly feeling worse than she put out for the sake of keeping polite company. He felt a little guilty for keeping her from her rest. "I'll tell them to keep the door closed so you can rest."

"Thanks," said Sandra, pulling the covers up over her chest, but watching Joe's buns intently as he walked out the door.

5

"I'll fly away, ol' glory, I'll fly away. When I die, hallelujah, by and by, I'll fly away!..."

William's shoved the curtain shut. "Good god, another charismatic service. I should have known the minute I saw that Reverend Bob Purswell," he whispered into the back room.

"Well, at least Aunt Millie is on her way out. Another half hour or so of revival and they'll move the uproar over to the cemetery where I won't have to nod and smile and pretend like I like it," he added, content to leave the old woman in the hands of the big shot TV preacher. "Purswell, the man had damned near declared himself on a par with Jesus. Says right on the back of his handouts, 'Purswell is God.' Now what's that supposed to mean?" William didn't favor one religion over the other, but for some of the preachers he had to make an exceptional effort to smile for. William walking back down the stairs to the preparation rooms.

There on the table was Mister Keeder. One cheek was pink, and the rest of his face was the stone grey of a man who'd melted off his cosmetic work.

"Good gravy man! I have to stop leaving these things out."

William nearly ran to the corpse. The face he'd tested the chemical on earlier in the morning was not only alive and rosy on one side, but he thought he could even see natural subtle variations in the pigment, an indication of depth to the color. All of that after one drop behind the ear, a drop that had chemically spread wildly, like a time lapsed skin cancer. Of course there were blotches of grey that had the look of liver spots. He'd had to do as much repainting on Aunt Minnie as he'd have had to do without the chemical.

Overall, the experiment had been a failure, although the stuff did seem to bring their flesh back to life, and with a minimal dose. Only a dab had been tried earlier near Mister Keeder's ear and the whole cheek had turned pink. Whatever it was, it spread or multiplied on its own when it met meat, like those experimental nanobots, or maybe just plain old virus or maybe even just enzymes, but enzymes that somehow regenerated. "Meat tenderizer," theorized William.

He put another pair of disposable surgical gloves on, and brushed the chemical over the rest of Mister Keeder's face. By the time he was done, Mister Keeder was starting to smell both of rot and chemicals, although he did look simply marvelous, even for a man with new white liver spots.

Upstairs, the crowd of burr haircuts and red ties, buns and long dresses was going strong on a resounding chorus of 'Meet Me on the Other Shore.' They were going on a little longer than William had specified in the contract, but that happened all of the time; more often than not with this kind of crowd.

On the table, Mister Keeder's sewn together lips smiled on the side made rosy earlier. Above that, the eyelid, sewn shut with one thread, started shaking. "Wow! I can see that your reflexes are working overtime, Mister Keeder. Let's get you back where you can do that in private." William snapped the rubber gloves off, and then shoved Mister Keeder back into the freezer with deft quickness. Done with that, he set the bottle of chemicals on the counter and sprayed the room with air freshener. The mortician hoped to God nobody changed their mind and had an open casket for the murderer. After all the fiddling around, even William doubted that he could make the man look natural again.

One floor up, Reverend Purswell spoke into the microphone. "Yes, brothers and sisters, uh huh, we are all going to meet the maker! Can you say, uh, hallelujah? Our sister here, uh huh, she's a goin home ta meet the maker! Yes, I said, uh huh, she's a goin' to meet the maker!"

"Hallelujah!" Screamed a thin lady in the back pew. She had her eyes closed and her head shaking yes. One hand was in the air, and the other holding a toddler on her knee. Everyone else joined in.

William crept back up the stairs and watched out from the corner of the curtain again. He looked at his watch, knowing he'd have to put up with the long service because he had nearly a hundred future customers in the chapel.

"We are so sad to see her go, uh huh. Our sister will no longer be at the pot luck. No, no! She will no longer be, uh huh, at the Bible studies. I say, uh huh, she will no longer be in section 8B with Sister Stella. No, no, but I can tell you folks, uh huh, she's a sitting at the feet of God, uh huh! Yes, I tell you, uh huh, and a, at the feet of our Jesus! Can a you see her there, a kissing the feet of our Lord? Can you see her there? Can you see her a standing there by our Lord Jeeeeeeeeeeeeessssssssssus?"

"Yes. I can see her there! Standing by our Lord!" Screamed Aunt Millie's nephew, who was three rows back. The nephew started dancing in front of the pew, waving both hands in the air. He banged row two with his knees, but didn't seem to mind. Half of the audience stood to join him, each with their own style of celebration. After awhile the pews couldn't contain them, and the crowd started forward, dancing around the casket. Reverend

Purswell was next behind the casket, the microphone abandoned, clapping his hand at a new round of, 'I'll fly away," as the organ blew to life.

William tightened his tie and stepped into the chapel. He nodded at Purswell with the smile and slightly bowed head of a professional mortician.

Over by the casket, the nephew leaned over the casket, imagining his Aunt Millie in heaven with Jesus. In fact, he could almost see her smile widening, and her face glowing like an angel, just a little. No, she is an angel now, he thought, leaning over and seeing the Holy Ghost on her face, shining through with new life. Born again, he thought! Her glow was a sign. She's been born again in Christ, and is now born again in heaven. God's signs are all over her, just to tell us all that she's got, "New life in the holy city! Hallelujah!"

The nephew leaned over and kissed his aunt on the forehead. The skin under his lips was soft and compliant, but cold. There was this taste too. He had to purse the lips to keep the foul taste out of his mouth. The nephew rubbed his lips with his fingers, but even that didn't help much, him soon squinting his eyes in an effort to hide the bitterness and ruin the otherwise good feeling of spiritual exuberance. Taking the backside of his other hand, he managed to rub away most of the rest of the taste, but then he looked at his hand and it was turning pinker than normal; pink with white liver spots!

He stopped dancing, and just stared at the back of his hand, the pink smear an inch long and twice as wide. Inside of that the white spots were becoming grey splotches that he touched, the splotches cold and tough like the skin of well done chicken that had sat in the refrigerator too long.

The man rubbed an eye with his fingers, using the same hand that he'd originally wiped his mouth with. The nephew looked again. The pink smear seemed a little larger, but suddenly his eye started to sting. It dawned upon the man that the mortician's chemicals were toxic and he might need medical attention. He Looked up at Purswell for support. There he found Purswell looking back with an accusatory frown, suggesting to the nephew that he wasn't in the proper spiritual frame of mind.

Around them both, the crowd kept right on celebrating.

Between them, Aunt Millie sat up in her casket.

Aunt Millie was the most surprised person in the room. One minute she'd been in a slow, horrifying and decaying state, fighting for each and every breath as her body grew cold. There'd been such a source of pain that she couldn't bear to wear it. Things had faded and suddenly felt much, much better as she'd finally died. That had been two days ago, but to Aunt Millie, it had been the very last second. Then, in another second she'd become crisply awake, slapped by a chillingly bright world. All of the old pains and horrors were gone. In their place she had a different, freezing feeling, that had the extra horror of both detachment and emptiness. Whatever was gone was so sorely needed that she couldn't bear being without it, and yet she didn't know what it was that was missing, her mental faculty just not what it had once been.

Her hands went to her belly, exploring the sunken mass of gutless stomach, clawing at the dress viciously. Never in her whole life had she felt so empty, so hungry, so in need of warm, pulsating comfort. It was as if she needed a massage from the inside out. Somehow she had to get something warm between her teeth and swallow it before she froze solid.

Trying to lick her lips, the tongue was a prisoner of her own mouth, her lips sewn shut. There was a foul taste of chemicals that was coming from so deep inside of herself that it was impossible to avoid. Her tongue had to get out, she understood. Her teeth bit at her own mouth from the inside out, seeing a way to allow the tongue to escape and find another taste. Her hands came up. They pulled at the threads on her eyes and mouth. When a few threads didn't come free, she banged her head across the side of the casket, hammering at the threads until they pulled free of the battered face.

Aunt Millie's mouth flew open. The tongue thrusted into the cold air. Expecting to taste the delights that she smelled, Millie's first reaction was utter disappointment. Her lips snarled into a scream that came out horse and almost as empty as a scratch of chalk across a blackboard. She had to taste something normal, something not chemical, something human like before she'd died when she could taste herself!

She sniffed the air over and over again, drawing in warmth and almost tasting the aroma. She heard the beating of the hearts of game all around her. One eye could only half open against the threads, but it looked at Bob Purswell and saw nothing but pure taste. It was unimaginable that she could be so lucky. This was not only a means to restoring a familiar taste sensation; it was also as if she'd found a deli in her own kitchen. She had to have him inside. She had to feel his humanity inside of her utter emptiness!

Millie raised her upper body toward Purswell. The preacher fall back across the podium carpet as the casket toppled over and Millie fell to the floor a step in front of his feet.

"Oh my God, Aunt Millie!" Screamed the nephew as he stepped over the casket and knelt beside the woman as she wreathed upon the floor. She was laying face down, fighting the blankets, her eyes still cast upon the shoes of the reverend as he retreated.

"Someone call an ambulance," said the preacher as he gained his feet. Not waiting for an answer, he ran over to where William was standing. "A phone, man! Call 911!"

William broke from his shock and nodded toward the curtains to his back. The preacher shoved past the mortician, and found the wall phone, quickly dialing.

In the mean time, several of the church members recovered. Half ran out of the front door, but a few of the sisters and brothers knelt around her, some praying and others trying to help the nephew roll her over onto a part of the floor where the medics could get at her when they arrived.

One of the sisters combed Millie's head with her fingers, finding the hand coming away with several dozen hairs. Another brother held her neck, him remembering them doing that on TV shows whenever someone fell and the TV medics had to insure against a neck injury.

Aunt Millie was a little dizzy from the fall and from being turned over, but then regained her purpose. Her head shot up, capturing the man's wrist in her jaws. She bit quick and hard, right to the bone, and held on for keeps. Blood immediately started to flow into her mouth, the taste of a live human being again upon her tongue. She closed her eyes and moaned a sickening gasp of putrid stomach gas as she tasted the heavenly flow. Her teeth weren't nearly as good as she'd hoped they'd be, but the blood alone was pure ecstasy.

The man pulled for all his worth, others looking on in terror. The arm seemed stuck, the jaws of the woman incredibly strong for someone so sickly. She started to grind the jaws back and forth, sawing upon his bone, wanting more than just blood. Her eyes suddenly shot wide open, brought to excitement by the taste and energy feeding trickle. The man and Millie's nephew, groped at her jaw, pulling it open so that the man could pull free, Millie's teeth cutting both men's fingers. The men broke free, and the small, lingering crowd drew back.

"Uhhhhhhh," wailed Millie, crawling up to all fours. She tossed herself at Sister Helen. Helen flew back, then fell back as Millie captured a foot. Helen cracked her skull across a pew. Helen's shriek was cut short by the fatal blow. Millie took one of Helen's thighs into her lips and ate away the skin. She looked around at the remaining crowd, her head darting, and her body curled over her food as if keeping it from being dragged away by the rest of the pack. The look in her eyes was that of a dog warning away other predators. Then she leaned back and ripped some muscle out with her teeth. She chewed, and then, the meat half chewed, swallowed. "Ohhhhhhhhh!" She moaned contentedly before chewing out a second helping. Helen's heart was in its last half minute of pumping. Blood from an artery flowed out as if it were shot out by a squirt gun. Millie drank a little, and then ate another chunk of leg.

Under her, Helen's heart stopped beating. The next bite didn't seem quite as good to Millie. "Ahh, ahh, ahh," she moaned, her voice taking upon itself a vibrating quality. Then she noticed all of the rest of the food around her, it still quite fresh. Helen's body, while still OK, seemed nothing compared to fresh meat. She stood, her legs wobbly. Then she took a step, her legs a little less wobbly. Then she ran at the half dozen who'd not yet left the main aisle. They turned, and while screaming, beat her out the door.

"What have you done?" Yelled Purswell.

William turned, and shook his head no at the preacher. "I..."

"What kind of place is this? Don't you check? How can a thing like this happen?" Screamed the preacher.

"Embalmed..." the mortician tried to explain, his stuttering words again interrupted.

"Embalmed my ass. You did no such things. You cut corners. Christ, if you'd have cut her open, you'd have seen her bleed. You'd have seen her heart beating. What you did was paint her up and put her in a casket. How many people have you buried on the cheap? I'll have your license. I'll see you in jail!" Screamed the preacher, backing William further into the main church.

William sat in the pew, repeatedly mumbling, "embalmed."

"Right!" Spit the preacher, rushing by the mortician. He went to Sister Helen and knelt at her side as another returning man checked her pulse.

"She's gone," declared the man, dropping Sister Helen's arm.

"What a mess. What about Sister Millie?"

"She took one look at the sun and it seemed to hurt her eyes more than ripping the stitches had. She lunged at people for awhile, but you know, she's old; not too nimble. Then she took a look around and ducked into the woods up the creek. The way things were, there wasn't anyone particularly excited about running after her. I guess she'll run out of steam before she gets too far. I don't know, but maybe she'll kill herself before the authorities find her. It ain't right, what's happened to her," explained the man.

"God help her."

"Help her find peace, pastor; that's what I'm praying. Dead or crazy, I wouldn't think it much different if it was me. Ain't no wonder she's gone off her rocker; waking up in a coffin,"

"Ain't no wonder indeed," added the man of God as he cast an accusatory eye toward the mumbling mortician.

****

"There's a ten-eight causing a disturbance at the Wilson Mortuary. Several people bitten."

Baker was on the wrong side of town, but his cruiser was aimed in the right direction. Within seconds his V-8 pushed sixty miles an hour in the twenty-five zone. A couple of those precious pedestrians his cops had spent years badgering in the name of safety, jumped back onto the curb in the nick of time. The cruiser zoomed by.

Baker was oblivious to anything but the emergency. He thought about those murders and the mayhem of the previous day, and now, added to the list was this call about a crazy at the funeral home. He knew a funeral was in progress, having arranged the overtime for the escorts himself. It was a quarter till ten, the escort supposedly on duty in ten minutes, assuming they weren't early enough to catch the last of someone's showing snacks like they usually were.

****

"Gee, thanks. That's the second time you've saved my life," said Sandra.

"Nah, he'd have probably missed you anyway. Besides, it's only a car. It could have been something dangerous, like maybe a skateboarder," said Joe.

Sandra looked at him with curious eyes. "You don't like police officers very much, do you?"

"Oh, I don't know. I like some of them, I guess. Just like anything else that includes people; some are worth a damn and some aren't. Except, of course, with cops you have these rare opportunities where you find yourself confronted by more of the latter than the former. One of the components of bad cops is they're the ones the general public are most apt to encounter. Good cops aren't all that conspicuous. I like you though, so I promise not to say another word about it," said Joe.

"You just like me because you've seen me in one of those flimsy hospital gowns," she said, stepping off of the curb, again leading.

Joe could tell that her hectic pace was mostly show, her ribs still heavily taped.

"Ok. I confess. Now what about breakfast?" asked Joe, catching up to her as she crossed the street.

"Maybe later. Let's go find out what's up first," asked Sandra, slowing down enough so that Joe could point out his car.

They drove down High Street, right through the center of the little town. Red and blue lights reflected off of the bridge just beyond Poplar Street. Joe and Sandra shared a shudder. They remembered the trauma of the day before down in the creek as they passed over the bridge and wormed to the right toward Dead Man's Turn. Joe's car passed by the cemetery, the cop cars just ahead in the parking lot of the mortuary.

"Watch out!" Yelled Sandra. At the same moment, Joe jerked the wheel and hit his brakes. The woman had run up the embankment and out into the road so quickly that she seemed to have come from nowhere. Her body slammed across the hood. One of her hands smacking the windshield with enough force to start a crack that slowly spread until it reached end to end across the glass. Aunt Millie bounced thirty feet back into the shrub obscured ditch she'd come from. Joe fought his car as it swerved another couple of feet to the left.

****

Millie only had sketchy memories about how she'd gotten back into the ditch. It had something to do with running toward the sun lit road, she guessed. That will never do, she decided. The ditch and the woods were better. It was darker in the woods. Not dark enough, but darker.

She put a hand up over her eyes, shielding them from the blinding sun that trickled through the loose canopy of leaves. Her hand dropped pitifully, an ulna bone freshly sticking out just behind the wrist. The bone was white, the end jagged, but there was no blood dripping from the ragged rip in her skin. There was a dull little pain, but Millie was becoming immune to the inconvenience; the pain of hunger for the taste was far bigger. She paid little mind to the cantankerous wrist, compensating by holding her arm over her eyes and letting the hand droop down past the opposite ear.

The sun was bad—very bad—she decided again. It had given her head a sharp kick the first time she'd looked up at it. Mostly because of the sun, Millie had been traveling with her head down even when she'd run out of the woods and into the street.

Darkness was what she needed, Millie determined. The ditch was darker than the road, but the woods were even darker. She got up, her body not feeling as cooperative as it had been when she'd first woken up with that bad taste in her mouth. Several freshly broken vertebrae ground in Millie's lower back. It took awhile for her body to adjust to the new damage, but in time she managed a reasonable walking stride as she ducked through the first canopy of the forest just upstream from the cemetery.

****

"My God, she came out of nowhere! Are you alright?" Asked Joe.

"Just give me a second," answered Sandra, holding her chest where the seat belt had pressed into her broken ribs.

"Are you sure?" He repeated, his door already open.

"Just check on that woman," answered Sandra, smoothing out her breaths.

Joe had a foot out of the door. He looked in front of the car and was surprised to notice that a body wasn't there. Over by Sandra's side of the car the ground was equally vacant. He stepped beside the road and looked down into the drainage ditch. The grass was pressed down, but the ditch was empty. There was no blood.

"How is she?" Asked Sandra.

"She's not here. The woman must have run off. Did you see her? Did you get a good look at her? A direction maybe?"

"How could I miss? My face was only a couple of feet from her's when she slammed across the hood. I have to tell you, Joe, she looked sick. I don't know if it was the fright or what, but.... Like rabies, or..." Sandra's voice trailed off as she failed to find the words.

Joe filled in the pause. "I can't believe it. I've hit a pedestrian. This is supposed to be a nice, quiet, stay at home vacation. I end up being shot at, killing a man, running down an old lady. Sweet Moses!" He stepped into the brush, and crossed the ditch.

"Come back here, Joe. We'll get help. She'll at least need an ambulance," shouted Sandra. Sandra felt a chilling premonition.

Joe looked into the edge of the woods that stretched north and yet he paused there at the edge of the road. Something isn't right, he sensed. No more than a hundred feet south, he could still see the broken guardrail where the madman's car had crossed into the graveyard the morning before. "Yeah, we'll report it and form a search," he said as he backed up the embankment, returning to the car.

They drove into the mortuary lot. A few of the mourners loitered around in small groups. Chief Baker walked in a circle around the funeral home, directing a trio of equally confused deputies in a search of the grounds.

"Chief! I just ran into a woman down the road. She ran right into my car, and bounced into the ditch," said Joe as soon as he got close enough.

"Where?"

"A hundred yards down. I'm surprised you didn't see it happen. A block down, in plain view."

"So you left the scene." There was delight in the statement.

"Not exactly. Officer Anderson was with me. We stayed there a minute, and looked for her at the brush edge, but the woman ran off, we guessed. I figured it would be best to get help. That something you guys do, or is being dumb and lazy the only parts of the training you've been through?" Joe said, exasperated.

Sandra got out of the car. "That's the way it happened, Chief. He looked for the lady, and she was gone. We're pretty sure she's hurt badly, so it's important that we get some people down there to help find her."

"What did this lady look like?" Asked the Chief. That drew the attention of a couple of men Joe didn't know; people from some funeral party, he gathered, though the pair hung back.

"She was old, kind of a dumpling, but not tall. Dressed in a light blue dress, kind of formal for her age; like she was at her own funeral," answered Joe.

"Damn! Guys! Let's get on down the road. It's probably the same woman; over by the cemetery. We'll spread out and comb on down that side of the creek," the Chief said to his men.

Jimmy came out of the mortuary just then and yelled over to his dad, "Hey Chief, you'd better come in here and have a look at this."

The Chief sighed and waved the other three deputies off to do the search on their own. One of the two men from the funeral party volunteered to help, going with them. The second man who'd wandered close, walked over to a black Cadillac with the name PURSWELL emblazed on the license plate. Joe remembered Reverend Purswell from his national telecasts, thinking him one of the world's biggest flies in the ointment. There, the man leaned into the window, Joe surmising that he was spreading the gossip.

Any minute now, a million reporters are going to be in on the latest, thought Joe. He wondered if they'd remember him from yesterday when they took their next photographs of the hit and run driver?

"Is this important?" Asked the harried Chief.

Jimmy saw Joe and Sandra together and cast a beam of disapproval. Still, there were other things pressing on the young cop's mind. "There's a mess down in the embalming room. This is going to make your week when you see this, dad."

"Chief!"

"Yeah, right Chief. This is really getting odd. You'll have to look."

"Not something else," moaned Chief Baker as he followed up the steps of the funeral home.

Sandra walked by both Joe and the Chief. Considering that Sandra was unofficially still his date, Joe felt compelled to follow the three cops into the dismal place. They went through a side curtain, and then down the steps. The basement workroom was in some considerable disarray. One of the metal tables had been knocked over. Above that, a cadaver storage door yawned. The door oozed a frosty chill. Finally, near the back of the room, a rarely used, but now damaged cellar door let in some much needed air. Morning light silhouetted a half dozen rickety cellar steps below that.

William waited in the middle of the room, pacing frantically, his hair a mess from his having combed it with his fingers once too often. He yelled at the Chief, "See! Someone's pulling some kind of stunt. It's probably some of those frat boys from Ohio State. I don't know why they just can't leave us alone out here in the suburbs. Think it'd be enough for them to burn up a dumpster or two after a football game, and leave us alone out here."

"What's going on?" Asked the Chief.

"They took Mr. Keeder. Imagine the news: Mass murderer's body stolen by frat boys. Jackasses like them live off silly shit like this," said William, who was actually glad to have the distraction from Aunt Millie's odd event. Anything to shift the focus, he thought, counting the theft as a blessing. Reverend Purswell's threats had startled him. He knew they weren't true, but he also knew that Purswell carried a lot more weight than he did.

Still, William needed to pump it up to turn the trick. "I think it might even be something satanic. Maybe all of this is somehow connected. You know, bodies stolen, including a mass murderer with maybe a special line straight to Satan. Shoot, Keeder might have been one of them before he died. I'm betting they came in here and stole Millie as a diversion. The woman who got up and caused a riot up in the chapel was probably someone made up to look like her. Fooled me even. One thing for sure, it wasn't Miss Millie. I embalmed her; have her guts in a bucket in the incinerator as we speak. How'd she do that getting up trick without lungs and a liver? No, this is really fishy. I think Aunt Millie was already stolen. The theft of Mr. Keeder is the icing on the cake; telling us what's going on. Ain't no doubt now. Some deranged freaks. This is just way out of control, Chief. You have to get on this."

The Chief went over to the drawers, and looked in. Then he checked the rest of the drawers for maybe a shuffle, not finding Mr. Keeder. "We'll get some prints on this one. Have radio put people in the know so they can be looking out for something suspicious. I think the satanic cult thing is quite plausible. Don't let that out," he told his son.

"Right, Chief," said Jimmy, running up the steps to get to his car radio.

Joe walked over to look up at the broken cellar door and then motioned for Sandra to come check it out. "See anything odd?"

"Yeah. Broken from the inside out." She whispered, "Maybe the mort did it?"

"No. Don't think so. He has no motive. This is bad for business. If he really needed bodies, he could cheat an incineration, and other than that, I can't imagine why he'd do it. Besides, the easiest way in here is most likely to have been through the front door. Getting a body out, however, well that's a bigger problem."

"So they broke the cellar door to get the bodies out," finished Sandra.

"Looks like it. Maybe someone in Purswell's crew? I don't know if that helps us solve the mystery though?" Mused Joe.

"Well, let's pretend he's right. If the lady that ran into your car is a sorority sister in makeup, she'd have left her makeup all over your window. If not, she'll have still left makeup, only it'll have been the make and model of that used by the mort," said Sandra loud enough for the Chief to hear her.

The Chief responded. "That's good. We'll be needing your car, Mister Jefferson."

"Oh, well of course. Any way I can help," said Joe, sarcastically.

"Hey! Don't get mouthy with me. I could run you in for the accident," said the Chief.

"No, I don't think so," said Joe, tossing his keys to the Chief, and leading Sandra up the first few steps.

"Why you so sure?" Asked the Chief.

"Well because I'm aiming on suing you for a hundred grand for the last time you did that. Now the way I figure it is, at twenty-five bucks a jaywalking ticket, you're going to have to bust four thousand skateboarders just to pay for that. There are only so many kids you pigs can pick on in this town, Chief."

"Right. Just don't leave town."

"I'll leave town whenever I damn well feel like it. But, it just so happens, I'm not in the mood for hitchhiking, now that you've impounded my wheels."

Sandra shrugged at her boss as Joe disappeared up the steps. She said, "I'll keep an eye on him."

"Yeah, you do that, honey. You get me a report on that accident too. And listen; don't forget you're a cop. You may be on leave, but that man is trouble, and I'm keeping an eye on you as long as you're with him."

"Yes Sir. I'll get you that report right away, Sir," she said with a practiced voice of detachment.

6

Sandra found Joe in back, looking around in the grass behind the funeral home. "You didn't have to be so negative in there. He's just trying to do his job," she said.

"Not very good at it, but yeah I know. It's just that in spite of that I've been shot, arrested, starved, verbally treated like scum, and now relegated to walking everywhere until the wheels of justice are done with me. I might as well just go out and buy another car, as quick as that is in America. I can't even go fishing; they have my tackle box. To top it off, I promised to take you out to breakfast and then home so you can get some rest. Some date I've turned out to be."

"Yeah. Some date. Big disappointment," she said, kneeling where Joe'd been kneeling and looking at the grass.

She is really good at saying things in a way that have me guessing if she is being sarcastic of truthful, thought Joe. She hadn't left, however, which gave him some hope.

"So, what are you looking for? Clues?"

"Um huh. See any tire tracks?" He asked.

"No, come to think of it," she agreed, looking closer.

"Not even footprints, except for that lonely little swipe of grass. See it? Get down close to the grass, and you can see where it's bent."

"Huh. What's that mean, Tonto?"

Joe explained, "Well, either we have one frat boy carrying a body all the way into that field where the closest access road is a quarter mile off, which would make our frat boy a pretty big man who didn't plan very well, or…."

"No. You don't think that Mr. Keeder just got up and walked out on his own?"

"No. That's…well that's not likely, I guess. I shot him dead center with your cannon, and then he was underwater for long enough to drown twice. The mortuary freezer isn't the kind of place one is likely to find invigorating either. No, the guy is dead. Two corpses coming alive in one day is even a bit much for the 'Inquirer'. Somebody's playing morbid little jokes on Pine Point is my guess. Maybe a witch." Joe got up.

Just then a group of three men broke from the woods along the section of the west river bank that ranged north. At first Joe thought it odd that three men in white shirts and ties pulled slack should be in the woods at all, but then he remembered the search parties of funeral attendees and how Reverend Purswell's people had volunteered to help. Joe waved, and one of the men waved back sheepishly.

"Find her yet?" Yelled Sandra.

"Yeah…" one man started to say.

A second man interrupted him, "Yeah, we think we saw her down toward the bridge, running along the bank for just a second. That's the direction the deputies went. They've got south where we had out sighting. We have this north section. She ducked into the tall weeds down there as fast as we saw her though. You mind relaying that down there?"

"Sure," said Sandra. She added, "Oh, by the way. We have someone playing games with us with a second body. Chief thinks Aunt Millie is someone faking to be her, so they might have her body too. Thinks someone snatched her body before the prank. A second body was carried off and the tracks make it look like they took it up from where you are, probably to that far road. Want to go on and see if you can spot something? Tire tracks on that access road and this field...maybe the guys we're all looking for. They got that crazy man who was in the news yesterday. The one shot in the chest! Good chance they have the real Aunt Millie too."

"Sure. No problem. Leave it to us. We got six more brothers helping in the woods down a piece," the second man said quickly.

They parted into the weeds. Joe and Sandra went to the front of the funeral home and told a recently arrived deputy to check out the claimed sighting.

After they'd waited half an hour, Joe said, "Let's go eat. This is taking way too long. I suspect the frat boys picked up the girl they'd planted as Aunt Millie. The cop's best bet at picking her up is at some hospital emergency room being treated for a concussion."

Sandra looked around. Even Purswell's gang had left, the parking lot only parking two cruisers and the mortician's hearse. Both deputies were nearly a mile downstream, finding nothing, but paid by the hour. A truck had come along and lifted Joe's car onto its back ten minutes previous; it no doubt off to the Columbus Crime Lab.

They walked a half mile west on the relatively unpopulated Cemetery Road, passing yet another large field of headstones. The Blue Fish Lounge was closed, it still being morning. Joe went around back and banged on a door.

Dolcy brushed a curtain aside on a window, and then opened the door halfway. "My god, Joe. It's morning. What's the matter with you?"

"I'm starving to death and the police took my car."

"Well, that sounds like a personal problem to me. Try Wendy's, it's not a mile down, or McD's; it's even closer," said Dolcy, she still in her bathrobe. Dolcy was a good fifty-five, and the owner of the Blue Fish. Nice enough most of the time, though Joe had seen her bounce more than one drunk out of her establishment under threat of claws.

"Too public. Come on; you got a grill. You see, it's a date I was on before they took my car, and this lady got shot yesterday, and we've been playing around all morning with these body snatchers, and I'm out of eggs at my place and..."

"Oh, shit Joe. If it isn't one thing with you, it's another. Just come on in and shut up. You make it yourself, and clean up after. Leave the beer alone. Stuff ten bucks on the counter," said Dolcy, shutting the door in his face.

They went around, finding the front door of the Lounge open. Dolcy had come and gone, her apartment through a back door that Joe could see was shut. She'd put the lights over the bar.

"Is she mad about this?"

"Oh no. That's just the way she is. I've known Dolcy for a long time. Play here every Saturday. It took me ten years to figure her out, but she's like the boss who fires you one day and then wants to know why you didn't show up for work the next."

"What do you play?"

"Bass. That's my stack in the corner. I just fill in, play with whomever needs me, do a few originals. It's an open stage thing on Saturdays. Mostly musicians. Some of it's good, and some of it's bad, but nobody really cares. I'm surprised that the crowd isn't bigger though."

"So, are you going to go over there and play me something?"

"No. It's hard to do with just a bass and a speaker cabinet. I'm going to whistle while I fix you breakfast," said Joe, popping open an under-bar refrigerator. He started to cook.

They were chatted about music over paper plates when they heard a bump that sounded like someone dropping a trash can right outside the front door.

"So, what was that noise anyway?" Asked Joe a full minute after the noise.

"You mean that banging noise?" Asked Sandra.

They both got up from their seats at the bar and looked out the front door window. A blue and rust holed pickup had its front finder bent around a telephone pole. The truck leaned into the ditch at a slight angle. A driver's door lay wide open. Strewn across their barely used portion of Deadman were half a dozen shovels, rakes and pickaxes.

A man in dungarees lurched into view from their right, and fell into the doorway. A splash of blood splattered on the glass where his head met the door window, and then streaked down, the glass painted by the man's black hair as he slumped. Joe pushed at the door, and after a third shove, pushed the body aside enough for him to wedge himself out and pull the man free.

"It's John Loews," said Sandra as she helped Joe pull him into the lounge. They laid his body out on the floor. Sandra took a pulse. "He's alive. The pulse is really pretty strong. I just think he probably knocked himself out with the glass. Maybe he was afraid of something. It sure looked like it. Call for a squad."

"Sure," said Joe, picking up the payphone and placing the call. He pulled the chord as taunt as he could while it rang. Looking out the opened front door, he couldn't see anything that might have cause the man to have lost his wit.

Dolcy walked in through her apartment door. She was in jeans and a decent shirt finally. "What the hell are you guys doing to my place now?"

"Some guy had an accident in front. I'm calling a squad," said Joe. The dispatcher's voice hit his other ear, and he gave them the story.

Sandra checked around the body, and found a gaping hole in the back of the man's upper arm. It looked mangled and a big chunk of muscle and flesh was missing, but no bones seemed broken, a fact she verified by seeing the white of bone where it had been scraped. The wound didn't show any sign of having been cut though, even as bad as it was, realized Sandra. That is odd, she thought, considering the half baseball size of the wound. Other than the ragged wound on the arm and the bloody bang on the forehead, John didn't look all that bad off. Still, the wound was bleeding profusely, and she knew he'd bleed to death in minutes if it was left unattended.

"I need something to wrap his arm with. Direct pressure won't work. We'll tie it right above the wound," said Sandra. Dolcy brought her a towel, and then got down on the floor beside her to help. Dolcy held while Sandra wrapped, the blood coming out so fast that Dolcy's hand was soaked before the first wrap. By the second wrap though, it seemed to be working, the bleeding having stopped seeping from just below the towel. A good pint was on Dolcy's floor, it looking like a gallon.

"Read that you was arrested for killing that family killer, Joe. You're bad luck, this week. Not all the time, but a lady would do well to wait until your Karma breaks," said Dolcy as she shoved a second towel under John's feet. She got a third, and started wiping her hands clean, all the time glaring at Joe as if it had all been his fault. Once done, Dolcy noticed an itch just over her left thumb knuckle. She scratched, and then looked at it, seeing a few white liver spots where she'd not thought she had them before. Shrugging it off, she got a blanket and covered John who'd started shaking.

"Where do you know John from?" Asked Joe.

Sandra replied, "He's the grave digger. The town uses him to bear caskets and cut the grass. He lives in the maintenance building. There's a two room section of the same building. A nice, cozy setup for an old bachelor. He's been real reliable at chasing away kids and keeping the cemeteries tidy too. I've seen him at a dozen funerals, usually standing off a piece, but sometimes being a friend to someone who needs an extra friend to get buried properly."

"Hum. Think he might have something to do with our two missing bodies?"

"Oh, no. Not John. He treats the cemetery as if it's his own yard," said Sandra as she adjusted the elevation of John's feet and checked the strength of his pulse again. "Hum!" She said, her face growing strained with worry.

"What's up?" Asked Dolcy.

"I can't feel anything." Sandra shifted her position, feeling for another vein on his wrist.

Joe knelt down and felt at the man's jugular. "Damn. Nothing. He's getting cold too. I'm not used to this trauma thing, but isn't that a pretty bad sign?"

John moaned and then shifted his head so it lay a little to one side, after which he moaned again.

"Shoot. Neither one of you know how to check for a pulse," scoffed Dolcy. John's head kept on rocking from side to side as if seeking a more comfortable position.

Sandra dropped the hand, and looked at Joe. She shrugged. "I could have sworn. Didn't feel a thing."

"Well, you're a cop—not a paramedic. They pay you to shoot people, not doctor them, I suppose," said Joe.

"I'm supposed to know how to feel a pulse, for crying out loud," said Sandra, her hand feeling his forehead, and it nearly ice.

"Look. Maybe he has low blood pressure. I hear that makes a big difference in what you can feel. It's not healthy, but it explains why you're not feeling much. Gets worse when they've lost a lot of blood too," said Dolcy.

Joe agreed with a, "Yeah. That seems like a good explanation," just as the medics came through the door and started their workup. Having seen the wreck, they went right to work.

They broke out their big red box and ran a workup. Medic Johnson was on the radio while Medic Bently called out a set of flat vitals. Bently gave a nod, and Johnson pulled an IV out of the kit for his partner. Between the pair, the man was on plasma faster than it would have taken a team of hospital nurses to accomplish in twice the time. Johnson worked the IV valve, tapped it, and shrugged, the fluid apparently not going in nearly as fast as he'd hoped.

"Man, I don't get any breath or pulse," said Bently.

"Check the lips," coached Johnson.

"They look OK. A little white, but not that bad."

"Fingernails?"

"Dirty, but fine."

"Must be the batteries in your vitals set. Do it manually," said Johnson.

His buddy put a stethoscope on and listened. "Nothing." He tapped the end of it, and heard his tapping banging in his ears. Then he checked again.

John moaned again, his head moving up and an eye half opening before his head fell back and he was again out.

"Low pressure. Look, let's just get him out of here. Let them deal with it at the hospital," said Johnson who was back working the radio.

"Sure."

"I've got a man down from an auto accident. Head injury, and gash on the arm. Vitals are…extremely weak. Am transporting to Mount Carmel East," Johnson said into the walkie handset.

They strapped the man onto a gurney and whisked him away. It was the first time either of the medics had ever been as baffled before, so they rushed, the medic unit peeling rubber and in a blaze of lights and siren.

In the medic's wake sat Jimmy's cruiser.

"Seems everywhere there is trouble, there is you," Jimmy said from across the lot while leaning on his fender. Jimmy had his highway patrol sunglasses on, and had even taken the time to put a wad of chew into his cheek, just to add to the look of a rough cop. Still, he looked like a wet cat in a starched blue towel.

"Seems like it. Maybe you boys should hire me. Look at my resume. I'm first on the scene, and I don't even need a dispatcher, or even a cruiser," said Joe, undaunted.

Behind Jimmy, his radio squawked, "I have a disturbance at the Westcare Asylum in neighboring Westpoint. Seems to have been a break-in, and several patients from their criminal unit have escaped. Two doctors and a security officer are down. Chief, the word is that at least one has been seen heading south. We're to be on the lookout for up to five males in white smocks and maybe straightjackets."

Jimmy turned, poking his head into the cruiser to hear it better. Then he got in. "Later," he said to Joe.

"Promise?" Asked Joe.

Jimmy drove past, nearly catching Joe's foot. Joe and Sandra watched him speed down the road at three times the legal speed limit.

"Well for once, I'm not anywhere near the ruckus. Thank god," said Joe.

"Don't spoil your luck by saying that too loudly, Joe. We have lunatics headed our way. That mental facility is only a mile down river. It could even be related," said Sandra.

Joe laughed. "Oh, you mean it gets crazier? Goodness. Well, not to change the subject, but how did you like our first date? You know, they have this book out; like, all about crazy first dates. You could, uh…"

"Exciting. Think I can get published?" Interrupted Sandra with a smile that Joe simply could not interpret. She walked back into the lounge to start with the cleanup, determined to not give him any clues. Joe took another look around. He saw no new crimes, so he followed to help with the chores.

Further in, Dolcy rubbing briskly at her hand, disappeared into her living quarters.

7

Down near the knee, one of the bones on the lower leg ground. It had been bothering him ever since that caretaker's truck had slammed into him on Cemetery Road. Too bad the man driving the truck had panicked and after only slowing, raced off down the road to who knows where. The dead man looked down, not because of pain, or even from curiosity, but because he thought the bone on bone noise might have come from something he could eat. The fact that the noise was his own leg bone rubbing against its own fracture, never entered his mind.

He stood up as straight as he could, and looked around, sniffing. Maybe he'd be doing better at the asylum, he thought. There had been lots of excellent smelling life there, back when...well, before that naked man with the hole in his chest had barged in and attacked him, causing him to feel...different. Regardless, he'd gotten hopelessly lost, and for now was just following his nose. As he looked, his left eye dangled before twisting around to examine the cinders for anything unlucky enough to move. Nothing did.

Where did that truck with all the shovels in it disappear to anyway, he wondered? He took another step into the cinders, finally realizing that the source of the grinding hadn't been food because things smelled pretty much the same. The grinding noise came back with the step, so he looked again, but this time didn't study as long before moving on.

A bird pecked at some gravel, waiting until the last moment to fly a line drive flight path away from the advancing man. The bird split through a seam between two boxcars, leaving his brief pursuer bent over the coupling.

The dead man stiffened, as if rejuvenated by a sudden rush of anger. Starved, as well as overcome with frustration, the creature thrashed against the restriction of his straight-jacket. After some merciless trashing of his body against the walls and turnbuckles, one arm snagged, ripping the fabric loose. Filled with infantile wonder, the man stopped to watch the bent arm swing. A foot of fabric and buckles dangled below the hand. The silver clasps fascinated him, as they swung, the buckle like a long tongue licking the air. He sat down to watch for a long time before beginning the slow trial and error of freeing the other arm.

Down the line, it was morning shift in the yards. Charlene wore her new light blues, leading Guy and Fred to the side-track of rusting boxcars. The Boxcar Graveyard, Guy had come to call this line. Companies that thought they might want to write an old car off, but weren't sure, parked their old cars on this set of rails. Guy imagined it wasn't a brainstorm of community relations that allowed the scrap line to nose its way into the edge of town, but saying so hadn't won him any friends in supervision, speaking of which, Charlene was the newest addition.

He had six immediate supervisors, in various capacities, counted Guy. He'd seen twenty on the revolving door of defection or retirement in the two decades he'd worked for the yard. This was the hardest to take. Charlene had been on the job for five months—her first job from what he'd been able to gather; he'd only half trained her; she was thirty years his junior. He figured she made a quota, was eager beaver, and didn't know enough to tell the higher-ups anything they didn't want to hear. Most depressing, however, was realizing that nobody had wasted an ounce of energy considering him for the job. Obviously he wasn't on the list. It didn't matter what he did from now on, Guy knew; he'd be wearing gray coveralls until they handed him his gold painted watch. Still, things could be worse; the job was a no-brainer at three times minimum wage.

Beside Guy, Fred carried a chain of 'Master' locks across his shoulder. He dropped them at the edge of the first car and waited. Guy had never been able to figure Fred out. He knew that if he'd been carrying the locks he'd have gone right to locking the first car, but to Fred everything was a power play. It might have made sense if someone had stepped on his ambition, but for Fred it really was just a job. Maybe the sluggish attitude came from some kind of code, imagined Guy. Maybe something had been passed down from grandfather to grandson, like someone's union had ordered a slowdown fifty years ago, and things hadn't been resolved. It was a zero sum thing, Guy knew, a hanger-on from the days when a union man held a joker or two up his sleeve. Just the three of them, standing out in the yard like this, Guy wondered if Fred knew how much of an idiot he looked like, taking a break before being told to do something, taking a break after being told to so something, and pretty near to taking a break in between all of that.

Awhile ago, Guy had told Fred the rules, "Kiss up a little, if you want to move up." It had taken six months for Fred to get over the insult to his much simpler code, 'Don't do anything unless told, and then don't do it very fast'.

Now Charlene was the boss, and Fred could say, "See; I told you so." So he did, and they were back on speaking terms because Guy had come to the conclusion that he was right; that being the most painful part.

Then there was Charlene. She'd handed Fred the locks without explanation, and led them here like it was the most natural thing in the world for railroad workers to follow dumbly. It reminded Guy of kindergarten, "Hold hands; follow along; no talking in the halls." Of course, by the time they'd gotten to the work site, Guy had figured out what they were going to do.

"I'll get this side," Guy said, risking Fred's wrath by picking up the locks and impaling the middle one with a key so he could take half of the chain.

Charlene finally explained, "The Sheriff called our dispatcher last night. He said we need to be extra sure to secure our cars."

"Well we mustn't upset our Sheriff," said Guy, going to the first door, and latching it down before moving on alone.

"OK, Fred, you take the other side then," added Charlene.

Fred spit on a rail. "They took my key. Last year. Some kind of security thing where only the wanna-bes got to keep em."

She took out a rusted ring, and handed it to the worker. "Here; use mine."

Unlocking the first lock off the half chain, Fred gave the key back to Charlene, then disappeared around the first car. After a couple of minutes, he came back, re-borrowed the key from Charlene and took a second lock. Down the row of cars, Guy was half finished by the time Fred turned the corner to lock his second door.

"For Christ's sake!" Said Charlene. She gathered up the locks, and fell in behind Fred. When does this end, she wondered? It wasn't her fault that they'd decided to put her on the fast track. The older guys were just bitter, she'd decided, but if these men were so great, why hadn't they shown their stuff years ago? Fred was taking his time with the second door when she walked past him and dropped the locks off in front of the open boxcar doors. She felt like Gretle, dropping bread crumbs on the trail.

At the last car she turned around to check on Fred's progress. Off to her right, cars whizzed by on the highway. Beyond that, a diner parking lot was half full of utility trucks and pickups, their drivers fueling up with breakfasts of grease, eggs and coffee. On her left, the brown ripple of freight car walls towered over gray cinders and an occasional spilled lump of coal. No Fred.

"Alright Fred!" She waited to hear him answer with another excuse, something like, "My medical says I can't reach more than twice an hour," or, "According to the state, my break should be two and a half minutes every half hour." Instead, she got silence.

"Damn!" A sense of hopelessness overcame her because she'd expected this. "Look Fred, we're going to get this done!" Still nothing emerged down the track. Fred appeared to have disappeared from the face of the earth.

Fifty yards straight ahead though, a black boot flipped from between two boxcars. It sailed before landing with a steel toed thump in a stack of termite eaten railroad ties. Fred has freaked, she thought instantly. She remembered Fred's eyes, and couldn't recall them ever having been too deep; a little glossy maybe. A second boot flew up through the space between the cars, then landed on a boxcar roof, loud like a rock.

"Alright Fred, that's not funny!" Charlene searched for the correct words: cut it out; let's get back to something constructive; hey, we can work it out; I'm not going to put up with this. She settled for, "I'm your Supervisor. I'm here to help you if there is a problem!" Jesus, she couldn't imagine a more lame thing to have said It was as if she'd been interviewing for a job; worse, it was Miss Americanese. No self respecting railroad man would miss the opportunity to chow down on a line like that! So she added, "You'll have to get to work, or I'll report you!" Universal, but late.

A guttural moan crept out of the space between the cars. She sensed neither fear nor pain in the voice, but rather pleasure, like the coming of an orgasm or the arrival of a feast. What was he doing? Masturbating?

"What's up?" Guy asked, inches from the nape of Charlene's neck.

Charlene jumped around. One of her hands fell flat at the top of her chest. An open mouth waited between reddened cheeks. After awhile she inhaled. "Good...God, Guy! Isn't there some kind of rule about sneaking up on a person like that? You could have given me a heart attack or something."

"Wouldn't do any good; they'd just find someone else for me to train," said Guy, matter of factly. "What's got you so antsy?"

"Oh Jesus, Fred's down there taking his clothing off. I think he's tooling up for the Postal exam or something," she answered.

Guy gave her a puzzled look between glances down the line.

"I think he's slipped a gear," she clarified. "Go down and check on him; will you?"

"Fred carried the locks. I put them on the cars. For two bucks an hour more, you get to check up on crazy people." He shrugged his shoulders. "Rough, ain't it. There is more to being a supervisor than a personalized stapler. Did I teach you that, or is this lesson new?"

"You jerk. I should know better then to expect your help. In fact, I bet you put him up to this. Fred's too stupid to come up with anything this devious, but you, you have a brain, and that makes you the dangerous one," said Charlene. She walked toward the crease from which the boots had been tossed.

Guy imagined he saw smoke coming out of her pink little ears. "Good. I'll be right behind you as soon as I put Fred's last five locks on. When you find Fred, tell him I'm tired of doing his work too. I still got one up on both you and Fred, besides experience that is; I still work for a living. I got relevance! Take that to the bank on payday when you cash in the money I'm making you." He knew he had her. Her stomach will be all tied up in nervous little supervisor knots for the rest of the day. The sensations of finally letting her have it made him all bubbly inside. Fred broke out into a seamy smile.

Charlene pretended she hadn't heard him, as she pretended to look at the closest car wheels for defects while she walked, the inspections slowing her progress. If she did it right, Guy would only be a few cars back when she confronted Fred. After all, she thought, Guy can be a jerk, but he is smart enough to know his limits. Fred, however, is a borderline fruitcake, all silent and sneaky. If it was up to her, she'd have fired Fred a long time ago.

"Hey Fred!" She yelled. "Guy needs some help over here. Can you give him a hand?" No need to tell a crazy man you're going to write a sixty-nine page report on him when you get back to the office, she figured.

Confident that Guy was safely close, Charlene turned the corner into the gap between the cars. She jerked to a stop, eyes wide. A man leaned over the coupling, only his back in view. Below him, draped backwards over the same coupling, lay Fred. The victim's legs were splayed out, but unmoving. Blood dripped out from under the two bodies. Her eyes followed the dripping blood down, seeing several pools of the thick, red fluid.

She couldn't scream or even move, shock having temporarily taken control of her body by the time she saw the red splatter on the boxcar walls. The man in front of her shifted, allowing her to see Fred more clearly. Fred's back was busted, inverted across the heavy metal couplers. Huge chunks of muscle had been eaten from his rib-cage. The chest rippled with neat, diagonally exposed bones. Tendons, arteries and flesh that had been ripped in random tears. The skin around the edges of the wound was slick with thin pink blood that no longer pumped from the open hole. In a flash, a head smeared with red wetness lifted, turned and leaned within an inch of Charlene's face.

The breath was rotting meat and stomach acid. The face was unbelievable, something human, something animal, something demonic. She felt her head spinning. That, of course, had to end; it would be a disaster if she lost consciousness, realized Charlene!

Charlene managed to jump back. The dead lunatic's hand lurched towards her chest. The punch dazed her and took her breath, even as the fist opened. Fingers tightened around the fabric of her new, light-blue, supervisor shirt. The creature did not hesitate. It pulled her across the space, lifted her off of her feet, and threw her against a boxcar wall. The concussion boomed off of the wall like a bass drum, shattering bones along the side of the woman's body.

Dazed senseless by the blow, Charlene slumped to the rocks between the rails. Everything was a blur. She fought to capture a breath after the blow to the chest, and the shattering of an arm, ribs and pelvis against the unyielding boxcar. Gasps came in short breaths.

The dead man now had two meals to choose from, one fresh, the other having not breathed for several minutes. Fred no longer moved, no longer held the aroma the creature recognized as life. The creature pulled the dead meat off of the coupler. Fred slumped to the rocks like a sack of potatoes. Then, leaning under the coupler, the dead man reached for the stunned woman, painfully hungry in spite of having already eaten half of Fred's chest.

Charlene's eyes had not yet cleared, but she could see the hand enlarging, coming towards her. Still breathless, she scrambled under the boxcar, kicking at the rocks in her wake. She crawled in spite of the pain and uselessness of one whole side of her body, dragging what wouldn't work. Her own involuntary sobbing made it even harder to scream for help or to get away, further clouding her vision, working against her efforts at sucking in more than small tokens of air. None-the-less, Charlene feverishly wormed her way under the boxcar with the savage, tight jerks of a cornered snake.

Having missed the first grope, the creature straightened. He moaned his displeasure before bending all the way over so he could see under the car. Awkwardly getting to all fours, bones crunching within his own body, he lunged for Charlene's leg.

She felt the blood slicked fingers slap around her ankle like folds on a thick, wet rag. Her working hand clawed at the ground, but then was raked back through the cinders. The cinders gouged deep long furrows into her skin and broke nails. Rail and ties banged against the newly broken bones on her side, making it even harder to fight. The hand at her ankle burned from the crushing slap. Bruised body heat rose from her own flesh. Then the ankle cooled before becoming a chill as the cold hand squeezed closer to the bone.

Charlene caught enough breath to force one weak scream of pain and alarm. To her it seemed pitifully weak, yet she knew that it and Guy were her only hope. Near to fainting, there were no more screams where that one came from. Once clear of the undercarriage, the monster that held her would waste no time in his final killing of his prey, she knew. The attacker had been mercilessly quick, brutally dogmatic, a thoughtless killer as it had stunned and now captured her, all in a few short seconds. Not like this, her mind screamed. Not eaten like an animal! I can't end up food! Completely stripped of her strength, Charlene measured the rest of her life by the unfocussed, blood soaked fingernails she left in the cutting, grey rocks.

A second cold hand slammed against the cloth at her back. Fingers closed, pinching a whole handful of skin. Using both the ankle and the skin on her back as handles, the creature lifted Charlene from the ground, banging her head as she cleared the undercarriage.

She had no control over what was happening to her at all as he spun her in the air. One of her arms flailed protectively in the vague direction of her flight; the other dangled numbly from a simple fracture, but it too struggled weakly to rise and protect her face. Her one able leg kicked towards the man ineffectively, while the other shot great gulps of pain up her spin, and was no more than an impediment. A half scream ripped through her lips, cut short by a shattering, frontal slam against the opposite boxcar wall.

Charlene's brutalized body crumpling to the ground. Everything was grey before her, coming and going like half sleep. She awoke seconds later though, screaming herself awake, as the dead man, who had never dropped the ankle, bit down on an Achilles tendon. Charlene willed the leg to kick, but nothing below the knee moved as the few muscles that were not too stunned to flex moved broken bones against one another. It was as if she'd grown new joints; the old ones above and below the breaks, no longer worked.

The bite stopped at the gristle of the tendon, frustrating the hungry man. He grunted. His head twisted and teeth grated until they met with a duel snap of both tendon and teeth. A sour expression of dislike distorted the mans face. He spit the meatless tendon into the dirt beside Charlene's useless right hand. Incredibly, she found her upper body going numb. In seconds, as the spinal swelling grew, she couldn't move anything below her waist.

Charlene's head flattened against the ground, and hazily looked at her own discarded gristle in disbelief, unable to accept it as once having been a part of her leg. She couldn't take her eyes off of it though, not having the strength or courage to move her eyeballs away, even as he bit once more, this time into flesh that suited his fancy much better. For some reason, the biting didn't hurt nearly as much as it had before, she thought. She was glad of that, that being more important than life itself since the agony of hitting the wall that second time. The pain that had been so high that she'd willed death, was ebbing to numbness. Struggle had within seconds turned to much easier acceptance. In fact, everything seemed to be dulling, as she watched the piece of tendon casually laying in the cinders where it had been spit mere inches beside her uselessly numb hand. The only thing not numb now, it seemed to her, was her sight, which for some reason seemed to clear, allowing her to see the finer details of nerve and vessel on the edges of the discarded bite. When she died, she imagined, she'd die with her eyes open like they always said people did.

Her body jiggled from the tug of the man above her twisting the leg to get at a better, higher spot of striped red meat. Still, it didn't hurt at all now. From within the state of shock she thought, it is going to be alright; it's not all that unusual for an animal to become meat. In her growing mental collapse she even gave a twitching little smile of acceptance.

Guy snapped the next to last lock in place, and looked down the line towards the sound of the ruckus. Fred had managed to do only two cars. It wasn't enough that Fred had let him do all of the work, but he was over there dancing on the turnbuckles, or something equally useless, thought Guy.

Guy muttered, "I don't know which is worse, an incompetent for a boss, or a Cro-Magnon moron for a friend."

He thought he heard a whimper. Fred had her crying, he imagined. Twenty years on the job and he'd never heard anything like it; the whimpering approach to supervision; it was a first for him, though Guy had always thought that most young, fast-tracked women got their high paying jobs through some sort of whimpering or from having sex with the boss. Guy shook his head.

"OK already! Cut it the hell out, Fred. You cross the line, and I ain't gonna cover for you. I already did your work, so you can call the damned show off. You hear me over there! I'm not messing with you, this time!"

That's when he heard Charlene's second scream. It ended with a bang that both cut the scream in half, and rocked the whole boxcar in front of him on its huge cast-metal wheels.

"Oh man! Now he's really done it! This is wrong, Fred! You jackass!" Guy looked for a weapon, but nothing appropriate was near. He turned in his tracks trying. Fred isn't much bigger than me, but Fred is crazy as a loon, thought Guy. He picked up two tennis ball sized rocks and put them into his pockets, then he added a third to his throwing hand. Charlene's scream died, as if a dimming light. It settled into a moan and then into nothing.

Crudely armed, Guy stepped to a spot directly adjacent to the seam.

Twenty years of rail yard work hadn't begun to prepare him for what he saw. A man stood in the space, although Guy couldn't understand how. One of his legs was bent at a nasty angle. A straight jacket dangled around his waist like a garter. The mans flesh looked, well, dead, realized Guy, except where blood had been smeared, which covered the greater percentage of him. The face, light grey behind the blood, was torn, with one eye dangling from a cavernous socket.

In a way, Guy was relieved that it wasn't Fred. It simplified the relationship. Fred lay dead, splayed out under the coupler. Beside him, Charlene was lying down too, looking towards her hand with lazy, stunned animal eyes, as if the perfect, cooperative victim. In a way, those eyes gave Charlene the deadest look of the group though, as if a part of her mind had simply accepted that she was dead, in spite of the fact that she wasn't...yet. Guy could see her chest heaving rapidly; he couldn't say the same thing for the one man still standing.

On an ordinary morning, three macerated people would pretty much top things off, Guy realized, but the stranger in front of him was still holding Charlene's foot, her whole body raised up except for her head and arms. He bit and chewed on a mouthful of lower leg. The man looked over at Guy, cleared a tooth with his tongue and then yanked Charlene up by her leg again, taking another bite into the thickest part of her calf. Her head jiggled on the ground, but didn't lose her continuous stare at her useless hand.

Guy could feel the mean look on the lunatic's face. Charlene's face remained expressionless as a psychological part of her mind had taken over; the part that told her that her body was best left undefended because it had been destroyed beyond wanting.

Guy's first rock whistled a foot high and to the right of the lunatic's head at eighty miles an hour.

The creature snarled, but otherwise remained content with his live meat.

Emptying both pockets, Guy tossed two more, taking a step closer with each. The last missile cracked the murderer at the base of his skull before bouncing into the train-car wall.

The zombie's head jerked around. It aimed a puzzled, one eyed stare at Guy. Guy could see the man's nose flair as he sniffed the air. What was left of the thing's eyebrows twisted into something like anger.

"Now lookie here, bubba." Guy took a few steps back, scanning the ground over for a few more of those hand sized rocks. "I'm going to mess you up if you don't lie down right there and..." All he could see close was a brick. "...take a load off!"

Charlene's leg had dropped. Her legs were piles of loosely connected tissue. She grunted weakly—almost like a last breath, thought Guy. It was amazing how much he wanted to help her; how much he was sorry for playing the tough guy and not helping her at the first noises he'd heard.

The crazy man ran towards Guy—sort of; while one leg stiffly ran, the other wobbled, threatening to give before the first leg took over each alternate stride. Still, the strides were wide, closing the gap quickly.

Guy jumped for the brick between them, rising and sidestepping with it in his hand just as his attacker rushed by. Using every muscle, Guy swung the brick, missing the head, but scoring a blow deep into several vertebra of the neck.

The neck bent. Both men fell. Guy jumped to his feet. The monster didn't move. Across the street, a woman was screaming. She yelled, "Fight," as she ran towards the diner doorway.

Guy wasn't sure if it was a man that he'd just killed, but it looked like one, and he'd never killed anything that looked like a man before. He realized the impact of what he'd just done. It had happened so fast. Ten seconds ago he'd not even imagined such an event possible. There hadn't been time to think. Maybe I'm in trouble, Guy wondered, confused for a second as his head swam. Lightheaded, he rolled over to his knees, and put his head between his hands to help him think. He had to focus.

The creature shook the bells out of his head. One more thing wasn't working right. He sat up. The head wouldn't straighten. Instead it hover above a shoulder at an angle. Everything he looked at looked uphill or downhill. Still, there remained that constant hungry pain in his stomach. He thought, good thing there's meat only an arm reach away!

Leaning over, the dead man bit three inches out of Guy's pulsing, pink neck.

Guy screamed!

Across the street, the diner door slammed shut, the diners soon roused and eyes at every window.

Blood gushed out of the severed artery on Guy's neck. He closed his hand over the wound, but with each heartbeat the blood kept moving out of his body. Streams spurted from cracks between or under his fingers, coating his shoulder and the side of his face. Guy was horrified by how much blood he was shooting out of himself. There was no stopping it, his fingers unable to plug the dike that was leaking his life. In only a handful of seconds, he was in a lake of his own blood. He knew he was dying, it all so shockingly sudden. Almost at once, everything dimmed. He barely had enough time to feel himself losing control, falling back against the ground. The last thing he saw was a terrifying shadow rushing over his face. Teeth lunged directly at him, biting off his nose just as he drifted into the sleep of death.

The creature let the tough, meatless nose dribble from his mouth. He sighed some gas. It hadn't been worth the trouble. This meal had been delivered dead. He'd been cheated! He looked over at the trains. There, in the cinders, somehow, the woman's chest still rose and fell, though her eyes were listless. He had to be quick. The zombie stumbled to his feet where he adjusted to the strange new sideways world, and walked toward the better cut of meat. As he walked, his leg bones finally cut the last tendrils of skin that held his broken foot on just above the ankle. The stump felt odd and made the sideways world wobble when he walked. Tired of the interruptions, he lifted the lady by an arm. He threw her across the shoulder furthest from his bent head. Crossing the coupler, he wandered into the seclusion of the fields bordering a wooded area. Responding to a brief rush of blood to her head, Charlene watched her civilized railroad yard vanish beyond the waist high weeds.

8

"Keys to the city?" Exclaimed Mayor Rhymeheart.

Dominique held her set of keys up in front of his face, dangling them as if reminding him what keys looked like. They jingled nearly on his nose. "My client gets a hero's medal, keys to the city for saving your officer's life, and a little ceremony. They do that all of the time in other places. I expect an effort, such as it might be. Not exactly a ticket tape parade, but it will do the city good. Of course, all of this after a quick, and tidy settlement. I'm going to let you call it a reward, if you like, and save a little face in the press."

"Seventy-five thousand dollars is a little steep for a reward, Marsha, and nobody is going to buy it when the press digs and sees that it's a settlement!" Mayor Rhymeheart said sternly.

"My word, for a slave boy, you've forgotten your place. This is going to cost you dearly," said Dominique. She swallowed the keys up in her left fist, and struck the mayor on his flank with the riding crop in her right one. He groaned—not like the moans he'd managed a few minutes earlier, but of course, this part of the lesson hadn't meant to be fun.

"Sorry, Mistress Dominique. It's just a little...unusual. Who will believe it's just a reward at that price?"

"Well, don't tell them about the settlement. If anyone asks, say the city just felt an obligation to pay for his medical expenses, considering that he is a hero. After all, your silly party owns the press in these parts, and city hall too, so burying it should be easy. Don't tell me the party infighting has gotten so bad that you're worried about oversight? I'm doing this as a favor, Rhymeheart. A showy lawsuit involving a town hero won't settle, come election day. Besides, I like working with you, and want to keep you around," Dominique said, proving her point by prodding him with her riding crop before swishing him across an upper leg.

"We should fight you in court. The number's a bit high, and besides, who ever heard of a lawyer making a settlement like this in a week?" Said Mayor Rhymeheart. He looked up at his hands, and jiggled them in the chains. The cuffs were looped through the tines in his office ceiling fan. Legs hurting from being made to stand in one place for the past half hour, he wondered what it was about himself that had let him expose his fantasies to the lawyer. At times like these, it seemed that she had her hooks in him a bit too deep.

Dominique walked around him, putting her riding crop down on a stool that was conveniently behind her submissive partner. She fussed at her leather mini-skirt, and pulled one of the straps of her low cut bra back up over a shoulder. Dan Rhymeheart glanced over his own shoulder to keep an eye on what she was up to.

Adjusted and more presentable, she asked, "And, what will the judge settle my hundred thousand dollar suit for, my little slave boy?"

"Shit, I don't know. Thirty thousand, I'm guessing."

"Oh, yes, right! That's for borderline police brutality cases; things like arresting school teachers for being a little flustered during a ticketing. Or, like when they run a woman in for going topless and then find out that it's protected by the courts," she explained, lifting her bra up in front to make sure she was covered. "This is different, and you know it. Fifteen to thirty is standard for petty things. My client has been harmed, however. Medical neglect cases, well, they can go into the millions. Don't get me too eager, my little wanker. You'll pay," she said, slapping his butt, "and you'll pay again."

"The man's just fine."

"Sure, for the most part, he'll recover. We know that, but there was still a need for surgery on something your stupid police force let fester. That dings the whole case up to that golden seventy to hundred thousand range, guaranteed. I'm giving you the lower number and a way to keep the embarrassment out of the papers. And, I'm offering you one more thing, my little man," said Dominique, her hand finding just the right place to squeeze.

"What's that, Mar...Mar...Mistress?"

"Well, let me put it this way: Ever since I brought up this topic, you've entirely lost your submissive headspace. Marsha is reserved for lunches. In here, slave, it's Mistress Dominique to you. You've been silly, thinking you can fight this thing in court, and you're being even worse by forgetting who you are talking to. You have no idea what a person like me might feel compelled to do to a slave like you under the prolonged stress of stubborn behavior." Dominique swiped upwards with her crop, like she was a one-handed golfing pro.

The Mayor swallowed hard as he looked down at his body. Other than his shoes and a ridiculous looking pair of thin, black socks, he was naked; vulnerable. "Yes, sorry Mistress Dominique. It's just as good that we settle," he said as a plea. His fear of her had risen, as had another thing, it making too good of a target out of itself.

Dominique hit him with the next stroke, the blow glancing off of a thigh.

"OK, Mistress. I'll see what I can do. Really."

"I'll expect an itinerary by tomorrow then," said Dominique, going to the door of his private office.

"Wait. You can't just leave me like this," the man said. Dominique held the door open, making him glad that he'd sent his secretary home early.

"What's the matter? Afraid your secretary will find you like you are. Or, maybe your wife might get curious and come looking for you?"

"Look, Mistress. I'll look into it. There are oversight people, like the President of the council. Eager for my job, that one, but they'll probably see it my way once I explain the opportunity to promote a hero. I'll just show them how it kills two birds with one stone. I don't think they'll go for a big show though; maybe something small in the office? An item at the next town meeting?"

"Well, fine then. As long as you're sure you can manage the settlement," said Dominique, tossing the keys up toward the Mayor's hands. The Mayor caught them, his chains rattling and making scratches in the ceiling fan blades as he concentrated solely upon the grab. It had been a lucky catch. He didn't hesitate, putting the key into one of the cuffs.

"Should I shut out the lights, slave boy?" Asked Dominique, putting her hand on the fan switch, which was just under the light switch.

"No, please! Watch that; it's not the light; it's the fan!"

"Oh, I know. Just teasing," said Dominique. She turned the lights off and then took her hand away from the switches. Closing the door, she left him in darkness. From the other side of the door, she could hear Mayor Dan Rhymeheart struggling to unlock his cuffs. He paid her half the regular legal consulting fee of a hundred an hour to do what she did to him every few days. For him it was sexual—though dry tease—but Dominique was still trying to figure out what it was to her? Power maybe, plain and simple, she wondered? No, just a means to connections, she knew. He spent his own money—she insisting upon it—not wanting to get into the mess of worms implied by using public funds, and just to make it right, she insisted upon a few minutes of real legalese upon each visit. Joe's lawsuit had fit nicely. There was something about the power exchange though that left her feeling as if it was the best money she made all week."

She stepped out onto the tiny town hall landing. About a mile down Hamilton Road, she saw blue and red lights flashing. Looked like an accident, she realized. There'd been a rash of them overnight, particularly when one measured in the rest of the county. Some of the wrecks had been fatalities. Since she'd gotten Joe out of jail, three people had died in separate accidents and even more oddly, several were hit and runs. The hit and runs were probably a gang thing, she guessed. Then there was that nasty business regarding the nuthouse up north and the grave robbing at the funeral home as well. Maybe there was something about life going to hell under a full moon, she wondered?

So much for the peaceful life of suburbia, she reflected, for once feeling a bit swamped by all of the law work that was dropping right into her lap. The new rash of cased to be had was one reason why she needed the Mayor to settle the Joe Jefferson case as quickly as possible. It was a solid case, but small potatoes compared to what might be found in a good old fatal car crash. Besides, dead people paid out a lot better than did injured people—that is unless the injuries cripple a person.

Dominique went to bed every night with visions of clients being wheeled into court with their heads bent over, their bodies plastered into body casts, drooling onto suits that had obviously been tossed on over hospital gowns by caretakers. Thoughts like that were positively orgasmic to her. It wasn't that she wished ill will upon the world, but rather that she'd grown to know that ill will was out there anyway, and that someone had to tap dance on its leavings.

While she poked her key into her car door, a Dodge Shadow raced by at twice the speed limit, brushed a light pole a little further down, and then disappeared down a residential side-street. The Shadow's passenger door handle was left spinning in the roadway.

Dominique shrugged, got into her car and drove down Hamilton. She poked Joe's number into her cell phone, and told him his money was nearly won. Then she rang the office to tell them she was on her way for a stopover before county court, each in fifteen second conversations that she'd gotten into the habit of specializing in.. She knew that her busy woman personality cut through doubts on the other end.

Business done, she sat back in the plush leather and turned onto High Street just in time to have to pull over and allow a streaking cruiser wail by towards Hamilton. It looked like Jimmy Baker to her, that numbskull son of the local Police Chief, recognized Dominique. She decided that she had to start liking Jimmy, considering that he was going to be around awhile, and mostly considering that his pig headed deputy act was likely to win her more than a few lawsuits before he grew up enough to hide his stupidity in even more insidious ways.

The car idled beside the curb, waiting for Jimmy's cruiser to clear.

A woman walked by on the curb side. Mostly legs, nicely overdressed in a body flattering grey dress, but too young for the look, thought Dominique, who was caught admiring the sexy outfit and wondering where the woman had bought it. The woman looked over, shifted her long blonde hair over a shoulder with a twist of the neck, and then smiled a little too much at Dominique. Earrings sparkled, seemingly diamonds. Tall at maybe five, four, the young lady was made taller by two inch heels. Maybe lesbian.. The little lady half, realized Dominique, though judging from the clothing, Dominique was guessing that the woman didn't know she was purely bottom half material yet.

The woman kept looking, her lips pursing out a tiny kiss. Dominique cringed, even the lesbians think I'm a lesbian now! Why does everyone think I'm a lesbian? Give me a break! Men have always thought that, or that I'm dominant, she realized, thinking, no wonder I'm single in spite of my handsome looks. She pulled out from the curb, leaving the young woman disappointed, no doubt.

She flicked the radio on and scanned over the endless parade of gospel and right wing gossip channels before landing on 820, NPR. She considered the channel the last radio station in American not flicking endless corporate buggers into everybody's ears, although she was perfectly aware of the fact that Congress was doing all that it could to change that. Not that Dominique was all that averse to the concept of making money. It was just that she preferred a little unpolished enlightenment along with her carpet bagging.

"...unusually large number of traffic accidents and violent assaults, particularly those involving fatalities. Is road rage out of control? With us, to help us with this topic is Doctor Roy Langley. Doctor Langley is a specialist in mathematical...uh...statistics, to be precise, and we have him here to give us his views on the subject. Good morning, Doctor. Callers, if you have any questions, or want to share your thoughts with us, dial regarding this subject, dial 402-9607. Now Doctor, is this a trend, or something more sinister that we need to be concerned about?"

"Well, as you've stated, it's out of the box, but in a way, to be expected."

"Expected? How does that work?"

"The best way to think of anomalies is to picture the bell curve. A bell curve is one way of expressing some statistical variations, like crime or accident rates for example. Things like that change seasonally, and due to other inputs, but generally speaking, we are used to a certain level that is represented by the bigger bulk bubble at the center of the statistical bell curve. If we have twenty accidents in a heavily populated county each day, for example, well, it's not really twenty a day. We have fifteen one day, and twenty-six the next. In fact, a day when there is exactly twenty is sort of unusual, though you might say it is more likely than any other number you might drum up, such as nineteen or twenty-one, each of which would be only slightly less likely to be the day's number. Everything kind of falls around twenty, assuming the freeways don't ice up." He laughed.

"So, you're saying that the freeways are iced up, maybe in a metaphoric way? I mean, that there is some sort of external factor that is causing the higher rates of assaults and accidents?" Asked the moderator.

"No. I'm not committed to that. It's possible, but what I wanted to say first is that numbers well removed from twenty are normal. Everything tends to remain within a few standard deviations, but it would be unusual if there were absolutely no days within which the unusual occurred, such as no accidents, or fifty on a perfectly calm day."

"Now wait a minute. What's a standard deviation?"

"A standard deviation is that sixty-eight percent tending toward mean average. Like if you had a hundred students take a test and you'd say, these sixty-eight students got the middle grades. That leaves thirty-two percent, half of which got really bad grades, and half of which led the class. The second standard deviation is sixty-eight percent of that remaining thirty-two percent, which means that if you aren't in the first two standard deviations, you either didn't study at all, or are destined for grad school with honors."

"Oh, so how does this relate to what you were saying?"

"Well, let's stick with the class grades, as an example. If you're in the fifth standard deviation, which means that out of a hundred students you're one of two people, the one who got the worst grade or the one who got the best grade; it's out there. It's not the normal student, but still, it's normal to have that best student, and it's normal to have that worst student. We don't say, "Gee, you're that unusual, best student, and therefore, you can't possibly exist." Certainly the unusual is normal. It's just so seldom seen that we think of it as unusual, maybe even mystical to some.

We can learn a lesson here about a lot of things. Homosexuality, for example: Some people contend that being gay isn't normal. The reasoning goes, "If it were normal, the species couldn't propagate?" From a scientific and statistical perspective, however, being gay is perfectly normal in ours as well as a number of other species. It just isn't average; not within the first couple of standard deviations of the general population. Most people are average, bunched in that first standard deviation, which leaves us with plenty of propagation. As for those outside of average, they are rendered the illusion of abnormality, you see, because they are judged against the average.

Lots of other examples abound. A psychic makes a dozen rough predictions, four or five seem close, while one hits some unlikely nail on the head. It must be magic, it's reported, but we know that the hit is just blind luck and considering the number and nature of the speculations, predictable in result because there will be fringe successes. Nostradamus made thousands of predictions, so it's perfectly normal that he had an occasional hit. Add the seemingly detailed guess to the wide range of less specific things, and he's a genius – not of predictions, but of human nature."

"So, we're having a lot of accidents and assaults, and it's just a couple of unlucky days."

"Exactly. On the other hand, it could be icy out there," said the professor.

Dominique looked out of her car door window, and in spite of the fact that she had her window up and the vent blowing, the weather was perfect. Only top leaves were tinkling in the sunlight.

"We have a caller. Don from Hilliard. Hi Don. You're on National Public Radio."

"Yes. I think that's a bunch of hogwash. I hear they had a breakout at the Westcare Asylum on the east side. That's near where most of the trouble started. I had a neighbor who came home after a run-in over there. Some woman just up and jogged into his car door when he was at a dead stop, like she couldn't tell where she was going. Then she started banging and clawed at the bottom of his passenger door when he was just sitting there. He got out to help her and she up and bit him on the arm. By the time the police got there, she'd gotten into it with half a dozen rubber-neckers. Traffic backed up all over the roadway. They had to strap her down before they could cart her off to wherever they house nutcases. Ain't that the craziest hit and run you ever heard of? Now he's up sick as a dog with the chills. You think maybe he needs shots for being rabid or something?"

"Ha. Well, I don't know about that. I've never heard of people passing rabies, but I have heard that bites can get infected," said the moderator.

"Well then, why do they give you shots for it if you can't catch it?"

The statistics professor ignored the comment, "I don't think that it's likely that we'd have a half dozen people escape a mental ward, and see them all running around being destructive. One person maybe. It's a common fallacy, thinking mental patients automatically dangerous."

"Yes, I agree. Mental patients have enough stigma; we don't need to add to it," said the moderator.

Dominique flicked the radio off. Well then, what can it be, she mused? Bad day. Good for business. Someone will either sort it out in the end, or it'll be exactly as the professor noted, a blimp on the radar screen. She thought, years from now we'll all be saying, "Did you remember that week when we had all those accidents? Big money!"

9

Patricia stood on the sidewalk, a bit miffed. That lady had looked right at her, clearly coming on to her, she thought. Then as if pleased that she'd caught her attention, the woman had toasted her with her eyes and driven off in a tizzy. Oh well, Patricia didn't know why she was thinking about sex this early in the day anyway, particularly with another woman, it not being her preferred orientation. After all, she had a full day ahead of her, hopefully including a man, after having hit up William for a couple hundred in cash.

Poor William, so trusting, so free with his money. It was like being married to the ultimate nobody and not having to deal with the tedious details that the formality of marriage entailed. Pulling up a sagging stocking, and hoping that the tidying looked both classy and provocative to whoever might be watching, she moved up to the tidy shop landing.

The front door chime tinkled in the specialty store of perfumes and wind chimes. Yeah, right there on the front counter is the little bottle of SEXSCENT. Unfortunately, the clerk isn't on the other side of the counter. Little minimum wage twerps, Patricia mused, spraying fifty cents worth of the fifty dollar perfume onto her wrist. Rubbing her two wrists together, she gave herself a smell, and loved it. She imagined herself, an hour from now, at the Muirfield Lounge, spending William's or some other man's money. Some rich hunk is dancing in front of her to the endless dance score. He's asking, "What's that scent your wearing?" She's answering, "Sex!" God, she was getting hot, imagining the tease. She was going to buy the stuff just so she could say that.

"Where the hell is that clerk?" She whispered, looking for one of those old fashioned bells to ring and finding nothing but fanciful perfume bottles.

She wandered around the little shop, occasionally brushing her fingers against a wind-chime, but taking care not to brush a bottle off of any counter. There was a little doorway in back, the opening covered by a plain brown drape.

"Yoo-hoo! Anybody home?"

Nobody answered. Maybe I should go in there, she thought?

Patricia walked right up to the curtain and looked through a tiny seam in the two halves of fabric. Directly ahead of her was a time clock and a table strewn with broken knickknacks, she catching pieces of the things as she pried by moving her head back and forth. The black toe of Patricia's shoe found its way just under the partition before she stopped. "Yoo-hoo!" Probably in the bathroom, thought Patricia, thinking better of going in and interrupting that.

Just one inch from the point of Patricia's shoe, petite Alice Norton was taking a prolonged nap on the hardwood floor. Everyone at Columbus Tech Night School liked Alice. She was the most flamboyant girl in her business classes. Sure, she had her little quirks, orange hair, butterfly tattoos and multiple piercings, but she had a way of making them into easily accepted additions to her fun personality. At the moment though, she was dead, which tends to put a damper on things.

Alice was lying in a pool of half dried blood, one portion of her left buttocks having gone into the stomach of one of Pine Point's enterprising new zombies. Her body had been twisted while she'd beaten and screamed against the man who'd eaten her, but in stark contradiction, she'd finally come to rest on her back, as if in the midst of a perfectly sound and quite temporary nap. The mortician himself might have laid her in the exact same accidental pose. Her eyes were open, staring up at the long pleats of the partition curtain that loomed slightly aside and above her. A pool of blood was spread under her lower half. Her skirt had managed to drape itself back over her legs as the zombie had dropped her, leaving her perfectly decent.

She closed her eyes, things sort of drifting and cold as she smelled something. The something she smelled had the effect of smelling salts, awakening a past need. As she came out of the misty black hole she'd been in seconds earlier, the smell of life compelled her closer to resurrection.

Patricia went back to the front of the store. Shoot, I can steal anything in here, she thought, looking into the corners of the tiny place for any hidden cameras. Glancing at the register, she shook her head no, realizing it was way beneath her dignity to do a thing like lifting a drawer full of cash. Still...she eyed the fifty dollar perfume. She did intend to buy it, she recalled. She had William's money right there in her purse, she thought, looking at her tiny handbag, as if its riches were some sort of seal of rights to whatever might happen. They just don't seem to really want to take my money....

"Honk! Honk!"

Patricia turned, the bottle of SEXSCENT still in her hand, and now with her back to both the counter and the more distant curtain. She realized that the bottle was hidden from anyone or any camera that might actually be around, assuming there was anyone or any camera in the store. Movement on the street shifted in the glass and metal of several wind chimes, as did the reflective shimmy of a curtain, but it was all just vague reflections to Patricia, who'd spotted her anticipated friend, Tammy, waving at her from the wheel of her car.

Patricia waved back and took a step toward the door. She had to put the bottle into her purse to catch the doorknob. That was all just how it had to be, not really a theft, and for sure she wasn't the one who'd done something wrong, thought Patricia. The people who ran the place were so incompetent, she thought as an excuse, walking out into the sun and getting into the car.

"Where to?" Asked Tammy.

"Where are all the pretty rich boys?" Replied Patricia. She took her new bottle of perfume out of her purse, spraying a dab on her friend's wrist.

Tammy smelled the perfume, saying, "Ummm," before driving off under the afternoon sun.

Alice stumbled against the glass pane of the front door. That smell was nearly gone, whisked away in that car, along with a second helping, she thought. Turning, she took in the store, not finding anything much that appealed to her. Taking a whiff of air, she smelled the departed meat as if her nose had bloodhound roots. Running her hands through her hair in a gesture of madness, the orange mane was quickly streaked with red.

That smell! She stepped from the door to the front of the counter. The perfume was overbearing, getting in the way of that sweet smell she so craved. Alice brushed several of the bottles aside, one or two breaking on the floor, causing the unwanted smell to get even worse and drowning out the last of the Patricia smell that had awakened and now so terribly enticed Alice.

What is this place? Alice wasn't too sure. It seemed familiar, but not all that recognizable as something she needed now. One spot in the room did seem to call to her though. Right there behind the counter. That's where you wait, she recalled. That's where you wait for the food. Yes! She staggered around to inside the counter spaces, the nonsensical cash register just off of her left elbow.

From that station, she facing the door just a few feet in front of her, ready to greet with a...oh yes, "How may I help you, ma'am?" She tried, "Hoo waaa a, weell, mmmmm! Ummmm! Umm! Ummmm!" Yes, that sounded pretty good.

She even tried to smile, her eyes big, bloodshot only on the bottom and hurting from the awful glare of the front window. Besides that, she showed way too much tooth, a whiteness that nearly matched her pale skin, save for the occasional liver spot. Of course, in Alice's mind she was just being attractive, presenting herself as the perfect...bait. She even took twenty fumbling minutes to fix the top button on her blouse, it having somehow gotten undone, she not knowing how. Shuffling from foot to foot like a worm on a hook, she craned her neck around, working out a number of rather noisy creaks. Do this awhile, she thought, and they just come right up to you. One just needs to be patient, she told herself, not particularly fond of that concept, but it was just too awfully bright outside to go looking for something to eat out there, she determined.

A string of spittle dripped from a brightly red lip she'd bitten in a forgotten struggle for life just that very morning. That, another lifetime ago.

****

"...rally against the death clinics is to be announced and coordinated through the ministry. Those interested in attending, call..." Reverend Purswell flicked the radio show off, content that his advertising dollars were being spent without a transmitter problem, or some other snafu. It was amazing that he had the time to check on such things, it having been so damned busy of late. Then there was the little emotional outburst at the office. He'd have to find something unique to help tide over.

That secretary! If he'd told her once, he'd told her a thousand times. "It's not a job requirement. I'm a married man, and you know it. I just needed some comfort, and it grew into something it shouldn't have. Ohhh!" He said to the mirror after parking. They were going to quit. They both knew they had to, but then, PMS time and boy, watch logic spit itself out the window, he scolded himself. He should have learned from the last one. It was more her than him, he felt, remembering how she'd come onto him at a moment of weakness. He repented for it every...single...day.

A little bottle of perfume, something special, will tidy things up a little; bring her back down to earth. She knew it couldn't go on, but you have to let a woman down gently, he understood. Women knew when perfume was the good stuff, the not necessarily what you'd find at the department store stuff. She'd appreciate the extra effort; not take the letdown so hard. He stepped up to the store landing and then boldly stepped inside.

Everybody in town, and half the people in the country knew him, so he'd have to say this right. "Do you have any perfume that really smells wonderful. You know, understated and classy, but pretty. My wife, you see, isn't a picky woman, but I want to surprise her with something nice that tells her how much I love and respect her," he told the clerk from just inside the doorway.

Alice stuck her tongue out nearly as far as it would go, and then, as slowly as the last drip out of a bottle, licked across her top lip. Oh god, the smell! She could taste it, it was that intense. If the guy just stood there like that all day long, she'd bust from just eating the smell of him.

Oh, but then she remembered that she'd forgotten what she was supposed to say to the customers, and then did, "Hoo waaa a, weell, mmmmm!"

She felt that she'd said that quite perfectly. He'd not be the least suspicious. Now all he had to do was just step one step closer, right up to the counter, and she could get a good bite out his plump arm, or better yet, couch potato belly. Just one...little...step, she pleaded, as if ESP worked. Her eyes were Houdini orbs.

Purswell was in the midst of that step, but then, in sudden recognition of the danger, thought better of it, rocking backwards.

She lunged across the counter. Her body spread across it, and then slid down the far side. Her skirt hiked up her waist, or more correctly, downward under force of gravity as she slipped forward toward the floor. Alice's mouth was open and aimed toward the black soled foot that was straight ahead. The bottles on the counter that hadn't been scattered earlier, went in all directions.

Kicking the side of her head, Purswell stepped to the side and made his way around the counter. "Jesus be with me," he spit, adding, "Look to God, girl. Find his strength!"

Dazed by the blow on her head by Purswell's shoe, she managed no more than to get up on all fours. Her skirt was up, displaying the naked and half eaten buttocks, but only for long enough for Purswell to see it and gasp.

Purswell backed up more, moving around toward the back of the counter and into the main store. Wind chimes jangled as he banged through them while struggling backwards. The woman got up onto one knee, and found with her eyes the meat that so tempted her with its powerful smell of life-force.

A weapon, thought Purswell. He picked up a boxed chime, and tossed it at April, the box banging against her side and settling near the door. Then he spotted the perfect weapon. A wind chime made of long, sturdy brass pipes was near the back. He moved back, and then pulled it down. Using the edge of a crystal chime piece, he cut the twine roping. A long pipe fell to the floor where he picked it up and brought it in front of his body like a sword.

April was up on two legs. At first she limped toward him, but then found a burst of energy, running with a wail of foul air.

Purswell side stepped, bashing her across the shoulder as she passed. Her body smashed through a display of tin knickknacks. April stopped with a sickening thud when her head butted into the wall, compressing her frail neck. She fell like a rag doll, a heap that didn't move.

With his pipe in front of him, Purswell kicked at her foot. She still didn't move. "God, she's barely eighty pounds, soaking wet. I've killed a near child. I only hit her once!" Mourned the preacher. Not killed her, no, he remembered how she'd looked when he'd come in, but it would look like it. Probably she was as good as dead already, out of her mind like Sister Millie had been. The woman had attacked me, not the other way around, he reasoned. Still, she was so tiny. Who'd believe she'd attacked me? Even if they learned the truth, I'd be questioned for weeks, then I'd be in the press, suspect, another Condit scandal that will never settle because people will believe what people want to believe. Does it even matter if I did it or not? "Televangelist found with dead woman half his age. The naked truth that the police didn't tell you," he imagined might read the 'Inquirer' headlines.

How did this happen, he thought? Someone attacked her. That explained the nasty gouging on her backside. Probably raped too, or maybe not, but she had no panties. Then I came in and she was half out of her mind from her trauma, realized Purswell. So, not being able to distinguish between me and the guy who'd done this to her, she'd attacked me. And then I'd finished the job; killed her, thought Purswell. "Jesus!" He sat down, but then quickly got back up, locked the front door and pulled down the shades.

Purswell pulled his cell phone out of his pocket and dialed, him pacing through the rubble as he told the man on the other end what had happened and what he needed from him.

Over by the wall, Alice moaned softly, and shifted a foot.

"My god, she's not dead yet!" The televangelist hung up his cell call and knelt over her. He felt for a pulse at her neck. Nothing! In fact, she was cold as the nose on a beagle, just like Sister Millie had been, and just like the reports he'd read about the strange deaths of late. Did it matter that she'd moved, he wondered? She was as good as dead anyway. She'd not be the same, and she was totally out of her mind too. It would be worse if she did revive, he understood. She'd pick him out of a lineup. Probably the guy who'd done her in had been disguised. Only one man would be recognized. They'd struggled. He'd hit her. It would be all one bad thing to her; all lumped into one really, really bad thing!

He grabbed some of the string that had been separated in the process of gaining his defensive pipe out of the tangle of the chime. Lapping her hands behind her, he tied her wrists. Then, careful to avoid the bloody buttocks, he pulled a little more twine out of the pipes and did the same to her feet. Thankfully she seemed only marginally lucid. No need to gag her; she couldn't speak in more than a mumble. Even when in not such bad shape, she'd moaned more than spoken, he recalled.

Purswell backed away and looked down at the slightly wiggling corpse as he waited. The door rattled in its frame. Purswell crouched. Someone knocked. Then, after half a minute, footsteps retreated down the front landing. He exhaled, not even aware that he'd been holding his breath, and then fought to slow his pounding heart.

10

"Hop in!"

Joe turned his lawnmower off. Not having heard what she'd said, he looked at the patrol car in front of his little house expectantly.

"I said, hop in. I have an assignment. I thought maybe you'd like to do a drive-along. After all, the Chief did say that I needed to keep an eye on you. I don't have to arrest you, do I?"

"Sure; that'd be fun. Just let me lock up."

"Oh, just leave it. I'm in a rush," said Sandra, leaning on the elbow that was hanging out of her patrol car. She was in jeans and a plaid shirt, looking more like a woman who'd stolen a patrol cruiser than an officer. The only official clue was a badge between her breasts, it dangling on a dog tag chain.

He went around and jumped into the passenger seat. The passenger seat was tight, much of the room between them consumed by radios, siren and light bar controls, as well as a complete mobile computer terminal. Completing the effect, a shotgun was locked upright in a cradle. To Joe the stuff seemed the perfect date chaperone. It was both an electrical and armory hazard just sneaking a hello kiss.

He said, "I thought you cops were supposed to tell everyone to keep things locked up and tucked away?"

"Oh shucks dear, these are the suburbs. Besides, with what's been going on lately, I long for the days of simple break-ins. Be the perfect excuse to check out your stuff."

"So what's up? Aren't you supposed to be on sick leave?" Asked Joe as she pulled away from the curb. The car had that old fashioned power of a Detroit engine before the invention of the energy crisis, he noticed as they raced up to forty-five in seconds.

"Chief called and begged. He said he'd officially keep me listed as on sick time if I'd do some light duty investigation. He's going to log the work I do now as overtime and add it to my clock when I come back so I don't lose my convalescence. Seemed like a good deal to me, as long as the duty's light. All time and a half or double-time. Besides, he is desperate. Three other officers called in sick, and everyone else is busy with other suspicious deaths, domestics and traffic accidents. It's like the whole town decided that today was the day they intended to go crazy."

She gave him a look of concern. Joe read her face and realized that she'd picked him up for two reasons. One: To get to know him better and spend some time with him. Two: She was scared. Something wasn't right, and she sensed it, just as he was starting to sense it. He made her feel a little safer. That was fine with Joe. She made him feel a little safer too, though he was thinking more than ever that he should have locked his place up. Maybe the town is under a spell, Joe thought, though he'd always thought himself not a superstitious man.

He answered her look more than her words, saying, "You're right. Something is in the air. The town seems strange."

"We drew that little thing with John, the caretaker, to look over. I've been told that he didn't make it, so it's now listed as a possible homicide. Something about the wounds not measuring up to what one might expect from a vehicle accident. It's the kind of job a team of detectives should have taken on immediately, but everyone's just that busy. It might be the full moon. I'm heading out to the cemetery. We'll see what might be found at his place. I'll pay you my overtime if you want to help?"

"Deputy Joe Jefferson? Woo hoo. That's a twist. Sure, I'll join the posse, but just think of me as the horse. Keep the money, dear; I'm on vacation, and besides, I don't mind going dutch on a date, but I'll be damned if I'm getting paid."

"Oh, goodness," said Sandra, amused.

They pulled onto Deadman. Pine Point's cemetery was pristine. Tiny cherry trees dotted the manicured lawn. In front, dark grey headstones of every description lined up behind a recently painted silver, chain linked fence. Beyond, newer headstones, those a more uniform formation of shapes, made themselves porcelain white soldiers in the sun.

The first gravel road led along the west boundary of the cemetery. John's cottage was really a long garage made mostly of block. The front half held the tractor and backhoe. A long dead Chevy Impala sat rusting on a patch of grass next to the back half's cottage. They stopped by the Chevy. A pair of doors, looking more like garden doors than the entrance to someone's house, hung wide open, one hanging from a single hinge.

"See. He didn't lock up, and look what happened to him," said Joe, the comment taking on a serious edge as the last few words drove his memory back to John's bleeding body. Just to make sure he'd not left the wrong impression, he added, "Let's be careful. I don't like the looks of this. Might be he had a reason to be out driving as crazy as he was. The Blue Fish is only a few blocks down. Surely he knew where that telephone pole was before he ran into it."

Sandra nodded and gave Joe the flashlight. She took the shotgun for herself.

Joe pulled one of the doors wider with the toe of his shoe. The glass rattled in its frame. There were streaks of dried blood on the inside glass, clearly finger drawn, as if the door had been clutched at before opened. The back of the room was dim, so Joe played the flashlight around while Sandra put on a latex glove and then popped the light on.

John's last meal had been corn flakes. A cat looked at them from over the upended box. Apprehensive, it paused in the process of licking up the last of the milk in a bowl. Corn flakes were all over the table, and over the edge, onto the floor closest to the entrance. The flakes had joined most of the rest of the contents of John's shelves there. John had been a heavy reader of private dick paperbacks, a library for them to wade through. No doubt the books had added mightily to the brick room's insulation before they'd spilled.

Typical of the finicky species, the cat jumped off of the far end of the table, ran under it, and then between Joe's legs on the way out the door.

"There was some kind of a fight, from the look of it. Looks like someone was after him. That's why he ran into the telephone pole. The guy he was fighting with might have even still been after him on the road."

"Seems like a good possibility, but the guy lives in a shack in the middle of a cemetery. What's to fight over here?" Asked Joe, walking past the table.

"Check this out," said Sandra, pointing out an inch wide smear of blood with her shotgun barrel. The smear ran right under the table. The bleeding had eased to intermittent as it led out the door. The route was the same the cat had taken. Either the bleeding had slowed, possibly due to some kind of temporary bandage, or John had been moving faster as he neared the door. The broader end of the smear disappeared into the further room.

The back room was partitioned, two thirds bedroom, one third shower and toilet. Joe probed with his light. There was blood all over the walls in the bedroom part, in stark contrast to the perfectly made bed.

"There's been a fight in here too. This is probably where it came to blood. Watch your step," said Sandra, pointing out the pistol Joe had nearly put his foot on. It was half covered by several tattered strips of t-shirt, as if someone had been making quick bandages. Sandra picked the gun up with a pen out of her pocket, and looked through the cylinders. "Empty, and smells heavily of burnt powder, so it's probably been fired lately."

"Did they find any gunshot wounds on John?" Asked Joe.

"No. I'm guessing that this is his gun. After the bad guy left, John probably bandaged his own arm up loosely and then dragged himself out, all of that after scaring his assailant off. He knew he was bleeding a lot, and was in danger of going into shock, where he'd no doubt bleed to death without assistance. The closest person is Dolcy at the Blue Fish. Bandage fell off in the wreck, and next, we saw him at the lounge in pretty bad shape. That wound on the arm was ugly," theorized Sandra.

"That's one possibility. But then again, how does a man empty a gun in a room this small, and end up missing what he's shooting at?"

Beyond the bedroom was one last door, this one leading into the tractor area. It was latched, a lock dangling in the latch as if tossing it on was all one needed to do. The lock didn't need to be locked to keep an intruder in the garage from opening it, realized Joe. Bloody fingerprints were on the lock, the prints more clearly visible when Joe put the beam of his flashlight on it.

"What do you think?" Asked Sandra.

"I think whoever he was shooting at ended up in there. John probably kept his gun in this bedroom. The fight started in the main room, moved in here as he fought to get his weapon, and the perpetrator ends up in there after John pastes him with his pistol. John locks the wounded man in there, bandages himself up, and makes for his pickup to get help. I didn't see a phone, the lucky bastard, but in this case it might have proven useful."

"I'm stuck on one thing. Why did John look so scared? Desperate, sure. Scared so badly that he couldn't drive straight, I don't know? The man lives in a cemetery. Makes a man hard, living next to the dead. Would be hard to spook a man like that," Sandra tossed back. She gingerly picked the lock up out of the hasp, and laid it on the bed for later prints. Then she turned the knob, and pushed the door open a crack. "Cover me," she said.

Joe took one look at his flashlight, and imagined it a pitiful club, nodding yes. He aimed the torch at the center of the door.

Sandra kicked the door open. It banged against the wall, having rotated half a circle. Rakes and shovels rattled in their wall nail cradles.

The garage only had one small window, the place dim. A bad smell hit them hard after a second's delay. Joe pointed his flashlight to the left, spotting a tractor grill, then to the right, pointing out the yawning scoop of a backhoe. Between the two vehicles, lying flat on his back with his arms stretched out under both undercarriages, was the deadest man Joe had ever seen. The guy was even dressed for dead, in his black, Sunday best, right on down to the black, gloss, spray painted shoes.

"Looks like your theory wins the cupie doll, Joe. God, it smells awful in here."

"Maybe we should open the window and let the flies out. Cruelty to animals," suggested Joe, pointing his flashlight at the dead man's face. There were half a dozen flies on it, as well as maggots crawling out of both eye sockets and a shriveled mouth full of teeth. The sockets were empty, as if the maggots had been at them for longer than the one day. Over that, two holes had been punched into the dead man's forehead, as if his head had been an easy target and John had hit it dead-on twice.

Sandra traded her shotgun for Joe's flashlight so she could look things over more carefully. "That's strange."

"What, like there can be something stranger than a dead man with maggots crawling out of his mouth?" Said Joe, fighting back his gagging impulse.

"There's no bloating. Look how thin and dried his skin is too."

"So? He looks old. Probably was thin and dry to start with," said Joe, not really wanting to look that closely.

"Yeah, but there's one more thing. Ever see a suicide victim? You know, one of those guys who've shot themselves in the head? They bleed. Goodness, do they ever bleed. You'd not believe how much blood is in a body, and the fastest way to get it out is to get shot in the head where a lot of blood is pumped to fuel all that thinking. They used to think that the head was a filter for the blood, you know, and for good reason; there's so much of it up there. It's not like in the movies. The heart keeps right on pumping even after a direct hit in the head, and the stuff shoots out in what looks like a gallon a second until there's nothing left. They bleed out first, and then the heart stops when there isn't enough blood left to keep the heart fed."

"Gee, lighten up with the graphics a little, sweetheart. I get the idea," said Joe, having had his share of the gory details.

"So, where's the blood?" She worked the flashlight around the body. There were two more holes that looked like bullet holes, but both of them were in the sleeve. The wounded arm showed no sigh of blood either.

"You mean, all that blood in there was just John's? Maybe some of it was this guy's. Maybe John dragged the man out here?"

"No heel marks on the dirt floor in this garage. Besides, what did he do, clean the man off? Wash his shirt with Tide? There'd be too much blood. Lots of punks think they can just shoot someone and clean it up. That takes a professional to do it right, not to mention, a lot of time. John didn't look to me like he was in a patient frame of mind when he ran up to that door begging for help."

"Yeah. Ok, so, where does that leave us?"

"I'm thinking that John shot a corpse," said Sandra after a minute's thought.

"Well, we pretty much had this whole thing figured out, and you had to go and say a thing like that. Now I don't have a damned clue how this deal plays out. My first day on the job as a city detective, and I'm bust. You know, next date, let's go to one of those dinner theatres where they have a cast that includes the audience, and the Mary Drew works out logically in the end. No messy bodies either."

"I'm baffled too, I'm afraid. But, we do have a whole cemetery. If this was a corpse, he most likely came from out there. Let's go check it out. Maybe John was into selling bodies? Maybe the fight was with an accomplice or with someone who found out what he was up to?" Suggested Sandra.

"Shall we?" Agreed Joe, eager for anything but the smell of the garage.

As soon as they stepped through the double doors, they saw them. Two men in white collared shirts and well cut jeans jumped out from behind a pair of headstones. They hurdled the far fence in seconds, and disappeared into the woods lining the creek.

Sandra and Joe took off after them, but pain hit Sandra in the chest, and she fell back to a bare jog. Joe got to the fence first, just in time to see the pair ford the creek, run up the other bank, and dive into the open back doors of a van. It sped away behind several buildings, Joe having not seen much more than the back of the thing.

Sandra came up beside him. "What did you see?"

"Looked like two well dressed white men, shirts untucked and dirty, but other than that, like a pair of Mormons out on mission. They ran into a white van and booked."

"Any license number?" Asked Sandra, between heavy breaths. She bent over, holding her taped, broken ribs.

"No. Too far. You know, this is supposed to be light duty. Let's just add this to our observations and not get involved in any more street chases. I'm worried about your chest." Just then Joe saw the line of headstones, second row from the back of the cemetery where they stood. Eight graves stood open, a ninth with a foot of dirt already uncovered. A pair of shovels lay on the ground beside the work in progress. "Huh! Maybe you guys can get some prints out of this," he added.

Sandra followed Joe's eyes.

"So this is the angle. John and two or three others are involved in body snatching. He got into a fight with one of the accomplices, maybe over payment, and ends up dead," decided Sandra.

"Persistent accomplices, I'd say. Well dressed, persistent accomplices. Well dressed, persistent accomplices with nice new vans," mused Joe.

"Sure. Doctor types, or medical students," guessed Sandra.

"OK. So, maybe that's what happened at the funeral parlor too. They're just stealing bodies wherever they're to be found, and doing practical jokes, and stealing more bodies, and murdering grave diggers," said Joe.

"Seems like a lot to bite off," said Sandra.

"That's what I was thinking too. And, one other thing."

"What's that?" Asked Sandra.

"John used at least four of his six bullets shooting a corpse. Let me ask you; if you were in a life and death struggle, ending up wounded so severely that it eventually caused your death, would you waste time and over half a load on a dead man?"

Sandra looked down into one of the eight empty graves and couldn't find an answer in the scarlet velvet of the yawning coffin at the bottom.

11

He took the confounding extra foot off of the table, and tossed it into the bucket, stuffing it down towards the bottom where Guy's guts met Fred's, and where the foot wouldn't be too obvious, should there be an unlikely snoop. Somebody had screwed up with the extra foot, big time. He had two bodies on the tables, and five feet. Let them figure that out! How sloppy can the cops get? The foot wasn't going to pay any different, that was for sure. He'd like to help out the coroner, who'd amazingly missed the detail, but the man had been nearly as busy as he had been over the last two days, reflected the mortician. He had to get things done, or he'd have to start putting bodies out and upping the air conditioning to something brutal. He already had them stacked two to a drawer, a totally unauthorized necessity, but at least he could blame it on the recent rush.

It wasn't all bad. William was kind of happy for the rush. It paid well, kept his mind off of his troublesome girlfriend, Patricia, and it helped smooth over the embarrassment of having lost the last load of corpses to pranksters.

Just minutes earlier, William had filled Guy's chest and stomach cavities with the mortician equivalent of Thanksgiving stuffing. Employing the aid of a four-inch, hooked needle, the flesh that had once housed a man named Fred was sewn closed. At the chest, where the skin had been ripped into jagged ribbons, William had been forced to use a sheet of latex. It's all going under the shirt, so what the hell, thought William. Odd that people wanted their bodies preserved in expensive caskets and eternally guaranteed vaults, while everything inside went down the drain or into the cooker. All that really got buried was the meat, he'd long since figured out.

"One down—one to go," said William, patting the wet belly. It echoed like a beach ball.

"I vant to be loved by you, by you, novody else vut you, I vant to dlink blood from you, from you, you, bo po pi do!" William sang, as he puttered around the workroom, cleaning and moving the instruments from Fred's to Guy's table. The singing was loud, but muffled behind his sterile mask. Once and awhile, a drop of water or body fluid dripped between the tables from his gloves and plastic apron as he moved about.

The mortician put his hand on the top of Guy's head, forcing it to turn so that he could see the wound better. The neck twisted with an audible snap, the rigormortis breaking. "This is a much nicer bust. I think we are going to have a lot of inspirational moments together," he told the corpse.

Fred was kind of fat featured, but Guy had a round little head that William thought might be pretty paint worthy. "Every wonder what it's like to be the fairer sex..." William looked at the nametag on the corpse's toe and added, "...Ginger? Oh, just kidding."

Minutes later, Guy looked like something between a circus clown and an elderly bar maid with a cheap hairdo.

William thought he heard a thump behind him. He looked around seeing nothing out of order. Those kids and their pranks had him jittery, he decided. One of Fred's arms was dangling from the edge of the table. Not having remembered being that sloppy, William lifted it back onto the table, and went over to the cooler drawers to unlock chamber six and get it ready for the newly done stiffs.

"Just hang on boys; I'll have you tucked in, nice and comfortable in no time at all. I've heard this here cooler can cures those jittery caffeine nerves of yours too. A few hours in here, and we'll have you that much closer to the last ceremony, and then it's on to the holy elevator. Going up? Going down? Either way, sure to warm you up after a stay in here. How's that? Sound nice? In the mean time, how do you want it, both sunny side up, or maybe sixty-nine? We're doing two at a time for the duration of the local witching season. Hee, hee!"

Just as William reached the drawers, a thump broke the silence of the hollow preparation room. Startled, William twirled. Fred's arm had fallen off of the table again. He looked at it, a little impressed with the way Fred twitched in such a specific way.

Rapping at the door shook William from his admiration of Fred's determined nerves. "Hey, is anyone in there? William! Open up; it's the Coroner," a man screamed. He seemed determined from the other side of the door.

"Oh, shit!" William threw a sheet over Guy and his incriminating makeover. Then he put Fred's arm back up on the table, not wanting the official to think that he ran an untidy shop. Finally, a can of floral spray trailed a foggy mist of room deodorant behind him as he briskly walked to the doorway. "Coming!" William screamed, to ward off the rapping that had resumed in an annoyingly steady way. Still in gloves, mask and plastic apron, William stuffed the spray can into an oversized smock pocket, and opened the door, making a point to look the part of a busy, but untroubled man as it swung wide.

"Yes? Can I help you gentlemen?" He asked the County Coroner, a familiar face. Beside him stood a stranger who looked technical, as opposed to political—yet still official—in a white uniform coverall with a state badge on the shoulder and a nametag buttoned over the heart.

"We've run across a problem from the lab with those three deliveries, I'm afraid," said the Coroner. William stood in the way, but it didn't seem that the officials noticed as they wedged their way inside. "Typical inter-agency screw up, Bill," the Coroner explained. He exuded casual, as if saying that mistakes and their cover-ups were an everyday occurrence for him.

"What do you mean?" William asked. "You need to make an appointment. I have my own schedule to look to," he tried.

"Oh hell, what have you done?" The state man in the white coveralls had slipped further into the room. William and the Coroner stopped negotiating and turned. The man was staring at the pail of organs between Fred's feet at the edge of the table. "This is going to be an all day job just sorting out the parts. You didn't spray the table into that mess, did you? Is there more than the waste from these two in that?"

William asked, "Will one of you please explain why you are here? Look, I'm not doing autopsies in here. I just make them ready to shovel six feet of dirt over."

"The Sheriff's office should have told you to put these two on ice for another round of autopsy, along with the woman, when she shows up. Actually, I'm kind of surprised that you couldn't surmise as much on your own, Bill. After all, they weren't a pretty set when they came in, from what I've already seen. This much damage in one murder, three dead, well…bound to be pressure for a complete inquiry."

"Hey, for all I know, they could have been run over by a lawnmower. Don't blame me for the County's mistake. You had all afternoon with them before you made the mistake of sending them to me."

The Coroner didn't answer. Instead he stepped across the room to where the technician was already standing over the first corpse. The arm had slipped off of the table again, a detail they were both inspecting—among other things. All William could think was, good thing I didn't paint Fred's face and had thought to cover Guy's with that sheet.

"That one's got the nerves. I should put them back in and let them cool up some before you have another go at them. Come back in a half hour," explained William.

"They usually move around when they've been left out to thaw too long," the state technician grumbled. "Is that air freshener spray I smell, or do you administer a gallon of after shave after a hack job?"

"Jackass," said William under his breath. "Look, I'll just tidy up in here. You can get some coffee in the reception room. Please; let me...."

The Coroner interrupted, "Coffee's good," before taking his suit coat off, and pulling a smock out of his briefcase.

"I'll get the portable lab," the state technician said, going for the door. "You can get some coffee," he advised William. "Then you can leave us to sort out what's left of the evidence." He paused to motion William out of his own door.

"Look, this is my business. I need a half hour," protested William.

"This is a murder investigation," corrected the Coroner, still acting polite, but serving notice that it could get ugly.

"But," William couldn't think of anything to add to his protest. He looked into the technician's eyes. Now there's a man with an overly active sense of duty, he thought, and an under active sense of cordiality. Boy, wouldn't he give a pretty penny to see that man and Patricia out on a date. The thought of too many Patricia faces sent a drop of sweat running down his forehead. What was the penalty for painting the face of a murder victim so that he looked like an all American Princess? William could only guess, as he shook his head, defeated, and aimed himself toward the door.

From out in the corridor, William watched the technician unload the back of a station wagon. Then William went into the pantry, pulling out the big coffee brewer, the one he usually saved for showings and funerals. William knew he'd have a long wait, and would be needing the caffeine, as he imagined their reaction to both the jumble of parts and the paint job. Hell, they even had cameras, he'd noted. He imagined one particular photo finding its way onto the front page of the local Dispatch, it right under a headline like, 'Local Mortician Dismembers Victims, Then Paints Female Faces on Corpses!' He couldn't even recall having read anything that weird in the National Inquirer. He imagined Patricia's surprise at the resemblance just before reading his name in the fine print! Bill sat and watched the little bubble on the top of the brewer; waiting for the coffee to perk.

Then on the other hand, he could sell his story to Nightline, Daywatch, A Current Affair, Howard Stern. Getting caught might include a penalty, but it might also be the publicity boost he'd not get otherwise. When the trial came, he could just claim stress. The penalty for painting a dead face could be a week without recess, William hoped? Hell, the worse that could happen is he could make a few million on the book and movie rights. They'd buy the art too. He'd need to make copies, run signed editions. This was his big break, recalling all of those women who had wanted to shack up with that ex-Marine Bobbit after he'd gone on the talk show circuit to tell about how his wife had cut his you-know-what off because he'd allegedly raped her every night; only now they would get product too, a regular show and tell. They couldn't show Bobbit's wang, but photos and paintings of corpses appear to be kosher. This is America: Sex is bad, but death is A-OK.

It could become the next big thing. Everyone might want their faces painted to look like Patricia. And, which made better copy, an ex-Marine with a deformed joystick or a real mortician that brought the dead to life, asked William? Everyone knows morticians are almost phallic; there are far more movies about the living dead than Marines, aren't there? Crazy ex-Marines are almost a dime a dozen. What did that professor say, ah, "Art dares not imitate life too well." Well, thought William, I'm not imitating life at all and my concept is nearly as romantic as Dracula.

His nerves were still on edge, but William felt a little better the more he thought about it. In the corner of his eye, the coffee finally perked.

The state man located a dozen kidney pans, and turned to sorting through the big pale. "He did it; all together into one pail. I swear, it's almost predictable the way these morts work. I have four lungs lying on top, slightly covered by every fluid known to mankind." He lifted a thick grey lung, and put it into a large pan. "I've got the intestines tied together next, and in multiple pieces, with feces swimming all over them; everything's been hacked on, and looks like it has been eaten on. You don't think this William is into that, do you? What kind of knife does that mortician use anyway? Damn!"

Nodding at each complaint, the Coroner busied himself with setting up a camera at the end of Fred's table.

"I'd at least like to isolate the organs and chill them before we transport them to the state lab," continued the tech.

"Hold on a minute, son. We slipped up shipping these too soon. We'll have to compensate by keeping to the parts of this autopsy that are likely causes. It's diversionary to get overly pushy about the mortician's mistakes. What if that leaks to the press, or some murderer's defense team? No need to bring in more spotlights than necessary. Whatever we find, this is a basic autopsy focused upon the wounds. I want your help, that's why we called you in, but it's going to look funny if we do out of county lab work on mixed up organs that have little to do with the case. Is there really any doubt that we have a trio of savage murders here? What do you think we'll find, a drowning? Just lighten up and let's leave this local. We won't be calling on lab work that sends our County over budget unless there's a pressing need, not to mention, sense of professionalism about what we're sending," lectured the Coroner.

"I hope you're right…about it being a simple multiple murder, that is. We'll need a few samples though, or my boss will have my head. I don't know what he's after, but he didn't sound flexible," said the state man.

The coroner nodded acceptance. Usually when the state was called in, it was anything but usual, the man had come to expect. His conversation with the state emergency control group that morning seemed to confirm what the tech was saying about needing a few samples. Still, it was the County's call, and he didn't wish work on himself, nor was he all that big on politics outside of his own campaign.

"Sure," answered the Coroner. "The Sheriff said there was a struggle. Look at the body. So far I have an act of violence. All we need to do is to document the insults to the body and get your best few samples in order to keep the bosses happy." He stopped, flicked on the camera and turned up the volume. Walking around the table so that both he and the body were in camera pan, he repeated, "So far I have what appears to be an act of violence." Then he went on to introduce himself and the subject of the inquiry.

The state guy finished sorting out the lungs and hearts, ultimately placing each into individually tagged sterile bags. Once done, he leaned into the view of the camera lense, and watched the Coroner muse over the rips and cuts to skin and muscle.

The Coroner went on in monotone for so long that the technician almost missed, "What would you suggest could have caused these insults?"

"Hum.... It's not a knife, or any other really sharp instrument, including our mortician's lawn mower." He smiled for the first time since arrival. A puzzle, and a dig at the mort. More important to him at the moment though, was the puzzle. He liked puzzles.

"I once saw odd rips like these in a farm machinery accident," injected the Coroner.

"Yeah, I was thinking that too. Again, though, there aren't enough clean cuts even for that, and machinery almost always affects a limb. What aren't cuts are actually rips. In fact, the rough cuts here are more like animal bites. See the moon shaped bite marks. Now, the way the flesh was stretched does seem familiar to something powerful and ripping, but not powerful enough to cause actual separation of joins and ligaments." He pointed to a row of rounded shapes and bloodied tissue.

"No large biting animals exist around here," challenged the Coroner.

"A small bear's bite is close together, but no, not all of these marks are incisors. Look on the skin here. The bruising," he leaned close enough to block the camera's view, "these are molar marks. Herbivorous or Omnivorous. There wasn't any penetration past the first few incisors. OK, I have it. Our vicious animal is an omnivore."

"An ape?" Asked the Coroner, with skepticism in his voice.

The technician looked up at the Coroner, and explained, "I don't want to be the first one to say this, because if I'm wrong they'll call me a quack. In fact, I know there has to be a snag in what I'm reading from a few marks, but it's my impression that we're looking at human bites here."

"A little odd, don't you think?"

"Well, it's not all that unusual. People in life or death struggles often bite," said the state man.

"Yeah, but, what about here? In the upper chest region. This whole muscle. This guy must have been dead by the time this bite was made. And, this kind of biting over here is just plain old eating," said the coroner as he pointed into the chest cavity.

"Well, one of them was crazy. We know that. So, this isn't our crazy guy. We've discovered who didn't do it," noted the state man.

A kidney pan fell from Guy's table. It banged and then rattled on the floor behind the pair. Both men jumped.

"What the hell was that," yelled the Coroner.

The empty pan lay on the floor beside the half empty organ pail. It rattled until it stopped, but the pail continued a slight vibration of its own with subtle, but even, rhythmic jerks. Both men leaned closer.

"What in tarnation is in there?" Whispered the County Coroner.

"It must be a rat or something. This operation is a pig's sty," explained the technician, although the pail was full of stuff that didn't look much like a rat, all of it under a brew of body fluids.

"Oh man, I've been in this business too long to get spooked by a few spasms," professed the Coroner, straightening back up. The vibration stopped.

The state man grabbed the tray off of the floor and loaded the bags of organs he'd been working on onto it. He tossed the tray and pail of vibrating organs into the open meat cooler. The state technician decided that he just didn't want to guess why all of those parts had such active nerves. Joining the Coroner, the pair of men stood over the body for awhile, speechless, unable to hear the rattle from behind the cooler drawer's insulation, and unwilling to be the first to propose an explanation for what they had seen.

"Spasms. Nerves," said the Coroner, factually.

"No. That wasn't like any spasm I ever saw," corrected the tech, looking into the hole in the body that had produced half of the guts that had been on the tray and in the pale.

"So what was it then? It only lasted a few seconds; maybe it was our imagination?"

"I don't know," confessed the tech.

"Come on. You weren't short for ideas a few minutes ago. I imagine you state guys see everything, " goaded the Coroner.

"I just don't have an explanation right now. In fact, I don't want to think about it for a few minutes, if it's all the same to you."

"Is that a profes..."

The technician interrupted, "Damn it! I said I don't want to think about it right now! Let's get on with this."

"Thin skinned.... Alright, ahum.... We have a preliminary cause of death due to some sort of animal attack, not excluding human bites of an extreme nature. The body is too decimated to make me believe large bites are the whole story, but I would guess, and I must emphasize guess, that the cause of death is blood loss."

"Preliminary," stressed the technician.

"Yes," agreed the Coroner. "I suspect we might never know which came first, the chicken or the egg, the mutilation of organs and vessels, or the loss of blood. It was an extremely quick and violent attack and in either case, both were at work as one. This particular victim shows little signs of fighting back, fingernails bloodless, although a total fracture of the seventh, eighth and ninth vertebrae will go a long way towards explaining the passive defense from the subject."

A chill ran up the state mans spine. "Where did this happen?" He asked, out of curiosity.

"Down at the yards."

"They don't have some maniac still running loose, do they?" He asked, looking towards the crudely repaired back door and wondering if it was locked.

It seemed to the Coroner that the state technician had lost that professional tinge. The more astute political mind, he shut off the camera, realizing that the video tape might well become a court document before this was all over. He wouldn't have some lawyer tainting the trial with allegations that the Coroner's inquiry had predisposed notions. "Well, off the record, a witness said she saw a pair of males, probably these two going at it. The Sheriff's version is slightly in disagreement, from what I've been told. Shall we judge for ourselves?"

They walked away from Fred's body, and over to Guy's. The coroner reached for the sheet covering the painted second cadaver.

It was dim under the sheet and below closed eyes, although not as dark as Guy felt things should be. His eyes stared up at the blank bottoms of his own eyelids, his mind buzzing like he was on some sort of electrical cruise control. Awhile ago, the idea of light had been pleasing. The light had guided him through the tunnel towards something comforting. He hadn't believed in any of the fashionable religions, but he'd always wanted to think that a beautiful continuation existed beyond the grave. The light had seemed to confirm it. He'd entered the light thinking his body was a prison, and the further toward that eternal essence he got, the more he loathed the idea of returning to earth. Yet, as the press of souls thickened and crowded the tunnel, fall he did.

With the fall came darkness. He opened and then closed his eyes in a flash, hoping to regain the tunnel of light.

He was back down upon the cumbersome land of the living. His body seemed more of a prison than ever, numb in areas, rock hard and rigid in several places, as if he were living within his own private jail cell. In the back of his head, there was that ceaseless buzz, like he could hear his fellow dead moan after their own rejection from the jam packed gates of the ether world. Yes, I'm dead now, he thought, shocking himself. It was more than a thought, he realized. It was frigidly real. The understanding of that hit him so abruptly that he opened his eyes. Then some sadist above him threw back the sheet, showering his senses with light. His rotting brain was overloaded with photons!

Violation! Rage! Hate! Hunger!

Two feet above his head was the smell and look of something warm. The steaming hot food of life-force! Guy licked his bloated, pink lips. He was so insanely cold. The chill burned of a frostbitten soul. Yes, steaming hot food; he could just about feel it entering him, coating his insides with rich red warmth! Guy threw himself up towards the feast, missing by an inch before the imbalance pitched both himself and his stainless steal bed to the floor.

"Good Lord! This man isn't dead!" The technician yelled, as the table barely missed his leg. The state man backed against the other table.

"Oh boy. What has happened here?" Agreed the Coroner. "Quick! Help me get this man onto his back." The coroner fell to his knees. His hands went to Guy's body, hoping to coax Guy into a more relaxed position.

Momentarily stunned, Guy let the men roll him over. Blinking the eyes on his painted, but otherwise dull face, Guy watched the furthest man mouth a recognizable, but meaningless sentence.

"Get a look at that face!" Screamed the state man.

Closer. Yes, closer, Guy found himself chanting, the words coming out all garbled. A second man knelt just above his forehead. Guy recognized it as the meat he'd reached for seconds ago.

"Are you alright?" The meat asked. "Can you hear me?" The cow continued.

Guy sniffed at the hot air that came toward him, and it made his absent stomach cramp with outrageous hunger.

Throwing his arms around the small of the meat's back, Guy's mouth opened as wide as he could get it. With mysterious new strength, he jammed the crotch of the Coroner to his mouth, sinking his teeth onto both fabric and flesh until the teeth met with a snap!

The coroner's head flew back with a pain stifled scream. His eyes filled with terrible misery as he pushed against Guy's head with both hands.

The state man grabbed at Guy's slick, naked body, his hands going into the open ribs. He recoiled in horror. God, the man has no organs, realize the technician. His partner was being pulled down, and although the coroner screamed, and stretched his arms for help, the technician found himself unable to move forward and touch the abomination that was eating his way through the coroner's crotch. A red stain filled the Coroner's groin, spreading like he was wetting his pants, seeping through the fabric, and filling the thirst of the resurrected man who bit. Inside Guys mouth, his tongue sucked and licked the warm blood. As he continued, the blood he'd just swallowed leaked out of his opened ribcage.

"No! Help me! Help me!" The tech managed to scream, as if it were him who was under attack, and not the coroner. He froze with fear. A step back earned him a pair of hands wrapped around his head. Suddenly the hands had him pinned in a viselike grip. The flesh upon the arms that had captured his head were grey and streaked with yellow chemicals. Yet they had the dried give of dead skin.

The technician tried to twist free while pushing against the impossibly strong arms. A pair of the technician's teeth cracked like nut shells, as one of the arms wedged itself between his jaws, cutting off his air.

"Ummm...." came the moan of zombie Fred from above his head, just as the piercing pain of teeth bit a four square inch section out of the center of the technician's scalp.

William tried the locked metal workroom door. He banged on it with a fist. OK, so I screwed up and painted the guy's face, he was thinking. They don't have to tear the place up and make pricks out of themselves by screaming over it, he reasoned.

"Come on; open up. It isn't that big of a deal, for crying out loud. It was a cosmetic thing I did for an art project; I never even touched the body. I was going to clean it up! Who would know? Gee, I didn't mutilated him or anything," William shouted, as the screams in the secured room suddenly went silent. He waited; nothing but a few banging noises, and then not even that.

"Well at least they shut the hell up," he said, walking back for his third cup of coffee.

It wasn't until an hour later that he walked around and found the cellar doors broken open again. Stepping inside, the coroner and state technician were long gone. With them, a half dozen paying corpses were missing as well.

12

"Nice digs," said Joe as they waited in the cruiser at the security gate of Bob Purswell's home.

"Yes. Not really a mansion, but three or four half million dollar houses on twenty acres in the wealthiest part of the county is pretty much the same thing, only easier to clean. Copper gutters, four car garages. All tax deductible because the luxury is paid for by church funds; an investment in God's work, which means he has an office in the study, I'm guessing," said Sandra

"Like him, do we?" Joe asked sarcastically.

They were in Muirfield, well out of bounds for a Pine Point cruiser, but Sandra had convinced the guard that they only wanted to check on any information the preacher had about the incident at the funeral home. Still, they'd been left waiting twenty minutes before the iron electronic gate opened.

They drove in past an odd sign that read, "Purswell is God." Joe figured there was probably some spin on that, that you had to be an insider to comprehend. The road ended at the best looking house, which they assumed was Purswell's place.

A man in a dark suit coat, white shirt, black tie and dark sunglasses met them at the door. His, "Right this way," seemed anything but evangelical.

"Are you packing?" Joe asked the man's back, having noticed a bulge under his arm. The man didn't answer, opened a door to an office and waved the pair in.

Joe let Sandra go first, and then told the guide as he passed, "Thanks. You can go on back to that little gatehouse and get back to wanking yourself, if you like." That didn't elicit an answer either, and after they'd passed inside, the man just stood there, as if he'd found something better to guard than the driveway.

"I'm Officer Anderson from the Pine Point Police, and this is my associate, Joe Jefferson. We're shorthanded, and he is helping with a case that we thought you might have some information on."

"Ah, I remember you. From the funeral home. What brings you to Muirfield?" Asked Purswell as a greeting.

"Yes. We're investigating that. Just generally we're looking into the strange disappearance of a few bodies," said Sandra, taking a chair that was planted in front of Purswell's dark oak desk. Joe stood to her side like a guard beside his queen, knowing the psychological advantage of elevation.

"Oh yes. Pranksters, I've been told. It was a most ghastly funeral," said Purswell from his chair on the other side of the desk. The man's eagerness to allay suspicion only raised it in Joe's mind.

Sandra continued, "There have been a few more bodies that have turned up missing. We came across a pair of men digging up several at the Pine Point cemetery this morning, I'm afraid."

"Oh, so they've been back. Persistent, I'd have to say. That doesn't sound like pranksters," said Purswell.

"White shirts, black ties, and riding in a van that looked amazingly similar to the ones we passed in your church parking lot, Reverend," added Sandra.

"There are a lot of vans the color of ours, and good dressing manners is hardly criminal as well, Officer Anderson. Are you aware of the fact that a disproportionately large number of well dressed, white men are villains in television shows?"

"No, not really. Anyway, there appears to be a pattern. Perhaps someone is interested in these bodies for some reason we've not yet discovered. It seems a lot of trouble for a group of pranksters. We're not just looking for bodies, but also a motive, I'm afraid. I thought that your men might have some ideas of their own regarding why this is going on, considering their involvement in the search, that is. Perhaps one of them found a clue?" Tried Sandra, hoping to get Purswell talking.

"I see."

"Confidentially, of course," coaxed Sandra.

"I see." The reverend paused, as if making a decision, and said, "Are you a Christian, Officer Anderson?"

"I was raised Methodist," she answered, not bothering to tell him that she'd not been to church in years.

"Then you'll know about the book of Revelations then. You know, about the last days. Wars, and rumors of wars. Famine, flood, pestilence. Has there ever been a time of more warfare, or famine. Look at that homosexual disease, AIDs, and tell me that we've not seen pestilence. Sin begets sin, and don't for a minute believe that God doesn't have his eye upon the things we allow in our country."

Joe bit his tongue. Wars, famine, floods, pestilence, homophobia? Hardly predictions, thought Joe; more like the status quo, not helped much by government policies administered by men just like Purswell.

Sandra nodded her head yes, and said, "Yes, these are troubling times. I've often wondered why, even after the fall of communism, we seem to have increasing difficulties with terrorism and wars. It's particular troubling to see the famine and disease in Africa."

"These are signs of the end times. One World Government is predicted in the Bible. Even the conflict in the Middle East, which ignited the entire idea of One World Government, you'll notice. I can't tell you who it is, but almost assuredly the Anti-Christ is alive and germinating somewhere; perhaps in our own country; perhaps as a collection of special interests instead of a man."

"Possible," said Sandra, leaning forward as if absorbed in the conversation.

"Not possible. There are already people with computer chips under their skin. Good reasons, they'd contend, security, finance, drug administration. It always starts that way, with a certain credibility. We have the UN, NATO, the Coalition of American States, the Pacific Rim States, the European Union, and even the old Soviet Union has become a confederation. All of this unity is predicted as an end sign. In fact, I can hardly find an end sign that isn't covered, save one, Officer Anderson."

"Yes. I can see your point. It does make sense. What is the last sign?" Asked Sandra.

"The dead shall rise. Demons shall walk upon the earth. All that are left shall be asked to take upon them the mark of the beast when this is done. I used to think that these were separate things, but no longer. I think the dead are rising, or at least awakening. They shall walk upon the earth as demons. If their fluids get upon your lips, that will be the mark, a curse that can only mean death. When this starts to happen across the globe, the Lord shall take his people home. That's for his people; those who have been born again in his spirit, Officer Anderson." The preacher sat back in his chair, folded his fingers in front of his face, and looked over at Sandra and Joe as if he'd checked their king.

"I'm following you, but this is just hard to visualize. It's not that I don't believe, Reverend Purswell, but it's just so surreal. I just don't know if I interpret Revelations so literally, or for that matter, at all," said Sandra, not wanting to look as if she was patronizing him.

"Yes. That's probably how most people are. God can be mysterious though. I have to tell you this; I know that I'm right. I've seen it. It is happening as we speak."

"The dead are rising?"

"Exactly. That thing at the funeral home. It wasn't a prank, I fear. I'm convinced that Sister Millie, as well as others in our congregation who have recently passed away, have been found wanting and are risen from the dead as demons. God does not accept lukewarm Christians. It is no longer a prophecy. It is here, though it will take some time for the unbeliever to come to grips with it. Even among us, there are those who have fallen short. God says to work your salvation daily. Salvation isn't easy, Officer Anderson. The evil portion of the promised resurrection of the dead is at hand, and as far as I'm concerned, it's not a terrible thing. You see, I'm saved and under His grace. When the demons take over this miserable earth, I'm going home to see my savior. Do you have that assurance? Where will you be spending eternity, Officer Anderson?"

"You've seen them. Dead people walking around?" Asked Sandra, she ignoring the question.

Purswell retreated, "A lot of people did. At the funeral home. That woman was full of formaldehyde, or at least that's what the mortician said. I, for one, believe him. I've dropped the lawsuit we filed in her behalf; that's how convinced I am of it. Now is the time to come to God, Officer Anderson."

"You've made an impression. I'll have to think about it," said Sandra, getting up to leave. She shook his hand. Joe didn't offer, and Purswell didn't as well, as if they both knew one another too well to be bothered.

The guard walked them to their car, and then followed on foot as they drove out the gate.

"Strange man. I can't believe that people in the thousands are so deluded that they suck in what he says like he's a slurpy and send him a check for the honor," said Joe.

"He's hiding something, that's for sure. That stuff about being eager to see the planet overrun by demons is just plain ill. I can't imagine such a thing."

"That fixation on One World Government had me stuck. Can you imagine what the world would be like today if governments didn't try to hash things out? It's not like the old days when time and travel allowed us to be isolationists. The world is a can of gasoline, and there are an increasingly larger number of easily available matches. If you ask me, his religious views are both ignorant and self fulfilled prophecies of doom. Politics and religion are as related today as they were during the dark ages. Be a thorn in the side all over the planet, and watch the world implode. When it happens, when the world blows up, he's standing on the sidelines, saying, "See. I told you so," as if it isn't mostly the fault of idiots just like him when it happens," said Joe.

"Well, we know one thing. He's into bodies. He likes this dead rising thing too much to not be involved. It all hits too close to home. I mean, why did he get into that with us? Sounded almost like an excuse for his actions to me; like he was saying, "Sure, I've been collection bodies, but this is why." I know he's doing something, but I don't know exactly what it all amounts to," said Sandra.

"Probably exporting demons," said Joe.

"Get real, Joe. You're supposed to be helping me think," protested Sandra.

"Hey! That's what he said he was into. He liked the idea that the dead are rising, so the stiffs could take over the planet and win himself a ticket to heaven. I mean, that's how I read it. People put money into his plate to hear him say shit like that. I tell you what. I think he's crackers, but I don't think for a minute that he doesn't believe the crap he's into. I don't know about you, but that scares me more than anything. We like sticking the label of hypocrite onto his ilk, but believe me, the honestly misguided are far more deadly. We see this sort of thinking from foreign religions, and we are not blinded by the cloth then. Religious freaks have always scared me; even when I was a kid and my ma and pa force me to be one."

"Should I play Fraud, and help you dig into that, Joe? Methinks you protest too much," Said Sandra.

"No thanks. I've been there. I'm content to know that I'm no longer among the deluded and I've gotten over the notion that I can deprogram the rest of the world. The real question is, what is Mister Delusion himself doing with seven, ten, twelve, who knows how many, bodies?"

"Assuming he's the one collecting them," injected Sandra.

"Well, yeah, right, maybe he's just selling them to medical schools like we originally thought. Kind of like the bake sale. Came up with that rising dead junk to throw us off. Raising a spot of change for the new Sunday School building. Could be he's not as dangerous as I was saying, and is a hypocrite."

After what she'd heard Purswell say, Sandra no longer believed that idea. No, he is really into that dead rising thing. If he's stolen them, he still has them, reasoned Sandra.

Joe read her silence. "I have an old suit, white shirt, red tie, slick shoes. They don't fit, but if I keep my coat buttoned on the one button that reaches, who'll know that? What you say we go to church tomorrow night?"

"I could get into trouble."

"No way," said Joe. "This is a free country. We can worship any way we want. Shoot, he invited you."

Sandra jacked her brakes. A man in an overcoat raced across the street a dozen yards in front of her car, his arms wrapped and rubbing around his body like he was freezing to death. He disappeared into a bakery, as if seeking the heat of the ovens. Sandra rolled up her window, and pushed the automatic door locks before turning on the air conditioner to compensate for the loss of air. "Odd. It's nearly shirtsleeve weather."

"So come on. You going?"

"I can think of a few better places you could take a date," she tried, but then relented, shaking her head yes.

13

Nancy bolted up in bed. Just behind her eyes, there was a fuzzy feeling, a cold, morbid vibration that took some time to control. Except for the phosphorous face-plate on the nightstand clock, the room was black. She used the clock to focus, and tried to remember a memory that was fading fast. Just a minute ago there had been a dreamy stellar whiteness, like she'd been looking at the dawn sun on the highway to someplace she'd always wanted to go, but that was all she remembered. Now this; normal, night, her room. She was back home. She felt numb, and eager both, as if she'd just gotten news of a terminal disease and was about to run the whole list of emotions. She nervously looked away from the all too familiar clock. If there had been just a little light, she might have glanced across the room and seen her face in the mirror. A hideous scowl of rage was frozen tight across her features, though she was not really angry at the moment. Nancy had died pissed.

Leaning over to pivot to her feet, she fell instead. As she fell, it seemed she was a bundle of bones, but the fall hadn't pained her, and once she realized that her left arm was missing, she quickly stopped trying to use it to get up with. Humans adapt. Nancy got to her knees, and then to her feet, finding one at a time. Her ankle bones ground as she tested her weight, some of the fluid between them a bit dry.

The dream had grown stiff, leaving behind one snapshot that would not escape her. The snapshot was more of a feeling than a vision, and it felt like the injection of a cold fluid through her veins. The fluid lingered past the dream, racing through her dry veins in the chill room. The room was as icy as her body, it seemed, but maybe that was part of the snapshot? Joints felt stiff, but they loosened some with the first step toward the door. Had she grown that much older in just one night, she wondered? One arm outstretched, she found the handle. At least that small capacity lingered.

In the hallway there was a little light from the creepy green runway lamps she'd had Fred put in a year ago after hearing about how many aging people died in their homes from broken hips in simple falls. Nancy looked down, seeing a green shoe on one foot, and pudgy, chipped, green toenails on the other. Her varicose veins were lost, blended into long oval pools of purple-green bruises where her blood had settled while she'd slept.

She turned the corner to her living room. None of the lamps were on, but the television illumination rose and fell at the whim of infomercials. A lady with a trustful, young, motherly face dangled a dazzling, synthetic diamond bracelet across an arm, saying the usual, "Now, you'd expect to pay over," sales pitch to her million captive phone order enthusiasts.

Nancy's husband, Fred, had become the latest shopping channel viewer, it seemed, having pulled his recliner to within a foot of the TV. The recliner was un-reclined, but Fred's upper back was leaning back on the seat anyway, his knees straddling the set as if imprisoning it. A half ham sat, still partially frozen, in his lap. In the kitchen, the freezer door was open, emitting ten watts of yellow light that diffused through a rectangle of thin, frig foggy air.

Between Fred and the freezer lay the contents of the refrigerator, each item chipped at, or bitten through once, but otherwise unconsumed.

Fred's wife looked upon this without much thought, other than an itch that something seemed missing. It wasn't anything in the living room, or even the hallway within which she still stood; rather, the feeling that something was missing had started way back in the bedroom. The thought had gotten stronger though. She touched parts of her body through a thick, sexless, corduroy nightgown. She let her hand feel her ragged stump, wondering why each part of her body felt alien, almost detached from the rest. The hand roamed across her swollen belly and hips. No, I seem to be mostly here, Nancy assured some of the less damaged parts of her consciousness. Yet, something that should be very close to her was definitely not with her. It was something she needed badly, and very much craved, realized Nancy; something unthinkable without.

Looking around the room, she couldn't see anything appealing; couldn't find the mysterious part of her that she longed for. Fred looked sort of like...maybe...but no, he didn't have any of whatever it was she needed either, she determined. In fact, from some internal primordial well of insight, she sensed that he might have been looking for it himself, and for some time now. If she waited quietly, it seemed likely that he'd give her a clue. So, she didn't bother to move. Instead, Nancy stood in the hallway opening. A line of spit crawled down her double chin, waiting for 'IT' to happen by. Her fat palm never stopped feeling at her belly. Two gray eyes waited, dull, wide and not once did those eyes blink.

After awhile, Fred will move, or someone else will happen along, and then she'd know.

****

Moria strolled up the worn suburban driveway, a brown briefcase in one hand, and a half dozen tiny pamphlets in the other. On the top pamphlet, 'Where will you spen...nity,' showed around a short, unpainted thumbnail. Under that there was a drawing of a screaming man who was engulfed by red flames. He seemed to answer the headline. She walked all the way around the rose bushes to the sidewalk, instead of cutting a shorter path through the yard, always wary not to offend anyone before informing them that she envisioned they'd be spending forever in a six hundred degree pit full of their fellow evil infidels. Sometimes it helped.

Of course, Fred already knew a thing or two about eternity, but had Moria known his perspective, she would have argued anyway. She was loaded for debate with a briefcase full of unquestioned answers. Moria raised her fist to the door, giving it seven short raps. Fred answered, his body a shadow on the dimmer side of the door. He pressed his face against the screen. Moria noticed, with a quick glance up, that he was a bit unshaven.

Witnessing to the lady of the house was the surest way in, Moria had come to realize. She began, "Excuse me Sir, but is the lady of the household in?"

Moria looked at the silver crosshatch of the screen where his whiskers stuck through. She missed the bulge in his eyes and the sniff of his nose, and even the rumble at his stomach. Fred's hand tightened on the door handle, squeezing instead of turning the knob. He grunted, "I want you." Even though he had no problem recognizing his own words, the sentence had actually rolled off his lips a lot like, "Nuh!"

Interpreting the nuh as no, Moria forged ahead, asking, "Do you have a personal walk with the Lord Jesus Christ?"

The word Jesus recalled some memory in Fred's mind, like an anthem that had been drilled into his consciousness from birth, like a long awaited event laden with a recent, sudden letdown—or relief. He had to answer, "No," which was close when it came out like, "Nuh," once again.

"Well if you don't mind, I'd like to tell you about Him. May I come in?" Moria asked, already turning the screen door handle that Fred seemed unable to budge simply by crushing the inside knob.

"Yes, please do!" He answered; another, "Nuh!"

Deeper in the house, Nancy watched all of this with the fascination of a cat who had spotted a bird digging for worms in the window box just opposite a pane of glass. 'IT' was at the door; life, the missing thing. The woman outside had hot flesh; she had her own imprisoned sensation of self. Warm, throbbing life, on the other hand, was completely missing within Nancy. Nancy craved a taste of what she was missing. Seeking confirmation that it wasn't so, that she wasn't really dead, her head bobbed down so that she could see her one arm. Raising the back of her arm towards her face, she saw the green tinged paleness of the flesh. As the hand slapped against her chin, she smelled its putrid emptiness, like a gangrened limb; foreign; as remote as a distant star. The hand dropped. Nancy raised her head, and saw the real deal walk into the door. It seemed a gift-wrapped turkey dinner; life. "I want some," she said, a gut whispered, "Nya om!"

As Fred's grip freed on the handle, he awkwardly stumbled backwards. Moria brushed by Fred, finding a seat on the only seat not a mess, the couch, knowing that finding an anchor was the first step towards garnering a lengthy conversation. It is one thing to say, "No thank you," but another to say, "Please get up out of my chair and get out of my house!" She knew. Smug with success, she put her tracts on the coffee table, where she could conveniently forget them if things got short, and opened her briefcase. Moria's arm dove into the briefcase, searching for her own version of the bread of life. In fact, she had a particular verse that popped into her mind for an opener; something like, "He that loveth his life shall lose it; and he that hateth his life in this world shall keep it unto life eternal." She wasn't sure if that was exactly how it went, but she aimed to look it up straight away. She reasoned, even the unbeliever is eager for a riddle.

A rotund shape expanded towards Moria from the green hallway opening. Moria looked up just in time to witness Nancy crashing across the glass coffee table. Glass shards roared to the floor. A painful cut slid down the front of Moria's shin. Looking down, Moria was surprised to see, not glass, but one of Nancy's fingernails had pealed away a foot long line of skin before falling to her foot. The gouge ran from knee to ankle, already beading red.

On the other hand, Nancy looked the worse for the fall, cuts and bruises all over her back, her face and upper body, all wedged into the empty space inside the coffee table frame. Realizing this, Moria reached down to catch the woman's arm, hoping to steady her and help her up.

Fred finally arrived at Moria's side. Just as slowly and meticulously as he'd done things in life, he lowered his teeth to Moria's back and took a great, big, delicious bite.

Moria screamed!

Thankful for the helping hand, Nancy's fingers sank into the arm that gripped hers, steadying the limb a little so that her watering mouth could get at a nicely flexed bulge of living meat. Fred's weight, and Nancy's tug, pulled the woman onto the glass littered floor, dropping her body between the table and couch. As the bites turned toward meals, Moria screamed beside the scattered pictures of a half dozen wailing men.

Fred settled in on a trembling leg. Taking his time, he used his fingers to strip strands of muscle off of a hamstring before cutting the fibers with small fastidious bites. Every so often the leg managed a weak kick, defeated each time by pain and weakness. Further towards the screams, Nancy bit savagely on a tense, struggling arm. It was her first time; Nancy wasn't quite as fastidious as Fred as she ate.

Wedged between the sofa and table, Moria lived too long. She willed death; in time, the screams became screeching pleas for an end. She felt slick, wet glass under her unbitten arm. Unable to pull the arm from beneath her, she slashed at the glass with her own wrist, managing no more than scratches. Finally, mindless, the sight of her own consumption faded into a thankful haze.

The haze shimmered, then blackened and muted. Time stopped—then returned with a sound like rain. A vision emerged, rushing forward in a field of whiteness. Neon colors streaked by. Her body was whole and flying! Everything was beautiful. Knowing this as death, Moria searched the passage and its lighted end. Friends and long lost relatives greeted her briefly in the flying ether.

As she neared the stellar light, shapes emerged. Three men stood, as if on an Olympic podium. Each man wore a white robe. In fact, everything about them seemed a shade of whiteness surrounded by a holy glow. Moria was sure that she knew who they were. These images must be the Father, Son and Holy Ghost. Nothing else could possibly fit the pre-disposition of her decomposing mind as it created one last fantasy.

Landing at the bottom of a dozen stairs, she took a step forward. As she neared, the flesh on the three gained color. Half way up the stair, the faces appeared harder, less than welcoming. She sensed something wrong. Had she failed them, she wondered? One more step, and the faces stiffened, as well as reddened. A pit grew in her stomach; something was definitely not right. Another step, and the faces froze, rose marble against the wistful, long, white hair, and equally pale clothing. Tinges of gray appeared on the cloth; dirt on the stairway. Where once the paleness seemed holy—now Moria sensed sickness and age. Two steps away, and she could almost touch the clothing now. Seeing the touch as both her goal, and dangerous, Moria reached out, convinced that this was the test of her faith. But, just as she reached, the figures turned, leaving her hand probing the air.

The sensation of invitation was totally gone now. Before, the light had seemed like a doorway, but as the figures stepped towards it, they merged with the void beyond. The void seemed to solidify, or, what is it, Moria wondered…yes, the word was full! A foul force pushed her backwards. The doorway forward was shut; the only path was backwards. There were no relatives this time; no happy faces. Her mind told her that this must mean hell! The lights were dulling, and they flickered, as if in danger of going out entirely. Flying back through the tunnel, the euphoria of the trip forward turned into an equal, but opposing shock of paradise lost. Memories of the terror she'd left were lost to her, but the realization of its despair grew as her mental awareness streaked towards the only home left it.

Moria's eyes opened with a salt encrusted pop. The room was numbing, claustrophobic, quiet—except for the television's background pitches. She was on her back in a sea of glass and litter. A broken table frame made her view difficult, but she could see a woman sitting with strange, watchful stillness on the other side of the room. For a moment, the presence of the other woman made Moria edgy, but after awhile both the edginess and the memories of paradise lost faded.

Brushing the table's skeleton aside with the bare bone of an upper arm, Moria got up after a few tries, made difficult by a half eaten hamstring. She stood, rocking with a noticeable wobble. Glancing around, Fred was back in his seat, watching the television lady selling trinkets, like he was waiting for her to come out and join him for dinner. He licked his lips dryly. It didn't take long for Moria to realize there was nothing here she wanted. In fact, there was an overwhelming feeling of impatience to get on with something she'd been doing. A missing thing to find; yes, something was lost perhaps, and had to be found.

Reaching down, her hand slipped through one of the handles on her open briefcase, which she lifted and carried to the door. The briefcase lid dragged on the floor. Pamphlets dribbled out, the thing soon empty. Moria stepped outside, looked around at the late night neighborhood, and walked through the grass and shrubs, straight towards the house next door.

14

Purswell's gate guard stood at the Southeast entrance to the huge hall, handing out four page handouts. Joe locked eyes with him as he passed, and shrugged, making the sign of the cross across his chest because he knew how much the Catholic sign annoyed protestant fundamentalists—particularly the zealous ones he figured the big guard to be.

He turned, and asked, "Hey, did you know a preacher named Jimmy Jones?"

The guy didn't get it, probably too young to remember the madman who had poisoned his whole congregation because the Feds were closing in and he'd grown an acute case of paranoia. Sandra got it though, and tugged at Joe's jacket sleeve so hard that he nearly tumbled down the short course of steps leading into the multi-million dollar cathedral. "Leave him alone. Gee Joe. We're supposed to be blending in."

"Yeah, you and I know that, but if they are serving punch after the service, don't offer me a cup."

"Seriously, what's the plan?"

Joe offered, "We sit next to as many young male types we can find. You know, twenty or so, fitting the profile of Reverend Purswell's grave diggers. Strike up some conversation, listen to the sermon for hints, and when the meeting is over, duck in between the vans for a look-see when the crowd clears."

"If that's the plan, I suggest you learn some acting, Joe. So far you've only managed to piss one of them off. Pretend like you're a convert. Do a little soul seeking, and mimic what everyone else is doing."

"Oh, don't worry about me, sweetheart. I've done this before. Raised in it," said Joe, finding a set of seats that were wedged in between several rows of young men in black suits and red ties. "Hallelujah! Praise the Lord," said Joe, even adding a shiver.

One of the men directly to Joe's right nodded.

Joe turned to him and said, "It's a good day to be one with the Lord."

"Yes, amen. Are you new here?"

"Yeah. Just moved into the community. Moved in to Lakeshore housing down the road, originally from the Cincinnati area and have always wanted to be a member. Do you know where they keep the membership forms? I should have asked the gentleman at the door. He was very helpful, but I went momentarily brain dead kidding around with him and I think he got the wrong idea about me. No sense of humor, and I'd forgotten I was new, I suppose. A very somber man, but praise god, we need men like him in these troubling times," said Joe.

"Yes indeed. Jonathon here. You'd be?"

"Joe, and this is Sandra Anderson. Joe and Sandra Anderson. Newlyweds. Nice to meet you. So, like those forms. We want to join right away. These are the end times, and he who hesitates is lost. Then again, speaking of lost, this complex is huge. I've only seen the tabernacle on television, and had no idea the property was so developed," started Joe.

Sandra hid her ringless wedding finger under an arm. She was a little surprised to see how quickly Joe assimilated. Apparently, his dry sarcasm did have an off valve when he felt it necessary. Then again, she thought, maybe a good con job was the ultimate sarcasm to Joe.

"We even have a high school. It's small, but it's dedicated to spreading the gospel, kind of like a seminary," The goon Joe was talking to gave Joe a virtual vocal tour of the facilities.

"Do they have everything a regular school has? I have a son. It might be just the place for him. He's good in math and science, but the public schools are ruining him," Joe Lied.

"You bet. None of that evil-ution or relative ethics nonsense exists here either. You can send your son here and know he's learning the truth. You know, we have our own banquet facilities, kitchen right behind this tabernacle, large hall behind that for dining, separate gym, that sort of thing. When you start thinking about it, a church this size doesn't need to do a lot of tinkering to make itself into a school during the weekdays....," said the man, rambling on. Sandra realized that the source was as good as any map.

Reverend Purswell preached after an array of singers who seemed more practiced than half of the vocalists on MTV. Purswell went on a roll, the sermon nearly a clone of the outburst Joe and Sandra had been privy to in the office. Near the end, out behind the baptismal tank, a hidden trumpeter blew a horn, scaring the teenagers into archangelic fits and filling the front alter with crying converts, some soon babbling in meaningless tongues that made the associate ministers happy as they announced a sting of saved drone to the mass hypnotic will.

Joe and Sandra pretended their involvement as long as seemed prudent, and then slowly slipped their way out a side door.

"Praise the Lord," said Joe as he shook the hand of a well dressed security man at the door. They got into Sandra's car, flipped on the lights, and pulled out of the main lot before killing the lights and backing their way between a pair of white church vans near the back of the main building.

"OK, time to be burglars," announced Joe.

"I can lose my job, doing this," said Sandra as she helped Joe retrieve his digital camera, crow bar and flashlight.

"Hey, we're not wearing ski masks. Just checking out the place can't be a crime. After all, we were invited here," said Joe.

"Yeah, right. You know, Joe, sometimes your sarcasm can be a little hard to take. I'm seriously reconsidering this relationship. I have a good job. I'd hate to lose it," said Sandra, showing him a different side of herself. They rounded the gym, making their way to the big dining hall and kitchen. "Besides, you're a lousy date. Look at what we've done, gone to a funeral, eaten bad eggs in a biker's bar, looked for bodies in a graveyard, and sat through a church service full of Arian Nation wannabes. I mean, I don't know about you, but I'm about ready for dinner, a movie and a foot massage."

"Oh, look who's being sarcastic now. After all the good times we've gone through together? Good show, girl," said Joe, easing up to a low back window.

Sandra pulled up her dress and tied it at the side like it was a shirt, revealing a practical pair of knee length shorts.

While she did that, Joe flipped his flashlight on, and looked through the window.

"What do you see?"

"It's a kitchen. A really, really big kitchen," said Joe. He trained his light across tables, a serving window, and big bottles of ketchup and mustard. His light stopped on a large set of freezer doors, each at least six feet tall and over half that wide. "And, the meat freezers. Enough for a dozen head of cattle."

"And, if I were keeping bodies, where would I keep them?" Asked Sandra, rhetorically.

"Exactly," said Joe, trying the back door. It was locked. "We could break a window."

"No. Let's wait before we commit ourselves to a crime. A stake-out is one thing; breaking and entry another," insisted Sandra. She led him back to the vans, where they waited, sitting side by side on a van bumper that was in moon shade. They had a completely open view to the kitchen and assembly hall area, as well as to the back of the church. Headlights streaked by occasionally as cars left the front lot; not enough to give them away, the pair a good hundred yards back from the main lot.

There was a little late night chill so Joe put his arm around Sandra, and they both realized that it was the first time they'd actually had the time to get cozy together. Time passed slowly as the lot emptied and they melted into one another. Then time dragged, no more passing headlight beams, only the crickets to keep them company as the first hours of morning passed.

Joe held Sandra while she slept. His arm was falling off, and he wanted to sleep too, but something about being close to her made it worthwhile. Then she awoke. "Um, this is nice," mumbled Sandra. She ran her hand through the seam of Joe's shirt, feeling his chest.

"I'm completely focused upon the job at hand, my sweet thing. Don't distract me or I'll lose my determination to keep an eye out," he teased, his own hand dropping lower on her back.

"Promise."

"Absolutely," said Joe, kissing her on the forehead, and then after thinking it too little, on the cheek.

Sandra looked up, and their mouths met. Lips parted. Tongues touched. Hands embraced bodies.

"Ouch," said Sandra. Joe had touched a broken rib on the hands way up to better things. It didn't seem to stop her though, as Joe moved his hand down and they both heated up all the more.

A door slammed, breaking the mood. Instinctively, the pair ducked off of the bumper, and huddled behind the tree that had been their shade. Three men walked down a concrete path connecting the back of the church with the other buildings. They headed straight for the kitchen building's door, the one Joe had tried and found locked. One guy had a burlap bag, and another looked along the lot with a long, heavy flashlight. The beam flashing by the pair just after Joe and Sandra pulled their faces behind the tree trunk. Next time they looked, the door was shutting, the trio in the kitchen proper. A weak neon light was flickering on.

"Bingo," said Joe, as a car crept up the back lot and stopped a few spots down from where Joe and Sandra crouched. Reverend Purswell got out, quickly making his tracks to the kitchen. Door unlocked, he walked right in.

"So far so good, Joe. Services done, everyone gone; Purswell's probably thinking, why not take the opportunity, while all the conspirators are here anyway, to put in a little night work," said Sandra.

They crept up to the building, and peeked inside. Over at the freezers, one door was open, a dim bulb lighting the men inside as they moved around like silhouettes. They took something down from what looked like a meat hook, and walked the hulk between them as they came out. Joe caught the outline of several other shapes behind them in the freezer, the shapes still on hooks, them gently swaying as if sent into motion by a bump, or perhaps, as if still alive. The hulk they'd taken from the freezer turned out to have legs as the plastic covering her body was removed. She was in what looked a lot like a straightjacket.

"Christ, it's just a kid," said Sandra. Alice looked up with frozen, seemingly glass eyes.

15

A cooler of iced 'Cokes' was belted into the passenger seat of Bancheski's cruiser. Four empty cans were ready to roll on the passenger floor. The glove box was open, its tray supporting a 'Mister Pib'. Between the shave headed deputy and his caffeine, an electronic tree divided the car with its radios, siren, light bar switches, data terminal, Vascar, and radio heads. On the hump, a loaded twelve gauge was clamped into its bracket and locked down. Sometimes he did this speed trap with Jimmy, but they were short handed, and besides, he kind of liked it best when he did it alone and the cruiser wasn't so cramped.

So far, the eight hundred Meg Sheriff's radio had kept ominously quiet, considering all the trouble they'd had the last few days. He'd been ordered home for eight hours of sleep, no matter what, hearing the radio reaching what sounded like some sort of climax on the drive home. Eight hours later, he'd gone straight to his job assignment. Not a peep came through the police net, he noticed, thinking, maybe people have just decided to give it a rest? More than likely, it was just a late night lull, though the net had quieted as if someone had turned off a faucet. Whatever it was, Bancheski was thankful for the first hour or two of reprieve.

The State radio, however, was busy, although its audio was unreadable, the mark of distant and, to him, irrelevant conversations. That was normal for state radio. It linked jurisdictions all over the state, but was only readable when the traffic got close. Still, to Bancheski, the static seemed far greater than normal, as if the trouble had moved just out of earshot. Maybe there were sunspots afoot, he imagined.

Bancheski kept his vigil, looking for cars coming over rises in front and behind him. This part of the north highway was a good fishing spot. The road sagged like the saddle between a camel's humps here, hiding the cruiser until too late. He wasn't the only one to realize the prime speed trap nature of the spot though; cars zipped by, most under Bancheski's twelve mile over the limit level of acceptability.

He'd only written two tickets so far, one to a ripe princess named Patricia. She'd done nearly everything in the book to get him to stop printing the thing out, leaning over to show cleavage; had her dress up nearly to her panties by the time he'd gotten to the car too. He had no doubt that it worked for her most of the time, but Bancheski knew she'd not have given him the time of the day otherwise, and thus even had some added thrill from writing her up. Let the girl's boyfriend have that fire and ice, he determined.

The second ticket had been a warning, him recognizing (Marsha) Dominique Sawyer by the DOM EUU license plate on her jet black Mitsubishi. He was sorry he'd stopped her the moment he'd read the plate, and opted for the warning because he knew she'd make the ticket into a five hour court case, complete with jury, and maybe even win on the sympathy-against-Gestapo-tactics vote. No raised skirt or unusually displayed cleavage from Dominique, that was for sure, though he'd have taken it as a compliment if she had. More like a raised eyebrow, as if she were scolding him as he wrote the yellow card. He'd found his, "Please drive more carefully and slow down," speech sounding a bit boyish for no explainable reason at all.

By the end of a shift, his cruiser ran up five hundred miles of idle time, none of it showing on the odometer. The car smelled of body odor, his shirt stuck to the back of the seat, and his butt ached from sitting. Most old timers Bancheski knew have had their hemorrhoids hacked on by a proctologist at least once in a career. Sitting on the side of a dark highway was not for the faint hearted, Bancheski had learned early on. Time went by very slowly. It was lonely, boring, and, well, spooky. Between the whine of passing cars, the roadside seemed a graveyard. Crickets kept him company occasionally; when they stopped chirping, he'd hold his breath, and count the seconds as he twisted his neck. When the moon wasn't full, or when the clouds were thick, the woods and marshes were solid walls capable of hiding anything the imagination might cook up.

Tonight wasn't so bad. He had some moonlight left, and could see the pond ten meters into the tree line on his side of the road. One night, at a time in the night when the moon had been fully up, he'd crept into the woods and strung a fishing line from a tree limb over the water. Then he'd sat in his car, and watched for people and catfish, all at the same time. He remembered pulling over a drunk, taking him in, and coming back to find his bobber dancing around the pond with an exhausted bluegill hooked to the gut. He'd felt sorry for the doomed baby fish, but the idea of stringing another line still tickled a bone, as well as promised relief from the monotony of the bone dull duty. When the light was just right, he spent as much of the night imagining the best place to put another line in as he did watching the hilltops for approaching cars.

A snapping sound broke the silence of the woods on the other side of the road. The crickets quit. It's just a raccoon; raccoons are all over the place out here, he told himself. As his ears straining for another sound, the radar beeped, signaling that a speeding car was approaching just over the hill ahead. Sixty-nine point four illuminated on the radar head, nearly twenty-five miles per hour over the limit, and that from a car on an upgrade.

The car lights broke into view at the ridge.

Something big shook the brush to the left, not more than forty meters in, guessed Bancheski. His attention was torn between the two intrusions. Half way down the hill now, the car's driver would have to be blind to miss seeing the speed trap. None-the-less, the speed climbed to seventy-four point nine.

Branches snapped, as if broken by two distinct footfalls from a heavy beast.

Every impulse told him to leave. There was the speeder after all, whoever it was didn't even have the respect, or faculty, to slow down! Yet Bancheski sat, determined to face down the noise that emanated from the woods. First he'd see what that noise was. As soon as the red glow of raccoon eyes beam, I'll catch the speeder, he told himself. If not, where will the fear stop? Shadows? Unreasonable fear like he felt didn't seem to fit the job description.

He waited, his eyes affixed on the other side of the road.

A blur of a speeding car ripped by his line of sight.

The dark gray outline of a tree shifted quickly to the side, against the light gray background of the sky. "That was no raccoon," the deputy swore. As the whine of the receding car's engine and wheels decayed up the rise behind him, Bancheski imagined he could hear a strained human voice. He fumbled for his flashlight, and aimed it into the trees and brush. The light gave a defused glow to the bushes beside the road, but was stopped by thick foliage only a few feet in.

Bancheski put the car into gear, and eased forward fifty feet. If it's a cop killer, maybe a little bit of movement is just what will cause the bastard to slip up, he imagined. In the back of his mind, he remembered that weird briefing about maniacs on the loose, which was no help to his nerves at all. The fact that he'd personally straight jacketed a half dozen citizens the last two days made it all too personal. It seemed like they'd captured a hell of a lot more maniacs than the powers-that-be told them had escaped. In fact, several had been people he knew; all of them bloody too. Shivers! Well, come noon, thing had settled, giving a break before rush hour. He was happy to have had that break too, in spite of the fact that half the department was out sick and he'd been told to pull this extra shift. No wonder I'm batty, Bancheski surmised, rubbing the sleep out of an eye.

Stopping the car, Bancheski looked over his shoulder, and could see the tree tops jerking one by one in his direction. The underbrush noise had grown deliberate, slashing.

"That's no raccoon for sure," he told himself. "Maybe an elephant."

He drove forward, then U turned to the other berm, bringing his headlights to bear on the forest. Bancheski still couldn't see through the first layer of bushes, but his lights clearly showed the moving trunks beyond.

A beep from the radar nearly cost him the contents of his bladder. He'd completely forgotten about that last car, probably out of the county by now. Two new headlights popped over the hill. The radar screen lit up a week's record, ninety-one point eight miles per hour.

The car shot over the hill, and landed in a sheet of undercarriage sparks. It bounced out of control across the oncoming lane, threw smoke off of the dirt berm, veered back onto the road, and ended up in the middle of the street, accelerating with the median strip lined up on the hood ornament. Still facing the oncoming speeder, Bancheski threw his red and blue strobes on, and waited.

Suddenly the driver hit his brakes, laying thick, smoking rubber across two hundred feet of highway. The car came to rest at an angle, still straddling the lanes, and still a hundred meters in front of the Deputy, its motor stilled by the sudden stop. Bancheski made the car as a four door Ford wagon, a family car, definitely not what he had expected. Glancing into the brush one last time, the deputy eased his cruiser forward.

Up ahead, he could hear the driver of the car trying to restart the engine. Every time the starter engaged, the lights on the wagon dimmed. It was eerie, his lights flashing bursts of blue and red light around the forest walls, the yellow line leading to the mystery straddling the lanes, and the cool wind in his window slapping him, reminding him of his own mortality.

The engine finally caught, and the wagon lurched forward. Bancheski could hear the engine roaring, but the car was barely moving. His radar showed, twenty miles an hour, then went blank as the car moved beyond the arc of the radar cone. As it started to pass, he could smell the smell of carbon brake pads still engaged; smoke crawled out of the wheel wells. Bancheski caught the outline of a driver and passenger, but the odd reflections on the angled windshield made that uncertain.

The deputy hit the manual button on his siren, delivering a second of warning as the car passed, still in the middle of the highway. "Pull it ov…" What he saw froze his last word. A face passed by, framed in the car window, and less than five feet from his own window. It was looking right at him, and it was white; the eyes were deep in purple sockets, pale gray, almost without pupils. As the car passed, the face kept right on looking at him. It even leaned out of the car as the window moved by, as fixated on the lawman as Bancheski was on it. The car moved in an arc, as if the driver's skills were too diminished to look away and work the wheel at the same time.

Then the man in the window lifted his foot from the brake, his head still out of the window, and the car shot off of the road like a jet being ejected from the launch ramp on an aircraft carrier. The car slammed into the ground, bouncing once before crashing into a fence of trees twenty feet off the road, and fifty yards behind the cruiser. Opening his door and looking back at the wreck, Bancheski saw the head still leaning out of the car, only now it was jammed into the wedge of the window.

He jumped back into the car, put it into reverse, and backed abreast of the wreck. One hand pulled the mike to his face. "This is car seven at the fifteen mile marker on highway fifty-three. I have a ten five, and at least one victim," he started.

Time passed without an answer from the dispatcher. A patrol Sergeant finally answered. "We'll get a squad to you. Do you need backup?"

They were seriously short handed, he knew. "I'll probably handle it alright if I can get those medics quick," he answered, instantly regretting not asking for a backup. Popping the hood button, he threw four flares on the road, then ran into the weeds towards the crashed station wagon.

Bancheski guessed the car had hit the trees at thirty or more miles an hour, and that meant the driver's neck had jammed into the window frame hard enough to nearly decapitate the victim. Playing his flashlight across the frame, he could see torn red muscles and deathly grey skin. The head fell loose from the window's corner, and lulled over the door like a saddlebag across a horse's back. He was surprised to see a shoulder still moving, and figured it was gravity doing the work, until the shoulder moved again, this time more up than down. His flashlight beam froze on the neck. I should say something, thought Bancheski; I should tell him to stay still. The words wouldn't come. That's when an arm reached out of the window, and lifted its own head by the hair. Responding to the movement, bones shot through the skin with pops of gristle. The hand turned the head so that it eventually looked at the officer. The lips tried to speak, but all of the air came out of the neck, making the sound of bubbles.

"God almighty! What am I supposed to do with this?" Bancheski pulled his gun. He checked himself, easing the gun back into the holster. The driver's dead, he thought. The man just doesn't know it yet because of the shock. What can I do? I can't move a man like that, the Deputy reasoned. Bancheski backed off. He walked around to the other side of the car, keeping some distance.

This far off the road, there were marshy spots that stuck at his shoes and gave off sucking sounds while he moved around behind the car. As if in harmony, the crickets in the tree line chirped tunes to the sucking rhythm.

Someone banged on the side of the car, shaking it from side to side, and everything else went deathly quiet again. A second bang thrust the passenger door open. Just behind the door, a body in a corduroy housecoat followed, falling into the weeds. The officer rushed to the lady's side. Leaning over her neck, he checked for a pulse. Nothing. He checked an arm, and discovered it missing; a fresh ragged hole at her shoulder was all that was left. He'd had to feel his way around the body to discover the hole before he registered it, coming away with a pestilent hand.

The officer jerked up, glanced to find the back seats empty, and backed away from the car. The dead lady in the grass started crawling around, darkly and lethargically, like a lazy gator in the weeds. Bancheski ran for his car. He flipped the door locks and windows shut with the automatic buttons.

From the safety of his cruiser, Officer Bancheski could see the two victims squirming around. He laughed a lunatic's laugh; victims? "Dead people. Die, you son of a bitches," he prayed. Watching them felt anything but real. Ironically though, they just seemed to be getting stronger—with not a scream from either of them as their battered bodies progressed. The man had gotten out of the car, and was standing beside it. His head dropped back across his bent back so that only the jagged edges of his neck were visible on top. The guy was buck naked. He turned, and Officer Bancheski's heart skipped when he saw the hole in the man's bare chest. The man wasn't just dead, Bancheski concluded; he was a broken shell. Then the lady stood, one knee at a time. She looked at the cruiser and smiled with chipped, bloody teeth.

Over the hill, the faint sound of a squad's siren carried in the crisp air.

A long ways off.

The man turned around, as if his thoughts were in tune with the woman's. His back toward Bancheski, he looked at the cruiser with an upside down head. It frowned with an upside down smile.

"Stay where you're at!" Screamed Bancheski. Then he rolled down his window, punched out a burst from his siren, and screamed it again. Nancy stumbled and then regained her knees, coming to the noise on all threes like a called, three-legged dog. Fred tried to walk toward the officer, but every time he tried to go a step forward the step took him in the wrong direction. Finally he did a little dance, and that seemed to orient him a bit. One cautious step at a time, he retraced his path.

Once more, Bancheski thought about his gun. Every instinct told him to shoot the monstrosities, but he couldn't come up with a crime for an excuse. He shifted the cruiser into reverse, and backed down the highway fifty yards, then stopped. The creatures stepped into the road, and slowly crept forward. (The emergency squad's siren was getting louder). At fifty yards, Bancheski backed again. Finally, his red and blue strobes were joined by a pair of red beacons just rounding the top of the hill. The big, square squad stopped just on the other side of Nancy and Fred, headlight to headlight with Bancheski's cruiser, framing the victims in the duel glow. Medic Bentley and Johnson leapt out, rushing obliviously towards Nancy and Fred.

Up until that moment, Bancheski had thought of the paramedics as if they were the Calvary coming to the rescue. Now he realized how preposterous that thought was. As the cop, he was supposed to be the Calvary, only he'd still not figured out what to do. In the street, the two creatures turned, not nearly as indecisive as he. They were only too eager to trade away an elusive deputy for a couple of fresh and willing medics.

"Get back!" Bancheski yelled as he worked his way out of his car.

Fred's arms clawed around his back, as his upside down face and back tackled the first paramedic. His teeth snapped on Johnson's arm. Bentley turned, and tried to pry the head off of his partner's arm, struggling with the revulsion of handling a head held onto a body by little more than a few tendons. Fred's teeth sank deeper, cutting, sawing back and forth, eating to the bone. As his teeth broke, the razor edges on his stubs continued to rent. Bentley wedged Fred's head in one forearm, and pushed Johnson's arm away with one great heave. Strands of muscles, arteries and veins snapped off, leaving the monster with a mouth full of paramedic. The whiplash finally ripped Fred's head free of its body. Everyone watched, horrified for a minute, as Fred's body wandered across the road and stumbled into the weeds before falling, arms still flailing and legs kicking for a few last seconds. The head moaned in the fireman's arms. Bentley shrieked and tossed the head down the roadway where it slid, and stopped on its side, still chewing. Fred's head swallowed, depositing a huge wedge of Johnson's arm out of the naked throat, and onto the road's yellow line. Licking at the lips, eyes ever frantic, Fred's head twitched its muscles and jaw, bouncing inches.

Nancy, still on her knees, grabbed Bentley's belt, ripped his pants loose with one good arm, and raked a jagged, chipped tooth across ten pounds of medic love handle.

As if renewed, Fred's body righted itself, turned out of the weeds and aimed itself at the carnage.

Bentley was barely able to move, while Johnson beat at Nancy with both arms and legs. Each blow drove Nancy further back and to the ground in front of the squad's headlights.

Bancheski fired a warning shot into the sky.

For a second, Johnson paused, startled by the shot. Nancy, on the other hand, sprang at the man just as Fred's body crashed into the pile. The four squirmed and fought a freakish dance. Shadows reached out and raced from the silhouettes, touching Bancheski, causing him to step back until his legs hit the front of his own bumper. It was black on black, like a modern dance. With the blackness, the strobes were pulsating red-like splashes of blood. Nothing about the group in front of him seemed real. Victims fighting rescuers, what is that? Nothing real, he thought. Nothing; just like at the range; paper targets. No, not the usual targets, he corrected, but one monstrous, cardboard shape.

Bancheski fired five shots into the mess. Smoke hung between the pairs of headlights, a little patch to match the fog that always seemed to hold at the tree-lines to their sides. Everything was still for a full count of ten—and then the collapsed cardboard shape started to rise.

"Oh, heck!" Bancheski yelled, bracing himself against the side of his car as he worked himself around the door and behind the steering wheel. "I'll show them! I'll take care of this right here and now. Permanently! Forever, you ugly suckers!" With instinct driven rationality, he snapped his seat belt on, pulling the strap tight. He even reached down, and took a quick sip of his Mr. Pib. Tossing the still full can out the door, it fell with a wet thud, rolling away heavily to the safety of the berm. Bancheski pushed the gas pedal so hard that he could feel it compress the floorboard. The tires squealed and smoked, then purchased and drove the deputy back against his seat. A body under the wheels launched his cruiser up over the squad's bumper before smashing it a foot into the squad's grill. Bancheski's airbag ignited, punching him back against his seat with a stunning blow. He had to fight the air down before he could see the torsos pinched, severed and wedged in the steaming kiss of metal. That's when he realized he wasn't as crazy as he'd thought he was, and had to lean out his door for a puke. Everything was clearing up; he'd just murdered four people, two of them innocent paramedics. What had happened really, he wondered; things still seemed a bit in a haze. There seemed on rational to it. He had to step outside and clear the air. No, it wasn't exactly murder he'd done, but what? And, what was he going to do about it? Call the cops?

His motor was still running, in spite of the tangled front end. The red idiot light on his radio was out. He turned it up, and couldn't hear the usual hiss. Punching his car into reverse, he gunned the motor. The car rocked, but the front bumper was locked over the front of the squad's and the wheels on his front wheel drive spun uselessly five inches off the ground. Some of the body parts on the hood shifted, but that was all that budged.

Bancheski jumped out of the car, and grabbed a jack out of the trunk. He crept around, keeping his gun handy, and slid the jack in under the front of his car with one hand. Christ, it isn't even loaded, he reminded himself, easing his spare cylinder into the chamber. He looked around. Nothing was moving too much, and that head was on the other side of the car. The decapitated body, at least, had stilled. The coast was clear. Putting his gun on the fender, at easy reach, he slipped the handle into the jack, and started to pump. Ten strokes later, the squad unstuck itself, as the front of the cruiser lifted. The gun fell. It hit on its handle, and true to Murphy's laws, clattered under the oil pan.

The motor was running. Steam was everywhere. Hot oil from the squad was pooling and running in his direction, mixing with the growing streams of blood he'd deliberately avoided looking at. Some of those body parts were getting the jitters worse than ever too, but he imagined that, that might only be his imagination. Bancheski wondered why cops had this thing about never losing their guns, like men in the military had about saluting the flag, and airline pilots had about checking the weather. This will only take a second, and then out of here, he thought! He fell to the ground, dove under the car, and groped into the black shadows until his fingers closed on the weapon.

"There it is," he told himself, breathing a sigh of relief.

All of a sudden all those body parts started moving. He could see the legs kicking at the underside of the car, sliding on the blood and oil like drunks dancing. Up above, the arms and heads beat on the metal drum of his hood. The car lunged back a couple of inches, and the jack took on a real ugly little angle. Bancheski scooted in reverse, but getting out was harder than diving in, and the body parts had become insistent, as if they knew his terror. The car lurched back a foot. He could hear the jack squeal in protest as it tore and twisted in its base. The whole works crashed down before he could get half way out. A wheel squashed his shoulder under its weight, missing his head by inches, which was saved by the wheel well. Bancheski went black with pain.

For ten merciful, but short seconds, he was out. He came to, fighting for breaths. Both his upper arm, and shoulder socket were about an inch of mush under the tire, which bled his blood out of its treads. The impact from the car's edge had bounced into a row of ribs, neatly busting a few, and making every breath an act of sadism. He tried to scream—couldn't scream—and even that, as unsuccessful as it had been, hurt worse than anything he'd ever imagined up to this point in his life. The engine was still running, its oil pan a blast furnace two inches from his forehead. The exhaust pipe exhaled a continuous cloud of smoke. The wind blew exhaust across his view.

And, out of the fog they came, first one, then two…

"Hey! Over here," he tried to yell, barely a whisper and between coughs of blood. Chest pain put him under for a second. The world came swimming back.

…then three, and as the first two neared, he thought he saw more at the edge of the tree line. The closest man limped a little, but it could be the steam and sweat in his eyes, Bancheski thought. Another had a nasty wound on her neck, he thought he'd noticed, as she got close enough for him to lose the top of her beyond the bottom edge of the fender. Well, they'd been in a wreck, he rationalized; if they can walk, hurt or not, they'll help. The pair knelt, one on a side of each hip. Each took a leg. They lifted the legs gently into their laps.

A new reason to be terrified filled Bancheski's mind as it wavered in degrees of consciousness. He wondered if they were going to try to pull him out without raising the car? Up front, the mashed body parts had mostly died, but one leg moved slightly, causing the tire to dig into his shoulder and pinch ceaselessly. Someone bit one of his legs like it was a drumstick and then as luck would have it, he was wide awake.

Bancheski reached for the gun he'd dropped, it just barely out of reach. One bullet, just one bullet, he prayed, his hand still those same two inches out of reach.

Short, breathless screams echoed across the peaceful bog as teeth found nothing but non-lethal bites of pure thigh meat.

16

Alice stood, enraged, in her bare feet. She'd been left in only panties and bra. Her skin, whitened by death, except for the occasional and faint, new liver spots, glistened sickly with thawing frost. Her lips were blue, her eyes deep, blue and black, raw with rage as she looked around at the food that was just out of reach due to her bonds. She told them over and over again to untie her and to let her taste them. She even promised sex. She'd been a decent girl just one day ago, but she was desperate to have just one bite. All other considerations paled. Still, the idiots just kept on ignoring her hunger, she realized.

All Purswell heard were weak, nearly airless grunts. "Alright, let's bag her. We run her by our friends at UPS and have her air cargoed out of here by two. Nice little present for our friends in Hebron. Plenty of evil in need of resurrection in those parts. Wouldn't want to forget to lay one of our Lord's presents on them," said Reverend Purswell to his men as they pulled a wooden packing crate out from behind a wall.

"Won't she suffocate in cargo?" Asked Jonathon, the young man Joe had been speaking to in the church.

"If God's seen to her raising from the dead, son, I don't think He'll take her back from the want of a little oxygen. We've had her frozen all day, and she seems fine from that; not much air in there either. Our tests show this to be a true miracle. The last six made it to their destinations easy enough, I've been informed. Started right in at their work too. Our duty appears to be to make sure the miracle makes it to the four corners of the earth, forthwith, including all the little nooks and crannies like the Middle East. A little of this, properly cultivated, goes a long way. Think of the resurrection that follows this work. First the evil, and then we saved shall rise, relieved of even our own deaths. When the dead shall rise and those with Christ resurrected, we shall return to rule the earth. The moment is here, and I for one cannot let it linger. Are we ready to meet our Master? Are we all eager to do his work?" declared Purswell to his disciple.

"Sure. Amen. Should we gag her, Reverend?" Asked the third man. It was the thug Joe had insulted twice that day already. This time the thug was in only white shirt and a loosened tie. He seemed still, all business and unlike Jonathon, experienced at handling the ambulatory cadaver.

"Sure. There are some hand towels behind the counter."

The thug went to get a towel while the younger Jonathon went back into the freezer and started the awkward chore of plucking another body off of its meat hook. Once off the hook, Jonathon staggered under the awkward and slippery weight.

Suddenly, the corpse shook himself free from Jonathon's grip. The man had untied his ankles by kicking them all day long, though his hands were still tied behind his back The dead man's eyes had been blinded white with frost, which made it hard to see when he made a dash through the freezer door. Plastic wrapping loosened, the stuff falling around the corpse's knees. Blinded and partially bound, his steps were short and choppy as he ran in a beeline towards the door Joe and Sandra were looking through. They ducked just in time as all eyes followed the fleeing corpse.

Reverend Purswell turned just in time to sidestep the naked corpse, who promptly stepped onto Alice's hip. Alice grunted, while the naked man stumbled to the ground, hitting the linoleum full force with his face.

Purswell stood back while Jonathon leapt onto the escapee. They tumbled on the floor, the corpse amazingly strong for a man with nearly no leverage due to the lack of free hands. It was like grabbing a greased pig. Jonathon found himself slipping, soon underneath the zombie, temporarily trapped within the dead man's legs in a scissor hold about his waist. The corpse's nostrils were unfreezing, water dripping off the end of a recently broken and crooked nose and landing in Jonathon's yelling mouth.

Purswell's thug arrived. He fought to find a handhold on the man's back, it dripping with thawed frost. He only managed to push the corpse into his younger buddy. Hungry teeth found an arm, digging into Jonathon's flesh, and then dislodging as the corpse was pushed even further to the ground by the bigger man on the dead man's back. The dead man's head shook from side to side, the motion allowing his teeth to rip into Jonathon's arm until an inch of flesh had been bitten out. Now food, a piece of Jonathon was chewed twice, then swallowed down the crazed zombie's throat.

"We can't just sit and watch this," said Sandra, her instincts taking over as she and Joe watched from outside. They'd only been able to make out half of the words, but the illegal activity was obvious.

"Like hell we can't. That thug in there is packing. Bring your gun? Didn't think so. We can't help those wounded folk in there; they look too far gone. Once he's taken us out, Purswell will fix it so he can lie his way out of everything. Besides, we're not supposed to be here. Everything we've seen might get tossed out of court. On the bright side, we've already gotten all the intel we came for and it looks like the people they've kidnapped have the upper hand for the moment. Let's bring on the Calvary," said Joe, holding her back with an outstretched arm. Of course, he'd been thinking the exact same thing as her, and was only voicing his devil's advocacy.

Just then the thug managed to kick the naked corpse aside. Thinking fast, he tossed a metal table over the squirming body, restricting the corpse's movements. The thug grabbed a rope, bent down and tied the legs as deftly as a cowboy doing a bull. Legs done, he lashed the rest of the rope through the tied wrists, hogtying the zombie. He finished the girl the same way, stepping back to help his buddy find a chair. Just like that, two hogtied zombies were subdued.

"Damned thing ate me," squeaked Jonathon.

"Looks like he only ate part of you," said his bemused accomplice as he opened a first aid kit and applied ointment to his friend's arm.

"Shit, that hurts!" Screamed Jonathon as the thug started wrapping the wound.

"Hold that tongue. This is the house of God," said Purswell.

"I got to go to the hospital. He bit off a chunk of my arm. I'm going to need surgery."

"Yeah, maybe, but not right now. Nobody said this was going to be easy, son. We need you to help us bag this up first. You can't stop the battle to tend to the wounded until the field is secured. We can deal with your arm later," said a determined Purswell.

"Oh God!" Screamed Jonathon, rolling over to the side in his chair as he fought the streaks of pain.

"OK. You and me then. Let's get this done. The sooner this one is off, the sooner we can attend to Jon over there," relented Purswell. They opened two crates that had their wooden lids painted green. They dumped the zombies into them. The thug pulled out a dozen cans of instant foam, and foamed them in tight, then dropped the wooden lids, nailing them shut. There was a side door that they unbolted and opened. Joe and Sandra noticed a van had been backed up to it.

"Got that license number?" Asked Sandra.

"Yeah, BLSED 7."

"Good. Let's get something moving on it. Those people can't last long in those boxes. God forbid he put them in cargo like that; they'd die. The man's deluded."

"My sentiments exactly," agreed Joe.

Sandra dialed her office with her cell phone, the call ringing twenty times before someone answered. By then the thug and Purswell had gotten into the van and driven off, leaving Jonathon to himself. Jonathon got off the chair and found a table to lie on, his face in intense pain as he pulled his knees up and fought it.

Sandra explained what they'd seen.

"What the hell are you doing over there?" Screamed Chief Baker.

"Just going to church. We were out strolling, you know, being romantic. No law against it. I've not interfered. I just happened to witness a crime. We have a license number, BLSED 7, and a probably destination, Port Columbus. Two body sized crates, marked with green lids. You see for yourself, Chief," said Sandra.

"Yeah right. When you get back, I'm sending you to a professional. Bound to happen, after the trauma of being shot at," said the Chief, hanging up.

"What did he say?" Asked Joe.

"Said he thought I was nuts."

"Well, I mean, besides that? Is he sending the troops?" Asked Joe.

"I guess he's going to check it out. Maybe not; I don't know?" Said Sandra.

"You know, I really do hate that man…and his boy," said Joe.

Just then, Jonathon fell off of the table.

"Look, we can use the same story on him that we used on the Chief. We're just passing by, and…." said Sandra, breaking a pane of glass and unlatching the door. They walked in, and Jonathon shrank back, startled.

"What? Oh, it's you," he said.

"Yeah, we were looking over the grounds, seeing what you was telling us about, and noticed the light. Kitchen huh? Nice. Seems you've hurt yourself. Oh my, that looks nasty. Need some help, buddy?" Asked Joe.

Jonathon nervously glanced over at the still gapping freezer door. Sandra noticed his apprehension, and stepped to the freezer. "Looks like the cooks left the freezer open. That's got to cost a pretty penny, electric alone; never mind what gets spoiled," she said, slamming it shut.

"Let's get a look at you, John," said Joe, completing the ruse.

Jonathon's apprehension eased the moment he thought that Joe and Sandra were clueless. "I just can't get comfortable. Had an accident and lost a chunk of flesh. My friends were going to come back and give me a hand, but they've gotten delayed. Can you take me to the hospital? I don't feel like waiting. I get these stabs of pain that send me nuts."

"Be our pleasure. Only Christian thing to do, I'd say," said Joe, feeling the man's forehead. "You're burning up, son. That wound must be infected."

Sandra helped Joe put the man into the back seat of their car. He rolled over, and started babbling incoherently.

"Let's go back and check the freezer," said Sandra after shutting the back door.

Joe whispered, "He needs to get to the hospital. I think he's going into a seizure. He's already half out of his mind. Oddest thing, but some people react to wounds a lot more severely than others."

"This won't take a second. There might be more hostages in there. We can't leave them like this. What if Purswell has enough pull to keep away an investigation? What if the police blow us off like they did before? Some of those people in there are alive. That's murder one. They'll freeze to death, and besides, Jonathon is with the bad guys. He's the last guy I'm worried about."

"Jon's just a kid; he only believes what they've force fed him. But, you're right, of course. Look, let's hurry though," said Joe, following Sandra. Sandra went straight to the freezer. She yanked it open, and stepped inside, searching for a light switch.

"Damn, it's freezing in here. How did those last two survive? It's full of meat too. Look at all that," said Joe just before she found the switch and lit the room.

Plastic sacks full of hanging meat draped both sides of a small aisle. Hooks pierced the packaging in back. The sacks were clear, but they'd accumulated a layer of frost that made it hard to see the meat inside.

"There must be two dozen sides of beef in here," said Sandra, running her hand across one of the hanging packages. The package she'd touched moved. That sent off a cascade of movements, like dominos, one package after the other, until the whole room was a solid wiggling mass of two dozen forms, each so close to one another that the lack of wiggle room alone kept the motions from becoming dangerous to the couple standing in the middle.

Joe ran his hands across the top of one of the plastic bags, rubbing away the film of frost. An elderly lady's face looked back at him, eyes wide and deep and surrounded by flesh that was almost the color of glowing moonlight. Joe instinctively jerked back, his back hitting another slab of plastic wrapped humanity.

"My god, there are people in there! All of them are people!" Screamed Sandra, meeting Joe nearer at the door as her instincts had them both retreating.

"Shit. Let's get them down," said Joe, grabbing one of the packages, and lifting. "Get the hook," he told Sandra.

She grabbed a chair from the main room, and took a grip on the nearest hook. It gave with a sickly slurp as Joe lifted the body high. The body was so frozen that the it didn't slump. Frost made it impossible to hold, as he dropped the body across several other packages of hanging humanity, and then onto the floor. They dragged the package out of the freezer, retrieved some knives from a drawer and ripped at the plastic and bonds.

It was Mrs. Keeder, naked as the day she was born. Her neck was slanted over with that one white bone protruding. In spite of the obviously mortal slant to her head, she opened her eyes and moved. Her mouth opened, and bit toward Joe's hand as he pulled away in just the nick of time.

"Hey. She tried to bite me."

"She can't bite you, Joe. She's dead," said Sandra, who'd last seen Mrs. Keeder when she'd been the first on the scene at her murder. The woman had bled out completely onto her bedroom floor, Sandra recalled with a queasy stomach. Hearing Sandra's voice, Mrs. Keeder rolled to her other side, and made a move to bite Sandra's ankle. Still half frozen, Mrs. Keeder's biting was slow. Joe shoved Sandra back, them soon standing well off of the body that moved of molasses, but with clear threat as it unthawed.

"Well, now that you mention it, dear. She is dead, isn't she? It's not like you can have your neck canted over at a forty-five degree angle, and be alive, is it? I mean to be asking, because I'm plum out of logical brain waves at the moment. Ever hear of something like that?"

Sandra just shook her head, no.

Jonathon appeared at the doorway. He staggered in, eyes wide with freight at having been discovered. "She's dead alright. Get back. If she bites you. It's…God, please get me to a hospital," he finished as he keeled over and hit the floor.

"We have to get the rest of them out of the freezer first. Some might still be alive. Damn, they might all be alive!" Said Sandra, not quite ready to accept that the woman they were looking at was a moving dead person.

"No, that's not going to work. There are too many of them. Who's going to believe us?" Said Joe. He walked over to the second freezer, and opened its door. More bodies lined the walls of the second freezer, all in the same plastic wrap. He found the electric box and tripped the breakers labeled freezer, leaving both doors open to let the cold out. "We'll call 911. Tell them it's a major fire. If we even as much as hint at what we're really looking at, nobody will come with all the crank calls out there lately. Let them deal with it when they get here. With all their personnel, they'd beat us at the job anyway. It'll take the two of us all night to pull those people off of those hooks alone, and Jonathon here is looking pasty. He's young, and not a zombie yet. Let's just do what we can handle, and leave the rest to the public servants. Kills all the birds with one stone. Remember how the Chief treated you when you first called?" Decided Joe.

"You're right. It's more likely that we'll get help if we don't tell them the truth," said Sandra, suddenly enlivened and in agreement with the decision to move out.

She gave one last look of inspection towards the reviving Mrs. Keeder. If anything, Mrs. Keeder looked more livid than ever, her hands clawing at the linoleum. Was she a zombie, wondered Sandra? That just didn't compute. What the hell is a zombie anyway, she thought, fighting for another explanation? Maybe the broken neck hadn't caused any vital damage, in spite of the evidence otherwise? Sandra caught a glimpse of the gaping hole the hook had made into the woman's upper back, seeing no blood. She gasped at the revelation her next thought contained. They'd all been hooked like that, and they'd all been moving, she understood. Perhaps a lucky person or two might live through such trauma, but not all of them!

Sandra rushed to the phone. Joe grabbed Jonathon while Sandra called in a fire run, referring to the kitchen behind the main chapel. She kept her eyes on Mrs. Keeder, who'd stumbled to her knees, though like a newborn fawn. Done with the call, Sandra ran to the door through which Joe was carrying Jonathon over his back. In spite of her desperate desire to convince herself that there had to be some kind of logical explanation, she ran with the feeling of panic.

They backed out of their parking spot, the first light of predawn creeping closer to day. Mrs. Keeder staggered to the backlit doorframe. The dead woman put her hand over her eyes to protect herself from the coming sun. As she did, she moaned a sorrowful goodbye towards the escaping meals of living flesh.

17

"Let's see these bastards do it one more time. Suckin put me out of business, will you! Three times. Three times! Can you believe it! And, what do the cops say? "Can't spare the manpower!" Well fine then, you overpaid pubic school dropouts with badges. I'll do it myself. No more, you, you, you preppie choir boys. Steeling stiffs right out from under my nose, will you! Meet Mr. Smith and Mrs. Wesson! Yeah, that's right. Mr. Smith and his momma, baby! Not to mention, Jr. and the boys."

William dropped the lid on the big metal coffin that was sitting on the top of one of his prep tables. He had a rapid fire shotgun, a civilianized M-16, two vintage forty-five automatic handguns and a law in there, all bought spur of the moment just that evening for four thou even at a Hilliard gun show. The modification to the M-16 came as a kit, the actual mod illegal—though it had only taken him five minutes to make the adjustments so that the weapon could go full automatic. As for the law, well, that had been out of a trunk in the gun show parking lot, illegal as hell, but who cares. "Can't spare the manpower, so like, who cares, for sure, Zippo" mouthed William. He had been in a bad mood when he'd bought it, thinking, you never know when you'll need to stop a tank, or some prep boy's van full of corpses. William flipped the morgue basement lights off. Only a pair of running board nightlights lit the cavernous room.

Actually, it was only a Smith and Wesson in William's mind. What was in his hand was a 1951 vintage M1 carbine that he'd purchased for three thousand extra due to its antiquity. He'd read about the reliability of M1s in countless Second World War novels, and had to have the relatively simple weapon as his mainstay. He dropped the weapon onto the opened drawer bed, and then crawled up beside it. Using his hands, he pulled the drawer and himself in until it was six inches from being closed. Through that he poked his rifle barrel. He'd disconnected his drawer's electric, but a little of the chill still seeped through from the drawers to his sides, making him wish he'd added a blanket. Oh well, he thought, not perfectly comfortable, but thinking, at least I'm not like the last guy who'd found himself in here.

"That's right boys. Stakeout time at the OK!"

William waited in the gloom, his eyes adjusting to the nightlights and the muzzle of his rifle barely peeking out of the end of the drawer he was lying in. He had a perfect view to each side, including the back cellar door with its few steps and the larger main stairway landing door. He'd left the back door barred with a six inch piece of one by one. Half an ounce will bust it loose, he hoped, really pissed and wanting to bag the culprit once the perp had broken in. The tables in front of him were obscured by the drawer face, but any 'guests' would be coming through a door, he knew. Time ticked by. William's head got heavy and nodded. They say that the darkest hour is just before dawn, but the sky lightened as seen through a partially painted over and barred basement window, proving that wrong.

William fell asleep.

Something scratched at the back door, as if a mouse was trying his nails. Suddenly, the door burst open, squeaking low on its hinges. A recent customer, middle aged, brown flowing hair, and no longer suffering from terminal cancer, stumbled in and then down the few steps. She sniffed the room, as if testing before taking the last step. She stood there in her long white gown, looking almost angelic in her heavily powdered, Patricia-like painted face. The place smelled of dead people and chemicals, she sensed. But then again, there was some small pleasant smell here too, though it was so mingled with the rest that she couldn't quite put a finger on it. Thus, William's smell mixed with that of the other chemicals and, his propensity to snore not yet having risen to the surface, William went unnoticed.

The woman turned around, immediately confronted with the faint glow of a nearly new sun. She turned back around, and looked for a place to stow away; someplace dark, preferably. Ah yes, she noted, staggering over to the body drawers. She fumbled at a latch, finally figuring out how to open one up—mostly through trial and error. It slid open, and she got on top of the drawer's little bed. How does this go, she reflected, seemingly finding something familiar about the thing, way back in the recesses of her mind. Oh yeah, she thought, pushing the sides of the rectangular cavity and shutting the drawer with a locking clank!

Only the clank was heard by William. In fact, scientists tell us that we hear every noise made while asleep, though we loft them out of short term memory well before awakening; except perhaps, the last sound, which in this case was close enough to recall. William blinked his eyes open, feeling insecure, as if the sound he'd dreamed had possibly been real. His eyes met the opened outside doorway in back of the room. He froze, wondering where the intruder might be. Maybe on the other side of the drawer face, where I can't see, he imagined fearfully.

Well, it's still fairly dark in here, he realized, though his own eyes were quickly re-acclimated. Whoever is in the room will show themselves, he imagined, straining his ears. Nothing, not ever a breath echoed back to him. William leaned out of the drawer, and found nobody else in the room. "Hell! Come and gone, four times. What is this; Grand Central Station?"

Just then a noise of something dragging reported from outside the back door. Still here then, thought William, leaning his head back into the relative darkness of the mostly closed body drawer.

A drunk! Some low-life, cheap-assed wino, realized William as the elderly male dressed in rags shuffled down the steps. At the last two steps he tripped, falling onto the hard basement floor with a series of bone jarring crunches. The wino got up. William trained his gun on him, and then with a second thought, flicked the safety off.

"Who are you and what do you want, Mister. I have a rifle aimed right at you, so make It good!" Screamed William.

The wino looked around, sniffed upwards into the air, and then glared right at William, as if he could see him. Yes, like a wave of heat, William's smell hit him. The wino imagined himself with infrared eyes as he noticed the source of the voice.

"Arah!" Moaned the wino zombie. He shuffled forward, being coy, blocking the main path through the maze of tables and utility carts. Have him trapped, I do, thought the zombie. His tongue licked at his cracked lips.

"You move one inch closer, and I'm shooting you. Get back! I'm warning you!" It struck William that he might actually get into trouble for shooting someone; even someone breaking into his place. Still, the man shuffled forward. Only in the event of self defense could he shoot, William remembered, feeling foolish. Stuck in the cooler, and alone, and particularly after all of the break-ins, a judge would see it as self defense, he rationalized. But then, do I want to kill a man and face his family, William wondered; another new thought?

The zombie was giving him no choice, having closed half the distance from the door.

"Shit!" William shot at the man's arm. The exploding bullet echoed across the walls far louder than expected. It missed the arm. Instead, the bullet ripped a seam in the zombie's side that under normal circumstances would have cost him two dozen stitches.

The wino zombie looked at the slash wound just under his armpit, and then slowly lifted his head back up, returning to the single minded business of closing the distance between himself and the tall sandwich lying in the serving drawer.

William shot at a shoulder next, hitting it squarely and severing the socket as well as two lethal arteries. The blow sent the zombie backward, turning him so that he faced to the side. Disoriented, the zombie sniffed the air again, and then turned to face his tormentor, taking another step.

"Jesus! Stay back!" Screamed William, shooting the man dead center. The bullet ripped through a lung, bounced off of a rib, chipped a chunk out of the back of the man's backbone, and lodged itself half an inch from the heart. The zombie staggered, then fell across a rolling table. The table slid, as did the unbalanced zombie, to the floor.

"Oh hell, I've killed a man," realized William, though thinking himself perfectly justified. He was about to crawl out of the rack he was lying in when the zombie moved. First on his arms, and then on his knees, and finally, standing one foot at a time, the zombie recovered. He turned, facing William; this time with a snarl on his face.

William shot him dead center mass again, causing the zombie to take a step back. The wino danced in place, a bit stunned. Then he again stepped unrelentingly towards William.

The zombie's head found William's crosshairs. When it was two feet away, William closed his eyes and squeezed the trigger. A bullet plowed into the zombie's face right at the nose and didn't stop until it struck the back wall a quarter second before sizeable portions of the zombie's brain landed across half the length of the basement floor. The zombie's head bucked back, and then his body fell back with it. The corpse landed in a heap of bones and flesh.

Leaning over the lip of the tray, William puked. Totally unprofessional, thought the mortician, though he knew it was mostly nerves that had him queasy. He jumped down from his table, and knelt over, catching his breath. Still leaning, he kicked the neutralized zombie. It didn't move. William stood and rolled the man over with his foot. For the first time, he noticed that the back of the man's pants had been ripped open right at the ass. One ham had been chewed clean to the bone. Arteries and all were gone. William held his rifle at a renewed ready, and stepped back.

"How did that man walk in here like that?" He wondered loudly. William knew a lot about death; enough to know that a wound like that was certainly terminal. "He was a damned dead man. I killed a dead man!" He smiled, and just as quickly lost the smile, not knowing what kind of emotion was right. Did I kill the man or not? "What is going on," wondered William as he walked over and hit the lights.

18

Amazingly, only three blocks since the mayor's office, and bang, chaos. Where were the cops, Dominique wondered? Had there been a riot and they'd missed it? It had been pure bedlam in front of her car, though the weakening fog made it hard to see much past a half block.

She had come to a rubber scorching halt in front of a baby blue upturned Volkswagen. After getting out to check, she found nobody in the car. Dominique backed away, and squinted through the fog to see further down the block. She barely made out several more heaps of rags, most of them fading in and out through the shifting haze. Out of one of the closer heaps of rags, she recognized a hand, and then a second later noticed the pool of blood. This wasn't her sort of neighborhood, she thought, nervously grabbing her way back into her car.

Picking her cell phone out of her purse, Dominique dialed 911. It rang for ten rings, and then gave her a message to try another number. Dialing that was no better. The whole time, her eyes looked around wildly while she held her cell phone to an ear. It was really early, the sun barely up enough to burn off another quarter block of fog, but in spite of that, there should have been the first trickles of rush hour. Instead, the town slept, literally; some permanently, she'd come to abruptly understand.

"Come on, come on," Dominique moaned, dialing 911 again. "Oh right! Two hours ago I get a warning ticket from some loitering fool out nowhere on the highway, and now nobody can answer the damned phone! Never a cop when you need one. Where's the closest donut shop? Hell! What a day I picked for getting up early. Feeling lonely and wanting to play with the submissive, dear Dominique? This is no way to find the right man!"

Well, I should maybe go back and untie the mayor. He might be able to roust the lazy crew next door at the police station, thought Dominique. The debris on the road made it hard to turn around without going past the upturned Volkswagen. As foggy as it was, backing was clearly unsafe. That meant going by the one heap she knew to be a body, but the only safe way through appeared to be just that — through.

She gingerly coaxed her hot Mitsubishi by the wreck.

Morning sun and lifting fog made it possible to see more of the heaps of clothing scattered about on lawns, sidewalks and suburban street, them taking on an increasingly lived in quality as they solidified.

"Oh my god," said a shocked Dominique as she passed at least a dozen victims. "Gas! What if it's gas," she thought, panicking.

She picked up a hanky and covered her lower face, picking up speed. Suddenly, a string of several new wrecks confronted her, one laid over a fire hydrant that was spewing water at a forced angle into a neighbor's front living room window. Spotting a driveway, she pulled in and turned her car around. As she backed between bodies, she felt a bump under a rear wheel and cringed. Putting the car back into drive, she gritted her teeth and pulled back over the body part on her way out. She'd made it back to the Volkswagen when she saw the arm on that first body shift.

Her car picked up speed as it whipped by the Volkswagen, putting distance between herself and the carnage. Turning onto Hamilton on two wheels, she swung into the mayor's office parking lot, skidding to a halt in a wheelchair slot.

She burst into his outer office. The idea had been to have some fun with him after a long night of utter loneliness. She'd called him in the wee hours, and convinced him to come to the office before dawn. There, she'd cuffed him up to the ceiling fan and walked out on the man, he in only boxers and she fully clothed, except for one missing stocking. The look of panic on his face had been too delicious, recalled Dominique. He'd had no way of knowing that she'd only intended to go for coffee. Saucers, his eyes had been, above the stocking gag. His moans had been forceful enough for her to hear even at the empty office complex's main door, which she'd locked with his keys. Now, however, the planned absence reduced to only ten minutes, and no coffee, she heard nothing as she made her way into the mayor's reception room. Had he had a heart attack, she worried, as she opened his office door?

The first thing she noticed as she reached for the light, was that the second switch was up. That meant the ceiling fan was on. Lights flickered, she seeing his body moving in a tight circle in the center of the room. Then she gasped! His toes brushed the floor as the mayor's body swung, head down limply. The red, heart-printed boxer shorts were dragging on the floor where they'd fallen to one ankle. An eight foot diameter ring of splattered blood was painted around his swinging body where it had been painted by a still dripping set of toes.

"Oh no. I've hit the wrong switch and killed him," was Dominique's first reaction. She looked around the room fearfully, then back to the dead mayor. Chunks of flesh were missing, all between his waist and knees. It looked like a couple dozen giant piranhas had found the perfect lunch, one inch chunks at a time. Alone, none of them were fatal, but they were all over him, each trickling their own tablespoon of blood, the combination coating his entire bottom half.

"My stuff," said a shocked Dominique. It was her stocking in his mouth, and her handcuffs holding him to the ceiling fan. They'd think I murdered him, she realized. With dread, she flicked the ceiling fan off, and pulled a chair up next to the slowing body. She uncuffed the cuffs and the body fell, toppling her chair. Falling hard, she counted her blessings, and crawled up to retrieve the cuffs, which she held in two timid fingers. She dropped the cuffs into the office trash can, which was lined with a plastic bag. Her hand grabbed the bag. Next, she untied his gag and dropped that into the plastic bag as well. She looked behind herself, and slowly backed out of the office, stopping at the office door to take one last look and see if anything else incriminating remained.

This is going to be bad, she realized, knowing that it had been her cell phone that had called him to the office. Surely, they'd trace that. She'd need a lawyer, assuming whoever did this wasn't still around, and ready to do her the nasty deed as well. It seemed an unfair burden to trouble her with both of those duties at once, particularly considering that she was an innocent woman on both scores. These are not pleasant thoughts, mused Dominique as she scanned the room while wiping the door knob with the hem of her dress. The dress was definitely going to find its way into the nearest incinerator due to having landed in the blood stains during her fall. As for the blood, her footprints and marks from the fall, and even her handprint were in the mess. She'd touched the chair as well. What else, she worried frantically?

OK, what do we have here, she considered? No DNA. Only a cell phone call. She could tell them they were having an affair, and when she got here, he was like this. She'd found him like he is now, on the floor and in her haste to help, she'd slipped, grabbing the chair on the way up. It would just be a scandal, no lying about it; the truth even, in its own little way. Then they'd investigate the means of death and it was a no brainer that she couldn't have done that…whatever it was that had been done to him. What had been done to him, she wondered with horror? Whatever it was, it wasn't the sort of thing a female murderer usually did to a man, she knew from court experience.

Yes, that was it; she'd have to confess having found him. Dominique put her fingers back onto the doorknob, knowing it best to be up front about that as well. She'd call in the death. Be right up front about it, like she'd found it all, but only after discarding the cuffs and stocking, she decided, taking off her other stocking and putting it into the bag with the rest. No, that wouldn't work, she decided, putting the bloody stocking on her leg. Just the cuffs would have to go; that was the only thing too weird to explain away easily. The story will have to be, I found him on the floor, the fan still spinning. I fell and got stained, trying to see if he was alive. In the mean time, I have to ditch the cuffs after wiping them clean, her mind finished.

Something bumped in the room. Her eyes raced around the furnishings as she backed a step, and then settled on the office's half bathroom door. Another bump, this time, the door shaking in its hinges.

"Oh, shit!" Dominique ran out of the office complex. She got into her car and ran the gears as she raced down the street. Stopping on the bridge, she opened the office trash bag, and tossed the cuffs into the brown, shallow creek, along with the keys that she belatedly fished out of her purse. Loosely putting a rock into the plastic sack, she sank that too. Still no traffic. There was a lot wrong with the morning, thought Dominique as she stood on the bridge and redialed 911. Nobody answered.

"Well, that works. I went for help. Nobody answers the phone at 911; they have records of that too! That's why I went to my car and it, of course, got bloody," she decided. Then she remembered the speeding ticket. There was a record of her driving toward town two hours earlier. How was she going to explain the lost hour and a half? Not only that, what will happen when they see the cuff marks and put two and two together. Kinky sex—dead body. She'd have to confess the whole thing, and then explain why she'd tossed the cuffs in the creek, realized Dominique. "Jesus, this sounds terrible. I have blood evidence everywhere. I'm going to need a really good lawyer!" Dominique stood on the bridge, stopped by her own indecision and sense of frustration.

She heard the sound of an oncoming car down on Deadman, and thought it best not to be seen on the bridge where she'd made her drop. Leaping into her car, she backed down the foggy road, accelerating frantically. At about thirty miles an hour, she turned her wheel sharply like she'd seen on TV. Amazingly, it worked, spinning the car a hundred and eighty degrees. Then she picked up speed, aimed back toward the center of town. The mysterious car pulled up out of the fog behind her. Looking in her rear view mirror, she thought she remembered the driver, and then noticed the passenger.

"Joe! Oh, thank god!" Dominique hit her breaks with both feet.

Joe got out to inspect the damage to the front bumper of Sandra's car.

"What's the matter with you," he half said before seeing Dominique who'd jumped out of her car. She was in a hysterical, blood splattered state. At first he thought it might have been the accident, but the cars had barely met, leaving only a crease in Sandra's bumper.

"Thank God it's you. I've been calling 911 all morning. Nobody answers. The mayor has been murdered, and there are a lot of people dead over on Eisen Street. Cars turned over, bodies in the street. It's horrible. I was going for coffee after seeing the mayor, and it's like the whole world has gone crazy and I've missed it. Something has happened to everybody, and we've all been sleeping. I raced back to get his help when 911 didn't answer, and he'd been murdered too. I'm just driving around, trying to find anyone who can help. Thank God it's you," confessed Dominique in words too fast to call anything but panic.

"Alright. Look, we have to get this guy in the back of our car to the hospital. Thought we'd try the one on our side of the county so we'd have the best crack at questioning him, or we'd have dumped him sooner. I guess we both have a bit of a complicated problem. I tell you what, let's all go to the police station and see what we can rustle up in the way of help. Maybe the medics can take this guy over and we can all get to the bottom of this mayor thing as well," suggested Joe.

Sandra nodded her agreement.

Dominique shook her head yes, but was numbed by the sudden letdown of adrenalin.

"You drive the speed limit, Ms. Sawyer. I think you've had enough excitement for the time being. OK? We'll be right behind you, absolutely promise; only maybe a little further back than before. Don't you do that thing with your breaks again either. I almost wet my pants when you did that," Joe winked a smile in both Sandra's and the Dominique's direction.

Dominique nodded her head yes, and got into her car.

"Try again," said Sandra as they got in.

Joe dialed 911, and then the direct line to the station, getting nowhere again. "At least that part of her story is right on the head. I dialed Columbus's police business line, and nothing seems to be working over there at all. I even dialed our local firehouse; zilch. It looks like our last call back at Purswell's was damned near the last run before everything went to dial tone, assuming the 911 center even got through with that one. Ma Bell must have taken one whale of a hit."

"So, what's really up with that woman ahead of us?" Asked Sandra, changing the subject to something she could deal with. All of the public safety lines being down seemed too much to fathom. Behind them, Jonathon moaned and rolled over, out of his head with a fever. His shirt was soaked with sweat.

"I think she saw a murder, like she said. That's my lawyer. Normally, she's pretty much in control of her emotions. In fact, I've never seen a woman so in control of her emotional side before. Fine difference between being a lawyer and representing victims or perpetrators versus being personally involved in a violent crime that sends your world spinning though."

"I have to tell you, Joe, if she's right, this IS out of control. Bodies by the dozen in freezers, endless traffic fatalities and serious domestic disturbances, and now the mayor dead. We've passed an endless stream of wrecks. Bodies in the streets.... What's going on? We don't have enough police officers to handle all of this. What happens when that happens?" said Sandra. It had been a long night, and the morning promised no relief.

"My guess is, you'll have to call in the state police, and maybe even the National Guard."

"I'll have to call them in?"

"Yeah, you. I don't imagine for a minute that Chief Baker has enough of a head on his shoulders to admit that his town is out of his control. Do you see any state officers here? See a green truck? Guys walking around with M-16s? I rest my case," said Joe.

A new wreck happened a block down from the police station, just as they turned onto Hamilton. Joe and Sandra watched both drivers run between the houses, as if the motorists had abandoned their vehicles and gotten into a mad chase. Realizing that there were too many problems at hand to solve yet another, they drove by. The police lot was nearly empty. Of course, it was late, or early, thought Sandra, but there was only one cruiser, and two personal cars, hardly enough to man the radio and make more than one personal call to arms.

"Let's get Jon here into the station," suggested Sandra. Joe took the arms, and Sandra the legs, as they carried him up the steps. The door was locked, so they propped him up in the corner of the landing while Sandra fished for her office keys.

"Why didn't you just drive over here. It's right next to the mayor's office," Sandra asked Dominique without hardly thinking as she unlocked the door.

Dominique thought, the story's already unraveled and I've not said a thing yet. "I panicked. When you see him, you'll know why. I heard a noise in the bathroom too. The guy who did it was still in the adjoining bathroom. He might still be in there, so whoever goes there has to be careful. You know, I'd called 911 about the bodies in the street, and had, of course, completely forgotten about the idea of going for coffee. I had to get back to the mayor so he could roust somebody. Then he was dead. I slipped, trying to help, ruining my outfit and then the noise in the bathroom, and I just ran. I called 911 again, and again nothing. My mind was already saying that there wasn't anyone at home at the police station. It just didn't strike me to try in person. I was looking for just anybody I could find at that point, thinking, just around the next corner, over and over again. Usually there are people on the streets, for crying out loud. You are the only two people on the road. Don't you think that's odd? You two are the only ones out. I can't believe that I had to drive around as much as I did before finding someone."

Joe looked back to the road, and realized that it was getting to be that time in the morning when one would expect more than a trickle of traffic. In fact, he thought back to when he'd been fishing the morning all of this seemed to have started and at how he'd been able to count the cars clanging across the bridge, a good two or more per minute by this time of day. Hamilton should be even busier, he understood. Yet, nothing moved. The place was eerie; as still as death.

"She's right," said Sandra, verbally confirming Joe's thoughts as they walked into the police waiting room. Nobody was at the desk. Sandra fished out another key, opening the door to the main wardroom. The first desks their adjusting eyes met sat empty. The curtains were closed, making the room's features dim pickings. She tried the lights, but they didn't work.

"Good lord, now this. Is anything going right in this town?" Asked Sandra.

A match lit in the deepest, furthest corner of the room full of desks. It lifted, lighting a cigarette and showing a face. Chief baker leaned back in a swivel chair, his feet up on a desk. A shotgun rested across his lap, while a police revolver sat to his side on top of a file cabinet. Jimmy lay lengthwise across the front half of the desk, his closest arm outstretched and his face aimed at the trio of intruders. His eyes and mouth were open, the eyes far too dull and unblinking.

Chief Baker answered, "No, Miss Anderson. I don't think a whole lot is, and at this point, all I've got to say about it is: Fuck em all!"

19

"William! I know you're hiding in there! You open this door, right now, buster!" Screamed Patricia.

"I'm not decent," tried William. What in the world is the matter with the planet, thought William. First the coroner and now Patricia, both at just the most perfectly awful moments. He dialed 911 again, trying to ignore Patricia's continued pounding. The phone no longer rang incessantly, going straight to disconnect and dial tone instead. Where the hell are the cops. How will this all look when someone else discovers it, and there'd not been a call to the cops yet, he worried.

"I don't care if you're decent. It's not like I haven't seen the itty bitty thing already! Now you open this door right now, or I'm going upstairs and kicking over all your precious coffins. I know you like them better than me; God knows you spend more time with them," Yelled Patricia.

"OK, fine then, but you're not going to like what you see," said William, pulling back the deadbolts.

"Like it was something special to look at in the f..." Patricia stammered as the door opened and she got her first look at the room around William. "...place."

"It's not what you think," he said, stepping over to the body that lay sprawled on the floor. In the process, he almost slipped on a piece of brain, the slip creating a foot long, grey skid mark on the floor.

Patricia put her hand over her mouth. She'd seen his stiffs before, but hadn't particularly gotten used to them. This one, on the floor, with his brains splattered all over the room, was too much to handle. She bent over the handrail, and tossed up three martinis, a vermouth, some beer nuts, two orders of tortilla chips and a little reminder from a guy named Mike; she doubted it his real name, though he hadn't been wearing a ring. To be fair, she'd taken her engagement ring off at the start of the evening as well.

"Sorry about that. I did warn you. It's not what you might think," repeated William.

"Well, what do you know about what I think?" Asked Patricia as William handed her a towel.

"There's some on your, uh, yeah," said William, brushing a bit of puke off of the top of her dress.

Patricia flinched, as if his hand was poison. "I can get it myself."

"Well, fine then. I don't know what you think. But…OK, just hear this and tell me what you think of it." William led her to a seat not too far from the door and well away from the stiff.

Patricia saw the gun and then the opened crate full of more weapons, and for the first time in her life, started to wonder if there wasn't more to William than met the eye. Like a really Hannibal Lecter sort of side. Should I run, she wondered, thinking it best to listen and make up her mind later, particularly since William was at a better angle relative to either door.

William started, "This guy on the floor is dead."

"Duh!"

"No, I mean, he was dead before he came in here."

"Jesus, William. They're all dead before they come in here! At least I'm hoping they're all dead before they come in here! What are you, an idiot?" Said Patricia rhetorically. She was not too scared to still be Patricia.

"OK...um...he was dead, and then he walked in here." William looked at Patricia with one of his eyebrows raised. Sometimes it's best to keep it simple, he decided.

Patricia just looked back with a new, patient sort of annoyance on her face that seemed to be saying either she was bored, or was waiting for the rest of the explanation that would help her make sense out of the first part.

William sighed, then walked over to the corpse. He kicked one leg around, and pointed. "See. That's the wound he had before he came in here. See how old it is; grey around the edges and soiled? The man attacked me. I had to shoot him. At first I was crazy, thinking, damn William, you've killed a man. Something about it didn't add up though. I mean, I shot him over and over and he kept coming. Fatal stuff, like right in the chest, and he didn't do much more than flinch from the weight of the blows."

William looked over with both eyebrows raised. He had her attention. "So, you know, I had to shoot him in the head. Right between the eyes. Punched his nose out, I did. That did the trick well enough. As you can see, he keeled over, but then I noticed this earlier wound. That's not something a man can survive. The second biggest artery in the body is right there. I know, I do this sort of work."

William prodded the wound with the rifle he'd just picked up. "See, severed! And, he's walking on that thing. A leg can't work without arteries, and it sure as hell can't walk without half an ass!"

"OK, so he was dead before you shot him. I'm relieved to hear that. It means you didn't do anything wrong. It's OK. We can call the police," said Patricia, deciding to patronize the man. Clearly, he's delusional, she thought, and armed as well.

"Well, yeah, sure. Don't think I didn't think of that myself, but it's not going to happen, Patricia," said William.

Patricia swallowed hard, suddenly stiff with freight. This, of course, was where William went completely bonkers and told her that she'd have to be shot too, now that she was a witness to his crime.

She said, "OK, William. Maybe you're right. We shouldn't call the police. Of course, that's silly. They'd jump to all the wrong conclusions. I'm sure they'd not understand like I do. I know you—they don't. We can clean this up and use the incinerator. It'd be like nothing happened. It's what you do, don't you see. You're the best at cleaning up this sort of thing. It's early; nobody's around. We can get this done. I'll help. It's just an old bum anyway; who cares about old farts?"

William looked at her with a crooked head. He'd never heard her so condescending in his whole life. Then it dawned on him. "Oh, shit. You don't believe a word I said. No, look…I can't call the police because they don't answer the phone!" He picked up his cell phone and tossed it to Patricia. "Yeah. That's right. Give it a try!"

It's a trap, thought Patricia, putting the phone down on a table next to her chair. "Do you honestly think that this town's police force is going to understand what you just told me? Look, William, there are vampires in town, and you have to shoot them in the head? There a million vampire movies and books out there, but nobody bel…"

"Zombies."

"What?"

"Not vampires, dear. Zombies. This is the real walking dead. Look at him. What do you see?"

"A dead man. Or, a zombie. That's fine. We'll just get rid of it," said Patricia.

William found it more frustrating to be condescended to than he'd ever been when she'd treated him like trash. At least the trash talk had been honest, up front Patrician. He tossed his gun on a close table, and said, "Patricia, dear. I'm not crazy, and I'm not afraid of the police. I am not going to shoot you. Do we understand all of these things?"

"Yes dear," said a confused Patricia, only willing to step so far into whatever William was getting to.

"Ok. Now look. What is missing here?" He stomped on the floor around the corpse, as if he were stomping out bugs.

In beat with his stomping, Patricia said, "I...don't...know. You...tell...me!"

"Blood. There's no blood. I've been to a million violent death scenes and never in my life have I ever seen someone die with a hole plum through his brain, and there's no blood! Not a dog sniffin lick of blood! Someone dies like this, and it looks like twenty gallons of blood all over everything. Just these grey blobs of brain, Patricia. I...killed...a...dead...man!"

Patricia's eyes went wide with recognition. Still, there could be an explanation. Maybe he'd done this to one of his corpses after having gone nuts, she wondered? On another note, being told to look at the brains all over the floor was not a good idea. Patricia leaned over the arm of her chair and puked again.

She recovered more quickly, using the same towel. Patricia had a bigger picture of what was going on in William's brain, but it still was most likely that William was nuts. She had a thought. "OK, so we put the zombie in the incinerator...and there you go. I mean, what else can you do? It's just a dead bum zombie! All the more reason to get rid of it."

That seemed to stop William's volatility. "Well! Hum. I guess that makes sense. OK then. I'll get him in and fire it up, and you can help by cleaning up the brains."

White faced, Patricia stood up, thinking, what have I just talked myself into? The brains were in one huge splash that covered maybe fifty square feet of the floor, not to mention some of the wall and a few of the steel tables. If she could have operated the equipment and lifted the corpse, she'd have offered to trade jobs.

William handed her a bucket, and pointed to another bucket with a mop in it in the corner. Then he started lifting the corpse onto a gurney.

Patricia found a rag and tiptoed in her heels over to the first chunk. She bent at the knees, lowering her hand over a chunk. Her fingers picked it up with the rag without actually looking at it. It was squishy, like Jell-O, she thought, as she dropped it into the pale. In her mind she was saying, "Oh, the things we women have to do to keep from being shot by our boyfriends!"

William wheeled the zombie out of the room and into an adjoining incinerator room. Once gone, Patricia looked around at both open exit doors. Damn, she thought, he has confused the hell out of me.

"Bump!"

Patricia froze.

"Bump, bump, bump! Scrape!"

One of the body coolers developed a bulge in the middle of the door.

He has put someone in there, thought Patricia. When he's done, I'm next. I should just run! No, if I open up the body cooler, the other person will distract him so I can get away, she decided. She ran to the body drawer, and unlatched the latch. It sprang forward, timed at the next kick. Patricia fell across the tables, them rolling aside and she falling on her butt. The next thing she knew, the cooler table opened just above her head like a top bunk to her bottom one. She looked to the side for an escape. To her side was a huge chunk of the bum's brain.

A pair of feet fell over the cooler's side. They were naked, white in places, yellow in others and splotchy everywhere else. A foot found her face, it cold as ice as it stepped.

Patricia screamed under the sudden weight!

As Patricia shifted, the woman above her fell. There, not three feet from her, separated by nothing more than a floor and a half dozen chunks of cranial matter, lay the whitest body Patricia had ever seen. For the first time, Patricia instinctively knew that William had been telling the truth. Now what, she wondered? What do zombies do? And, why is that zombie's face painted up to resemble a seventy year old me?

Patricia scampered away like a crab just in time to avoid finding out what zombies did. The zombie lashed out with her face, just missing a bite of Patricia's.

Behind her, footsteps, realized Patricia with relief. She backed further, William passing her in the opposite direction. He aimed his M1 at the zombie, and fired on an empty chamber. "Click, click, click," nothing.

Tossing the empty weapon aside, he cursed himself for not having reloaded it right away. Patricia screamed behind him, adding to the pandemonium. Putting his hand into the crate, he pulled out the first thing that hit his fingers, the law. There isn't time to be picky, he thought, remembering the instructions he'd read just that previous evening.

"Extend the tube. Pull up the sights. Set the range—forget that. Point in the direction of the arrow, and squeeze.

There was a whish that set a towel on a rack behind him on fire. Then, like an afterthought, the rocket leapt from the tube. It smacked the zombie in the middle of the stomach, sending her flying to the far wall where there was a surprisingly tiny, "Pop!"

The surprisingly tiny pop sent an amazingly vast quantity of body pieces in every direction. The tables, ceiling, floor, all four walls, and even Patricia and William were coated in chunks of bloodless flesh. On the wall, a wisp of smoke told of where the middle third of the zombie had been. Under that, the head and shoulders had fallen to meet the lower hips and legs. There, the whole mess slumped.

The instructions on the law said, "After use, break the firing tube in half." Always a man of order, he did.

The top third of the exploded woman, fell over onto the floor. William was amazed to notice the zombie's head starting to vibrate. "It's trying to crawl," said William when he noticed the jaw working at the floor. Behind him, Patricia had fallen to her knees, crying crocodile tears over the seemingly insurmountable mess.

After loading the M1, William shot the zombie in the head, sending head and shoulders spinning, and ending the sickening crawl. The towel burned down on its own, but it started the sprinklers raining. William laughed at the final insult to his tidy workroom, half dazed into lunacy by the accumulative events. "We're going to need a fire hose to clean this place up."

"Jesus, Bill, let's just get out of here!" Screamed his fiancé from where she knelt with trembling limbs.

"What? And leave all of this?"

20

Jimmy was a mess. It looked as if a thousand rats had taken chunks out of him. His back was the worst, the young police officer having had the sense to cower away from whatever had attacked him, they saw.

"You have to call the Governor. There isn't any choice any longer. Face the facts, Chief: It's all gone out of control. Dominique told us that we have a ton of people down in a riot only a few blocks away, the mayor has reportedly been murdered, and we have a gravely ill man propped up on the stoop. That's just what we can see at a glance right out of the parking lot, not mentioning two freezers full of stiffs at Purswell's and half the transportation in the city wrecked," demanded Joe.

"He's right, Chief. There isn't a single car moving out there. If this is the tip of the iceberg, we're all in serious danger. We have a duty to the citizens," said Sandra.

The Chief waffled. "Duty to the citizens? Hey, while you and lover boy have been out playing private dick on the other side of the county, I've been working this war zone. Last night was an entirely new thing around here. Things quickly got out of control. Those citizens, as you call them, killed my son. Forget them!"

"Not everyone killed your son, Chief. It can't be growing that exponentially. The bulk of the population is probably in hiding; just as scared as we are," offered Joe.

"Oh really? Not from what I've been seeing. It wasn't just a few who took down Jimmy." Something caught the Chief's eye. He got up from his chair, and walked to the window. "See. Look at that," he said before busting the window out with the butt of his shotgun.

Even as the glass fell clear, Chief Baker aimed and then shot a boy driving by on his bicycle. It was a long shot for a shotgun, the dispersed pellets mostly sweeping the bike out from under the youngster, but the boy had enough sense to stay down once shot.

Joe jumped Baker first, and then Sandra was on him. He must have been tired, because they gained the shotgun and tossed it to Dominique. Sandra cuffed her boss behind the back.

Once the Chief was seated into his chair, Joe ran out to the boy. He was about ten, and shaking like a leaf.

"You OK, son. The man who shot at you is cuffed now. Let me have a look at that," said Joe, leaning down. The boy shied away, but then, as if reading every expression on Joe's face, took some kind of measure and relaxed.

"My name's Joe. I'm not the one who shot you. I'm just a guy who works in a music store. What's your name?"

"Stanley. Ouch, that hurts," said the boy.

"Looks like a few of the pellets got your leg. Not going to be much worse than a couple of bee stings. Bet a doc can even get at the pellets without much work. Ever been shot with a BB? Could have been a lot worse, judging from your bike. Can you stand up? Once we get you inside, we can bandage it up."

"Are you taking me to jail?"

"What in the world for, son?"

"For killing people. I had to shoot my sister," he confessed, pulling a gun out from where he'd tucked it in his back belt.

"Woo. Better give that to me. What, um, what did you have to do that for?" Asked Joe, helping the boy up. At the same time, Joe was wondering why he wasn't shocked to hear the boy tell him such a horrible tale? It seemed that times had changed, and his rational side was a bit slow at catching up to his emotional side.

"She was one of them. I can tell by the way they look at you. I didn't want to shoot her, but she was one of them," said the boy hurriedly.

Joe helped the boy up the steps past Jon, who'd fallen stark still. "Do you know him?" Asked the boy.

"Met him. He's waiting for an ambulance, soon as we get around to calling one. Things have been a little hectic," said Joe.

"I can shoot him for you, if you want. He's going to turn," said Stanley.

"People have done enough shooting around here," said Joe, bending over to test Jonathon for vitals. His wrist was cold. Joe felt the man's head, and then put two fingers to his jugular. "Damn! He's dead. That bite wasn't fatal. Must have been shock. It's my fault; we should have taken him straight to the hospital. Don't look at him, son."

"See. I can shoot him now, if you don't want to," said the boy. Joe had never seen a person so eager to shoot someone before, other than perhaps the Chief. He ushered the boy into the offices.

Sandra came over and started working on the boy's leg right away. The Chief's eyes lit up like he'd seen a ghost, noticed Joe, but then when the boy yelped at Sandra's cleaning, the Chief seemed relieved.

"Jonathon outside is dead. Don't pretend that it's shocking. Everything is just basically crazy. What's going on here?" Joe finally asked.

The Chief gave his answer, "There's dead people all over, coming back to life, you ass. That's what the whole thing was from the start, with the mortuary, the graves and probably even your freezers. I wasn't onto it until all hell broke loose just after you called last night. We'd been out all night long, dealing with it, when they got Jim. You see things just a little bit different when it's sorted out to you wholesale, boys and girls."

"So you shot this kid because you thought he was a walking dead person?" Asked Joe.

"Hell, I admit a mistake with the boy, but last night, all of them were walking dead. He's the first live one I've seen in half a day, other than you," explained the Chief.

"Walking dead?" Asked Dominique.

"Zombies?" Sandra and Joe asked, both voices a chorus.

"I don't know what they are? I guess that's what they are," said the Chief.

There was the sound of a door shutting in the distance. The fact that Dominique, who was closest to the busted out window, could hear it at all, told volumes regarding how still the town had become. She looked out while the others argued. It was the mayor who'd made the noise, noticed an alarmed Dominique. He stiffly walked out between the administration building and Hamilton. With a hand shading his swollen eyes, the mayor sniffed the air. Then he turned around and looked at the police building. It appeared as if he was looking right at Dominique, she framed in the broken window. She swallowed a scream.

"What's the matter?" Asked Sandra.

"Oh my god, he's still alive. I can't believe it. There was so much blood, and I was so sure. If that was a prank, I'll kill the bastard," said Dominique, switching from a feeling of guilt to that of anger.

"I don't know about dead, but if he doesn't get back inside, he's dead politically," said Sandra, making note of the fact that he was completely naked. Given the size of his love handles, she decided that, that wasn't a vote getter. On the other hand, given the size of his blood swelled equipment, she imagined that he might gain a few votes in exchange.

"He doesn't know he's butt naked. He's already dead, and ain't half right upstairs. That's the way they get; they get crazy up in the attic," said Stanley, who'd moved up beside the women. "Where's my gun? I'll poke him for ya," the boy asked Joe. Everyone took a look at Stanley. He looked like a perfectly average ten year old suburban kid, striped t-shirt, jeans, a minor mop of blonde hair. Who'd have thought of him as such an outlaw, they all wondered? The mayor kept coming and everyone stopped wondering about Stanley long enough to notice.

"Uncuff me. Don't let that thing in here with me like this. A man's got a right to defend himself. Don't forget, I'm still the law around here," insisted Baker.

"Alright. But look, Chief, we test this theory of yours out before we shoot at them. Things got out of hand last night, but it's a new day. The whole deal that's doing this to people might be some sort of new disease. You stay unarmed until I know what's going on. Consider yourself on probation," said Sandra, unfastening his cuffs.

The Chief stood up, looking as if he was going to challenge the new arrangement, but then shrugged. "Fine then. You see for yourself. Just don't get bit by getting too close to one of them. When you see for yourself, you toss me my shotgun, hear!"

"Seems fair to me," said Joe, walking out of the office with the Chief's shotgun. On the way out, he put his evidence together in his head, starting with the story of Millie funeral resurrection. Then there'd been John; neither he nor Sandra had felt a pulse. At

John's place, the dead man hadn't bloated, nor had he bled, and then there'd been all of those people up on hooks, moving when they should have been dead. What had Purswell said about the dead rising, Joe tried to remember? Putting all of the facts under the mental microscope of what he knew about zombie movies, and it all made sense. And, of course, that didn't make sense at all, but it sure spooked him, knowing that nothing else did either, as he walked by Jonathon with one eye on the recently deceased zealot.

"Hi Mayor," Joe said after walking out onto the grass. Everyone else was framed in the window, looking out with great interest.

The mayor squinted at Joe, his eyes in pain from the glare of sunlight. He smelled Joe, licked his own lips and changed direction of travel so quickly that he fell down taking the first step towards the meat.

"Woo there, big guy. What's the rush. Now look, I can see you're having some trouble. If you're hurt, just lie still and I'll help you," tried Joe.

As if determined to do the opposite, the mayor crawled a few feet and then got up. He started to run at Joe, his knees too stiff to do it very well, but the distance closing just the same. Joe backed up quickly, doing his best to maintain some distance. "Hey. Now, stay right where you are, or I'm going to have to shoot you." No dice.

"Look. I just want to see if you're a zombie, OK! If you're a zombie, it's OK. We'll get you a doctor, but you have to stay back some," said Joe, thinking as quickly as he could. The mayor swept in. Joe sidestepped, tripped the man, and stepped backwards, this time away from the building. With the new view, Joe could see the steps up to the police building. Behind the mayor, Jonathon was getting up.

"Look out, Joe! Don't play with these guys!" Yelled Sandra, she suddenly at the front of the pack at the window. Her service revolver was at hand.

He'd checked Jonathon's pulse, Joe remembered. "Honey, I think these guys are dead. Can I shoot them? Is that like self defense or something?"

"Hell yeah! Shoot em, Joe," yelled Stanley, his face barely visible over the bottom lip of the window sill.

"Be tricky to defend, but my call is self defense; though I'm a lawyer, and I have a tendency to think of everything as self defense," added Dominique. Her voice trailed off due to her sadness.

"I think you're going to have to, Joe," agreed Sandra in the nick of time. Jonathon had gotten up. Barely hurt by the bite that had killed him, he ran past the mayor at a speed not all that much slower than a normal human sprint.

This is going to be a difficult shot, thought Joe as he fired the shotgun at Jonathon. It hit him in the chest, opening up a hole that would have killed any man. In Jonathon's case, it hardly mattered, only slowing him for half a stride. Joe jacked a new shell into the chamber and shot again, hitting the young man in the jaw, ripping it so that it hung by only skin on one side. A few of the pellets had hit his eyes, blinding the newly resurrected zombie. The damage was enormous, but none of the pellets had actually struck the core of his brain.

Ducking away, Joe let Jonathon ran right past. The blind man kept right on going across Hamilton Road. After awhile he slowed, but by then he'd gone upwind, well past the smell. Jonathon's jaw felt weird, but his eyes positively hurt. Joe watched the new zombie wander between some houses, clawing at walls as if looking for a way in.

In the brush with death, Joe had forgotten about the far less nimble mayor, him falling right behind Joe after a single explosion. Sandra held her revolver out of the window, it still aimed at the fallen mayor.

"Thanks dear. I guess I needed that. I got a bit distracted," said Joe as he cocked another shotgun shell into the chamber.

Joe walked back inside. Once through the door, he tossed the shotgun back to Baker. "OK, Chief. It's zombies. You're not crazy. So, now what do we do?"

Sandra answered for him, picking the phone up. She dialed, zero. Everyone watched as she waited. Then she called her own home number, not even getting her own answering machine. Sandra dialed 411. After a minute, she put the phone down, the other end having substituted the ringing with really boring background music.

"I bet you can dial time and weather and still get all of those advertisements before learning that the weather's what you're standing in," said a rather damper Sandra.

Joe laughed once, but everyone else was in too gloomy of a mood to do even as much.

"You know the direct line to the Governor?" Sandra asked Baker.

"Oh yeah, sure. I go over for tea every Thursday. We do crickets. Look, I've tried calling the hospitals, social services, even several of our own officers, and the whole phone system is broken. For that matter, I imagine everyone in this half of the county is fending for their own families about now. What makes public servants any different?"

Dominique was still drying her eyes, not really realizing how fond of the mayor she'd been. It was hard on her, being the crushed dame. She stood up, straightened her skirt and struck a regal pose. Then she sat back down, but straighter, her legs together, back up tall, showing some dignity. "This sucks," she spit, as if making a claim in court. "Bet the lawsuit for this is going to be big enough to make someone into a franchise player," noted Dominique.

Jimmy, back in the gloomier corner, sat up. He had the strangest dream running around in his head, and the even stranger cotton mouth. Something sure smelled good though, as if momma was in the kitchen doing Thanksgiving dinner. He cranked his creaky neck around and let his eyes focus upon the far too brilliantly lit room where everyone argued, them oblivious to his resurrection.

21

Doctor Adkins had never seen anything like it. She'd been called out to her sister's house just before nightfall, and had spent the rest of the evening fussing over her sister's husband, Hank. "It isn't flu season," her sister had told her the moment she'd arrived.

At first glance the doctor would have sworn that he had the flu, but like her sister had said, it wasn't flu season. Fine way to end two days and a night on her own back from a migraine, thought Laura Adkins, just thankful that it was night and she'd not have to test her receding headache on daylight. Hank's eyes looked like pinpricks, and his face was flush, also the sign of a migraine. There was more to it than that though, she could tell. Instead of the expected fever, he had chilled to an even more dangerous ninety-five, Laura noticed. Then she noticed the scratch. The skin had been only barely abraded, but the wound was clearly infected.

Betty saw her sister's worried look at the infection. "He was doing a job for someone in Glacklick, and this idiot ran by. Hank said the man just grabbed at him. Hank slammed his truck door and drove off. He said that he figured the guy was crazy, so, you know, what do you do? He made a cell phone to the cops about it. They were like, "big deal." You know how the cops are around here. Is it what's made him sick? It was nothing, I thought. Didn't even need a bandage, but look at it now. Maybe it's that anthrax thing? Maybe something's got in him," said her sister while Laura opened her bag.

"So, why didn't you take him to the emergency room, Betty?" Asked Laura.

"Well, it costs a fortune with our deductible, and besides, where have you been? The news said it's crowded from all the accidents and mental patients that have escaped. They aren't taking anybody. Besides, Hank wasn't feeling this poorly when I called you. Oh my god. Is he bad? How much worse can he get from just a scratch?"

"The hospital is closed?"

"Well you're the doctor. Don't you know that?"

"I've been sick. They can't close the hospital, or at least not all of them."

"Maybe not, but that's what the anchor said on TV too. They went on and on about it, with pictures of people nearly rioting at Riverside's emergency entrance. It seemed like they meant it was that way at all of the hospitals, and I don't think I want Hank anywhere near there, not unless he is really bad. He's not really bad, is he?" Asked Betty.

"Holy mother of god, Betty, he should be in a hospital right now. Here; just hold the end of this," Laura said to her sister after plopping a thermometer into his mouth.

Hank seemed to waken. He looked over at his sister in law. "I feel like…." He didn't bother to finish, setting his attention upon breathing.

"We're going to see what's up. You just take it easy," said Laura, listening to his chest. She had been betting on pneumonia as a second guess, which sometimes sent a person from hot to cold, and yet his chest sounded perfectly clear, as if there wasn't an ounce of fluid on the lungs. Blood pressure, however, looked a good quart or two low.

"What's wrong with him," said Betty after Laura did all of her tests a second time.

"He's in a mild shock. Infection, probably, along with a headache; they can be debilitating and they coexist nice and nastily. It's just why that is hard to determine? This infection really has taken off quickly. I don't know why. It could be a number of things. Let's start working the infection. At least I can see that clearly enough. In the mean time, you go call the hospital. Tell them that I have a medical emergency, and won't take no for an answer, and then give the phone to me if they say otherwise. We'll need an ambulance if we can get one."

Betty went to the living room and dialed the phone while Laura stuck Hank with an injection of antibiotics. Hank didn't feel a thing, having lapsed into a coma. His breathing was even more shallow, and when Laura extracted the thermometer, it read ninety-four. This is a lot worse than five minutes ago, she thought, startled.

"The hospital said that it wasn't safe to come to the hospital, and to do what we can," said a frightened Betty.

"I told you to let me talk to them," shot back Laura.

"I know, but the line went dead and then wouldn't connect." She took one look at her husband's worsening condition, and then added, "Why don't we just take him?"

Hank started shaking from the spine out until Laura feared he'd shake himself off of the bed. She looked around the room, finding several boxes of pantyhose. She opened the tiny boxes as fast as she could open them. "Here, help me tie his legs and arms. We'll have to keep control, or he's liable to become a danger to himself as well as us. He's going into seizures. Put a pillow under his feet, and get several blankets. We need to warm him up and get his blood into his head."

Once Hank was secure, Laura tried the hospital herself, getting nothing. She dialed 911, receiving a busy signal. "911 isn't taking our call. This could be some kind of plague; maybe even biological warfare. Whatever it is, it has overloaded the system. We're going to have to do this ourselves. It isn't safe to move him until we have a place we know we can move him to quickly," rationalized Laura out loud.

"What can we do?"

"Keep him warm and his feet elevated. If he gets warm enough, he'll come out of his, (she caught herself from saying coma), sleep. He isn't nauseous, which is both good and highly unusual. I don't know these exact symptoms, but it's probably new and it might have something to do with the hospital being swamped. It doesn't look to me like they're doing much better than we are here, so let's get busy," said Laura as she found a t-shirt in another drawer. She folded it in half and tied it around her face as a mask before handing one to Betty. "This acts like a disease, only in so far as it's quick. We'll have to watch ourselves."

Betty took the mask, soon only her eyes showing the new, more personal level of fear. Laura listened to Hank's heart, it so weak that she had to try several places. Whatever was wrong was killing him, she understood. Blood pressure nearly nothing, pulse weak, shallow airflow, bone cold, and into a coma in minutes, were a sum that told a morbid tale. She went for her bag, sticking him again, this time with heart medication, just in case it was all due to a heart attack that she'd not detected in the usual way. What could it hurt; the heart was going anyway?

Laura was worried about Hank, but Hank was as good as gone, she realized. One minute later, his temperature was down to ninety-three. She'd never even heard of a temperature that low on a live human being. She was sure his brain was suffering for it, the continuous shakes a visible sign of the damage going on in there. No, Hank was as good as dead because he was falling too fast, she understood, and now Betty was going to have to be treated.

"You go get some rest. He has settling down now. Here's some medication to help you sleep. I'll watch over him, OK?" Indeed, Hank's shakes were settling, but only Laura knew that it meant he'd slipped into that bottomless coma from which no mortal escapes.

Betty gave one worried look, bent down to kiss his cheek, and then thought better of it when Laura's masked face shook a vigorous no. "He might be contagious. There's a lot we don't know. You just go lie down. I'll watch him and call around. Sooner or later the crisis at the hospital will pass and it'll be our turn to get some help."

Betty went to the spare room while Laura watched Hank die. Die he did, and quickly. Within ten minutes of Betty's departure, Hank's skin was room temperature, an unusually fast fall even for a dead man. His heart had stopped two minutes sooner than that, a fact that Laura attributed to Hank's good health. Laura pricked his finger with a pin, and it didn't bleed; pressure zero. It just didn't seem real that a fully grown, healthy adult should die so quickly from virtually nothing, worried Laura. There seemed only one explanation, and that was unthinkable: Biological or chemical warfare. His skin was blotchy in some spots, a very unusual symptom, which Laura photographed with Betty's cheap digital camera.

"Well, if it's a biological thing, I have to isolate it," mused Laura. She put on a fresh pair of latex gloves, and scraped his skin near the wound, putting that into a baggie. She scraped the worst of the blotching as well. Then she took a blood sample, which wasn't easy, considering that there was no pressure and the vessels had all gone flat.

Getting some large leaf bags from the kitchen, she wrapped his stiffening legs and tied off the bag restraint at his waist. Using a second bag, she made a hole for his head, and worked the bag over him like a shirt. The pair of trash bags made a reasonable body bag. Then she rolled him up tight in a blanket for appearances sake. A second blanket formed a shroud that made him look like he was comfortably sleeping with his head covered, that for when Betty came in.

Poor Hank; wasn't a bad guy for a brother-in-law, she thought as she sat down to look at her work. Dialing around, she found every number she dialed to be a dead line. After awhile, she couldn't even get dial-tone.

The lights flickered, setting several appliance LEDs back to zero.

"Oh, come on. Something has to be working," she told herself, turning the small bedroom television on.

"This is a test of the emergency broadcast system. You are advised to stay tuned to this channel for further instructions." It was the same empty promise of information on all four channels, the others apparently completely off the air. The radio was equally useless, which surprised her, considering how many radio stations existed. This late at night, I should be getting New York or Chicago, she thought.

"This is a big problem, Laura. Something is very wrong out there in Indian country," she told herself, turning the volume down and then looking out the window, barely cracking the curtain. A dog barked in the distance, and then suddenly yelped as if struck before going silent.

"Yeah," she said, confirming a thought. It struck her that without the public safety net, everyone was a potential victim. She scurried around the house, making sure that all of the doors and windows were locked. Then she doused the lights, except for the one where Hank slept, where she reinforced the curtain with some towels to make sure the light stayed in.

It's going to smell like hell in here soon, thought Laura after waking up from a four hour nap. It wouldn't do to have Betty walk in and smell Hank ripening, so she went into the kitchen. She flipped a light on. Finding a big can of floral air freshener, she turned the kitchen light back off and returned to her chair by the corpse.

"Sssssssssssssss!" The spray landed on the shroud. Laura sat down, and tried to relax her tied up nerves.

A bang on the front door startled Laura, who had nodded off. Her finger twitched, wetting a spot on her knee with a short blast of floral air freshener. She had to hold her other hand to her chest in order to keep her heart in her chest. Nothing like a knock, the bang had sounded more like someone's body was trying to break the door in.

Creeping into the living room, Laura got there just in time to see the door bulge from a second pounding. She jumped back into the corner between a chair and a corner side table.

"What's going on?" Asked Betty as she exited the room she'd been sleeping in at the end of the hallway. The intermittent electrical service had the bedroom light flickering around the woman. Between her and Laura, Hank's green trash bag wrapped body fell into the hallway and crashed to the wall adjacent to his room. Hank tripped to the floor.

"My god, you stupid bitch! What have you done to my husband?" Screamed Betty.

Someone's body slammed into the living room door again, this time accompanied by the sound of the door frame cracking. One more blow and whoever is out there is going to be in here, understood Laura.

Betty had fallen to her husband, her hands flailing at the trash bags. "Hank, are you alright?" Trash bags ripped aside, she bent to hug him.

"Betty. There's someone trying to break in. I'm sorry about the bags, but Hank is...." She'd meant to say that Hank was dead, but then she saw his eyes looking up at Betty and the words wouldn't come. Hank is, somehow, alive, she understood. Of course he's alive, she had to tell herself; after all, he has just walked into the hallway!

No, no, no, this isn't right. Nothing about this night is right, Laura told herself, remembering the lack of radio and public services. "This is all wrong!" She managed to say to Betty just before the front door slammed open and two teenaged boy zombies toppled into the unlit living room. Then, to herself, she said, "I'm dreaming! Wake up!" Exactly the opposite was in the works though because Laura's head growing light, swimming in a sea of fainting stars.

Out of the corner of her fainting eyes, Laura saw Hank's head reach up and capture Betty's nose so tightly that she could hear the cartilage crushing. Blood squirted out in all directions as Betty screamed into Hank's neck. Hank's head shook like that on a mad dog, ripping. Betty's hair waved in concert, like a mop being shaken out. Blood splashed across the walls in the hallway, seemingly far too much for one little nose. Suddenly Betty broke free, her head snapping back to upright, where Laura could see the ragged hole where once Betty's nose had been.

"Oh," moaned Laura. She'd finally seen enough and succumbed to the faint, falling the last few inches between the chair and side table. Her hand still clutched the can of air freshener. Both the hand and air freshener were soon wedged against the wall. The wall pinched against the button. A plume of air freshener rose above Laura's fainted form, as if she'd become the base of Old Faithful. The can sprayed for a whole minute until the propellant ran out.

In the mean time, Hank ate a little of his wife's arm. Betty watched herself being consumed. The hallway was too cramped for her to get away, leaving her no options other than to watch him lunch. She thought her life already over since she no longer had a nose and blood from it was soaking the entire front of her night shirt. Still, in spite of all of the bleeding, it wasn't enough to kill her through the meal. She fought desperately for balance, but couldn't find it. She didn't pass into her final faint until Hank came away with one of her pinky fingers. He decided the finger wasn't the best of pickings, and spit it out in perfect time with the nodding of Betty's head.

The teenaged zombie boys found their feet. There'd once been movement, they knew, but now the living room was silent. Only an inorganic hiss could be heard, it soon fading. In the hall though, there was some activity, which they promptly joined, ignoring the snarls of Hank who guarded his meal. The hunger was greater than Hank's threat though, all three zombies knew.

They all three munched on arms and legs. Betty, though in her last coma, lasted long enough for the legs and arms to all be substantially chowed upon. Then, of course, she grew cold and the fun was over; the life they craved, and only imagined obtainable through the mortal act of eating, was gone.

Noses coated with dripping blood sniffed.

The zombies wandered through the rooms.

Betty, as if eager to set a record as the shortest transition between human being and zombie, got up and though poor at the craft, sniffed through the huge nose holes in her skull. One by one, they wandered through each of the rooms, and then back into the dim living room, sniffed with crunched up faces of displeasure. Satisfied that the cheap floral smell that reeked in the living room couldn't possibly be that of a life, they found their way back out the front door, thinking, maybe next door.

When the sun came up, Laura woke, her head again splitting. Nobody was about, and the street was deserted. Half of the houses on the block had their doors standing open. Across the street, a window was splattered with what Laura could only guess was blood.

Laura sank back into her sister's house, truly frightened. It felt unreal, as if she'd awoken in hell without a welcoming committee. She was too tired to think about what might be the best thing to do, or even to mourn her recently dead sister. The head was back to that migraine condition. I have to find a dark room, a bottle of pills, and a bed, she knew, working her way past the pools of blood to the room her sister had slept in the night before. She locked it, stuffed some rags under the seam and propped a chair up against the handle. Twice the normal Darvon swallowed, she slept.

22

Something about those legs, thought Jimmy as he stood on the grey office linoleum for the first time since he'd died. The legs were rubber, he thought as he wobbled, giving his mind a few seconds to adjust to the new equilibrium. Damn if the room isn't bright, he thought as he lifted his eyes a bit and scanned the place. Um, but it sure smells positively great, like a barbecue in full smoke. His nose got into the act at about the same time that his legs adjusted and his eyes started to pick out the pickings.

Joe bluntly said, "Uh oh, Chief. It looks like your boy is a zombie."

Sandra pulled her service revolver from a freshly acquired shoulder holster, but the Chief slapped it out of her hand with the butt of his shotgun.

"Now wait a minute, here Chief!" She screamed, as she held her pained hand. The Chief kicked the pistol into a remote corner and held his shotgun on the crew as he backed out of reach.

"Ain't nobody going to shoot my son, now. You hear me!"

"Damn, and I was so looking forward to it," said Joe.

"You would, you prick. I haven't liked you since the first I laid eyes on you," said the Chief, waving the business end of his shotgun at Joe's chest.

"Well look, I was just speaking figuratively. No offense. Just my way of showing my dissatisfaction for the man who lied and said he saw me murdered a man. People like that deserve issues."

"Hey guys. We have bigger problems. We can work this out," said Dominique in her best lawyer voice. Jimmy had just banged into a desk and was looking for a way around.

"You all get over there with him," said the Chief, waving his shotgun at them.

"What, and let him chow down on us? You have to be insane! I'd just as soon you shot us! You can't get us all before we get to you," Said Sandra.

"No need for that. You just catch him, but be careful. I don't want him hurt," said Baker.

"You don't want him hurt? Hell, Baker, he's dead; haven't you noticed the green complexion?" Asked Joe.

"That's the disease. You don't know he can't be fixed."

"That's not the tune you were spouting when we came in here. Nothing but excuses for why you spent the night gunning down the neighborhoods. It took all of half a second to shoot Stan here. Far as we know it, your men gunned down as many innocent people as zombies last night. What, your son has a disease? Be careful, he bruises easily, but the peasants are terminal? What's different Chief?" Asked Joe.

"Just get!" Baker's barrel waved threateningly.

Joe saw that Dominique was closest. She's a tough lady, but not necessarily a street brawler, he realized. He jumped between her and Jimmy.

"This is not a good idea, Baker. You know what you have to do with these things. That's what you convinced us needed down just a minute ago. Well, I'm convinced. Jimmy's dead! Jimmy doesn't want to be like this."

"That's with a lot of them. Jimmy's only one boy. We can isolate him. Take him to the doctor when this is over and the squads aren't so busy. Their tissue sticks together pretty good; I've seen a lot of them. He wasn't hurt so bad. It was just a few grazing bites. When this is over, they can fix him up," said the Chief optimistically.

Joe whispered, "Have him fixed. Now there's an idea. Should have had that done yourself, Bevis," as he ducked Jimmy's first attempt to grab him. Joe backed around, hoping to keep the zombie's attention, and keep him away from the kid and women.

Sandra saw an opening. She kicked Jimmy in the small of his back from behind, knocking him onto his face as Joe leapt back. Joe finished the job by shoving a desk over onto Jimmy. A drawer fell open, coating Jimmy in a wash of pens and paper, but the desk had him pinned to the floor. It was nearly the same trick they'd seen Purswell's crew use.

"Stop being so useless and toss us some cuffs, Chief," said Sandra. Joe helped her cuff the hands, remembering how Jimmy had overly tightened his. He made sure to return the favor, though he had doubts zombies concerned themselves with such trivialities.

"Don't let him scratch at you, Mister Joe," offered Stanley. Joe took the hint, unbuttoned Jimmy's shirt, and pulled the material down to help cover his cuffed hands and upper arms with the loosened material.

"We need a leash," said Joe.

Sandra pulled the coffee pot chord free, handing it to Joe, who used it to tie up Jimmy's ankles. The squirming zombie soon looked like a legless alligator, thrashing around, chomping threats with his teeth.

"Now you get back over toward there," said the Chief, nodding towards the cellblock door with his weapon.

"You're kidding me?" Said Sandra.

"You heard me! Get!"

They walked back toward the main block door.

Dominique tried, "This is illegal, Chief. You do this; it's not just a civil case."

"In!"

"Thought you said you still represented the law around here?" Asked Joe.

"Bam!" The Chief shot a hole in the roof as an answer. They opened the door and walked into the cellblock. Chief Baker kicked the door closed behind them, it automatically locking.

They were in the main cell room, the cells themselves a step or two further in and separated by an aisle. Sandra looked out through the ten inch square cellblock window, seeing Baker move his son over by a steam pipe. Baker tied the boy's ankle restraints to the pipe. Then the Chief dialed the phone awhile, but gave up after several minutes, choosing to wait it out and set post just inside the office's broken out window.

"Asshole. Out of all the towns to pick to be a cop in, I picked this one. That's just totally lame. I thought police officers were supposed to be heroes. I didn't know that we still had Smoky and the Bandits," said Sandra.

"I think we all made that mistake, sweetheart. And trust me, cops are like everybody else, some good, some apathetic, some crooks with licenses. The only way I make money on civil cases against the cops is because most of them do a reasonable enough job to make the bad ones stick out," agreed Dominique.

"Joe! Buddy! Hey, thanks for the meal. You have no idea how good the eating has been here since you left, cept' for maybe the last couple. Seems the jail keep is on vacation. Wouldn't happen to have a sandwich on you, would you?" Asked Truck.

"Hey, Truck. You still in here? Thought you'd be long gone by now," said Joe, walking up to their old cell.

"Just me and Andy here. They took the drunks out yesterday. Smell's much improved since, if you ask me," said the big man.

"Steaks and onions! Steaks and onion! Joe, the murderer is back, yep, yep, yep!" Said Andy. Andy grabbed his cup, but Truck put a fist over his wrist and shook his head no. Let go, Andy found a bunk, which he sat on. He smiled picturesquely and with adamant attention.

"I used to think Andy was nuts. You should have a look outside," said Joe.

"What's up? All we hear in here are gunshot and a yell or two," said Truck.

"I don't expect for you to believe this, but there seems to be a problem with zombies. People are turning into stiffs and then the stiffs are coming back to life; hungry. They as much as wing you, you're one of them," said Joe.

"Cool," said Andy.

"You know, Andy, you'd best watch out. You look and act a lot like a zombie. Get you out there, and someone is apt to get confused, so stick with us, once we leave. It's one of those kill or be killed sort of things out there, as best I judge it. There may even be authorities paying for pelts," said Joe.

Truck said, "Hey, well, doin in zombies can be a living, I suppose. I never was much for telling a person how to earn a buck. So, what are they doing, shooting them in the head like in the movies?"

"Yeah. That's what we've been doing. We do have another small problem, however. This isn't a visit. The Chief has locked us in here because his boy, Jimmy, has turned, and he has gotten a bit paranoid about it," said Joe.

Sandra spoke, "We can work on these hinges, Joe. This door isn't as secure as the ones on the cell. They've only put the lock on it as an afterthought." She fiddled in her purse and extracting a wicked looking Swiss pocket knife.

"OK. Then, once out, we can get the keys and let these two out. We'll need their help. They've already been in here longer than their original offenses warrant, and besides, the Chief can't leave them to the zombies," said Joe.

Dominique agreed, "The most important part is that we need them. What if there are a lot of those things out there, like Baker said? Are there any guns in this office?"

"In the safe room. We can get to that with the keys too. Just have to get this door off and wait for the Chief to bugger off," said Sandra.

"You with her or her?" Asked Truck.

"Her."

"Good. That means I'm free to put the moves on your lawyer," whispered Truck.

"Hey, I'm not a wishbone, boys," protested Dominique with the small voice of someone distracted by bigger thoughts.

"We have bigger problems, Truck. I'm not going to tell you to not think romance, but uh, the town may well be full of zombies, and for the time being, we're all stuck in jail with the only man close to the keys, out there. He, unfortunately, is completely off his rocker."

"Um, yeah. I guess I'll just have to wait until evening. I mean, ma'am, I'm just asking for a date. Dinner, maybe?" Asked Truck.

"Sure. We get out of here; we get dinner," yielded Dominique.

Dinner was delayed through the day. Joe and Sandra worked at the bolts holding the three hinges on, managing two out of the nine. The problem was that the bolts were far bigger than the screwdriver on the knife, forcing them to chip out concrete.

"We can all starve to death in here," observed Dominique.

Stanley had gotten friendly with Truck, his first real life prisoner encounter. "You know, I once saw in a movie, this guy took his shirt off and wrapped it around two bars and then took a stick and twisted the shirt. The bars just bent and the prisoners walked right out."

"Huh," huffed Truck, who promptly tried it and ripped the sleeve off of his shirt in the process. "Are we getting anywhere?" Truck asked as the room started to get dark.

"No! Well, we'll get out before we starve to death, but I've been thinking: That might be too late," said Joe as he rested from working a bolt.

"Why?" Asked Sandra, taking a rest as well. She sat beside Joe, close, resting her head on his shoulder.

"Purswell! We've forgotten all about him, but I've been thinking about those crates and in particular, what they might mean to us. What was that paper taped to them? Do you remember the color?"

"UPS! Damn, he's shipping those zombies out of town!"

"Yeah. That's it. We could barely hear what they were saying. At the time we were thinking differently about his angle with the corpses too. Now though, considering what we've learned since, new pieces are fitting together. It just all makes too much sense. The man is nuttier than we thought, maybe even nuttier than Baker. He's exporting zombies," said Joe.

Dominique asked, "Why would someone want to ship zombies? That's totally stupid!"

"The dead in Christ shall rise. But, before that, according to Purswell, the evil dead will inherit the earth. Only the saved and righteous shall be spared for the great resurrection, which he is banking on happening as soon as the evil dead take over the planet."

"That's a bunch of hogwash!" Said Truck.

"That's pretty much what he told us in his office," agreed Sandra.

"Yeah, and the sooner the better, as far as he's concerned. Ship the zombies all over the country, or who knows, maybe all over the world, and it's part one of the plan in spades. Imagine these things all over the place, coming at us from all directions at once? It is going to be hard to stop them in places where things aren't as organized as they are here in Ohio, like West Virginia, Michigan and Indiana, for example," said Joe.

"We have to stop him," said Sandra.

"Shoot, we've spent the whole day in here. How far has he gotten? Some of the meat was already packed and driven off when we jumped in and found the freezer of zombies! Vans moving! The fire department probably never made it. He has probably come back for more since the last load. We're way behind the eight ball on this," Exclaimed Joe.

"We could at least find out where he sent them and contact the authorities," offered Dominique.

"I like the thought, dear, but it still leaves us right where we're at. We need to get the hell out of here! I am hungry!" Said Truck.

"Give me that chair leg you used to rip your shirt up with," said Dominique, making reference to Truck's failed attempt at bending his cell door bars. In spite of the insult regarding his failure, he handed it through the bars with a smile at the gorgeous, middle aged lawyer. Dominique wasted no time in swinging the stick, startling everyone as she smashed the small door window out in one blow.

She yelled through the new opening, "Listen up, Baker. I'm going to give you one chance to get this right, otherwise, the lawsuit you face is going to make you into my little puppy dog throughout all of those long awaited retirement years! Here doggie, doggie, doggie! Am I making contact? Yoo-hoo, alien mind!" She was feeling better.

"You just leave me alone, bitch!" Yelled Baker. At first he'd flinched at the glass's breakage, but had gone back to his vigil of looking out the window. The sun was nearly gone, but since he'd not turned on the lights, his face was an orange, sundown glow.

"Fortunate for you, however, I'm a good lawyer. Do you know what good lawyers are known for, Mister Baker? I'm going to tell you. Good lawyers settle nearly everything out of court. Neither side is perfectly happy, but they end up with most of what they want, and most importantly, nothing nearly as bad as they feared. Case closed, allowing each party to get on with new business."

"Your point, bitch!" Said the Chief, no longer bothering with diplomatic language.

It was better than being told to leave him alone, Dominique noticed. "We don't need your kid. He's your problem; he always was. What the hell would we do with him if we had him? Your whole reason for putting us in here never made sense from the start. As for us being locked in here, which is quite literally a kidnapping charge that carries a sentence sure to spell the last time you'll ever eat at whatever your favorite Porkie's is, we can forget it. Why? Well because we want out; simple as that. Things need done that aren't even remotely connected to your little family problem. We chalk it all up to your being distraught. So, from ground zero, we deal. Do you read me? You get our word that we ignore your kid, and we go our way, and we all forget your moment of utter stupidity. Otherwise, you have to worry about us, one way or the other, which can't be a pleasant thing, I imagine, given we'd all like to strangle your ugly ass!"

"You go away, and I stay here knowing you keep your yaps shut about Jimmy. Is that what your saying? How can I trust you?"

Joe jumped to the small window, having had a thought. "It's easy, Chief. We have a bigger problem than this. Remember that preacher, Purswell?"

"Yeah. What's his problem?"

"We've put two and two together in here, and the only thing that makes sense from what we know about him is that he is shipping these zombies all over the place. He's the one who is robbing the morgues and gravesites. The man's nuts. Our problems aren't about this little town anymore, nor are they about the few of us. If he ships those zombies around, what's the world going to be looking like when it's morning? We have to stop this, Chief. We have to go find somebody who is in contract with the rest of the world and warn them," Joe explained.

"It ain't my problem. Not our jurisdiction either. You had no business poking around in someone else's town in the first place."

"OK, fine; it's not our jurisdiction, but that still leaves us with an entire organization shipping zombies around the country and aiming them at the general population. Terrorism is everyone's problem, Chief. If you don't see that, then at least let us take it on. What do you have to lose? With us out there, how long do you think it'll be before we're attacked? You'd do better without us, because, like Ms. Sawyer says, if you pass up this chance, we're going to break out of here and put a bullet through your head."

"Big talker!"

"Just don't go to sleep. Either us or them will get you. Can't keep your face to both doors forever," threatened Joe.

"Alright. You walk, but I'm giving you two minutes to clear the lot. You got that?"

"We're taking your prisoners with us too," said Joe.

"No way"

"Fine. No deal. We'll wait you out. Hell, Chief, it's not a law thing; its a simple humanitarian gesture. What are you going to do with your prisoners anyway; leave them to the zombies?" Asked Joe.

The Chief grabbed the keys out of his desk, and handed them through the broken cell door window. "Just make it fast. Anything to get rid of you. I'm counting those two minutes off starting now!"

Joe freed the prisoners and then reached through the window to unlock the block door. They walked out, escorted by the barrel end of Baker's shotgun.

"No pauses. Just keep right on walking out the door," he said, waving his weapon.

Sandra chimed in, "We'll need some weapons."

"Well, of course you will, honey. You'd be entitled to one too, assuming I'd not fired you, which, I'm delighted to say, I just have. These things get real active, come nightfall. Too bad you've made your lot with this sort," said Baker.

"Don't push it, dear. Fine enough; a deal's a deal," said Joe, holding her back and making his way out of the police office door.

Chief Baker was waiting for them when they walked out of the building door. He was at the window, still aiming his shotgun at them as they made the lawn.

"Just keep on walking, right on across Hamilton, and through those houses over there. There used to be a whole bunch of them milling around about there, and I want to personally introduce you to them," he insisted.

23

Baker watched dusk crawl around the edges of the town, and then make its way into the police station. Sandra, Joe and their gang had been gone for most of an hour before Chief Baker realized that the street lights weren't going to come on either, telling him that both public and private electric companies were out. Every so often, human-like shadows danced between the rows of houses across Hamilton until even that wasn't easily seen.

"I've played this wrong," he told himself, realizing the mistake of making enemies out of Officer Anderson's group for no gain. They might have let him keep Jimmy and kept guard as well while he slept, he grew to understand, remembering the lawyer's words. Now he was alone, and it was night; night in a whole different sense of the word than what he'd grown up believing in. Night, last night, was when it had all gone to hell, he recalled. These things don't like sunlight much, though they don't melt entirely away from it like vampires. I've been up for nearly two days straight, he bemused, excusing himself for having lost his head with the group, and at the same time, making a connection with his own mortal exhaustion.

Baker shook his head, having found himself sleeping with his eyes open, only to awaken seeing a zombie standing right in the middle of Hamilton Avenue. He recognized the dress as a formal sleeping gown, the kind one might put on a body before burying it. Picking up his binoculars for a closer look, he saw no blood, other than a trickle or two on the middle aged woman's chin. Yeah, this is a clean one, probably from the graveyard, he determined, remembering how Sandra had gone on about Purswell's grave robbing. He'd only half believed her, but now, with a reduced sense of skepticism regarding the impossible, he knew she'd been telling the truth.

Setting a bead on the female zombie with his shotgun, he thought about shooting, but decided better of it. He'd have dropped her; having reloaded with slugs, a better kill potential for long range shooting. However, the noise will attract others, he decided, looking over at Jimmy. They'd done that last night, he remembered. Some of the fresher zombies had focused in on the shooting, and had even gotten a little calculating about it. Some primordial instincts and even a few sparks of higher level thinking might still be active in the things, he realized. Just the fact that they'd been so successful against the general population, and were multiplying so swiftly, spoke to the folly of underestimating them.

He smacked himself on the cheek, waking again. The zombie wasn't in the street anymore. "Jesus, Baker. We have to get out of here. We can't do this alone. You have to find someone to help you out," he told himself as he want to the drinking fountain to slosh some water over his eyes. Water pressure was still there, but he'd passed an open hydrant, turned fountain, the night before, and wondered for how long?

So, what are the options, he thought? I can try to find the group I've just vanquished, he thought. Jimmy has a hard-on for them; scent and all. They'd be going for the west bridge. Chances are, they've found a car and driven off, well out of town by now, or maybe been eaten? Or maybe holed up, waiting out a crowd, he wondered?

They'd be grateful for a rescue. No, that's stupid, he thought; they're not my kind of people, any way a man spells it. I've jerked them off too much to expect their help anyway. Best find another use for the pricks.

Then Baker filled out the idea that had been forming in his head. He looked at his son. Joe's group had written him off, but Baker couldn't imagine writing off his own son. If not a write-off, then what? A helper? Could he win the boy's trust? How? What might a zombie's heart and soul be purchased with? What's their currency? "OK, Jimmy. We're going to have to help one another. I need your instincts. I need your radar. Can you smell them? Can you smell out the living?"

Jimmy looked over, just like always, a hunger and hurt in his deep, dark eyes. "Umm!"

Baker reworked Jimmy's bonds. He fastened a chain around his son's waist, and then cuffed his upper arms to it so that Jimmy had flexible use of only his forearms. The cuffs were tight, cutting off all circulation above the elbows, but Baker knew that was no longer an issue, or at least not until he could get the boy to a doctor and have him cured. The chains on Jimmy's ankles were set, using two pair or chains in order to give him a long stride, long enough to walk, but not to run.

The boy's hands were apt to be a problem. Chief Baker was aware of the effect a single scratch might have. He had a thought about that. Done with the bondage, he cuffed his son's leg shackles to the steam pipe again, and then opened the arsenal in the far corner of the room.

"M16, thirty round banana clips, duct tape." He brought that and some other gear over to his son, and pushed the boy over onto his face. Loosening some duct tape off the roll, he taped the fingers on Jimmy's right hand, and then his three small fingers on his left hand. Rolling Jimmy over, Baker taped the boy's hands to the M-16. The right hand was duct taped to the hand guard. His left fingers were secured near the trigger area. With nowhere else to go, Jimmy's left trigger finger fell into the finger well. Baker righted the boy, patting him on both shoulders in salute.

"Ha! Now you're a trooper again. Now listen up! We're going to go out there and find our way out of here. We're going to get you fed, and then get you some help, and we're going to get you fixed. Understand?" Jimmy looked at his dad as if trying to understand, and then suddenly leaned forward. "Snap!" His jaws tried for a bite.

Chief Baker jumped back, having half expected it.

"That's alright, son. I know you have an impulse to eat me. Just know this: It ain't gonna happen. We can work together, and you can eat whatever else you want. Just not me. Think about that. You hear me? We've got a deal. Anything we find out there is fair game. You and I together can find more targets than either of us alone. You take me off your snacking list, and I'll help you find all the food you ever wanted. Now, we're going to work our way out of here. When I say shoot, you're going to help me by shooting this thing. Just like when we used to go hunting. You remember that? We got it down to instinct then, you and I."

Jimmy furrowed his brows, and moaned.

"When I say shoot, you shoot. Listen up.

Shoot!"

"Uh!" Jimmy moaned, clearly responding to the command—though barely.

"That's a good start. Now you understand that you need to do something. Now the finger!" Baker tapped Jimmy's left hand. "The finger, when I say shoot.

Shoot!"

"Click," the M-16 fired on a dead chamber.

"There you go. You and I are going hunting for food. Eat! Food! Eat!" Baker pointed at his own open mouth. "Shoot! Eat!"

"Umm!" Jimmy said, pulling the trigger, but without results since the firing chamber hadn't been set by his father nor from the gas off of an exploding round.

Baker recharged the rifle's charging rod and said, "Shoot!"

"Click!" The rifle hit another empty chamber.

"That's my boy!" Baker slapped Jimmy on the shoulder.

Using one last piece of duct tape, he taped Jimmy's mouth shut while saying, "Sorry, son, but I can't have you biting me. When we shoot something, I'll take that off and let you have the first bite, hear? Now let's go hunting, son."

Chief Baker got himself ready with a backpack half full of food, ammunition and a throw-down pistol. He then slung his own shotgun. Baker led Jimmy out into the star and moon encased world, and helped his son into the cruiser. Jimmy's barrel extended out the passenger window. Baker got behind the wheel. He slapped a banana clip of bullets into Jimmy's weapon and charged the chamber. Their cruiser pulled out onto Hamilton where it soon turned towards the route to the west bridge.

Jimmy sat in the car, the smell of food next to him excruciatingly tempting. Still, he knew just barely enough to know that he couldn't get at it all bound up and with the tape on his mouth, and besides, a little bird in his head was telling him that the man beside him would help him find even more food. It didn't make the least bit of sense that the man would do that, but he'd wait a little bit before going for the ready meal. There was other food out there too, he knew. Smells blew in from outside the window. Every so often one of them bore a brief whiff of the living, which sent his head jerking to keep up with the wind as each sniff found the back seat.

Words rambled in his mind around the exciting blend of aromas. Eat! Food! Shoot! “Bam!” he fired a round through the open window as they turned down High Street.

24

"Maybe we should get up and run through them. They don't look too fast to me," Stanley said to Joe. He patted his baseball bat. It was the smallest of four they'd found in a back yard, but was nearly as tall as Stanley.

"Some are faster than others, and we don't know who's around other than the ones we see. Do you know how long you can run without getting tired, son? What if there are others on the other end of the bridge. What happens when we get there tired and find out that since they don't breath like we do, they don't tire either?" Asked Joe.

"They don't seem to get winded, that's for sure. In fact, they ain't even breathing, so maybe they can't get winded at all. Of course, they're kind of slow too, so it might just be that," said Truck.

"Good points. We have a lot to learn about their limitations and capabilities. One thing for sure, they're determined and have caught the town with its collective pants down. All the more reason that we should give our move a little thought," said Joe.

"Whatever you say, Mister Joe, but I don't like hanging in these shrubs; they got jiggers nipping at me in here."

Somewhere across the river, a house fire lit the scene before them. There was another grind as a dozen of the zombies shoved another car into the middle of the three way intersection in the middle of Pine Point's old town hub. The automobile came grudgingly, first the back and then the front, it being forced sideways, zombies apparently not all that savvy at car pushing skills. This one was a minivan, a lady's arm still hanging out of the driver's side window. Fresh blood was smeared on the outside of the door from where one zombie had recently taken a lethal chunk out of her wrist. The woman had bled out in two minutes, wasting the meal for the others, who apparently had no interest in dead meat.

Joe had seen enough such scenes, growing wary to keep their group downwind and in the shadow side of the raising moonlight. That seemed to be an edge that had helped kept them alive, he realized, noticing that there were either a lot more dead people around than living ones, or else the other living ones were doing a spectacular job of hiding. Apparently some of Pine Point's residents were still alive though. For example, he knew that the woman in the minivan had met a recent demise; she'd not yet turned.

"We can't just wait them out. Someone will come in behind us and smell us out before daylight. It's like they all have their noses in the air," said Dominique.

"Why don't we just hike a car?" Asked Stanley.

"We will, but we need one with the keys in it, and with not a lot of their tainted blood. Not to mention, it'd be easier if we grabbed our car on the other side of this barricades, given there are so many of them around the bridge at this intersection. I think they're aware of the fact that this is a likely choke point," said Sandra.

"That's right about the choke point, as well as the blood. We don't know how far this infection goes. One scratch did in Jimmy. Maybe one drop of blood does it as well," said Joe.

Sandra said, "I don't know, Joe. We touched some when the caretaker died. It must be like AIDS. You just don't want anything getting into a cut, or a lot of it ingested."

"Still, the very thought of getting too close to these monsters freaks me out, ever since I saw Jimmy come back; not that it couldn't have happened to a nicer guy," said Joe.

"We can hotwire a car. I bet I can. Just cross some big wires, and see what happens," said Stanley.

"Yeah!" Agreed Andy. Truck slapped a hand over Andy's mouth before the man could say anything else.

Sandra explained, "They do that in the movies. Cars are a lot different than they used to be. Steering wheels lock; keys are magnetic. Lots of things are different. We'll need one of those out there on the road; one with keys in it."

Joe noticed, "This roadblock is nearly right in front of the bridge, and it's closing up fast. If we're going across in a car, we'd better do it fast. If we don't cross here, we're going to have to go back through town or downriver to the next crossing. That's a long way to go and I'd expect more zombies and more obstacles. At least what we see in front of us is upwind and in the open. These things seem to have a single thought, and a comparably singular skill; catching people."

"Like spiders," agreed Truck.

"Eating them too, huh Truck. They catch them and then they eat them, huh?" Said Andy, as if it was really good news that he'd made that discovery.

"Make up our mind for us, Joe. First you say we should wait, and now you say we need to make a run for it," noticed Dominique, a woman not used to wasting time.

Joe said, "Well, that van is tempting. Big enough for us all. Keys likely to still be in it. The lady's still dead and as long as she stays that way, it's an edge. She bled mostly on the outside of the vehicle. Problem is, the van is surrounded by three dozen cannibals and none of us can afford to take strikes with these bats with that kind of a crowd going for us."

Truck decided, "We need a diversion."

"I was thinking the same thing, but just didn't want to be the one to suggest it and make it look like I was volunteering," said Sandra.

"Good god, have none of us any valor," said Dominique. She shook her head and ducked back into the taller shrubs.

"OK, so what's your plan," Joe asked Truck.

"I say some of us run and hit one of them and play it by ear while someone goes for the van," said Truck.

"Not very creative, Truck," said Joe.

"You got a better idea?" Asked Truck.

"Yoo-hoo! Zombies!"

Dominique had worked her way between a couple buildings, and was tossing her shoes at the crowd of living dead. "Yoo-hoo! Tasty lady lawyer here! Nice legs! Lawyer! Everyone hates lawyers; especially you slow, ugly, dead people! "

Truck looked at the rest of the perplexed group and said, "Well, what do you say to attract a bunch of zombies? Problem is, that's the love of my life out there doing our dirty work for us. I ain't even got one kiss out of her yet. Shame to waste something so pretty."

Joe and Sandra were too preoccupied with the shifting events to ask Truck how he'd come to the conclusion that Dominique was the love of his life. As far as they knew, the pair had hardly spoken.

The closest two zombies fell over each other turning around and scrambling toward the voice of the breathing lawyer. In seconds, the whole crowd hurdled the cars and formed a gang that worked its way toward the new meat. Only a pair of zombies wandered perplexed, or perhaps just fatalistic regarding their chances at getting to Dominique in time to grab a living bite. Within seconds, all but two of the zombies disappeared between the buildings where Dominique had fled.

"Well, let's get at it. No point in wasting a good ruse," said Sandra, stepping out into the open and holding her baseball bat in front of her as she advanced.

"The women have more balls than we do, Joe. This is getting embarrassing. I'm going for Dominique. I'm kind of keen on her," said Truck, ducking back through the shrubs. Andy followed Truck like he was the bigger man's puppy.

"OK. You and me, sport. Watch my back," Joe said to Stanley as they stepped out and moved beside Sandra.

"I won't let nobody eat you, Mister Joe!"

A dead man in a green business suit saw them first. He stumbled forward, one leg crooked from a break that he apparently didn't feel. His yellow tie wobbled with each stride, the gait no more than a walk, though it looked far more energetic due to the wobble. Sandra laid the first swing against the zombie's head. A sickening bash only slowed the man's next stride. Sandra stumbled back, not expecting the dead man's determination.

Joe connected with an overhead pop that disoriented the zombie. It started a slow rotation in the street, as if he'd slipped a gyro.

Stanley smacked under the knee on the man's crooked leg, folding the leg over in a place where there wasn't supposed to be a joint. The zombie fell. The boy hit the fallen zombie again, right over an ear. It jittered a few seconds and then stilled, as if returning to the beautiful slumber of death. "Gotta get them down on the ground where you can deal with them," said Stanley. Clearly, he was the veteran in their outfit.

Joe barely heard the child's words of advice, having his hands full with the second zombie. He hit the second one with all of his strength, realizing that he'd held back the first time out of respect for the humanity he'd been unable to dismiss. The skull caved. Zombie number two sank to the ground with the one lethal blow right over the eyes.

Sandra grabbed a rag from the ground, and whipped the blood off of the van's door handle. Jerking it open, she saw the shoulder strap that held the dead woman in place. All I have to do is lean in and push the release button. Piece of cake, Sandra tried to tell herself, yet she held back. What if the woman comes back to life while I'm leaned all the way over her, she had a hard time not thinking about?

There was a commotion in the dark space between two buildings. They looked over, seeing Dominique rushing at them. Truck and Andy were one step back, the fastest half dozen of the zombies another thirty meters behind the trio.

"Oh hell. This is going to freak me out," said Sandra, reaching in and fighting at the button that held the woman's dead body in the driver's seat. The lady's arm slipped off the seat, causing Sandra to bump her head on the overhead from sheer fright. After ten more stabs at it, the seat belt released, sliding into its holder. The body fell over into the center of the van.

Joe grabbed a leg and pulled, the woman becoming a wishbone before she fell to the pavement. She lay in a heap, and then started to groan, feeling the first pains of being born again.

Sandra was already behind the wheel, churning the engine to life. Everyone grabbed at a door at once, them all being locked. Sandra hit the lock switch, all three remaining doors jerked open at once and everyone but Joe, who was too close to the zombies to turn, piled in. Stanley was pulled in by the seat of his pants as Truck dove for his back door.

Outside, Joe took a swing at the first zombie, making contact like he'd hit a fastball. He tossed his bat onto the roof of the van, and climbed up a fender as the van rolled back, braked, and slid into drive. They were off, Joe climbing onto the roof with the help of the luggage rack.

Joe grabbed his bat, wondering how it all came about that he'd ended up on the roof instead of in a seat. Worse than that, they were going up the main drag, away from the bridge. One fast zombie, a teenaged boy of maybe fifteen, ran steadily behind them. A skateboard under the teen's arm attested to a past hobby.

Sandra yanked the wheel around, doing a U-turn that sent two wheels over the curb and then back down into the street. Once again, they aimed downhill toward the bridge and closer road-block of automobiles and animated dead.

Joe had a perfect swing to the teenager's head, but decided against it as the van passed. Was that compassion, Joe wondered as he let the teen slip by? The young man is dead, he reminded himself; was it better to leave him a member of the walking dead than to put him out of his misery? While Joe worked the puzzle out, the dead teen stopped, turned, stepped onto his skateboard and started skating downhill towards the van as it speeded to thirty. He was a fresh one, only slightly damaged, good and fast on the board. The teenager's speed told Joe that he'd made the wrong choice. Sure, a relatively healthy skater might work the board faster than the zombie was doing, but what if they got stopped and were delayed by the others? It was just one more zombie to worry about, Joe realized.

While Joe looked back, Sandra drove onward, leaving the teen further behind. There were at least two dozen zombies in the road ahead of her, some milling around the roadblock, some on the other side, and a few right in the gap. She yelled out the window, "Hold on, Joe!" She floored the accelerator. They headed for the last clearing between cars before the bridge, it not more than the width of a Pinto.

"Oh, great!" Said Joe, looking back to the front and stuffing his bat under his body. With his good hand, he ripped away the last of the bandages on his wounded hand and then held onto the luggage rack with both fists just as Sandra slammed into the first zombie.

A rapid bouncing sound riddled the undercarriage of the speeding van. To Joe it felt like they'd run over a squirrel; a really big squirrel, followed by a leap of a real wheel. Joe was glad that he couldn't see what they'd run over as he fought to pull his left leg up onto the roof after it bounced off in the collision.

Dominique looked over at Sandra as she drove. She noticed the determination in her eyes and sensing no lift of Sandra's right foot off of the accelerator. The next three stiffs stood as one, right before the gap, saw Dominique as she looked back to their destination. Grabbing the seat belt, she snapped herself in just in time.

A head and two hands split the windshield and then stuck there as if glued. Two more zombies bounced into fenders, shaking and slowing the van another five miles per hour. The zombie slid aside and under, leaving a smear, as the other two zombies glanced off of the fenders, aiding its fall. That misaligned the van a few degrees, but Sandra was committed, still well over thirty miles per hour at the brink of the gap.

The left fender plowed into a pickup, having missed the gap by inches, but just enough to stop the van in its tracks. The pickup slid back a couple of feet, its fender sprayed by fluid from the van's punctured radiator. Airbags exploded in Dominique and

Sandra's faces. Truck, Andy and Stanley were thrown into the back of the front seats.

Up top, Joe's bat sailed out from under him. The bat flew like a missile. Its fat end caved the skull of a seventy year old zombie Wendy's clerk who had abandoned his post at the Wendy's cash register a day earlier when a customer came in with a special biggie order. Through chance, the bat ended the man's short zombie career in the center of the roadblock gap.

Joe held on for dear life, but at the moment of impact found himself sailing over the front luggage rack bar as if he were an Olympic gymnast going over the parallel bars. He closed his eyes and groaned, knowing what was coming next, and then slammed back first into the front of the now stopped van. Joe bounced off and fell to the ground, his wind gone. He coughed, struggling for a breath, finding himself alone in the gap and knowing he'd not have a lot of time to find a little wind.

Joe wanted the bat back, seeing it embedded in the skull lying a few feet in front of him. He fought for air and crawled on the oxygen borrowed from his last gulp of air at the same time, seconds ticking by as if hours. There were shoes and legs just beyond the tangle of cars, he saw from down low as he crawled, coughing and sucking in air with short audible gasps. Amazingly, his hand found the bat, pulling it out from where it was embedded into four inches of brain. He sucked in a whole lungful of air just in time to keep himself conscious. Behind him, the van rocked. Ahead, a half dozen zombies were stepping into plain view, looking down at him and licking their dry, purple lips.

25

"There we go, boy. Plenty of food right up ahead. Didn't I tell you? A whole van full of tasty fritters, you see. Now you just help me clear out your competition some with that M-16 so we can both better get to what we're after, and you can chow down on the live stuff all you like before we move on and get you some professional help at Saint Ann's, or even Delaware if we have to drive that far, but by god, boy, we're going to get you fixed. You hear? Just a snack to tide us for the trip though; that's the deal for you helping me clean up a little before the trip. Shoot if you hear me, boy!"

"Bam!"

Jimmy smelled them a block before his father had mumbled whatever he'd mumbled. All Jimmy heard was the word shoot, but mostly all he heard was his own head screaming at him that food was close. Daddy was bringing him closer to that food too, so maybe his patience had been a good idea after all.

The heavy cruiser passed a pedestrian violator skating down the street. Ignoring the pet crime, the cruiser banged over a couple of wasted stiffs before punching aside a much more ambulatory former housewife.

Chief Baker skidded to a stop, his lights flashing blue and red as if he were on official business. He got out with his bag of supplies in one hand, and his shotgun in the other. Putting the bag of supplies on the roof, he cocked his shotgun, and shot the brains out of three zombies that just so happened to have been both on the wrong side of the roadblock and on his side of the cruiser.

Baker picked a couple of fresh shells out of the bag on the roof and reloaded casually, sure that he was solely in charge of the scene. He looked over the top of his car. Two more stiffs were close to Jimmy's door.

"Shoot, son!"

"Bam!" The M-16 round fired out of the passenger window, missing the closest zombie by ten feet.

"You gotta aim, son. Ain't no use shooting if you don't aim at something. Now aim, boy. Shoot!" Repeated the Chief.

"Bam!" The second round missed by twelve feet. Jimmy's eyes were fixated upon the back door of the van as it swung open, not the least bit interested in a couple of foul smelling fellow zombies.

"Shit! I don't have no more time for lessons," said the Chief, aiming his shotgun at the closest head on the other side of the van and ending another zombie career.

Stanley fell out of the van. He knelt on all fours, found his head as it stopped spinning, and then after noticing the first zombie fall beside him, scooted under the van.

Only one zombie remained standing by the roadblock, other than the twenty or so on the other side. Baker walked over to the other side of the cruiser, and grabbed the hot barrel of his son's M-16. He pulled it over so it was aimed toward the second zombie. The zombie was a young lady, no more than twenty, and pushing a hundred pounds. In the melee of her death, she'd lost a blouse, and one strap on her bra. Below the waist, however, her jeans were clean, and shoes neatly polished black. A hairpiece fell over one ear, held in by only one bobby pin. It seemed a pathetically sympathetic target.

"Now let's try this one more time. See, this is how you aim. Shoot, boy!"

"Bam!" A bullet snapped into the meat of the zombie's shoulder, sending the girl spinning and down to one knee.

"See. You do it," said the Chief, letting go of the barrel.

Truck and Andy crawled toward the back of the van, only to witness the next round from Jimmy's M-16 miss the girl zombie by another ten feet. Suddenly, it dawned upon Truck what was going on. "What are you, some kind of crazy assed mother fucker? That boy's dangerous," Truck yelled to Baker as his feet fell to the pavement.

"Now you just stay right where you're at. You're an escaped felon, and I'm not screwing around with you. I'll shoot you where you stand, if you butt in," said Baker, aiming his shotgun at the big man who stood ten feet away.

The Chief continued, this time grabbing the M-16 barrel again. "We'll work on this some more, boy. Now shoot!"

"Bam" A quarter of the girl's skull cap bounced into the street a half block behind her. Tufts of hair flew like feathers. The shot had just grazed the brain itself, but it was enough to cause her to bend over onto all fours and forget how to do much more than drool onto the brickwork. As zombies go, she was out of the game, figured Truck.

"That's a good one, boy. Now, just one more. I think you have the bead. You plug her a good one, and I'm going to give you that nice big one over there first. You see how big that is, son? Can you imagine wrapping your lips onto that? Now, just aim for me, boy, and I'll serve it up," explained the Chief.

Jimmy, whose eyes had never left the contents of the van in front of the cruiser throughout, suddenly realized that the man beside him was offering the treasure chest of food to him for some sort of deed. The rifle in his hand wavered under the steady guidance of his father's hand. A weak ancient thought prodded him to look down the top of the barrel and find the head of the girl in the street down his sights. It wasn't too steady, and it took all of his willpower to look away from the food, but he had a thought that it was important to look over the barrel for just a few seconds.

"Shoot!"

"Bam!" The top of the girl's head turned to mush as the power of the round shoved her down so hard that her upper body bounced.

"Now that's my boy! Didn't even have to help you much."

Chief baker renewed his concentration upon Truck. His shotgun found the spot right between the big man's eyes and wavered from left to right. The shotgun fell, aimed towards Truck's crotch. "Here's the deal. You come over here and give my boy a little bite off your arm, and I won't shoot your dick off and serve up your friends for desert. He's in need, and I aim to keep him healthy until I can find some medical help to cure him. Just a few bites on the forearm might be all that the boy needs to top off his cravings. You take your chances from there. I'll even let you tie it off; maybe the blood won't reach the rest of you and you won't turn—maybe not. Don't matter to me, either way."

"That's crazy," said Andy, a more lucid comment from his lips than usual.

"Yeah. It's crazy, but hey, this whole deal is crazy. The strong adjust. I'll admit to a bit of a breakdown when it all hit me, but right at the moment, I've no doubt that I'm on a roll. I've the upper hand and I'm just being practical. I'm also running out of patience," said the Chief.

Punctuating his comment, he fired his shotgun into the space between Truck and Andy. The slug passed through the van and blew out the front windshield. Pellets punctured the still deflating airbags in front of Dominique and Sandra, filling their view with a half dozen advancing zombies just twenty yards outside of the suddenly shattered window.

"Now get over here; you're wasting my time, and when I run out of time, so do you and your friends. I'm going to take them out one at a time until I get what I want," he insisted. Baker reached into the passenger window, and ripped the tape off of his son's face with one violent pull, as if signaling everyone that it was lunchtime.

Truck walked forward, sensing that time was running out for all of them. How long before the zombies on the other side of the roadblock work their way around, or through the van? He pulled his belt out of his pants, and wrapped his left arm at the elbow.

"No, you're my friend. You can't let them eat you, Truck," said Andy, stepping forward.

Chief Baker fired his shotgun at Andy's feet, splattering his toes with a few stray pellets. Andy fell to his knees, holding his feet.

"Five seconds, and I'm offing your monkey. Five, four..." said Baker, prompting Truck to move closer to the window. Baker backed up, making room as Truck put his arm out and stepped nearly within munching distance of Jimmy. Jimmy had figured out what was going on and he had his head literally on the sill.

"Ha. Yeah, that's right. Just put it in there, and let Jimmy do the rest; easy as pie. You don't even have to do a thing. My boy always was a quick eater. Three, two..." gloated Baker. Grunts of zombies working their way toward the front of the van were getting louder. At the same time, a rumbling noise was getting louder, all of that background, too many seconds away to mean anything to the fast developing situation, thought Baker. Baker's lips started to form the word, one.

"Don't do it, Truck. I'm looking forward to that dinner you promised me," yelled Dominique, who'd managed to crawl over her seat and was halfway through the van. He turned to see her concern, oddly pleased that she'd finally noticed him as he put his arm into the window. Jimmy's mouth watered, nodding toward the offering. The half second seemed eternal. Truck watched the attractive Dominique crawling towards him from inside the van, using the sight of her for strength as he awaited the teeth. Her eyes lifted as she crawled, full of pain for him, and then her eyes looked slightly aside and froze.

****

Thirteen seconds earlier:

Joe knelt up with the bat in his hand, having used the strength in his last breath to just get that far. Three fully grown male zombies dripped drool and puss onto the ground just in front of Joe as they advanced.

Glass showered around him as the front window of the van exploded under the force of Chief Baker's shotgun blast. Joe had no idea what was going on behind him, but he had his own hands full. In fact, he wasn't going to make it, realized Joe, thinking it impossible to fight off three zombies and escape before being rushed by the rest who were pressing into the opening. Another gasp of air filled his lungs, enough for one or two last surges of strength before they'd have him and start eating him alive. Up until that moment, he'd not imagine that he'd end up as fast food, but so it seemed; the moment was upon him.

Stanley emerged from under the van, filthy as a rat from a sewer grate. Bat in hand, he bashed the closest zombie on the knee, sending it to the ground, the head falling within inches of Joe's legs.

Joe jumped back against the grill of the van, and then lashed out with his own bat, smacking one zombie on the side. That one fell into another. They were clear for a few feet, another trio of walking dead about to replace the three that had been brushed aside, but the ones down were also recovering quickly.

Stanley took the lead, hopping onto a bumper and then up to the top of the pickup they'd crashed into. He turned, hit another zombie above an ear and attracted attention as Joe pulled himself up onto the top of the car opposite the gap from Stanley. Both slashed down with their bats, both ending the quest of two zombies as the two skulls fractured.

Giving no more than a second to fight, they scrambled away on parallel auto tops.

Both Stanley and Joe turned in time to see the long forgotten skateboarding zombie plow into Chief Baker like a bowling ball into a pin.

The teenager slammed into the fender of the cruiser. Baker fell forward, ending the distance that separated him from Truck.

Truck pulled his arm out of the car just as Jimmy's teeth closed on the suddenly empty space. Truck yanked the barrel of Baker's shotgun past an armpit where it fired a glancing load across the hood of the cruiser. The big man stepped aside, and shoved the torso of Chief Baker, shotgun and all, into the window.

Jimmy was beside himself with hunger. He chomped down on the shoulder that presented itself to his lips. His mouth came away with shards of shirt and skin. He spat out the wrapper, and sunk his teeth into the real stuff, squirming meat.

"Jimmy! No, no. It's your dad. Listen to me boy! Let me go. Come on. Come on, son! No! Ah! God damn it, boy! Listen to me! Ah! We can handle them. Nooo!" Screamed the Chief as Jimmy swallowed an ounce of flesh and dug his lips in for more, gnawing with enough effort to break a tooth, which only gave him a sharper edge with which to cut.

Truck was delighted to hold the cop right where he was, particularly when he noticed Joe jump down off of the top of the car and land on the teenaged zombies back before dispatching the threat with a couple of sharp raps. That gave him enough time to hold the Chief still for two more bites.

"Shoot, son. Shoot," screamed an increasingly desperate Baker. The M-16 fired a round by his unbitten shoulder and out the window, missing both Joe and Truck by inches.

"Shit!" Spit a startled Truck. He pulled the Chief out of the window, and yanked the shotgun out of his hands. With a second hand, Truck pulled Baker's service revolver out of his holster and tossed it to Joe.

The Chief staggered back, holding his shoulder and swearing, "You can't get away with this. I'm the law. You're all escaped felons. This is a big mistake. Every cop in America will be after you."

Joe ignored the Chief's comments, saying to Truck, "Get Jimmy out of the car. We're going to need it."

"You heard the man. Out of the car, pig. Go join daddy," said Truck, opening the door and unfastening the seat belt. He yanked the police zombie out by a fist full of hair. Truck punched the clip release on the M-16, sending the clip to the street, and then, still holding the hair to keep the boy steady, set his boot into Jimmy's back. Jimmy fell at his father's feet. Chief Baker shirked away as if Jimmy were the plague.

"Maybe you should tie that arm off, Chief. The way I figure it, you're already a zombie, but you might not turn if the blood doesn't get to you. Were those your words? I didn't believe it, but maybe you did," tormented Truck as he unfastened his own belt from around where he'd tied it around his arm and in seconds, looped it back through his pants loops.

"Fuck you!" Said the Chief.

"I tell you what. I'll be nice and plug you with a quick little head shot. If it was me turning into one of these freaks, I'd consider it a favor. Just ask me," mused Truck as Dominique finally found his side, checking his arm for the scratches that were thankfully not there.

"I'll take my chances."

Dominique butted in, "Leave him alone, Truck. What's happened so far is all on his back. Perfectly legal. He has to live with his own justice now."

Truck looked at her and nodded. "The lady has spoken. Sure you don't want fixed, Chief? Oh well, suit yourself," said Truck, opening the back doors of the cruiser and smashing out the windows. "Can't have anyone riding behind the cage in the back of one of these things and not being able to open the door. You don't mind if we take your batmobile, do you Baker?"

"Nah, he doesn't mind. He's busy calling in the FBI, CIA and Delta Force due to us escaped felons messing up his plan to murder us all," Joe answered for him as he helped Stanley, Andy and Dominique into the back of the cruiser. Sandra, who was still working her way out of the fog from having been sucker punched in her injured ribs by the airbag, sank into the passenger seat.

"What's the plan," asked Truck to Joe and the others in the car.

Joe pulled a box of flairs out of the cruiser trunk. "I'm going to light it up around here and on the other side of the van. These things don't like light. Then I'm going to see if I can work my way into the van. I'll back it out of the hole. Then I'll give it another go, and if I make it, fine. If not, I'm counting on you in the cruiser to push me through. Don't be afraid to bash me in the ass nice and hard if I get stuck. We get on the other side of the bridge, and you pick me up; this van isn't going very far, all beat up and with a hole in the radiator, but it'll make a nice battering ram."

Truck shot a zombie off of the top of the van, and answered, "Sounds like a plan. We use the van as a battering ram to widen the gap and preserve the cruiser for our big escape. I'll pick you up at the funeral home over there."

Time was precious. Truck ran to the other side of the cruiser and quickly got behind the steering wheel. He backed off a good two blocks, Baker's bag tumbling to the ground from where he'd left it on the top of the cruiser.

Creatures stirred between the buildings, making Truck antsy enough to rev his engine. Baker had abandoned his son, and found a hole to hide in, Truck noticed, Jimmy wandering around, trying to figure out which car of meat to go for first. They watched Joe stroke the pavement with the end of a half dozen flairs and when lit, toss them over the heap of cars. Jimmy ran to the sidewalk. Zombies cringed away, but only far enough to allow Joe to crawl through the van.

"Seems like the perfectly wrong destination," said Sandra from Truck's side in the cruiser.

"What's that?" He asked.

"I know that it's the logical stop for regrouping, being out just far enough from the bridge, but a morgue and funeral parlor? Not exactly where one would think to go to get away from dead people," she finished.

"Um. Now that you mention it..." nodded Truck.

Ahead, Joe's van started grudgingly, the exhaust smelling of oil and radiator fluid. Smelling that, Joe knew that he had precious time before the engine seized.

The van creaked back to the tune of twisted metal and the clang of a bumper falling to the bricks and asphalt. Soon enough, he was back a half block. A few of the braver zombies had wormed their way past the horrible light of the flares. Joe tugged at his seat belt, and then floored the accelerator. Instead of a surge of power, the engine backfired, and then the mess rolled forward at a pathetic ten miles per hour before plunging into the gap like a limp noodle.

During the short trip, zombies banged against the van, barely injured and barely thrown off balance; some stuck like flies to a cinnamon roll. The van stuck too, like a stick in mud, square, but half in and half out of the space. Zombies landed on the hood. That was particularly unsettling, considering that the van no longer had a front window. Joe ripped the belt off and lunged for the back of the van just as a zombie dove in toward him after pulling the back doors open.

"Wam!" The cruiser cut the zombie in back in half when it hit the van's bumper dead center. The van's back door was still open. Joe fell against the grill of the cruiser, and then next felt himself in space, the van free, and the cruiser slowed by the collision. Joe grabbed at the van's door, and pulled himself back into the moving platform. The top half of the zombie had disappeared out of the same gap Joe had fought to recover from. Up front, the hood had also cleared.

The van's engine hadn't stopped. Joe found himself several feet back from the wheel, his ride accelerating toward the bridge and doing so without a driver. He jumped forward, leaned over the seat and awkwardly steered the van straight across the bridge. Something in the linkage had stuck, and the van only got faster, up to forty before he reached the other side and pulled the wheel hard to make Deadman Road on little more than two wheels.

The zombies were secondary at the moment, them being brushed aside by the speeding vehicles, or rolled over in ways that launched both cars recklessly. It seemed like there was an endless number of them, far more than the two dozen they'd had to deal with earlier, but then they were through the bulk of them, and Joe managed to regain his driver's seat. Up ahead, the funeral home loomed, its lot empty of all but a hearse and a convertible. Behind in the rear view mirror, the cruiser drove steadily through the same wake of eager zombies. Joe hit the breaks, but they failed. At the last second, he pulled the emergency brake handle, and the van slipped to the side as the brakes jammed and rubber baked black streaks into the parking lot pavement. A zombie he'd not seen before in the confusion, slipped off of the roof and flew into the side of the funeral home with a splatter of broken ribs and collar bones.

Joe fell out of the driver's doorway. He'd lost the bat, but the police pistol was still in his pocket. In the headlights of the steaming van, the broken zombie squirmed. It looked like every bone in his upper body had been smashed when he'd hit the funeral home, but the head still wobbled over the pulp of muscle and bone. The zombie kicked with his legs, barely moving, wormlike, towards the two car loads of food. More out of pity than need, though mostly without much thought, Joe put the monster out of its misery.

26

"Did you hear that?"

"Duh! It sounds like hunters, Billy. There are a billion acres of woods out back along the creek," said Patricia.

"This isn't hunting season. What if there are more of those things out there? Could be someone in trouble. Could be other people fighting off the same things we've fought off. Could be that this isn't the only such incident."

"I certainly don't think so. I'm not so sure I believe this zombie idea anymore either. That woman, the way she looked dead; anyone who has been sick and stuffed into a meat locker might look that way. It would make a person crazy enough to go on fighting after being shot too."

William countered, "And, what about the way she moved after we'd more than cut her in half?"

"You. After you cut her in half with that, that...bazooka. Don't blame an ounce of this on me. Hell, Billy boy, it could have been nerves twitching. Maybe the brain can live without a body for awhile. I read that people executed by guillotines can sometimes live long enough to see their own bodies for several seconds if their heads fall in the basket just right," said Patricia.

"Where'd you read that kind of crap? On the internet?" Asked William, shocked, but then again, thinking that she'd probably made it up or heard it from one of her dense friends.

"Never you mind where I read it. There's just probably a logical explanation like that. You're a ghoul, not a doctor, Bill! You don't get to see when people actually die, so you don't know everything about it; you just think you do. We don't know what goes on in the end. It might be different than on TV. We might die harder than they want us to believe. Saving us the worry, don't you see, or keeping us happy. Don't worry, be happy; you know, shit like that," said Patricia.

"Suit yourself if you want to believe in the impossible, but it's not like it changes anything soon if my suspicion is right and there are more of these things stomping around. As for shooting the zombies we shot, we still had to do what we did," said William.

"You did. You forced me to be here too, you moron," said Patricia, the last part under her breath. She was back to no longer trusting him, having endured the last part of the long day of cleaning while back under the suspicion that her boyfriend was crazy and could resort to anything, including murdering her to keep her quiet.

Too unsure to actually leave him, she still managed to whine, "I've never been so tired in my whole life. We've spent the whole day cleaning up this dump. Look at my clothes. Everything in here is sopping wet. Shoes ruined, because of you. How in hell are we going to clean that ceiling? It's Stucco, for crying out loud. Dripping wet Stucco! Jesus, George, I don't know why I put up with you."

Several more shots rang out, those frightfully near the back cellar door, which they'd propped up to fight the smell of bodies and antiseptic cleanser.

"See. It's not hunters," said William, picking up his reloaded M-1 carbine.

"Those things can't shoot, can they?" Asked a startled Patricia as she ducked behind a metal table.

"What things? You don't believe in zombies. You don't believe in things." He paused, and then answered her, "No. Zombies can't shoot. They're too stupid to know how to shoot a gun. All they know how to do is grunt and stumble around and eat pretty women who drive day-glow convertibles. Don't you watch TV?"

"OK. I believe in zombies or whatever you want me to believe in. Now, do something," scolded Patricia from where she'd ducked.

A figure nodded into the doorway, aimed a shotgun at William, and then ducked back outside before William could shoot him.

"You a zombie in there?" Yelled Truck from just outside the elevated cellar door.

"No!"

"Are you sure?"

"See," William said to Patricia without looking at her. His heart was speeding, him having realized that the man outside might well have beat him to the draw the way he'd scoped out the room in half a second. "Of course I'm sure. Isn't anyone in here but us live people. The zombies have all run off or been shot. State your name and your business."

"Name's Truck. I have some normal people with me. We thought to check your place out when we saw the cars and heard arguing. Bunch of zombies milling around the grounds and we're nearly out of shells. Even a pitchfork would be helpful. If you don't know it yet, we're all in a fix together."

"Come in peaceful with your gun pointed down," said William.

Truck shrugged towards Dominique.

"Let me go first. I won't scare the man to death," she said, stepping into the doorway before Truck could stop her.

"My god, you look a lot different than your voice," said William when he saw her.

"Hey! Don't let your eyes fall out of your head," scolded Patricia as she smacked the back of William's head, a possessive practitioner of the cuckold's trade to the end.

Everyone followed, the last one Joe, him hanging by the back door as lookout. "We're not staying. This place is like a dead man's magnet. We're going to have to all start moving out of here as soon as we get organized and supplied," Joe said to the crowd below.

"I can't leave my place. What if someone breaks in?" Protested William.

Sandra looked the place over. The basement was humid from all of the wet work of cleaning. One speck of blood dripped from the ceiling, spoiling the freshly mopped floor in front of her feet. "Looks like someone already has."

"Hey, I remember you from the investigation," said William.

Sandra nodded, "The investigation's over. We know what's going on, but seem powerless to do a lot about it. Reverend Purswell is apprehending the stiffs. He has this idea that he can create the end time by shipping zombies all over the place, spreading this disaster to far away places. We have to get to Columbus and see if we can find someone in contract with emergency forces and the rest of the planet so we can stop him."

"You think he started all of this?" Asked William.

"Probably. Looks like it," said Sandra.

"I'd sure like to get my hands on the bastard who started this; that's for sure. Do you have any idea how devastating this has been for the funeral business? Who wants the services of a mortician when your dearly departed gets up in the middle of the service and bites your ear off?" Asked William.

"I can imagine. Lots of zombies out there with missing fingers, ears, toes, whatever. Everyone's a Mike Tyson meal. That does seem to be the new spin on things too. Back to the main point though: We've spotted a lot of them coming through the cemetery from the bridge. They're like bloodhounds. Can smell a living person from a few blocks away, so we're not safe here and neither are you two," said Sandra.

"OK. I'm convinced. I've seen enough to know I don't want to be alone here with a bunch of them milling around outside," agreed William. What good is a funeral home if nobody stays dead, he conceded to himself.

Sandra noticed the coffin full of weapons. "My god, where did you get all of this?"

"Been on my own little stakeout. Seemed to me that the cops were useless; no offense. Up until the day before yesterday I didn't even own a gun."

"None taken, and it looks like we came to the right place, assuming you don't mind us pooling our resources so we can all up our chances of making it out of here alive? We should arm and move on as quickly as possible," said Sandra, picking up a shotgun and half of the boxes of shells.

"Looks like we came to the right place all right," said Truck, stuffing his pockets full of the other half of the shotgun shells.

"Speaking of looks like; looks like we're out of time. They're moving," warned Joe. Two zombies moved into dark view at the back edge of the tree line. Joe fired, missing the heads on the first two shots, and ending two zombies with the last two. "I'm out! Any forty-five ammo?"

William tossed him a box, and Joe reloaded while everyone collected back to the door.

"We're not going out there, are we?" Asked Patricia.

"There are too many of them out this way now, and they know where we are by now too. Another exit perhaps. We'll never get to Columbus out the back, and if we don't, the Purswells of the world win, which is the least of our problems by the time they do, but hey, we can still try," said Sandra.

Patricia injected, "Say that again; I lost you? No, forget it, it's your problem to make sense of what's going on. We're not going to Columbus. We're just going somewhere quiet and far. Tell them, Bill. Tell them it's there problem."

William Answered, "It's not their problem. It's everybody's problem. We have to help stop this thing too. How will we live in a world like this? No place safe! Always looking over our shoulders! All that we've learned to take for granted, gone. No more funerals!"

"You bastard!"

"Hey, let's fight later. We need to make a break for the cars," said Joe from the back doorway as he slammed the door and secured William's makeshift braces.

Truck handed Dominique the M-16, explaining to her that the thing was both lethal and not all that hard to use once a person learned how to chamber a round. "Not a whole lot of kick either. Wouldn't want to bruise that pretty little shoulder," he said in his typically un-PC way—though he intended to be smooth.

"Hum," said the unflappable Dominique as she adjusted the sling like a professional biathlete.

Truck turned, saying, "Here Andy. You use my bat now. It's a Louisville." Andy's eyes lit up, his lips smoothed over his upper lip and he smiled while holding his bat up high like a flag.

Crazy as hell. What would it be like to see Andy shoot a gun, wondered Truck? The bigger bat seemed lethal enough.

Patricia somehow found the time to quickly fix her lipstick during the preparations, perhaps from a habit of thinking it always the last step before going out.

Truck handed one 45 to Stanley and gave the other to William, since it was technically still the mortician's property. Truck had run out of what he considered to be intelligent bodies to arm. William tucked the 45 into his belt at the small of his back so he'd have his hands free for his M-1. Thinking that neat, Stanley did the same. With all of his pockets quickly filled with bullets, Stanley took on a dwarfish posture that resembled an old picture of Billy the Kid in baggy hand-me-downs.

Sandra noticed, and walked up to the boy. "Now listen up, Stan. There isn't anything cool about a gun. It's nothing more than a tool to help us survive, like matches or a car. Yesterday it was a dangerous thing to have around the house. Today it's a necessary evil—nothing more, yet still dangerous. You understand what I'm trying to tell you?"

"Yes ma'am," said Stanley, nodding rapidly with a big, 'I'm one of the big boys now,' smile on his face.

"There are only two rules for that weapon. First, you don't shoot anyone who's still alive. Second, you don't ever aim the barrel at anyone you don't intend to kill. That's like, not even by accident even. Keep the barrel down, period. You got that? That gun should be invisible on you until you positively need it. And, leave the shooting to us unless it gets hairy. I don't want you shooting any of us by accident," finished Sandra.

"Yes ma'am. I can shoot a gun. I've got Nintendo!"

Truck laughed. Sandra groaned. The zombies started the process of kicking and beating down the back door.

"Well, as suggested, we might consider taking the front way out," offered William, leading the way up the front basement steps. Everyone followed except Patricia, who upon finding herself alone in the cavernous, blood dripping lower morgue, decided to scoot along after the rest.

She nearly crashed over Andy as she hit the top of the steps. Instead of moving through the dark and forbidding main funeral cathedral, William sidetracked them through a series of casket showing rooms. Highly polished, the caskets seemed the only thing visible in the dark, other than the vague shapes of one another as they stumbled forward, each bunching up to keep from getting lost or feeling alone in the symbolic surroundings.

"Don't worry. These are models. Just for show. Everybody's gone anyway. I should know. Wrong business for this sort of disaster, you know," William whispered back as he got to the last room, his business office. The side door led into the sanctuary again, but this time close to the front door.

Joe led the way, pulling the front door open without bothering to check through the stained glass windows that framed it. What good will it do to check, he thought, barging out barrel first with his forty-five. Just as he'd suspected, the zombies had nearly all wandered out back, chance leaving only a couple of pathetic slowpokes to guard the front. He thought about shooting them, but then had another thought.

"Hey Andy. We don't want to make too much noise, so your bat's our ticket out of here. Let's see how you can handle that bat of yours," offered Joe. Andy worked forward, and with a smile the size and shape of Kentucky, lit into the chore. A couple more zombies came around from the side of the business, Andy waltzing right up to the new task as the others sorted things out.

Joe explained, "The van's toast. We take the cruiser and William's hearse. Sandra, Stanley and I will go with William and his friend in William's hearse. Truck, you, Andy and Dominique man the cruiser. We'll head straight west on Deadman. The Columbus outer-belt is less than two miles out and it's too wide for a few half organized zombies to block. From there we can figure out the best way to get into the city. It'll be a good view up on the overpasses."

"Sound's like a plan," said Truck, rushing toward the cruiser with Dominique in hand.

Andy looked around, seeing nothing left that was close enough to hit. He swayed a minute, indecisively, before rushing to the cruiser. It took him a few seconds to find his second gear as he stood by the door, but then he dove through the cruiser's broken back window without bothering to try the door.

"Go on. We're right behind you," said Sandra as William led the way to the hearse. William always parked it out of the way due to the effect it sometimes had on new clients.

"Wait! What about my convertible?" Screamed Patricia, far too loudly. She stomped her heel and stood in the middle of the lot while the others gathered around or mounted the two heavier vehicles.

Joe explained, "We need to stick together. Besides, what happens when one of those things jumps on top of your car. There's no protection without a top. Trust me; I drove in here on top of a much bigger car than that."

"Come on dear. Don't make a fuss. We have to get out of here. When this blows over, we'll come back for it," coaxed William as he opened his door.

"No way. Besides, you're all a bunch of losers. Go on to Columbus. Join the crusades. Whatever floats your boat, but I'm heading the other way, towards the country. I have a friend east of here," insisted Patricia, turning and briskly walking to her convertible. She got in and fumbled in her purse for her keys while the others wondered what William was going to do about it. William shrugged and got into the hearse.

Patricia knew when her boy was giving up. "Oh, and William! You were always such a wimp. And, a lousy fuck!" Patricia smiled as she started her engine with a roar that was an exclamation point. The zombies were out of sight, but then again, it was darkest around the edges of the funeral home. Surely her fuss had cut their staying time considerably, they all felt.

Hitting the accelerator, Patricia's car shot out of her parking spot. Joe was about to warn her that going for the bridge might make for a tight squeeze on the other side, but then he thought that maybe the smaller car might make it through the gap with little trouble. They had attracted a lot of the zombies away from the bridge, he knew. Her car was making too much speed and noise for him to be heard anyway. Even more compelling, he guessed that their little group was better off without her.

Suddenly, just as it passed them, the car swerved, nearly finding the ditch before regaining control. Patricia's car swung back toward the town bridge. The figure she'd just missed stumbled forward, no less than thirty yards from where Joe and Sandra stood. An arm was bandaged near the shoulder. A throw-down pistol was in his hand, the man's tattered bag of supplies in another.

Chief Baker said, "Didn't think you'd see me again, huh! Now it's my turn to play! Toss the guns."

Sandra and Joe looked at one another, and lowered their weapons to the ground. They stuck their hands up at the insistence of Baker's barrel.

Baker added, "You in the car. Mortician, aren't you? Stay put. Let me see your hands." William stuck his hands out of the car window. Baker stepped forward to point blank range, facing Sandra and Joe. Rage and the sweat of quickly spreading infection moistened his face. His veins stuck out at the temples, and the skin at his neck was splotched along one side. Every so often, he shook his head, as if chilled, in utter contradiction to the perspiration. Stanley sidestepped a little towards the rear bumper of the hearse.

"Got your runt still, I see. Little pisser. Couldn't wait to poop one of your own, I imagine. Well, that's good, cause they're not letting any family visits where you're going; unless it's Beelzebub waking up with a hard-on," cursed Baker, waving his weapon towards the boy. Stanley backed away into the gloom behind the car, his hands up like he'd always imagined they should be when captured by the enemy.

"Look, Chief. We didn't ask for any trouble. You..." tried Joe.

"Where's the fat fuck! I owe him a big one. Tell me that and I'll plug you easy; otherwise I'll hole your knees and leave you groveling in the parking lot where the freaks can get at you," said Baker, out of his head with a combination of dizzying spells and uncontrollable anger. His gun hand wavered, but then returned with the renewed focus of his eyes.

"Generous of you, I suppose. Maybe you'll regret the offer though, once you get the cravings. Wasted meal if you kill us, and if you shoot that thing to wound us, a billion competitors are going to beat you to us before you change," said Joe, hearing the sound of zombies advancing behind him.

Baker seemed to not really hear Joe's advice. "Even let the little spike go, just to up the incentive. I'm fond of thinking of the brat running around like a little rat in a world full of anacondas." Baker waved his gun at Stanley, and the boy hurriedly backed into the woods adjacent to the lot. "See. On his way already. Not much loyalty in adoption, is there."

"Listen Chief. I wasn't your favorite officer, but I always did my job," tried Sandra.

"What the hell are you talking about? This isn't about your job. This is about Jimmy. You think I forgot about my boy, just like that. It was you people who got us separated. It was that fat boy who turned Jimmy on me too and got me bit. All to hell, cause of you!" Screamed Baker. He shuddered, a chill biting him to the bone.

Joe had a thought. "You're a zombie already, Baker. I feel for you; no bull, but you're wasting everybody's time. Be best if you shot yourself. Be best for all of us. You most of all. It'd be an act of goodness; a fine way to leave the world. Once you've turned, you'll not think clear about it again. Other forces will drive you that aren't of this earth. Then you'll be stuck like them..."

"Like Jimmy? What kind of madman are you, asking a favor after what you bunch of criminals done did. Fuck it. I'm just going to shoot you and hunt for him on my own!" Interrupted Baker. His hand trembled as he aimed his weapon at Joe's knee.

Time for talk was over.

27

(Ten minutes later on the road to the outer-belt)

"Isn't necessary to cry, Stanley. He had it coming," said Joe from the front seat beside William as William drove the long black hearse. They'd shoved a casket out the back and reconfigured the back for back seats.

"Hush Joe. Let the boy cry," scolded Sandra from the back seat where she held an arm around the boy. His face was buried in her bosom, a place Joe realized he'd never had the pleasure of nestling his own face quite so comfortably. It seemed like he and Sandra were an item, but it occurred to him that things had been too hectic for either of them to actually add sexual intimacy to the equation. Joe turned around, least he have inappropriate thoughts at what seemed to be yet another completely inappropriate time.

"I ain't crying," sniffled the boy.

"Joe's right though, Stanley. It had to be done. You had no choice," said Sandra.

William spouted, "Big old hole, right dead in the heart. Damn. That forty-five can rip. I'm plum amazed that it didn't crack the kid's wrist when he pulled that off. They got kick like that in those plastic guns they sell for Nintendo? Vibrasonic – whatever! Heh!

The blood in that man was amazing too. By the time they get to me they're not pumping like that any more. Thought I'd seen it all. Man, it was a fountain; shooting out there." William put his right hand to his own chest and then swung it out towards the windshield, demonstrating and saying, "Swish!" The hearse swerved just a little, adding to the gesture. William nodded to Joe as if he were making an important observation.

"Oh god, will you men quit!"

"He weren't a zombie yet. I ain't never killed a real live human being before. You told me not to shoot if he weren't a zombie yet," said Stanley, seeking forgiveness.

"Hey, he was a zombie in my book," said Joe.

"That's right, Stan. He was a zombie for sure by the time he got to us. His head was already messed up. You saw him shake with cold. You saw whose side he was on," lied Sandra, though only a little.

"Really?"

"Sure. OK now?" Asked Sandra.

"OK." Stanley got quiet for awhile, and then sat over in the center of his own seat, his eyes drying. "But how do I know for sure? I mean, for next time," he asked.

"Can't know for sure, Stan. You just look them over and see how they act. If they're looking hungry at you, it's a good bet. If they want to kill you, like Baker did, it's a lot safer bet," said Joe.

"Zombies don't bleed," thought Stanley out loud.

"No, I guess you caught us in a little lie, but people who are trying to kill you sometimes do. That's just about the same thing as being a zombie, and I'm not lying when I tell you that Baker was about ten seconds from being both a murderer with a zombie mind and a zombie in the flesh as well. You did doubly good back there, Stan. I'm not telling you to shoot everything you see. You looked over the situation, and did the good thing. There was a cost, but it was good at heart. That's judgment. You know about wisdom, Stan. You ever dream about being a wise man when you grow up?" Asked Joe.

"Yes sir, Mister Joe," said Stan, all ears.

"That's good. You're going to grow up fine enough if you just want a little of that," said Joe.

"You listen to Joe. He's telling you something important," said Sandra.

"What's he gonna be, now he's out of blood?" Asked Stanley.

"He's gonna be a zombie," said William with a laugh. He had a big smile on his face for the first time in awhile.

"What's got you go giddy," said Sandra from the back seat of the hearse. She hit the back of the driver's seat.

"Just happy. I'm guessing that becoming a zombie is a step up for some people. That's a little humorous, don't you think?" Explained William as he made his way around a wrecked wrecker. A car dangled precariously from the hook, but nobody was around.

"We should have shot him in the head. That's the only thing I regret," said Sandra. Joe didn't tell her what he thought because he knew that Sandra wouldn't like it. After all, it wasn't that Sandra was wrong; it was just that he didn't mind one bit that Baker was going to wake up in the living hell of the walking death.

William had a thought, "No, I'll tell you why I'm so slap-happy. It's that girl of mine. I spent two years thinking how lucky I was to have such a good looking chick calling me her boyfriend. Now that she's gone, I can't believe how incredibly happy I am. I know that the current subject at hand is zombies, but that woman was a vampire sucking up my soul faster than that crooked Sheriff bled out. Christ, right about now you could tell me that I'm the last living man on earth, and I'd consider it a lucky day."

"Speaking of which; when are you and I going to have a decent date?" Joe asked. He leaned over the seat and looking at Sandra.

Sandra batted her eyes and turned a rosy cheek, mocking something nearly May West. "Soon as I get a two hour bath, turn over two straight days in a goose down bed and swallow enough Valium to help me forget our first few dates."

"Not exactly been the most romantic first few days, I suppose," said Joe, turning back to keep an eye out the front window.

"I'm not complaining. Just tired. I'll let you make it up to me because I know how much you have to make up for," said Sandra.

"I appreciate that, dear. I'll be in the motel room right next door. We'll see who can sleep the longest. It'll be like the anticipation of sailors when we get to it," said Joe with some relief that she was still game.

"Stop that; I'm just a kid," said Stanley.

"Wow. What's this," said William. He swerved the giant black auto around Dolcy, who was crudely swinging a bass guitar around in the middle of the road in front of the Blue Fish. She took a swipe at the hearse, scraping a dint into the back fender as they passed. Dolcy ran after them a few strides, and then beat the guitar on the road in frustration when she realized that the hearse had gotten away.

"Did you see her face?" Asked Joe sadly.

"Sorry Joe," said Sandra, sympathetically.

"Sorrier than you can imagine. That was my guitar she was beating to a pulp."

They passed a McDonalds. There was a string of cars in line, some doors standing open. A few bodies laid around the ground, those having either taken too much damage to the head or haven not yet made the change. Nothing ambulatory was in line, no doubt due to the lack of a particular kind of meat that had suddenly come into fashion, but had not yet made the Mcmenu.

A short left and then right took them to a finger off the freeway that led to the outer-belt interchange. They broke free of the trees and the houses of the suburb. Up on the rise, the cruiser shined as it reflected the rising sun to their backs. Three of the doors were open, but they were still too far away from the car to tell much more. What they could tell was enough. Several miles behind the cruiser rose the morning greeting of a city engulfed in smoke. In places, the dim morning plumes glowed red and orange. There was a growing smell of burning ash. Everyone's heart sank at the signs of fire and at the sight of grey soot that extended nearly across the entire western horizon. They closed, ash speckling the windshield.

"My god, the whole city is burning. I can't even see where the skyscrapers are. They should be clear as day from here," said Sandra who'd leaned up between the seats for a better view.

"I thought I caught a glimpse before I lost them in the smoke. One looked like it was adding to the smoke; like a big rectangular chimney. All of this explains a lot. I thought the ash smell I'd been smelling all night was just the fires we'd passed," said Joe, pointing between mini-forests of trees where there was a small break in the near wall of smoke.

"Radio stations, television stations, public services and phones, all burnt or trashed in one heap of chaos. Maybe most of the people got out? The road we're on isn't exactly the best escape route. Could we have missed this much chaos?" Asked Sandra.

Joe didn't answer, thinking the spread of the zombie curse faster in the city than it had been out in the relatively open suburbs. Several wrecks were evident, but there were no cars running on the causeway to 270, a certain clue that things had spun out of control, and that they were now driving into the lag edge of the disaster.

"And, if this metro area, what else? Columbus is the crossroads to the entire Midwest. Seventy runs straight and clear to the mountains in Colorado. Seventy-one is an hour from Cleveland and Cincinnati," said Sandra.

"Purswell can't have helped with his seeding program, " said Joe.

"I don't see any planes. Won't the Guard be flying choppers or something?" Observed William. Everyone looked over the brightening horizon, seeing nothing in the air.

Sandra guessed, "Maybe the FAA grounded everything. Maybe we're all quarantined? The Guard's probably busy setting a perimeter. They've written Central Ohio off. I would. It would be insane to let this disease spread."

"A quarantine around the whole Midwest? Ending where? Clear to Colorado? Are there resources enough to do that? How do you set boundaries in endless rolling plains? These things don't need roads; they walk," said Joe. Nobody dared guess how a thing like that might be done or what it might mean for them, as they approached the cruiser.

"It just makes sense to try to close this off. If the airport is closed, that eliminates the need to warn anyone about Purswell. He can't get out any more than we can," said Sandra.

"Unless he already has. Look at the head start! He's had nearly two days to do his ilk. Those freezers at his church grounds are probably empty by now, but you're right; who needs warned now? This is clearly out of control," said Joe thoughtfully.

"What are we going to do?" Asked William.

Joe thought, and then answered, "We'll have to hole up. If we're under quarantine, we're not going to be allowed out, and they might shoot us on sight. Worse, if this problem has spread half as far as it looks like it might have, which is at least out of radio range, I'm assuming, we'll have zombies to deal with all along the road. Our luck will run out sooner or later. The problem might even outrun our best efforts to find an edge to it. Shoot, we've only done three miles since last night, and that's been tough going."

"I don't know. We might be wrong. They might have a safety zone set up right over the next hill? Who is to say how far this has gotten?" Wondered Sandra.

"Even if we made it past a quarantine, we'd be refugees. Those camps get crowded. We'd be in a controlled environment. Guards watching us like we're the enemy. What are the odds of the government keeping the disease out of a place like that? It'd be a death camp, is my guess, and any sane governor wouldn't let the contamination out. Best to find our own out of the way place to wait it out or at least figure out what's happening before we move on. Someone is bound to get the emergency radio system working. Scrounge for what we need in the mean time. The zombies have no use for most of the things we'll need, so I'm guessing it isn't hard to find things, as long as we stick to day raids. At least that way we'd be in control of our own destiny."

"OK. That gets my vote; or at least until we find something out. It's getting to be full lightness. If what you say is true and they don't like the daylight, we might have some time to settle and put out some security," agreed William as he drove over debris in the roadway.

"Fine with me too, as long as this place we end up at has running water," offered Sandra.

"We going to a motel? I want a place with cable TV." Asked Stanley.

"There they are," said Joe, pointing to the right side of the road.

Everyone got out, joining Truck, Andy and Dominique on the firing line at the rail beside the freeway. Truck and Dominique were firing at a layer of zombies who coated a station wagon like cheese over a fast food hamburger patty.

Dominique took aim with her M-16, plucking another zombie off. The zombie got up and resumed his fight for the goods.

"My shotgun doesn't do much more than rain pellets at this range. There must be fifty of them, and they're wasting my woman's ammunition," said Truck.

"It's getting to be daylight. These things don't like the light much. Must be that the pickings are getting slim and they're desperate for a snack before the sun starts hurting their eyes and they go for cover," said Joe.

"Seems like it. So, what are we going to do? If we take that on, it'll waste most of our ammo," asked Truck.

"Maybe we should leave it," thought Joe.

"We'll have to drive right past it if we do. That ramp goes north. From what I see, it's the only direction that makes sense. We can cut off of the outer-belt and out of the county faster that way than we can going south from here. Less zombies to deal with too," suggested Truck.

"We can't just leave and drive by! There's a real live human being in that car," protested Sandra as Dominique finally hit one in the head. Dominique was clearly the trained marksperson in the crowd. The other distant zombies nudged the dead zombie aside, and kept right on trying to tear the automobile in half with their bare hands.

"Look. I've got an idea. Let's go. I'm driving. Truck, you stay back a little. Anything gets in your way, drive over it," said Joe, getting behind the wheel of the hearse.

28

Doctor Laura Adkins ducked down as far as she could squeeze into her front seats. Every nerve in her body was shaking her apart as she wished that she could pass out like she'd managed before. Two windows in back were already cracked. The safety glass held the windshield, but that was going to last only for a few seconds, and she knew that any second now one of those things she'd managed to elude all day long was going to find a rock or stick, and it would finally be all over with.

On the other hand, it wasn't going to be all over with, she knew, because being eaten alive was going to be a very painful and prolonged death. Being a doctor and having seen tragic deaths wheeled into emergency rooms, she understood that her instincts would force her into a fetal position, where they might chow down for some time before hitting something vital. Under the circumstances, that was a very masochistic instinct, survival. Then, finally, she'd end up like them, she'd already figured out, that state of living death decidedly not over with. They didn't look like happy people. In fact, they looked nearly as miserable as she felt, though at the moment she'd have gladly traded them places for the duration of the upcoming meal.

She heard herself screaming over and over again, the screams sprinkled with the occasional plea of a mind out of control, "Don't eat me!" To the zombies, the pleas and screams only served as a dinner bell.

Her car jerked forward, compressing her against the back of the seat. Some of the zombies slipped off of the smashed front window, giving her some light as the station wagon accelerated in a slow arch.

Laura pushed up, fighting for balance before grabbing the wheel. A speck of the freeway ramp showed between zombie limbs, so she did her best to aim as the car picked up speed. The smell of burning brakes filled the car. Laura slipped the car into neutral and the car picked up speed much more easily.

As they picked up speed, zombies fell away. Only a half dozen or so managed to keep a handhold as the cars slipped onto I-270.

She adjusted the rear view mirror, finding a huge black car with deeply tinted windows pushing her along. "Oh god, a hearse! I'm in hell!" She screamed. Laura hadn't missed the connection and was not really sure what a hearse from hell meant in context with her mind numbing nightmare. Maybe she had gone mad after all, she imagined, kind of liking it, considering.

Finally, the contact ended and she was coasting alone at fifty miles an hour. The hearse pulled up beside her. Laura saw Officer Sandra Anderson open a window and then aim a shotgun out. One by one, the remaining zombies were shot off of her car without a missed shot, leaving behind gristle and flesh as it was left splattered across the metal and broken glass.

Her heavy car eventually slowed and then stopped, the needle still on empty. The hearse beside her stopped, and then Laura noticed the police cruiser behind it. She laughed, imagining them both having been pulled over for speeding. It had been an insane thirty-six hours, and from the looks of it, things were getting crazier. Why not a clueless cop eager to write out a ticket? On the other hand, Laura basked in the overwhelming relief that she'd not ended up breakfast for a crowd of crazed zombies.

Her door was jerked open and all she could manage was to look out and start laughing hysterically, an outpouring of raw emotion that held a few tears as well, though she'd nearly been drained of those.

"Take it easy, sister. It's the cavalry. Can't have zombies eating my favorite doctor, now can we?" Said Dominique as she bent down and looked the woman in the eyes to comfort her.

"Doctor Laura!" Said Joe, surprised to see someone he knew.

Laura looked at the man, gaining some recognition. Oh yes, the guy with the hand wound, she recalled. She looked down, and said, "Didn't I tell you to keep that wrapped. What do you want, an infection?"

"Oh, thank God she's back," said Dominique, helping Laura out of the car and eventually into the back of the cruiser.

Sandra, Andy and Stanley fanned out around the cars, keeping guard. Andy watched the freeway fence line like an Eagle Scout. Stanley stood in the middle of the road, swinging his bat as if swatting invisible flies.

Sandra stood lookout towards the rear. Back from where they'd come, about half of the zombies were giving chase, but the way they moved, it'd be ten minutes before any of them got close, she guessed. Up ahead were the northern suburbs. Yeah, right over the trees, she could see the Grandville Road water tank. She'd been up there doing security once, when they'd had a rash of kids spray-painting the sides of the tower's base. It was one of the new big ones, she knew, as wide as it was tall, and fully enclosed at the bottom. The kids hadn't been able to climb it because it was climbed from the inside, but that hadn't stopped them from misspelling words of sophomoric wisdom along the bottom, she recalled.

Everyone piled in except Sandra. Engines started behind her as she paused.

"Wait. I have an idea. Let me drive," she said, motioning for Joe to scoot over and give the hearse it's third driver since their trip began.

"What's up?" Asked Joe.

"The water tank. We can hole up there," said Sandra as she drove.

"Gee. When you say you want running water, you're not kidding," scoffed Joe.

"That's only part of it. The thing is metal. Nobody can get in without a serious effort. To these things it'd be a fort. It has a steel garage door, so we can hide the cars too, and it's completely open in there under the water tank part, which is at least fifty feet up to the bottom of it. It even has a false ceiling. If they get in, we just go up to the second level, taking the ladder with us after we replace the one they have with our own. If it gets worse than that, we can climb up above the water, or even onto the roof. There's a hatch up there. Perfect for seeing half the county. We'll put in a rope up there for an escape over the side. Golly boys, it is a fort."

"That's brilliant. The water and metal might even mask our smell. If we get in there quietly enough, they'll not even have a hint we're there," said Joe enthusiastically.

"Exactly. If we go out during the day to raid for supplies, and are careful to hide our tracks, we can hole up there for years. The things are offset from the road and fenced in on several acres. We might not draw any attention at all," said Sandra.

"What's this about years? I suggested holing up for a day or two, not necessarily playing the Caruso family," said Joe, not wanting to imagine the need.

"Yeah, or days; whatever. Get our hands on a generator, some wire and a short-wave radio. We can pick up Moscow on a coat hanger from the top of a tank. We'll know soon enough what the score is. It's perfectly logical from an intelligence perspective as well, considering the line-of-sight," added Sandra.

"How do we get in?" Asked William.

"Graffiti. Kids were spray painting the ones up north. I pulled extra duty. I have a key on my ring that nobody asked back. Thought I'd pull the duty again, probably. It's good for the back door and the fence. I can get us in, even without the key; it's not that secure, but the key makes it harder for the zombies since we can lock down. Once we're in the tank, we manually open the garage door, and drive the cars right in. Lock us down, and make us forgotten until this blows over," said Sandra as she pulled up the exit ramp.

"That's a good idea, the more I hear of it. In the mean time, we medical types can maybe find out what we're up against," said William from the back seat.

"You mean you and Doctor Laura?" Asked Joe.

"She acted nice. It's been awhile since a woman was nice to me. All I know for sure is, I'm tired of young, bitchy women. No sticking power. One or two little zombies and, phew, off they go. Besides, the doctor and I can work at the science of undoing this mess somebody made of the world. Give us something to do anyway, while we find out if we're compatible."

Sandra and Joe managed a small laugh in the midst of the stress, while Stanley dozed off in his seat—it having been a long night.

Joe looked up at the water tower as they closed towards it, thinking about his own romance. It seemed always on the launching pad, and never in the air. What kind of place was this water tower going to be, he wondered? No wine and linen, that's for sure. Concrete floor, steel walls, a billion pounds of water right over their heads, assuming they can close off the valves before all of the opened faucets and hydrants drain it?

Joe said, "I'm warning you. This is your date. You picked the place. It's on you, sweetheart. When we get in there, I don't want to hear it! You have no idea what I had planned for our next night out. Two pound lobster dinner. Violins. Fat woman singing in an opera dress. Roses and candles on the table..."

Sandra gave him a stern look and said, "Shut up, Joe. Just squeeze over here closer; in there I might be the only thing warm."

Joe shrugged at himself in the side view mirror, and moved to her side.

They wove their way up the hill past bodies and wrecked cars. The sidewalk was clear, making for surprisingly easy going beside the endless string of cars that hadn't made it up route 161. At the top of the world, they turned into the long, winding road to their new, green, steel home.

Conclusion #1

"Get you anything to drink? Perhaps some nuts?" Asked the male flight attendant.

They hadn't even gotten me off the ground yet, and they are already pumping me for alcohol, thought Reverend Purswell. I certainly will not miss this sinful world, he thought as he let his eyes wander away from the flight attendant so that he could look out of his tiny window.

They'd been delayed while the cargo loaders put the last casket into the plane's hold. It had been close, but he'd managed to empty the freezer just in time before things had gotten ugly in Ohio. How fitting that the last five should accompany him to his final destination, not that they were particularly needed where he was going. His friends abroad had all told him of an astonishing level of success. Apparently god's vengeful zombies were motivated. He'd not even need to stick around to retrieve these five. Let the authorities find them, he reasoned, that as good a place to start as any.

Seems that only a handful of the teamsters showed, due to the crisis, so the going had been slow. If the few who had managed to make their way to work this morning didn't hurry up, they'd not make it off the ground before the authorities cancelled the flight; that wouldn't be good.

Purswell looked back into the plane and cast his eyes protectively over his flock. They'd decided to follow him on this last journey, although only he and the man beside him knew about the contents of the five caskets. One hundred and seven of his most faithful had helped him charter this last flight out of Reagan Airport. As best he could tell, it was the last plane leaving before the authorities shut the airport down. If it hadn't been for the fact that it was charter and an overseas carrier, he doubted they'd be lifting off either. It had come to be just that close. Of course, that is assuming that the lumbering thing left now!

He looked back up at the flight attendant. A male flight attendant, he could not help but notice, checking for tale-tell mannerisms. "Are you gay?" Purswell asked the man who was waiting patiently for orders in Purswell's row.

"What did you say, sir?"

"I asked you if you were a fag? It's a simple question."

"No sir. If you don't mind me saying though; isn't it a little rude to ask a person a thing like that?" Said the attendant, leaning back up from where he'd been bending.

"Non-PC, you mean? I suppose it is, but these are the end times, son. Haven't you noticed the headlines: dead rising? No, of course you have noticed, but you will soon see the meaning behind it. We'll all have to adjust to straight forward questioning from our lord Jesus Christ, quite soon. Those in perdition will have bigger worries than being politically polite. Oh, and as for drinks, we are all non-drinkers on this charter. Drinking is a sin of the flesh," explained Purswell.

"I see. Well, I'm afraid that I'm Jewish, so we're probably a few thousand years behind you in the waiting for Messiah department. All is not lost though. We have non-alcoholic drinks, so if you change your mind, I'll still be glad to serve you and your fellow travelers. Oh, and if you notice, as I walk the aisle, I'll have a perfectly heterosexual stride." He winked to Purswell and the goon sitting by his side. The goon chuckled until Purswell gave him the evil eye. The attendant chuckled as well, inside, as he moved forward and hit up the next passenger for a beverage.

The goon at Purswell's side shrugged.

"Don't take it so lightly, brother. That's a lost soul who has as much as said, "Almost thou hast persuaded me to be a Christian,"" said Purswell to his disciple. Purswell returned his focus to the movement of the ride, the aircraft shaking back inches.

The plane engines roared. It backed out of the gate. Then the engines reversed panels reconfigured, and they were racing down the runway.

"Click!" The speaker spoke, "Ladies and gentlemen. Thank you for flying the safest airlines in the world, El Al. We are about to fly non-stop to Madrid, where we will take on fuel. After refueling, we will continue to Tel Aviv, Israel where it is a balmy eighty-six degrees under the palms. Due to the current state of emergency in the US, I've been informed that this will be the last flight out of Reagan International today. For us this is lucky because we will be making a quick turn at the end of the runway and be off post haste. Make sure that your seat belts are fastened, and we ask that you all remain in you seats until the seat belt light is extinguished. We are committed to making your flight as comfortable as possible. Enjoy the trip."

The attendant found an empty aisle seat, and buckled in as the plane turned. The pilot found the adjacent runway, and without the need for further clearance, rumbled to air speed. The nose rose. The wing wheels lifted from the blacktop, and they were several hundred feet over the Atlantic in seconds.

"I wonder if anyone has ever liked any of the magazines you find in the back cubby of these seats," complained Purswell after perusing the flap in front of him. "Airways News. What in the world is that?"

"Kachunk!"

"What the hell was that?" shouted Purswell, looking out at the wing and surprised to see that it was still there.

"Kachunk!"

Purswell joined several of the other passengers, noticing a bounce from the panels in the aisle flooring.

"Kachunk!" The flooring bucked up a fraction of an inch before settling.

The co-pilot raced out of the cabin ahead. Purswell watched him huddle with the gay flight assistant. They parted, scrounging in opposite crew areas, first and second class.

"Kachunk! Kachunk!" Purswell felt that in his feet. Several of the passengers were talking frantically with a neighbor.

The plane kept rising past cloud layers over the Atlantic.

"Kachunk!"

A lady several seats up screamed. That got the whole passenger list talking.

"Click!" The speaker spoke, Purswell saw the co-pilot at a microphone several seconds after he'd started to speak. "Try to not be alarmed. It appears that something has broken loose in the cargo area. The plane is not in any danger, but clearly the noise is startling, so I'm going to pull up the deck plate hatch and secure the loose item. Hopefully we'll be able to secure the cargo without much difficulty."

The flight attendant raced past with a flashlight in his hand, handing it to the co-pilot.

Purswell got out, "Hey, wait a minute. You can't open that," before the co-pilot pulled up the trap door in the floor. The door flew up and open, as if on a spring. Arms pulled at the co-pilot, who'd been leaning in towards the hold. The co-pilot and the arms dragging him, disappeared into the floor. The trap door closed, leaving the male flight attendant alone. Only the attendant had seen what had pulled the man in. His face was ghostly white; his eyes the size of golf balls. Purswell thought the man was going to pass out from shock and plain old indecision.

"Kachunk, Kachunk! Kachunk!" Then deafening silence.

People started to scream, some moving to seats further from the hatch.

Two female attendants came to the tail end of the cabin, standing as if waiting for the co-pilot to return.

"Oh, for peat's sake. Go give them a hand," Purswell told the thug beside him.

The man looked reluctant, but then got up gingerly and made his way to the front. "Got a weapon or something?" He asked the male attendant.

The attendant looked at the big man a second, and fell backwards. He scrambled up, groping for the pilot's door. Jabbing the keypad, the door opened, and he disappeared into the pilot's cabin.

"I didn't mean to freak him out," said the goon, who stepped forward and stood on the cargo hatch door to keep it shut after it started banging upward.

"What's going on? Sir, I'm going to have to ask you to take a seat," said the pilot as he banged into the passenger area. A loaded thirty-eight pistol was in his hand, aimed at the gut of the big man standing in the aisle. The flight attendant moved slightly to the Captain's side, offering support.

"Hey, I just asked the man if he had a weapon. Seems like someone is down there doing some damage," explained the goon.

Purswell walked up beside his bodyguard, saying, "Yes, it's apparent that we have a problem. You'll have to shoot him in the head."

"We'll have to what?" Asked the pilot.

"Shoot him in the head. Whoever is down there is probably a member of the living dead. You'll have to shoot the demon in the head. That's the only way to stop these things. You see, the dead are rising from their graves, as prophesized," repeated Purswell.

People in their seats got loud, debating their ordeal and the likelihood that the minister they were following to the end of the earth just might be completely insane.

"Kachunk!" The floor buckled, and this time didn't recover, several seats back, leaving a bulge in the floor that was two feet long and eight inches high. People screamed.

"OK. You're crazy right! Just get back. In your seats. Don't you get up! I'm paid to handle this," said the pilot, waving the business end of his gun at the men. Purswell and his goon backed up past the bulge in the floor. They found their seats, hoping for the best.

The pilot leaned over, carefully unlatching the recessed ring in the floor. He lifted the floor panel gingerly.

"Kachunk!" The hatch flew open, bashing the pilot on the chin so hard that everyone heard the bone crack. The attendant banged back against the front wall. The gun fell to the floor, while the pilot's head jacked backwards. A sack of bones, the pilot hit the deck, out cold. Blood poured from his chin, forming a wide pool of shocking dimensions. Luckily, the trap door in the floor banged closed, only the hinge a bit twisted as the door self latched.

"Who's flying the plane?" Purswell asked his big friend, who shrugged an answer.

"Kachunk! Kachunk!" The banging started in earnest, this time all of it at the trap door, the plate bouncing and the hinges twisting.

El Al kept reaching for altitude, now two hundred miles out of US airspace and well over the last layer of clouds. People's ears popped.

"Damn it. Do something. Get the gun!" Purswell screamed to the big man sitting beside him.

"Kachunk! Kachunk!" The gun bounced on the cargo hatch as whatever was beneath it popped neat little bulges into the door's carpet covered aluminum plating.

Racing across the floor, the big man grabbed the gun, checking to make sure that it wasn't on safety. Now this is more like it, he told himself, a long standing member of the NRA. "You get my gun when you pry it out of my cold, stiff hand," he yelled to the trap door as it bounced upward, lifting the frame an inch.

"What in the world are you talking about. Get your head out of the clouds, boy. Just open the hatch up and shoot that thing," commanded Purswell.

The goon kicked the pilot aside to make room, breaking a couple of ribs, but what the hell, he was out cold and bleeding so badly that it was unlikely he'd ever know, thought the lout. Then the goon leaned to the side, assuring that the door wouldn't bang him in the head as well, and pulled it up by the ring. Expecting the zombie, he raised up, and stepped back, aiming the gun at the first head he saw.

"Bam!" Smoke filled the tight cabin, but the forehead of the man below was punctured where the bullet struck, and the body fell back. Not a single word escaped the co-pilot's lips as he finally died from the fresh head wound.

"Oh, shit! Shot the wrong guy!" Muttered the goon.

"Watch your damned language," said Purswell out of habit and pure nerves.

Another head looked up at the big man, this the head of a stout old woman who looked a lot like the goon's own mother-in-law before his ex had sinned and divorced him. "Be a pleasure," he said, finding a little bit of comfort in shooting the representation of the woman who'd spawned that woman.

"Bam! Bam!"

Air hissed from a hole in the exterior wall in the lower compartment, made when the second shot, missed due to the head jerking back under the first shot's impact. The neutralized zombie was sucked towards the air hole, filling it with flesh and stopping the flow.

"Get in there, and see if there are any more of them," said Purswell, who'd edged up behind the man. The males flight attendant had come to enough sense to crawl up to the edge of the trap door as well, hoping that his help wouldn't be needed.

The jet's engines sucked in increasingly thinner air, automatically slowing the plane's ascent. It leveled just under the stratosphere.

The goon looked at his pastor as if he were mad, but then realized that the work had to be done and that he was probably the strongest of the lot. It made sense that he finish the job. He stepped down the little ladder to the four foot high space.

It was dark as hell in the bone cold hold, and the co-pilot's flashlight was nowhere to be found. With every freezing breath, the goon exhaled fog, the tiny clouds only hampering his view. In the thin air, he got a little light headed.

Up above, Purswell and that attendant cast shadows into the hold. There! One of the caskets had its top open, explaining the mess. But, shadows from the light up and behind the goon were everywhere, playing across the other caskets and the mounds of luggage. "What's that," he whispered. His head jerked around at every flicker of reflection and shadow. "Something's moving! I think."

Purswell leaned down, watching closely, a cabin light just behind his head; doing more harm than good as he blocked half the light. Back, behind some boxes or luggage or something square, the goon saw the shadow of Purswell's head in the deepest part of the hold!

"Bam! Bam! Bam!"

"Sssssssssssssssssssssssssssssssss! Wack! Wack! Sssssssssssssssss! Wack! Roar!" Thus began the tornado of boxes, luggage, caskets, incapacitated zombie, goon and, eventually, seats as the tail panels buckled and stripped themselves from the back of the plane one by one.

The big airliner did a slow, steady roll.

Conclusion #2

The sun had come up a tad. It was still a bit dark, but the first haze of sun was a good sign, thought Patricia as she wormed her convertible through the little gap at the roadblock. William was five minutes behind her, but good as forgotten. Good riddance. In his place, lots of stinky dead people were around and about, but she was used to that—at least that formaldehyde stinky William was history. As for the zombies, it appeared that the ones that had turned were off doing, well, whatever zombies do when they're not making a nuisance of themselves, she mused. Seems that Joe's group had thought the day safer. The zombies must sense it's getting lighter out, or maybe they'd mostly all been attracted to the funeral home. Be like them to want to hang with William, she imagined.

This isn't all that bad, once past the roadblock. I'll just travel by day, she decided. Hell, in a day on the freeway, a person can make six hundred miles and I've decided to start at the crack of dawn. The coast is closer than that. Washington might be cool. The President will have that secured, she imagined.

Still, the boys had made a point about a convertible being a little, well, out there in the open. It'd be nice to have a bit of protection, she imagined, noticing that the White Castle was closed as she neared. "Jesus, the Castle never closes! Is that legal? No food.

I'll have to make it myself. Lunch meat, yuk!" She made a pained sneer on her face.

A zombie with a hole in the middle of her head was propped up against a car as if the person who'd holed her had cared about her enough to put her out of her misery, but set her straight. "Huh. That's the second time that I've seen a dead person with makeup that makes her looks fantastic." Weird, thought Patricia!

Up ahead, a guy was walking in the same direction that she was going in, him on the right sidewalk. Just a short, but steady gait, holding a rifle. Zombies don't do complicated things like shoot rifles, she remembered being told. It was half dark still, but.... "A cop! Thank god!" Patricia pulled over.

"Want a lift?"

"The cop looked at her from under a shady spot on the sidewalk. He curtly nodded yes. The single, mechanical nod reflected off of the top of his head in the growing angular daylight, and he then jumped over the door without opening it, taking a seat. Cuffs and chains jingled throughout the seating. Cops and their appliances, snickered, Patricia.

The cop's rifle barrel tilted out of the passenger window as if ready and his left hand rested firmly on the pistol grip like a well trained and ready trooper.

James Dean, imagined Patricia, not bothering to ogle too soon and seem too interested. She pulled back out into the street and carefully steered around the nearly endless wrecks.

They edged towards the eastern edge of town as she rambled, "How in the world did you manage to make it through last night, walking around like that? I know. Big boy; big gun. You know, we were armed to the teeth too. My boyfriend, or should I say, ex-boyfriend, he shot one of those things with a bazooka. You should have seen that! What an idiot! Cleaning up forever, duh. I'm normally not this shabbily dressed,, but it just got everywhere when he did that! He always was a little strange. Well, anyway, I'm glad you made it. I can use a real man for a change. I totally need someone riding shotgun for awhile. It's going to be a long trip to Washington DC, and a girl needs protection. You're game, aren't you? Going that far? The way I figure it, this place has gone to the dogs. I've got to get out of here. Everybody's got to get out of here. Should have done it years ago, personally. If you're smart, you'll get out of here with me. Damn, but even White Castle is closed in this town. What kind of life is that? I need coffee! We get on a little bit, and we'll find some food. The whole country can't be closed down."

The passenger remembered that if he waited patiently, just a little bit, then maybe it was best. The driver might help out? The last one did. Yes, it had worked out very well last time, though he was still powerfully hungry.

Patricia added, "Oh, listen to me. My name's Patricia. Shoot! I don't even know your name?" She passed her right hand over in front of his chest, hoping for a handshake.

Though the clip was missing, there was one last bullet in the M-16's chamber.

"Bam!"

The End

0-595-22051-7

Printed in the United Kingdom
by Lightning Source UK Ltd.
103967UKS00001B/272